Praise for *New York Times* bestselling author **Brenda Jackson**

"Brenda Jackson writes romance that sizzl~~e~~ ~~an~~d characters you fa~~ll i~~n ~~...~~

~~...~~*AY*
~~...~~er

"Jackson's tradem~~...~~ characters and sid~~... together~~ makes shocking truths all the more exciting."

—*Publishers Weekly*

"There is no getting away from the sex appeal and charm of Jackson's Westmoreland family."

—*RT Book Reviews* on *Feeling the Heat*

Praise for author **Reese Ryan**

"Familial obligations and years of emotional baggage provide realistic obstacles to their romance... This well-executed romance is sure to please."

—*Publishers Weekly* on *A Reunion of Rivals*

"I really enjoyed this story!... I'm a big fan of this series and look forward to what's coming next!"

—*Harlequin Junkie* on *A Reunion of Rivals*

"The author has a fun and fresh writing style and intertwines the lives of her main and secondary character with vivid detail."

—*Contemporary Romance Reviews* on *Making the First Move*

Simply Irresistible

NEW YORK TIMES BESTSELLING AUTHOR
BRENDA JACKSON

Previously published as *Temptation*
and *Playing with Seduction*

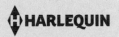

Recycling programs
for this product may
not exist in your area.

ISBN-13: 978-1-335-40635-4

Simply Irresistible
First published as Temptation in 2011.
This edition published in 2021.
Copyright © 2011 by Harlequin Books S.A.

Special thanks and acknowledgment are given
to Brenda Jackson for her contribution to the
Texas Cattleman's Club: The Showdown miniseries.

Playing with Seduction
First published in 2017. This edition published in 2021.
Copyright © 2017 by Roxanne Ravenel

This edition published by arrangement with Harlequin Books S.A.

For questions and comments about the quality of this book,
please contact us at CustomerService@Harlequin.com.

Harlequin Enterprises ULC
22 Adelaide St. West, 40th Floor
Toronto, Ontario M5H 4E3, Canada
www.Harlequin.com

Printed in U.S.A.

CONTENTS

Brenda Jackson is a *New York Times* bestselling author of more than one hundred romance titles. Brenda lives in Jacksonville, Florida, and divides her time between family, writing and traveling.

Email Brenda at authorbrendajackson@gmail.com or visit her on her website at brendajackson.net.

Books by Brenda Jackson

Harlequin Desire

The Westmorelands

The Real Thing
The Secret Affair
Breaking Bailey's Rules
Bane

The Westmoreland Legacy

The Rancher Returns
His Secret Son
An Honorable Seduction
His to Claim
Duty or Desire

Visit the Author Profile page at Harlequin.com for more titles.

TEMPTATION

Brenda Jackson

To the love of my life, Gerald Jackson, Sr.

To the cast and crew of
Truly Everlasting—the Movie,
this one is especially for you!
Thanks for all your hard work!

Though your beginning was small,
yet your latter end would increase abundantly.

—*Job* 8:7

Chapter 1

Some days it didn't pay to get out of bed.

Unless you had a tall, dark, handsome and naked man waiting in your kitchen to pour you a hot cup of coffee before sitting you in his lap to feed you breakfast. Sheila Hopkins smiled at such a delicious fantasy before squinting against the November sun that was almost blinding her through the windshield of her car.

And the sad thing was that she had awakened in a good mood. But all it had taken to spoil her day was a call from her sister that morning telling her she wasn't welcome to visit her and her family in Atlanta after all. That message had hurt, but Sheila really should not have been surprised. What had she expected from her older sister from her father's first marriage? The same sister who'd always wished she hadn't existed? Definitely not any show of sisterly love at this late stage. If she hadn't shown any in Sheila's twenty-seven years, why had she assumed her sister would begin showing any now? Not her sister who had the perfect life with a husband who owned his own television station in Atlanta and who had two beautiful children and was pregnant with her third.

And if that very brief and disappointing conversation with Lois wasn't bad enough, she had immediately gotten a call from the hospital asking that she come in on her off day because they were shorthanded. And of course, being the dedicated nurse that she was, she had agreed to do so. Forget the fact she had planned to spend the day working in her garden. She didn't have a life, so did it really matter?

Sheila drew in a deep breath when she brought her car to a stop at a traffic light. She couldn't help glancing over at the man in the sports car next to her. She couldn't tell how the rest of him looked because she could only see his profile from the shoulders up, but even that looked good. And as if he'd known she was checking him out, he glanced her way. Her breath caught in her throat and her flesh felt tingly all over. He had such striking features.

They were so striking she had to blink to make sure they were real. Um...a maple-brown complexion, close-cut black hair, dark brown eyes and a chiseled jaw. And as she continued to stare at him, her mind mechanically put his face on the naked body of the tall, handsome man whom she would have loved to have found in her kitchen this morning. She inwardly chuckled. Neither she nor her kitchen would have been able to handle all the heat her imaginary lover would generate.

She saw his head move and realized he had nodded over at her. Instinctively, she nodded back. When his lips curved into a sensual smile, she quickly forced her gaze ahead. And when the traffic light changed, she pressed down on the gas, deciding to speed up a little. The last thing she wanted was to give the guy the impression she was flirting with him, no matter how good he looked. She had learned quickly that not all nicely wrapped gifts contained something that was good for you. Crawford had certainly proven that.

As she got off the exit that led to the hospital, she couldn't get rid of the thought that she didn't know there were men who looked like him living in Royal, Texas. Not that she knew all the men in town, mind you. But she figured someone like him would definitely stand out. After all, Royal was a rather small community. And what if she had run into him again, then what?

Nothing.

She didn't have the time or the inclination to get involved with a man. She'd done that in the past and the outcome hadn't been good, which was why she had moved to Royal from Dallas last year. Moving to Royal had meant a fresh start for her. Although, Sheila knew that where she lived was only part of the solution. She had reached the conclusion that a woman didn't need to be involved with a no-good man to have trouble. A woman could do bad all by herself. And she of all people was living proof of that.

Ezekiel Travers chuckled as he watched the attractive woman take off as though she was going to a fire or something. Hell, she wasn't the only one, he thought as he watched her car turn off the interstate at the next exit. Whoever was trying to ruin his best friend, Bradford Price's, reputation had taken things a little too far.

According to the phone call he'd received earlier from Brad, the blackmailer had made good on his threat. Someone had left a baby on the doorstep of the Texas Cattlemen's Club with a note that Brad was the baby's father.

Grabbing his cell phone the moment it began to ring, he knew who the caller was before answering it. "Yeah, Brad?"

"Zeke, where are you?"

"I'm only a few minutes away. And you can believe I'll be getting to the bottom of this."

"I don't know what kind of sick joke someone is trying to play on me, but I swear to you, that baby isn't mine."

Zeke nodded. "And a paternity test can prove that easily, Brad, so calm down."

He had no reason not to believe his best friend about the baby not being his. Brad wouldn't lie about something like that. He and Brad had gotten to be the best of friends while roommates at the University of Texas. After college Brad had returned to Royal to assist in his family's banking empire.

Actually, it had been Brad who suggested Zeke relocate to Royal. He'd made the suggestion during one of their annual all-guys trip to Vegas last year, after Zeke had mentioned his desire to leave Austin and to move to a small town.

Zeke had earned a small fortune and a great reputation as one of the best security consultants in all of Texas. Now he could live anywhere he wanted to, and take his pick of cases.

And it had been Brad who'd connected Zeke with Darius Franklin, another private investigator in Royal who owned a security service and who just happened to be looking for a partner. That had prompted Zeke to fly to Royal. He'd immediately fallen in love with the town and he saw becoming a business partner with Darius as a win-win situation. That had been six months ago. When he'd moved to town, he hadn't known that his first case would begin before he could get settled in good, and that his first client would be none other than his best friend.

"I bet Abigail is behind this."

Brad's accusations interrupted Zeke's thoughts. Abigail Langley and Brad were presently in a heated battle to win the presidency of the Texas Cattlemen's Club.

"You have no proof of that and so far I haven't been able to find a link between Ms. Langley and those blackmail letters you've received, Brad. But you can bet if she's connected, I'll expose her. Now, sit tight, I'm on my way."

He clicked off the phone knowing to tell Brad to sit tight was a waste of time. Zeke let out a deep sigh. Brad had begun receiving blackmail letters five months ago. The thought nagged Zeke's mind that maybe if he had been on top of his game and solved the case months ago, it would not have gotten this far and some kid would not have been abandoned at the club.

He of all people knew how that felt. At thirty-three he could still feel the sting of abandonment. Although his own mother hadn't left him on anyone's doorstep, she had left him with her sister and kept on trucking. She hadn't shown up again until sixteen years later. It had been his last year of college and she'd stuck around just long enough to see if he had a chance in the NFL.

He pushed that hurtful time of his life to the back

of his mind to concentrate on the problem at hand. If leaving that baby at the TCC with a note claiming she was Brad's kid was supposed to be a joke, then it wasn't funny. And Zeke intended to make sure he and Brad had the last laugh when they exposed the person responsible for such a callous act.

Once Sheila had reached her floor at the hospital, it became evident why they'd called her in. A couple of nurses were out sick and the E.R. was swarming with patients with symptoms ranging from the flu to a man who'd almost lost his finger while chopping down a tree in his front yard. There had also been several minor car accidents.

At least something good had resulted from one of the accidents. A man thinking his girlfriend's injuries were worse than they were, had rushed into the E.R. and proposed. Even Sheila had to admit it had been a very romantic moment. Some women had all the luck.

"So you came in on your off day, huh?"

Sheila glanced at her coworker and smiled. Jill Lanier was a nurse she'd met on her first day at Royal Memorial and they'd become good friends. When she'd moved to Royal she hadn't known a soul, but that had been fine. She was used to being alone. That was the story of her life.

She was about to answer Jill, when the sound of a huge wail stopped her. "What the heck?"

She turned around and saw two police officers walk in carrying a screaming baby. Both she and Jill hurried over to the officers. "What's going on, Officers?" she asked the two men.

One of the officers, the one holding the baby, shook

his head. "We don't know why she's crying," he said in frustration. "Someone left her on the doorstep of the Texas Cattlemen's Club and we were told to bring her here."

Sheila had heard all about the Texas Cattlemen's Club, which consisted of a group of men who considered themselves the protectors of Texas, and whose members consisted of the wealthiest men in Texas. One good thing was that the TCC was known to help a number of worthwhile causes in the community. Thanks to them, there was a new cancer wing at the hospital.

Jill took the baby and it only screamed louder. "The TCC? Why would anyone do something like that?"

"Who knows why people abandon their kids," the other officer said. It was apparent he was more than happy to pass the screaming baby on to someone else. However, the infant, who looked to be no more than five months old, was screaming even louder now. Jill, who was a couple of years younger than Sheila and single and carefree, gave them a what-am-I-supposed-to-do-now look as she rocked the baby in her arms.

"And there's a note that's being handed over to Social Services claiming Bradford Price is the father."

Sheila lifted a brow. She didn't know Bradford Price personally, but she had certainly heard of him. His family were blue blood society types. She'd heard they'd made millions in banking.

"Is someone from Social Services on their way here?" Sheila asked, raising her voice to be heard over the crying baby.

"Yes. Price is claiming the baby isn't his. There has to be a paternity test done."

Sheila nodded, knowing that could take a couple of days, possibly even a week.

"And what are we supposed to do with her until then?" Jill asked as she continued to rock the baby in her arms, trying to get her quiet but failing to do so.

"Keep her here," one of the officers responded. He was backing up, as if he was getting ready to make a run for it. "A woman from Social Services is on her way with everything you'll need. The kid doesn't have a name…at least one wasn't given with the note left with her."

The other officer, the one who'd been carrying the baby, spoke up. "Look, ladies, we have to leave. She threw up on me, so I need to swing by my place and change clothes."

"What about your report?" Sheila called out to the two officers who were rushing off.

"It's completed already and like I said, a woman from Social Services is on her way," the first officer said, before both men quickly exited through the revolving glass doors.

"I can't believe they did that," Jill said with a disgruntled look on her face. "What are we going to do with her? One thing for certain, this kid has a nice set of lungs."

Sheila smiled. "Follow procedure and get her checked out. There might be a medical reason why she's crying. Let's page Dr. Phillips."

"Hey, let me page Dr. Phillips. It's your turn to hold her." Before Sheila could say anything, Jill suddenly plopped the baby in her arms.

"Hey, hey, things can't be that bad, sweetie," Sheila

crooned down at the baby as she adjusted her arms to make sure she was holding her right.

Other than the times she worked in the hospital nursery, she'd never held a baby, and rarely came in contact with one. Lois had two kids and was pregnant with another, yet Sheila had only seen her five-year-old niece and three-year-old nephew twice. Her sister had never approved of their father's marriage to Sheila's mother, and Sheila felt she had been the one to pay for it. Lois, who was four years older than Sheila, had been determined never to accept her father's other child. Over the years, Sheila had hoped her attitude toward her would change, but so far it hadn't.

Pushing thoughts of Lois from her mind, Sheila continued to smile down at the baby. And as if on cue the little girl stared up at Sheila with the most gorgeous pair of hazel eyes, and suddenly stopped crying. In fact, she smiled, showing dimples in both cheeks.

Sheila couldn't help chuckling. "What are you laughing at, baby-doll? Do I look funny or something?" She was rewarded with another huge smile from the baby. "You're such a pretty little thing, all bright and full of sunshine. I think I'll call you Sunnie until we find out your real name."

"Dr. Phillips is on his way and I'm needed on the fourth floor," Jill said, making a dash toward the elevator. "How did you get her to stop crying, Sheila?" she asked before stepping on the elevator.

Sheila shrugged and glanced back at the baby, who was still smiling up at her. "I guess she likes me."

"Apparently she does," a deep, husky male voice said from behind them.

Sheila turned around and her gaze collided with the

most gorgeous set of brown eyes she'd ever seen on a man. They were bedroom eyes. The kind that brought to mind silken sheets and passion. But this wasn't the first time she had looked into those same eyes.

She immediately knew where she'd seen them before as her gaze roamed over his features. Recognition appeared in his gaze the moment it hit hers, as well. Standing before her, looking sexier than any man had a right to look, was the guy who'd been in the car next to hers at the traffic light. He was the man who'd given her a flirtatious smile before she'd deliberately sped off to ditch him.

Evidently that hadn't done any good, since he was here, standing before her in vivid living color.

Chapter 2

This was the second time today he'd seen this woman, Zeke thought. Just as before, he thought she looked good…even wearing scrubs. Nothing could hide the wavy black hair that came to her shoulders, the light brown eyes and luscious café-au-lait skin.

He wondered if anyone ever told her she could be a very delicious double for actress Sanaa Lathan. The woman before him was just a tad shorter than the actress, but in his book she was just as curvy. And she was a nurse. Hell, she could take his temperature any time and any place. He could even suggest she take it now, because there was no doubt in his mind looking at her was making it rise.

"May I help you?"

He blinked and swallowed deeply. "Yes, that baby you're holding…"

She narrowed her eyes and clutched the baby closer to her breast in a protective stance. "Yes, what about her?"

"I want to find out everything there is about her," he said.

She lifted an arched brow. "And you are...?"

He gave what he hoped was a charming smile. "Zeke Travers, private investigator."

Sheila opened her mouth to speak, when a deep, male voice intruded behind her. "Zeke Travers! Son of a gun! With Brad Price as quarterback, you as split end and Chris Richards as wide receiver, that was UT's best football season. I recall them winning a national championship title that year. Those other teams didn't stand a chance with you three. Someone mentioned you had moved to Royal."

She then watched as Dr. Warren Phillips gave the man a huge bear hug. Evidently they knew each other, and as she listened further, she was finding out quite a lot about the handsome stranger.

"Yes, I moved to town six months ago," Zeke was saying. "Austin was getting too big for me. I've decided to try small-town life for a while. Brad convinced me Royal was the place," he said, grinning. "And I was able to convince Darius Franklin he needed a partner."

"So you joined forces with Darius over at Global Securities?"

"Yes, and things are working out great so far. Darius is a good man and I really like this town. In fact, I like it more and more each day." His gaze then shifted to her and her gaze locked with his as it had done that morning.

The clearing of Dr. Phillips's throat reminded them they weren't alone.

"So, what brings you to Royal Memorial, Zeke?" Dr. Phillips asked, and it was evident to Sheila that Dr. Phillips had picked up on the man's interest in her.

"That baby she's holding. It was left abandoned at the TCC today with a note claiming Brad's the father. And I intend to prove that he's not."

"In that case," Dr. Phillips said, "I think we need to go into that private examination room over there and check this baby out."

A short while later Dr. Phillips slid his stethoscope into the pocket of his lab coat as he leaned back against the table. "Well, this young lady is certainly in good health."

He chuckled and then added, "And she certainly refused to let anyone hold her other than you, Nurse Hopkins. If you hadn't been present and within her reach, it would have been almost impossible for me to examine her."

Sheila laughed as she held the baby to her while glancing down at the infant. "She's beautiful. I can't imagine anyone wanting to abandon her."

"Well, it happened," Zeke said.

A tingling sensation rode up her spine with the comment and she was reminded that Zeke Travers was in the examination room with them. It was as if he refused to let the baby out of his sight.

She turned slightly. "What makes you so sure she's not Bradford Price's child, Mr. Travers? I recall running into Mr. Price a time or two and he also has hazel eyes."

He narrowed his gaze. "So do a million other people in this country, Ms. Hopkins."

Evidently he didn't like being questioned about the possibility. So she turned to Dr. Phillips. "Did that social worker who came by while you were examining the baby say what will happen to Sunnie?" she asked.

Dr. Phillips lifted a brow. "Sunnie?"

"Yes," Sheila said, smiling. "I thought she was a vision of sunshine the moment I looked at her. And since no one knows her name I thought Sunnie would fit. Sounds better than Jane Doe," she added.

"I agree," Dr. Phillips said, chuckling. "And the social worker, Ms. Talbert, is as baffled as everyone else, especially since Brad says the baby isn't his."

"She's not his," Zeke said, inserting himself into the conversation again. "Brad's been receiving blackmail letters for five months now, threatening to do something like this unless he paid up."

Zeke rubbed the back of his neck. "I told him to ignore the letters while I looked into it. I honestly didn't think the person would carry out their threats if Brad didn't pay up. Evidently, I was wrong."

And that's what continued to bother him the most, Zeke thought as he glanced over at the baby. He should have nipped this nasty business in the bud long ago. And what Ms. Hopkins said was true, because he'd noted it himself. The baby had hazel eyes, and not only were they hazel, they were the same shade of hazel as Brad's.

He'd asked Brad if there was any chance the baby could be his, considering the fact Brad was a known playboy. But after talking to Brad before coming over here, and now that he knew the age of the baby, Zeke was even more convinced Brad wasn't the father. Warren had confirmed the baby's age as five months and Brad had stated he hadn't slept with any women over the past eighteen months.

"To answer your question, Nurse Hopkins," Dr. Phillips said, breaking into Zeke's thoughts, "Ms. Talbert wants to wait to see what the paternity test reveals. I agreed that we can keep the baby here until then."

"Here?"

"Yes, that would be best until the test results come back, that is unless Brad has a problem participating in the test," Dr. Phillips said, glancing over at Zeke.

"Brad knows that it's for the best, and he will cooperate any way he can," Zeke acknowledged.

"But it doesn't seem fair for Sunnie to have to stay here at the hospital. She's in perfect health," Sheila implored. "Ms. Talbert has indicated the test results might take two weeks to come back."

She then glared over at Zeke. "Whether the baby is officially his or not, I would think your client would want the best for Sunnie until her parentage is proven or disproven."

Zeke crossed his arms over his chest. "So what do you suggest, Ms. Hopkins? I agree staying here isn't ideal for the baby, but the only other option is for her to get turned over to Social Services. If that happens she'll go into foster care and will get lost in the system when it's proven my client is *not* her father."

Sheila nibbled on her bottom lip, not having a response to give him. She glanced down at the baby she held in her arms. For whatever reason, Sunnie's mother hadn't wanted her and it didn't seem fair for her to suffer because of it. She knew how it felt not to be wanted.

"I have an idea that might work, Nurse Hopkins, granted you agree to go along with it," Dr. Phillips said. "And I'll have to get Ms. Talbert to agree to it, as well."

"Yes?" she said, wondering what his idea was.

"A few years ago the wife of one of my colleagues, Dr. Webb, was hit with a similar incident when someone left a baby on her doorstep before they were married. Because Winona grew up in foster care herself, she hadn't wanted the baby to end up the same way. To make a long story short, Winona and Dr. Webb ended up marrying and keeping the baby to make sure it didn't get lost in the system."

Sheila nodded. "So what are you suggesting?"

Dr. Phillips smiled. "That you become Sunnie's emergency foster parent until everything is resolved. I believe I'll be able to convince Ms. Talbert to go along with it, and given the fact the Prices are huge benefactors to this hospital, as well as to a number of other nonprofit organizations, I think it would be in everyone's best interest that the baby's welfare remain a top priority."

Sheila looked shocked. "Me? A foster parent! I wouldn't know what to do with a baby."

"You couldn't convince me of that, Ms. Hopkins. The baby won't let anyone else touch her and you seem to be a natural with her," Zeke said, seeing the merits of what Dr. Phillips proposed. "Besides, you're a nurse, someone who is used to taking care of people."

Although Brad swore the baby wasn't his, he would still be concerned with the baby's health and safety until everything was resolved. And what Zeke just said was true. He thought the woman was a natural with the baby, and the baby had gotten totally attached to her.

He had a feeling Ms. Hopkins was already sort of attached to the baby, as well.

"And if you're concerned as to how you'd be able to handle both your job and the baby, I propose that the hospital agrees to give you a leave of absence during the time that the child is in your care. My client will be more than happy to replace your salary," Zeke said.

"I think that would be an excellent idea," Warren said. "One I think I could push past the chief of staff.

The main thing everyone should be concerned about is Sunnie's well-being."

Sheila couldn't help agreeing. But her? A foster parent? "How long do you think I'll have to take care of her?" she asked, looking down at Sunnie, who was still smiling up at her.

"No more than a couple of weeks, if even that long," Zeke said. "The results of the paternity test should be back by then and we'll know how to proceed."

Sheila nibbled her bottom lip, then Sunnie reached and grabbed hold of a lock of her hair, seemingly forcing Sheila to look down at her—into her beautiful hazel eyes, while she made a lot of cheerful baby sounds. At that moment Sheila knew she would do it. Sunnie needed a temporary home and she would provide her with one. It was the least she could do, and deep down she knew it was something that she wanted to do. This was the first time she'd felt someone truly, really needed her.

She glanced up at both men to see they were patiently waiting for her answer. She drew in a deep breath. "Yes. I would be happy to be Sunnie's emergency foster parent."

After removing his jacket, Zeke slid into the seat of his car and leaned back as he gazed at the entrance to the hospital. He felt good about Sheila Hopkins agreeing to take on the role of foster parent. That way he would know the baby was being well cared for while he turned up the heat on the investigation to clear Brad's name.

He intended to pursue each and every lead. He would not leave a stone, no matter how small, unturned. He intended to get this potential scandal under total control before it could go any further.

Now if he could control his attraction to Sheila Hopkins. The woman was definitely temptation with a capital T. Being in close quarters with her, even with Warren in the room, had been pure torture. She was a looker, but it was clear she didn't see herself that way, and he couldn't help wondering, why not? He hadn't seen a ring on her finger and, when he'd hung back to speak with Warren in private, the only thing his friend could tell him was that she was a model employee, caring to a fault, dependable and intelligent.

Warren had also verified she was single and had moved from Dallas last year. But still, considering everything, Zeke felt it wouldn't hurt to do a background check on her, just to be on the safe side. The last thing he wanted was for her to be someone who'd be tempted to sell this story to the tabloids. That was the last thing Brad needed. His best friend was depending on him to bring an end to this nightmare, and he would.

Zeke was about to turn the ignition in his car, when he glanced through the windshield to see Sheila Hopkins. She was walking quickly across the parking lot to the car he had seen her in that morning. She looked as if she was dashing off to fight a fire. Curious as to where she could be going in such a hurry, he got out of the car, walked swiftly to cross the parking lot and intercepted her before she could reach her vehicle.

She nearly yelled in fright when he stepped in front of her. "What do you think you're doing?" she asked, covering her heart with the palm of her hand. "You just scared me out of my wits."

"Sorry, but I saw you tearing across the parking lot. What's the hurry?"

Sheila drew a deep breath to get her heart beating back normal in her chest. She looked up at Zeke Travers and couldn't do anything about her stomach doing flips. It had been hard enough while in the examination room to stop her gaze from roaming all over him every chance it got.

"I'm leaving Sunnie in the hospital tonight while I go pick up the things I'll need for her. I'm going to need a baby bed, diapers, clothes and all kinds of other items. I plan on shopping today and coming back for her first thing in the morning once my house is ready."

She paused a moment. "I hated leaving her. She started crying. I feel like I'm abandoning her."

A part of Zeke was relieved to know she was a woman who would feel some sort of guilt in abandoning a child. His own mother had not. He drew in a deep breath as he remembered what Sheila Hopkins had said about needing to go shopping for all that baby stuff. He hadn't thought of the extra expenses taking on a baby would probably cost her.

"Let me go with you to pick up the stuff. That way I can pay for it."

She raised a brow. "Why would you want to do that?"

"Because whether or not Brad's the father—which he's not—he wants the baby taken care of and is willing to pay for anything she might need." He hadn't discussed it with Brad, but knew there wouldn't be a problem. Brad was concerned for the baby's welfare.

She seemed to be studying his features as if she was trying to decide if he was serious, Zeke thought. And then she asked, "You sure? I have to admit that I hadn't worked all the baby expenses into my weekly budget, but if I need to get money out of my savings then I—"

"No, that won't be necessary and Brad wouldn't want it any other way, and like I said, I'll be glad to go with you and help."

Sheila felt a tingling sensation in the pit of her stomach. The last thing she needed was Zeke Travers in her presence too long. "No, I'll be able to manage things, but I appreciate the offer."

"No, really, I insist. Why wouldn't you want me to help? I'll provide you with two extra hands."

That wasn't all he would be providing her with, she thought, looking at him. Besides the drop-dead gorgeous looks, at some point he had taken off his jacket to reveal the width of his shoulders beneath his white dress shirt. She also noticed the way his muscular thighs fit into a pair of dress slacks.

"We could leave your car here. I have a feeling you'll want to come back and check on the baby later. We can go in my vehicle," he added before she could respond to what he'd said.

She lifted a brow. "You have a two-seater."

He chuckled. "Yes, but I also have a truck. And that's what you're going to need to haul something as big as a box containing a baby bed. And in order to haul the kid away from here you're going to need a car seat tomorrow."

Sheila tilted her head back and drew in a deep breath. Had she bit off more than she could chew? She hadn't thought of all that. She needed to make a list and not work off the top of her head. And he was right about her needing a truck and wanting to return tonight to check on Sunnie. The sound of her crying had followed Sheila all the way to the elevator. She hated leaving her, but she had to prepare her house for Sunnie's visit.

"Ms. Hopkins?"

She looked back at Zeke Travers. "Fine, Mr. Travers, I'll accept your generosity. If you're sure it's not going out of your way."

He smiled. "I'm not going out of my way, I assure you. Like I said, Brad would want what's best for the baby even if she isn't his."

She arched a brow. "You certainly seem so sure of that."

"I am. Now, it's going to be my job in addition to making sure the baby is safe and well cared for, to find out who's trying to nail him with this and to clear his name."

Zeke paused a moment and stared down at her. "And speaking of names, I suggest you call me Zeke, instead of Mr. Travers."

She smiled. "Why, is Mr. Travers what they call your father?"

"I wouldn't know."

Sheila's heart skipped a beat when she realized what he'd said and what he'd meant by saying it. "I'm sorry, I didn't mean anything. The last guy who told me not to call him by his last name said the reason was that's what people called his daddy."

"No harm done, and I hope you don't mind if I call you Sheila."

"No, I don't mind."

"Good. Come on, Sheila, my car is parked over here," he said.

Sheila felt her stomach twist in all kinds of knots when she heard her name flow from his lips. And as she walked beside Zeke across the parking lot, a number of misgivings flooded her mind. For one thing, she wasn't sure what role he intended to play with her becoming Sunnie's foster parent. She understood Bradford Price was his client and he intended to clear the man's name. But she had to think beyond that. If Bradford wasn't Sunnie's father then who was? Where was the mother and why had the baby been abandoned with a note claiming Bradford was the father when he said he wasn't?

There were a lot of questions and she had a feeling the man walking beside her intended to have answers for all of them soon enough. She also had a feeling he was the sort of person who got things accomplished when he set his mind to it. And she could tell he intended to investigate this case to the fullest.

His main concern might be on his friend, but hers was on Sunnie. What would happen to her if it was proven Bradford wasn't the child's father? Would the man cease caring about Sunnie's welfare? Would it matter to him that she would then become just a statistic in the system?

He might not care, but she would, and at that moment she vowed to protect Sunnie any way she could.

Chapter 3

While they were on their way to the store to pick up items for the baby, Sheila clicked off the phone and sighed deeply as she glanced over at Zeke. "I just talked to one of the nurses in Pediatrics. Sunnie cried herself to sleep," she said.

There was no need telling him that she knew just how that felt. She was reminded of how many nights as a child she had lain in bed and cried herself to sleep because her mother was too busy trying to catch the next rich husband to spend any time with her. And her father, once he'd discovered what a gold digger Cassie Hopkins was, he hadn't wasted time moving out and taking Lois with him and leaving her behind.

"That's good to hear, Sheila," Zeke responded.

There was another tingling sensation in the pit of her stomach. She couldn't help it. It did something to her each and every time he pronounced her name. He said it with a deep Texas drawl that could send shivers all through her.

"So how long have you been living in Royal?" he asked.

She glanced over at him. "A year." She knew from his conversation with Dr. Phillips that he had moved to town six months ago, so there was no need to ask him that. She also knew he'd come from Austin because he wanted to try living in a small city.

"You like it here?"

She nodded. "So far. The people are nice, but I spend a lot of my time at the hospital, so I still haven't met all my neighbors, only those next door."

She switched her gaze off him to look out the window at the homes and stores they passed. What she decided not to add was that other than working, and occasional trips to the market, she rarely left home. The people at the hospital had become her family.

Now that she'd agreed to a fourteen-day leave of absence, she would have her hands full caring for Sunnie, and a part of her actually looked forward to that.

"You're smiling."

She glanced back at him. Did the man notice every single thing? "Is it a crime?"

He chuckled. "No."

The deep, husky rumble of his chuckle sent shivers sweeping through her again. And because she couldn't help herself, when the car came to a stop at the traffic light she glanced back over at him and then wished she hadn't done so. The slow smile that suddenly curved his lips warmed her all over.

"Now you're the one smiling," she pointed out. "And is that a crime?"

Grinning, she shook her head. He'd made her see just how ridiculous her response to him had been. "No, it's not."

"Good. Because if I get arrested, Sheila, so do you. And it would be my request that we get put in the same jail cell."

She told herself not to overreact to what he'd said. Of course he would try to flirt with her. He was a man. She'd gotten hit on by a number of doctors at the hospital as well as several police officers around town. Eventually, they found out what Zeke would soon discover. It was a waste of their time. She had written men off. When it came to the opposite sex, she preferred her space. The only reason she was with him now was because of Sunnie. She considered Zeke Travers as a means to an end.

When he exited off the expressway and moments later turned into a nice gated community, she was in awe of the large and spacious ranch-style homes that sat on at least thirty acres of land. She had heard about the Cascades, the section of Royal where the wealthy lived. He evidently was doing well in the P.I. business. "You live in this community?" she asked.

"Yes. I came from Austin on an apartment-hunting trip and ended up purchasing a house instead. I always wanted a lot of land and to own horses and figured buying in here was a good investment."

She could just imagine, especially with the size of the ranch house whose driveway they were pulling into. The house had to be sitting almost six hundred or more feet back off the road. She could see a family of twelve living here and thought the place was definitely too large for just one person.

"How many acres is this?" she asked. "Forty. I needed that much with the horses."

"How many do you own?"

"Twelve now, but I plan to expand. I've hired several ranch hands to help me take care of things. And I ride every chance I get. What about you? Do you ride?"

She thought of her mother's second and third husbands. They had owned horses and required that she know how to ride. "Yes, I know how to ride."

He glanced at his watch. "It won't take me long to switch vehicles," he said, bringing the car to a stop. "You're invited in if you like and you're welcome to look around."

"No, I'll be fine waiting out here until you return," she said.

He got out of the car and turned to her and smiled. "I don't bite, you know."

"Trust me, Zeke, if for one minute I thought you did, I wouldn't be here."

"So you think I'm harmless?" he asked, grinning. "Not harmless but manageable. I'm sure all your focus will be on trying to figure out who wants to frame your friend. You don't have time for anything else."

He flashed a sexy smile. "Don't be so sure of that, Sheila Hopkins." He closed the door and she watched as he strolled up the walkway to his front door, thinking his walk was just as sexy as his smile.

Zeke unlocked his door and pushed it open. He had barely made it inside his house when the phone rang. Closing the door behind him, he pulled his cell phone off the clip on his belt. He checked the caller ID. "Yes, Brad?"

"You didn't call. How was the baby?"

Zeke leaned up against the wall supporting the staircase. "She's fine, but she cries a lot."

"I noticed. And no one could get her to stop. Did they check her out to make sure nothing is wrong with her?"

Zeke smiled. "She was checked out. Just so happens that Warren Phillips was on duty and he's the one who gave her a clean bill of health, although she still wanted to prove to everyone what a good set of lungs she had."

"I'm glad she's okay. I was worried about her."

Zeke nodded. "Are you sure there's nothing you want to tell me? I did happen to notice the kid does have your eyes."

"Don't get cute, Zeke. The kid isn't mine. But she's just a baby and I can't help worrying about her."

"Hey, man, I was just kidding, and I understand. I can't help worrying about her, too. But we might have found a way where we don't have to worry about her while I delve into my investigation."

"And what way is that?"

"That way happens to be a nurse who works at Royal Memorial by the name of Sheila Hopkins. She's the only one who can keep the baby quiet. It's the weirdest thing. The kid screams at everyone else, but she's putty in Sheila Hopkins's hands. She actually smiles instead of crying."

"You're kidding."

"No, I saw her smile myself. Warren suggested that Sheila keep Sunnie for the time being," Zeke explained.

"Sunnie?"

"Yes, that's the name Sheila gave the kid for now. She said it sounded better than Jane Doe and I agree."

There was a slight pause and then Brad asked, "And this Sheila Hopkins agreed to do it?"

"Yes, until the results of the paternity test come back, so the sooner you can do your part the better."

"I've made an appointment to have it done tomorrow."

"Good. And I'm going shopping with Sheila for baby stuff. She's single and doesn't have any kids of her own, so she'll need all new stuff, which I'm billing you for, by the way."

"Fine." There was a pause, and then Brad said, "I was thinking that perhaps it would be best if I hired a nanny and keep the baby instead of—"

"Hold up. Don't even consider it. We don't want anyone seeing your kindness as an admission of guilt, Brad. The next thing everyone will think is that the baby is really yours."

"Yes, but what do you know about this nurse? You said she's single. She might be pretty good at taking care of patients, but are you sure she knows how to take care of a baby?"

"I'm not sure about anything regarding Sheila Hopkins, other than what Warren told me. She's worked at the hospital about a year. But don't worry, I've already taken measures to have her checked out. Roy is doing a thorough background check on Sheila Hopkins as we speak."

Suddenly Zeke heard a noise behind him and turned around. Sheila was leaning against his door with her arms crossed over her chest. The look on her face let him know she had heard some, if not all, of his conversation with Brad and wasn't happy about it.

"Brad, I need to go. I'll call you back later." He then hung up the phone.

Before he could open his mouth, Sheila placed her hands on her hips and narrowed her eyes at him. "Please take me back to the hospital to get my car. There's no way I'm going anywhere with a man who doesn't trust me."

Then she turned and walked out the door and slammed it shut behind her.

Sheila was halfway down the walkway, when Zeke ran behind her and grabbed her arm. "Let me go," she said and angrily snatched it back.

"We need to talk and I prefer we don't do it out here," Zeke said.

She glared up at him. "And I prefer we don't do it anywhere. I have nothing to say to you. How dare you have me investigated like I'm some sort of criminal."

"I never said you were a criminal."

"Then why the background check, Zeke?"

He rubbed his hands down his face. "I'm a P.I., Sheila. I investigate people. Nothing personal, but think about it. Sunnie will be in your care for two weeks. I don't know you personally and I need to know she's not only in a safe environment but with someone both Brad and I can trust. Would you not want me to check out the person whose care she's been placed in?"

Sheila sighed deeply, knowing that she would. "But I'd never do anything to harm her."

"I believe that, but I have to make sure. All I'm doing is a basic background check to make certain you don't have any past criminal history." After a moment he said, "Come on in, let's talk inside."

She thought about his request then decided it might be best if they did talk inside after all. She had a tendency to raise her voice when she was angry about something.

"Fine." She stalked off ahead of him.

* * *

By the time Zeke followed her inside the house, she was in the middle of the living room pacing, and he could tell she was still mad. He quietly closed the door behind him and leaned against it, folding his arms across his chest, with one booted heel over the other, as he watched her. Again he was struck by just how beautiful she was. For some reason he was more aware of it now than before. There was fire in her eyes, annoyance in her steps and the way she was unconsciously swaying her hips was downright sensual. She had taken center stage, was holding it and he was a captive audience of one.

Then she stopped pacing and placed her hands on her hips to face him. She glared him down. The woman could not have been more than five-four at the most. Yet even with his height of six-four she was making him feel shorter. Damn. He hadn't meant for her to overhear his conversation with Brad. Hadn't she told him she hadn't wanted to come in?

"You were supposed to stay outside. You said you didn't want to come in," he blurted out for some reason. He watched as she stiffened her spine even more.

"And that gave you the right to talk about me?"

His heart thudded deeply in his chest. The last thing he had time or the inclination to do was deal with an emotional female. "Look, Sheila, like I said before, I am a private investigator. My job is to know people and I don't like surprises. Anyone who comes in contact with the baby for any long period of time will get checked out by me."

He rubbed his hand down his face and released a frustrated sigh. "Look. It's not that I was intentionally questioning your character. I was mainly assuring my client that a child that someone is claiming to be his has been placed in the best of care until the issue is resolved by way of a paternity test. There's no reason for you to take it personally. It's not about you. It's about Sunnie."

Had you been the president's mother-in-law I'd still do a background check. My client is a very wealthy man and my job is to protect him at all costs, which is why I intend to find out who is behind this."

He paused for a moment. "You do want what's best for Sunnie, don't you?"

"Of course."

"So do I, and so does Brad. That baby was abandoned, and the last thing I would want is for her not to have some stability in her life over the next couple of weeks. She deserves that at least. Neither of us know what will happen after that."

His words gave Sheila pause and deflated her anger somewhat. Although she didn't want to admit it, what he said was true. It wasn't about her but about Sunnie. She should be everyone's main concern. Background checks were routine and she would have expected that one be done if they'd hired a nanny for Sunnie. She didn't know Zeke like he didn't know her, and with that suspicious mind of his—which came with the work he did—he would want to check her out regardless of the fact that Dr. Phillips had spoken highly of her. But that didn't mean she had to like the fact Zeke had done it.

"Fine," she snapped. "You've done your job. Now, take me back to the hospital so I can get my car."

"We're going shopping for the baby stuff as planned, Sheila. You still need my truck, so please put your emotions aside and agree to do what's needed to be done."

"Emotions!" Before thinking about it, she quickly crossed the room to stand in front of him.

"Yes, emotions."

His voice had lowered and he reached out and tilted her chin up. "Has anyone ever told you how sexy you look when you're angry?"

And before she could take another breath, he lowered his mouth to hers.

Why did her lips have to be so soft?

Why did she have to taste so darn good? And why wasn't she resisting him?

Those questions rammed through Zeke's mind as his heart banged brutally in his chest at the feel of his mouth on Sheila's. He pushed those questions and others to the back of his mind as he deepened the kiss, took it to another level—although his senses were telling him that was the last thing he needed to do.

He didn't heed their advice. Instead, he wrapped his arms around Sheila's waist to bring her closer to the fit of him as he feasted on her mouth. He knew he wasn't the only one affected by the kiss when he felt her hardened nipples pressing into his chest. He could tell she hadn't gotten kissed a lot, at least not to this degree, and she seemed unsure of herself, but he remedied that by taking control. She moaned and he liked the sound of it and definitely liked the feel of her plastered against him.

He could go on kissing her for hours…days…months. The very thought gave him pause and he gradually pulled his mouth from hers. Hours, days and months meant an involvement with a woman and he didn't do involvements. He did casual affairs and nothing more. And the last thing he did was mix business with pleasure.

* * *

Sheila's first coherent thought after Zeke released her lips was that she had never, not even in her wildest dreams, been kissed like that. She still felt tingling in her toes and her entire body; her every limb and muscle felt like pure jelly, which was probably the reason she was quivering like the dickens inside.

She slowly drew air into her lungs, held it a moment before slowly letting it out. She could still taste him on her tongue. How had he gotten so entrenched there? She quickly answered her own question when she remembered how his tongue had taken hold of hers, mated with it and sucked on it.

She muttered a couple colorful expletives under her breath when she gazed up at him. She should not have allowed him to kiss her like that. She'd be the first to admit she had enjoyed it, but still. The eyes staring back at her were dark and heated as if he wanted a repeat performance. She cleared her throat. "Why did you kiss me?"

Why had he kissed her? Zeke asked himself that same question as he took a step back. He needed to put distance between them or else he would be tempted to kiss her again.

"You were talking," he said, grabbing the first excuse he could think of.

"No, I wasn't."

He lifted a brow. Hadn't she been? He tried to backtrack and recall just what was taking place between them before she'd stormed across the room to get in his face. When he remembered, he shrugged. "Doesn't matter. You would have said something you regretted and I decided to wipe the words off your lips."

Sheila frowned. "I suggest that you don't ever do it again."

That slow, sexy smile that she'd seen earlier returned, and instead of saying he wouldn't kiss her again, he crossed his arms over his chest and asked, "So, what brought you inside? You said you were going to wait outside."

He had changed subjects and she decided to follow his lead. "Your car began beeping loudly as if it was going to blow up or something."

His smile widened to emphasize the dimples in his cheeks. "That's my fax machine. It's built into my console in a way that's not detectable."

She shook her head. "What are you, a regular James Bond?"

"No. Bond is a secret agent. I'm a private investigator. There's a big difference." He glanced at his watch. "If you're ready, we can leave. My truck is this way."

"What about the fax that was coming through?"

"I have a fax in the truck, as well. It will come in on both."

"Oh."

She followed him through a spacious dining room and kitchen that was stylishly decorated. The living room was also fashionably furnished. Definitely more so than hers. "You have a nice home."

"Thanks, and if you're talking about the furniture and decorating, I can't take credit. It was a model home and I bought it as is. I saw it. I liked it. I got it."

He saw it, he liked it and he got it. She wondered if that was how he operated with everything in his life.

"Where do you want me to put these boxes?" Zeke asked, carrying two under his arms. One contained a baby car seat and the other a baby bath. He hadn't wanted to tell her, but he thought instead of purchasing just the basics that she'd gotten carried away. The kid would only be with her for two weeks at the most, not two years.

"You can set them down anywhere. I'm going to stay up late tonight putting stuff up."

After placing the boxes in a corner of the room, he glanced around. The place was small, but it suited her. Her furniture was nice and her two-story home was neat as a pin. He could imagine how it was going to look with baby stuff cluttering it up.

"I'm going to call the hospital again to check on Sunnie."

He bit down on his lips, forcing back a reminder that she had called the hospital less than an hour ago. And before that, while they had been shopping in Target for all the items on her list, she had called several times then, as well. It was a good thing she knew the nurses taking care of the baby, otherwise they would probably consider her a nuisance.

While she was on the phone, he went back outside to get more boxes out of the truck. Although she didn't live in a gated community, it was in a nice section of town, and he felt good about that. And he noticed she had an alarm system, but he would check the locks on her doors anyway. Until he discovered the identity of the person who'd tried to extort money from Brad, he wasn't taking any chances. What if the blackmailer tried to kidnap the baby back?

He had made several trips back and forth into the house before Sheila had finally gotten off the phone. He glanced over at her. "Is anything wrong?"

She shook her head. "No. Sunnie awakened for a short while, but she's gone back to sleep now."

Hell, he should hope so. He glanced at his watch. It was after nine o'clock. He should know since they'd closed the store. He figured that kid should be asleep by now. Didn't she have a bedtime?

"Okay, all the boxes are in, what do you need me to do now?"

Sheila glanced over at him, tempted to tell him what he could do was leave. He was unnerving her. He'd done so while they'd been shopping for the baby items. There was something about a good-looking man that could get to a woman each and every time, and she'd gotten her share with him today. Several times while walking down the aisles of the store, they had brushed against each other, and although both had tried downplaying the connection, she'd felt it and knew he'd felt it, as well. And he smelled good. Most of the men at the hospital smelled sanitized. She was reminded of a real man's scent while around him. And then there was that kiss she was trying hard to forget. However, she was finding it difficult to do so each and every time she looked at his lips. His mouth had certainly done a number on her. She thought every woman should spend the day shopping with a man for baby items at least once in her lifetime. Sheila couldn't help remembering the number of times they'd needed assistance from a store clerk. Finally, they'd been assigned their own personal clerk, probably to get them out the store sooner. She was sure the employees wanted to go home at some point that night. And she couldn't forget how the clerk assumed they were married, although neither of them was wearing a wedding ring. Go figure.

"You can take me to get my car now," she said, tucking a loose lock of hair behind her ear and trying not to stare at him. She shouldn't be surprised that he practically dominated her living room by standing in the middle of it. Everything else seemed to fade to black. He was definitely the main attraction with his height, muscular build and overall good looks.

"What about the baby bed?"

She quirked a brow. "What about it?"

"When are you going to put it together?"

She nibbled on her bottom lip, thinking that was a good question. It was one of the largest items she'd purchased and the clerk had turned down her offer to buy the one on display. That certainly would have made things easier for her. Instead, he'd sold her one in a box that included instructions that would probably look like Greek to her.

"Later tonight."

A smile curved his lips. "I should hope so if you plan on bringing the baby home tomorrow."

She wrapped her arms around herself. She hadn't told him yet, but she planned on bringing Sunnie home tonight. It was getting so bad with her crying that the nurses hated it when she woke up. Her crying would wake all the other babies. She had talked to the head nurse, who would be contacting Dr. Phillips to make sure Sunnie could be released into her care and custody tonight. She was just waiting for a callback.

Zeke studied Sheila. Maybe his brain was overreacting, but he had a feeling she was keeping something from him. Maybe it was because she was giving a lot away. Like the way she had wrapped her arms around herself. Or the nervous look in her eyes. Or it could be the way she was nibbling on the lips he'd kissed earlier that day. A kiss he wished he could forget but couldn't. For some reason his mouth had felt right locked to hers. He crossed his arms over his chest. "Is there something you want to tell me?"

She dropped her arms to her sides. "Sunnie is keeping the other babies up."

That didn't surprise him. He'd heard the kid cry. She had a good set of lungs. "She's sleeping now, right?"

"Yes, but as you know, she probably won't sleep through the night."

No, he didn't know that. "Why not?"

"Most babies don't. That's normal. The older they get the longer they will sleep through the night. In Sunnie's case, she probably sleeps a lot during the day and is probably up for at least part of the night."

"And you're prepared for that?"

"I have to be."

It occurred to him the sacrifices she would be making. His concentration had been so focused on the baby, he hadn't thought about the changes keeping Sunnie would make in her life. When she'd been on the phone and he'd been hauling in the boxes, he had taken a minute to pull his fax. It had been the background check on her. The firm he used was thorough and he'd held her life history in his hand while holding that one sheet of paper.

She was twenty-seven and every hospital she'd worked in since college had given her a glowing recommendation. She was a law-abiding citizen. Had never even received a speeding ticket. One year she had even received a medal for heroism from the Dallas Fire Department because she'd rushed inside a burning house to help save an elderly man, and then provided him with medical services until paramedics got there. That unselfish act had made national news.

On a more personal side, he knew she had a sister whom she didn't visit often. She had a mother whom she visited once or twice a year. Her mother was divorced from husband number five, a CEO of a resort in Florida. Her father had died five years ago. Her only sister, who was four years older, was from her father's first marriage. Sheila had been the product of the old man's second marriage.

"Tell me what else I can do to help," he said.

She released a deep sigh. "I want to bring Sunnie here tonight. The nurses are contacting Dr. Phillips for his approval. I hope to get a call from him any minute. Either way, whether I get Sunnie tonight or tomorrow, I'll need the bed, so if you really don't mind, I'd appreciate it if you would put it together. I'm not good at doing stuff like that."

He nodded. "No problem." He began rolling up his sleeves. "You wouldn't happen to have a beer handy, would you?"

She smiled. "Yes, I'll go grab one for you."

And then she took off and he was left standing while wondering why he couldn't stop thinking about the time he had kissed her.

"We're glad you're here," one of the nurses in Pediatrics said anxiously. "We have her packed up and ready to go," she added, smiling brightly.

"She's been expressing herself again, eh?" Zeke asked, chuckling.

Sheila glanced over at Zeke, wondering why he was

there. It hadn't taken him any time to put up the baby bed, and he'd taken the time to help with the other things, as well. Except for the fact Sunnie was a girl and the room was painted blue, everything else was perfect. By the time they'd left, it had looked like a genuine nursery and she couldn't wait for Sunnie to see it.

That brought her back to the question she'd wondered about earlier. Why was he here? She figured he would drop her off and keep moving. She had a baby car seat, so as far as she was concerned, she was ready to go. But she couldn't dismiss the nervous tension in her stomach. Sunnie had clung to her earlier today when the police officers had first brought her in. What if she no longer had that attachment to her and treated her like the others and continue to cry all over the place? She drew in a deep breath, wanting to believe that that special connection between them was still there. "Where is she?" she asked the nurse.

"Down that hall. Trust me, you'll hear her as soon as you clear the waiting area. You won't be able to miss it. All of us are wearing homemade earplugs."

Sheila knew the nurse had said it as a joke, but she didn't see anything funny. She was ready to get Sunnie and go home. Home. Already she was thinking of her place as the baby's home. Before tonight, to her it was just a place to eat and sleep. Now, taking Sunnie there had her thinking differently.

True to what the nurse had said, Sunnie could be heard the moment Sheila and Zeke passed the waiting room. He put his hand on her arm for them to stop walking. He studied her features. "What's wrong? Why are you so tense?"

How had he known? She released a nervous sigh.

"I've been gone over eight hours. What if Sunnie isn't attached to me anymore? What if she sees me and continues to cry?"

Zeke stared at her. The answer seemed quite obvious to him. It didn't matter. The kid was going home with her regardless. But he could see it was important for this encounter with the baby not to constitute a rejection. He wondered why he cared. He reached out and took her hand in his and began rubbing it when it felt cold. "Hey, she's going to remember you. She liked you too much not to. If you recall, I was here when she was clinging to you like you were her lifeline, her protector and the one person she thinks is there for her."

He saw the hopeful gleam in her eyes. "You think so?"

Hell, he wasn't sure, but he'd never tell her that. "Yes, I think so."

She smiled. "Thanks, and I hope you're right."

He hoped he was right, too. They began walking again and when they reached the door to the room where Sunnie was being kept, he watched her square her shoulders and walk in. He followed behind her.

The baby was lying in a crib on her side, screaming up a storm, but miraculously, the moment she saw Sheila, her crying turned to tiny whimpers before she stopped completely. And Zeke wasn't sure how it was possible, but he wouldn't believe it if he hadn't seen it for himself.

The abandoned baby she'd named Sunnie smiled and reached her chubby arms out for her.

Chapter 4

The alarm went off and Zeke immediately came awake. Flipping over in bed, he stared up at the ceiling as his mind recalled everything that had happened the night before. Sunnie was now with Sheila.

He had hung around long enough to help gather up the baby and get her strapped in the car seat. And the kid hadn't uttered a single whimper. Instead, she had clung to Sheila like she was her very last friend on earth. He had followed them, just to make sure they arrived back at Sheila's house safely. While sitting in his truck, he had watched her get the baby inside before he'd finally pulled off.

At one point he'd almost killed the ignition and walked up to her door to see if she needed any more help, but figured he'd worn out his welcome already that day. Hell, at least he'd gotten a kiss out of the deal.

And what a kiss he'd had. Thinking about that kiss had made it very difficult to fall asleep and kept him tossing and turning all night long.

His day would be full. Although Brad was his best friend, he was also a client; a client who'd come to him for help. Zeke wanted to solve this case quickly. Doing so would definitely be a feather in his cap. It would also further improve his reputation and boost the prospects of his new partner, Darius.

He eased out of bed and was about to slide his feet into his slippers, when the phone rang.

"Hello."

"Hi, Zeke. I just want to make sure the baby is okay." He smiled at the sound of Darius's wife, Summer's, voice. Darius was presently in D.C. doing antiterrorism consulting work. "She's fine, Summer. The nurse who's going to be taking care of her for the next two weeks took her home from the hospital last night."

"What's the nurse's name?"

"Sheila Hopkins."

"I know Sheila."

He lifted a brow. "You do?"

"Yes… She and I worked together on a domestic abuse case six months ago. The woman made it to the hospital while Sheila was working E.R. I was called in because the woman needed a place to stay."

Summer was the director of Helping Hands Women's Shelter in Somerset, their twin city. "I hope things turned out well for the woman," he said.

"It did, thanks to Sheila. She's a real professional." He agreed. And he thought she was also a real woman. Before they'd gone to pick up the baby and while he was putting up the crib, she had showered and changed into a pair of jeans and a top. He wasn't aware that many curves could be on a woman's body. And he practically caught his breath each and every time he looked at her.

Moments later, after ending his call with Summer, Zeke drew in a deep breath and shook his head. He needed to focus on the case at hand and not the curvaceous Sheila Hopkins, or her sleep-stealing kisses.

The first thing he needed to do was to check the video cameras around the TCC. According to Brad, there were several, and Zeke was hoping that at least one of them had picked something up.

Then he intended to question the gardeners who were in charge of TCC's immaculate lawns to see if they'd seen or heard anything yesterday around the time the baby had been left on the doorstep.

And he had to meet up with Brad to make sure he'd taken the paternity test. The sooner they could prove that Brad wasn't Sunnie's father, the better.

As he made his way into the bathroom, he wondered how the baby was doing. Mainly he wondered how Sheila had fared. Last night, it had been evident after taking several naps that Sunnie was all bright-eyed and ready to play. At midnight. He wondered if Sheila got any sleep.

He rubbed his hands down his face. The thought of her in jammies beneath the covers had his gut stirring. Perhaps she didn't sleep under the covers. She might sleep on top of them the way he did sometimes. Then there was the possibility that she didn't wear jammies, but slept in the nude as he preferred doing at times, as well.

He could imagine her in the nude. For a moment he'd envisioned her that way last night when he'd heard the shower going and knew she was across the hall from where he was putting the crib together, and taking a shower and changing clothes. Strong desire had kicked him so hard he'd almost dropped his screwdriver.

And there was the scent he'd inhaled all through her house. It was a scent he now associated with her. Jasmine. He hadn't known what the aroma was until he'd asked. It was in her candles, various baskets of potpourri that she had scattered about. But he'd especially picked it up when she'd come out of her bedroom after taking her shower. She had evidently used the fragrance while showering because its scent shrouded her when she'd entered the room she would use as the temporary nursery.

Last night it had been hard to get to sleep. To take the chill out of the air he'd lit the fireplace in his bedroom and then couldn't settle down when visions of him and Sheila, naked in front of that same fireplace, tortured his mind.

As he brushed his teeth and washed his face, he couldn't help wondering what the hell was wrong with him. He knew the score where women were concerned. The feeling of being abandoned was something he would always deal with. As a result, he would never set himself up for that sort of pain again. No woman was worth it.

A short while later he had stepped out the shower and was drying off when his cell phone rang. He reached to pick it up off the bathroom counter and saw it was Brad. "What's going on?"

"Abigail Langley is what's going on. I know she has a meeting at TCC this morning and I'm going to have it out with her once and for all."

Zeke rolled his eyes. "Lay off her, Brad. You don't have any proof she's involved in any way."

"Sure she's involved. Abigail happens to be the only person who'll benefit if my reputation is ruined."

"But you just can't go accusing her of anything without concrete proof," Zeke said in a stern tone.

"I can't? Ha! Just watch me." Brad then clicked off the phone.

"Damn!" Zeke placed the phone back on the counter as he quickly began dressing. He needed to get over to TCC before Brad had a chance to confront Abigail Langley. He had a feeling his best friend was about to make a huge mistake.

Sheila fought back sleep as she fed Sunnie breakfast. She doubted if she and the baby had gotten a good four hours' sleep. The pediatric nurse had been right. Sunnie had slept most of yesterday, and in the middle of the night while most of Royal was sleeping, she had been wide awake and wanting to play.

Of course, Sheila had given in after numerous attempts at rocking her to sleep failed. Now Sunnie looked well-rested. Sheila refused to think about how *she* looked half-asleep and yawning every ten minutes. But even lack of sleep could not erase how it felt holding the baby in her arms. And when Sunnie looked up at her and smiled, she knew she would willingly spend an entire week of sleepless nights to see that smile.

And she could make the cutest sounds when she was happy. It must be nice not having any troubles. Then she quickly remembered Sunnie might have troubles after all, if Bradford Price turned out not to be her daddy. Sheila didn't want to think about what could happen to her once Social Services took her away and put her into the system.

"We're not going to think about any of that right now,

cupcake," she said, wiping Sunnie's mouth after she'd finished her bottle. "Now it's time for you to burp," she said, gently hoisting the baby onto her shoulder.

Dr. Phillips had referred Dr. Greene, the head pediatrician at Royal Memorial, to the case, and he had called inquiring how Sunnie was doing. He'd also given her helpful hints as to how to help Sunnie formulate a sleeping pattern where she would stay awake during most of the day and sleep longer at night.

A short while later, she placed the baby back in the crib after Sunnie seemed to have found interest in the mobile Zeke had purchased at the last minute while in the store last night. She had almost talked him out of getting it, but now she was glad she hadn't.

Sheila had pulled up a chair to sit there and watch Sunnie for a while, when her phone rang. She immediately picked it up. "Yes?"

"I was waiting to see if you remembered that you had a mother."

Sheila rolled her eyes, fighting the urge to say that she'd also been waiting to see if her mother remembered she had a daughter, but knew it would be a waste of time. The only reason her mother was calling her now was because she was in between husbands and she had a little idle time on her hands.

"Hi, Mom," she said, deciding not to bother addressing her mother's comment. "And how are you?"

"I could be better. Did you ever get that guy's phone number?"

That *guy* her mother was referring to was Dr. Morgan. The last time her mother had come to visit they had gone out to lunch, only to run into one of the surgeons from the hospital. Dr. Morgan was ten years her mother's junior. Did that mean her mother was considering the possibility of becoming a cougar?

"No. Like I told you then, Dr. Morgan is already in a serious relationship."

Cassie Hopkins chuckled. "Isn't everybody…except you?"

Sheila cringed. Her mother couldn't resist the opportunity to dig. Cassie felt that if she could get five husbands, her only daughter should be able to get at least one. "I don't want a serious relationship, Mom."

"And if you did want one, then what?"

"Then I'd have one." Knowing her mother was about to jump in about Crawford Newman, the last man she wanted to talk about, she quickly changed the subject. "I talked to Lois the other day."

Her mother chuckled again. "And I bet you called her and not the other way around."

"No, in fact, she called me." She didn't have to tell her mother that Lois had called to tell her not to visit her and her family in Atlanta after all. And that was after issuing her an invitation earlier in the year. There was also no need to tell her that Lois had only issued the invitation after hearing about that heroic deed Sheila had performed, which had gotten broadcast nationwide on CNN. She guessed it wasn't important any longer for Lois to let anyone know that she was her sister after all.

Her mother snorted. "Hmmph. I'm surprised. So how is the princess doing and has she said when she plans to share any of the inheritance your father left her with you?"

Sheila knew the fact that her own father had intentionally left her out of his will still bothered her mother, although it no longer bothered her. It had at first because doing such a thing had pretty much proven what she'd always known. Her father hadn't wanted her. Regardless of the fact that he ended up despising her mother, that should not have had any bearing on his relationship with his daughter. But Baron Hopkins hadn't seen things that way. He saw her as an extension of her mother, and if you hated the mother then you automatically hated the child.

Lois, on the other hand, had indeed been her father's princess. The only child from the first wife whom he had adored, he hadn't been quite ready for the likes of Cassie. Things probably wouldn't have been so bad if Baron hadn't discovered her mother was having an affair with one of his business partners—a man who later became husband number two for Cassie. Then there was the question of whether Sheila was even his child, although she looked more like him than Lois did. She was able to get her mother off the phone when Cassie had a call come through from some man. It was the story of her mother's life and the failed fairy tale for hers. She got out of the chair and moved over to the crib. Sunnie was trying to go to sleep. Sheila would have just loved to let her, but she knew if she were to sleep now that would mean another sleepless night. "Oh, no, you don't, sweetie pie," she said, getting the baby out of bed. "You and I are going to play for a while. I plan on keeping you up as much as possible today."

Sunnie gurgled and smiled sleepy hazel eyes up at her. "I know how you feel, trust me. I want to sleep, too. Hopefully, if this works, we'll both get to sleep tonight," Sheila said softly, rubbing the baby's fingers, reveling in just how soft her skin was.

Holding the baby gently in her arms, she headed downstairs.

* * *

Zeke walked down the hall of the TCC's clubhouse to one of the meeting rooms. The Texas Cattlemen's motto, which was clearly on display on a plaque in the main room here, said, Leadership, Justice and Peace. He heard loud angry voices and recognized Brad's and knew the female one belonged to Abigail. He wondered if they'd forgotten about the peace wording of the slogan.

"And just what are you accusing me of, Brad?"

"You're too intelligent to play dumb, Abigail. I know you're the one who arranged to have that baby left with a note claiming it's mine, when you know good and well it's not."

"What! How can you accuse me of such a thing?"

"Easily. You want to be the TCC's next president."

"And you think I'll go so far as to use a baby? A precious little baby to show you up?"

Zeke cringed. He could actually hear Abigail's voice breaking. Hell, it sounded as if the woman was crying. He paused outside the door.

"Dang, Abigail, I didn't mean to make you cry, for Pete's sake."

"Well, how could you accuse me of something like that? I love babies. And that little girl was abandoned. I had nothing to do with it, Brad. You've got to believe me."

Zeke inhaled deeply. The woman was downright bawling now. Brad had really gone and done it now.

"I'm sorry, Abby. I see that I was wrong. I didn't mean to get you so upset. I'm sorry."

"You should be. And to prove I'm not behind it," she said, still crying, *"I suggest we suspend campaigning for the election until the case is solved."*

"And you'll go along with doing that?"

"Of course. We're talking about a baby, Brad, and her welfare comes first."

"I agree," Brad said. "Thanks, Abby. And again, I'm sorry for accusing you earlier."

Zeke thought it was time for him to make his entrance before Brad made a bigger mess of things. At least he'd had the sense to apologize to the woman. He opened the door and stopped. Brad was standing in the middle of the room holding a still-weeping Abigail in his arms.

For a moment Zeke thought he should tiptoe back out and was about to do just that, when they both glanced over at him. And as if embarrassed at being caught in such an embrace, the two quickly jumped apart.

Zeke placed his hands in the pockets of his jeans and smiled at the pair. "Brad. Abigail. Does this mean the two of you are no longer at war?"

A short while later Zeke was getting back in his car thinking that he hadn't needed to put out the fire after all. Brad and Abigail were a long way from being best friends, but at least it seemed as if they'd initiated a truce. If he hadn't been a victim of abandonment himself, he would think something good had at least resulted from Sunnie's appearance.

Sunnie.

He shook his head. Sheila had deemed the baby be called Sunnie for the time being, and everyone had pretty much fallen in line with her request. He had refrained from calling her earlier just in case she and the baby were sleeping in late. But now it was close to two in the afternoon. Surely they were up by now. While she had been upstairs taking a shower last night, he had opened her refrigerator to grab another beer and noticed hers was barer than his. That meant, also like him, she must eat out a lot. Chances were she wouldn't want to take the baby out, so the least he could do would be to be a good guy and stop somewhere, buy something for her to eat and take it to her.

While at the TCC he had checked and nothing had gotten caught on the video camera other than a woman's hand placing the baby on the doorstep. Whoever had done it seemed to have known just where the cameras were located, which meant the culprit was someone familiar with the grounds of the club. Could it have been an inside job? At least they knew they could erase Abigail off the list. She had been in a meeting when the baby had been dropped off.

Besides, to say Abigail Langley had gotten emotional as a result of Brad's accusation was an understatement. He couldn't help wondering why. He knew she was a widow. Had she lost a baby at some point while she'd been married? He'd been tempted to ask Brad but figured knowing his and Abigail's history, he would probably be the last to know. He'd heard from more than one source that the two of them had been butting heads since they were kids.

After buckling his seat belt he turned his car's ignition and eased out the parking lot, wondering what type of meal Sheila might have a taste for. Still not wanting to disturb her and the baby, he smiled, thinking, when in doubt, get pizza.

Sheila cocked one eye open as she gazed over at Sunnie, who was back in the crib toying with her mobile again. She sighed, not sure how long she would be able to stay awake. It had been almost eighteen hours now. She'd done doubles at the hospital before, but at least she'd gotten a power nap in between. She didn't know babies had so much energy. She thought of closing her eyes for a second, but figured there was no way for her to do something like that. Mothers didn't sleep while their babies were awake, did they?

She had tried everything and refused to drink another cup of coffee. The only good thing was that if she continued to keep Sunnie awake, that meant when they both went to sleep, hopefully, it would be through the night. She glanced around the room, liking how it looked and hoped Sunnie liked it, as well.

Zeke had been such a sweetheart to help her put the baby equipment together and hang pictures on the wall. Although he hadn't asked, he had to have been wondering why she was going overboard for a baby that would be in her care for only two weeks. She was glad he hadn't asked because she would not have known what to tell him.

She tried to ignore the growling of her stomach and the fact that other than toast, coffee and an apple, she hadn't eaten anything else that day. She didn't want to take her eyes off the baby for even a minute.

She nearly jumped when she heard the sound of the doorbell. She glanced at the Big Bird clock she'd hung on the wall. It was close to four in the afternoon. She moved over to the window and glanced down and saw the two-seater sports car in her driveway and knew who it belonged to. What was Zeke doing back? They had exchanged numbers last night, merely as a courtesy. She really hadn't expected to see him again any time soon. She immediately thought about the kiss they'd shared...not that she hadn't thought about it several times that day already. That was the kind of kiss a girl would want to tell somebody about. Like a girlfriend. She'd thought about calling Jill then had changed her mind. On second thought, maybe it was the kind of kiss a girl should keep to herself.

The doorbell sounded again. Knowing she probably looked a mess and, at the moment, not caring since she hadn't anticipated any visitors, she walked over to the bed and picked up the baby. "Come on, Sunnie. Looks like we have company."

Zeke was just about to turn to leave, when the door opened. All it took was one look at Sheila to know she'd had a rough night and an even rougher day. Sunnie, on the other hand, looked happy and well-rested.

"Hey, you okay?" he asked Sheila when she stepped aside to let him in. And he figured the only reason she'd done that was because of the pizza boxes he was carrying.

"I'm fine." She eyed the pizza box. "And I hope you brought that to share. I've barely eaten all day."

"Yes, I brought it to share," he said, heading for the kitchen. "The kid wore you out today?"

"And last night," she said, following on his heels. "I talked to the pediatrician about her not sleeping through the night and he suggested I try to keep her awake today. That means staying awake myself."

He stopped and she almost walked into the back of him. He turned inquisitive dark eyes on her. "Sunnie hasn't taken a nap at all today?"

"No. Like I said, I'm keeping her awake so we can both sleep tonight."

He found that interesting for some reason. "When do babies usually develop a better sleep pattern?"

"It depends. Usually they would have by now. But we don't know Sunnie's history. Her life might have been so unstable she hadn't gotten adjusted to anything." She glanced at the baby. "I hate talking about her like she isn't here."

Zeke laughed. "It's not as if she can understand anything you've said."

He shook his head. Sheila had to be pretty tired to even concern herself with anything like that. He glanced around the kitchen. It was still neat as a pin, but baby bottles lined the counter as well as a number of other baby items. It was obvious that a baby was in residence.

"Why did you stop by?" she asked.

He glanced back at her. Her eyes looked tired, almost dead on her feet. Her hair was tied back in a ponytail and she wasn't wearing any makeup. But he thought she looked good. "To check on the two of you. And I figured you probably hadn't had a chance to cook anything," he said, deciding not to mention he'd noticed last night she hadn't had anything to cook.

"So I decided I would be nice and stop and grab something for you," he said, placing the pizza boxes on the table. He opened one of them.

"Oh, that smells so good. Thank you."

He chuckled. "I've gotten pizza from this place before and it is good. And you're welcome. Do you want to lay her down while you dig in?"

She looked down at Sunnie and then back at him. "Lay her down?"

"Yes, like in that crib I put together for her last night."

"But…she'll be all alone."

He frowned. "Yes, but I hooked up that baby monitor last night so you could hear her. Haven't you tried it out?"

"Yes, but I like watching her."

He nodded slowly. "Why? I can imagine you being fascinated by her since you admitted yesterday that you've never kept a baby before, but why the obsession? You're a nurse. Haven't you worked in the nursery before?"

"Of course, but this is different. This is my home and Sunnie is in my care. I don't want anything to happen to her."

He could tell by her tone that she was getting a little defensive, so he decided to back off a bit, table it for later. And there would definitely be a later, because she wouldn't be much use to Sunnie or anybody if she wore herself out. "Fine, sit down and I'll go get that extra car seat. You can place her in it while you eat."

A short while later they were sitting at her kitchen table with Sunnie sitting in the car seat on the floor between them. She was moving her hands to and fro while making sounds. She seemed like such a happy baby. Totally different from the baby that had been screaming up a storm yesterday. Every once in a while she would raise her hazel eyes to stare at them. Mainly at him. It was as if she was trying to figure him out. Determine if he was safe.

Zeke glanced over at Sheila. She had eaten a couple slices of pizza along with the bag salad he'd bought. Every so often she would yawn, apologize and then yawn again. She needed to get some sleep; otherwise, she would fall on her face at any minute.

"Thanks for the pizza, Zeke. Not only are you nice, but you're thoughtful."

He leaned back in his chair. "You're welcome." He

paused for a moment. "I got a folder with stuff out there in my car that I need to go over. I can do it here just as well as anywhere else."

Her forehead furrowed as if confused. "But why would you want to?"

He smiled. "That way I can watch Sunnie." She still looked confused.

"Look, Sheila. It's obvious that you're tired. Probably ready to pass out. You can go upstairs and take a nap while I keep an eye on the baby."

"But why would you want to do something like that?" He chuckled. She asked a lot of questions. Unfortunately for him they were questions he truly couldn't answer. Why had he made such an offer? He really wasn't sure. All he knew was that he liked being around her and wasn't ready to leave yet.

When he didn't give her an answer quick enough, she narrowed her gaze. "You think I can't handle things, don't you? You think I've taken on more than I can chew by agreeing to be Sunnie's temporary foster parent. You think—"

Before she could finish her next words, he was out of the chair, had eased around the baby and had pulled Sheila into his arms. "Right now I think you're talking too damn much." And then he kissed her.

For some reason he needed to do this, he thought as his mouth took possession of hers. And the instant their mouths touched, he felt energized in a way he'd never felt before. Sexually energized. His tongue slid between her parted lips and immediately began tangling with hers. What was there about kissing her that was so mind-blowing, so arousing, so threatening to his senses? This kind of mouth interaction with her was stirring things inside him he'd tried to keep at bay with other women. How could she rouse them so effortlessly? So deeply and so thoroughly? And why did she feel so damn good in his arms? Even better today than yesterday. Yesterday there had been that element of surprise on both their parts. It was still there today, but surprise was being smothered by heat of the most erotic kind.

And it was heat he could barely handle. Not sure that he could manage. But it was heat that he was definitely enjoying. And then there was something else trying to creep into the mix. Emotions. Emotions he wasn't accustomed to. He had thought of her all day. Why? Usually for him it had always been out of sight and out of mind. But not with Sheila. The woman was unforgettable. She was temptation he couldn't resist.

He felt a touch on his leg and reluctantly released Sheila's mouth to glance down. Hazel eyes were staring up at him. Sunnie had grabbed hold of his pant leg. He couldn't help chuckling. At five months old the kid was seeing too much. If she hadn't gotten his attention, he'd probably still be kissing Sheila.

He shifted his gaze from the baby back to the woman he was still holding in his arms. She was about to step back, so he tightened his hold around her waist. "I'm going out to my car and getting my briefcase. When I come back inside you're going to go up those stairs and get some rest. I'll handle Sunnie."

"But—"

"No buts. No questions. I'll take good care of her. I promise."

"She might cry the entire time."

"If she cries I'll deal with it." He then walked out of the kitchen.

* * *

Sheila couldn't stop her smile when Zeke walked out. She glanced down at Sunnie. "He's kind of bossy, isn't he?" She touched her lips. "And he's a darn good kisser."

She sighed deeply. "Not that you needed to know that. Not that you needed to see us lock lips, either."

She then moved around the kitchen as she cleared off the table. She was standing at the sink when Zeke returned with his briefcase. "How long do you plan to be here?" she asked him.

"For as long as you need to rest."

She nodded. "I'll be fine in a couple of hours. Will you wake me?"

Zeke stared at her, fully aware she had no idea of what she was asking of him. Seeing her in bed, under the covers or on top of the covers, would not be a good idea. At least she hadn't reminded him that she'd told him not to kiss her again. But what could she say, when she had kissed him back?

"I won't wake you, Sheila. You have to wake up on your own."

She frowned. "But Sunnie will need a bath later."

"And she'll get one, with or without you. For your information I do know a little about kids." She looked surprised. "You do?"

"Yes. I was raised by my aunt and she has a daughter with twins. They consider me their uncle and I've kept them before."

"Both?"

"Yes, and at the same time. It was a piece of cake." Okay, he had exaggerated some. There was no need to tell her that they had almost totally wrecked his place by the time their parents had returned.

"How old are they?"

"Now they're four. The first time I kept them they were barely one."

She nodded. "They live in Austin?"

"No. New Orleans."

"So you're not a Texan by birth?"

He wondered why all the questions again. He had made a mistake when he mentioned Alicia and the twins. "According to my birth certificate, I am a Texan by birth. My aunt who raised me lives in New Orleans. I returned to Texas when I attended UT in Austin."

He had told her enough and, when she opened her mouth to say something more, he placed his hand over it. Better his hand than his mouth. "No more questions. Now, off to bed."

She glanced down at the baby when he removed his hand from her mouth. "Are you sure you want to handle her?"

"Positive. Now, go."

She hesitated for a minute and then drew in a deep breath before leaving the kitchen. He glanced down at Sunnie, whose eyes had followed Sheila from the room. Then those same hazel eyes latched onto him almost in an accusatory stare. Her lips began trembling and he had an idea what was coming next. When she let out a wail, he bent down and picked up the car seat and set it on the table.

"Shh, little one. Sheila needs her rest. Come on, I'm not that bad. She likes me. I kissed her. Get over it."

When her crying suddenly slowed to a low whimper, he wondered if perhaps this kid did understand.

Chapter 5

Something—Sheila wasn't sure exactly what—woke her up, and her gaze immediately went to the clock on the nightstand: 7:00 p.m. She quickly slid out of bed and raced down the stairs then halted at the last step. There, stretched out on the sofa was Zeke with Sunnie on his chest. They were both asleep and, since the baby was wearing one of the cute pj sets they'd purchased yesterday, it was obvious he'd given her a bath. In fact, the air was filled with the fragrance of baby oil mixed with baby powder. She liked the smell.

She wished she had a camera to take a picture. This was definitely a Kodak moment. She slowly tiptoed to the chair across from the sofa and sat down. Even while sleeping, Zeke was handsome, and his long lashes almost fanned his upper cheeks. He didn't snore. Crawford snored something awful. Another comparison of the two men.

She wondered if he'd ever dumped a woman the way Crawford had dumped her. Good old Crawford, the traveling salesman, who spent a lot of time on the road… and as she later found out while he'd been on the road, in other women's beds. She remembered the time she would anxiously await his long-distance calls and how she would feel when she didn't get them. How lonely she would be when she didn't hear from him for days.

And she would never forget that day when he did show up, just to let her know he was marrying someone else. A woman he'd met while out peddling his medical supplies. He had wanted her to get on with her life because he had gotten on with his. She took his advice. Needing to leave Dallas, the next time an opportunity came for a transfer to another hospital, she had taken it.

She continued to stare at Zeke and wondered what his story was. He'd told her bits and pieces and she figured that was all she would get. So far he hadn't mentioned anything about a mother. His comment yesterday pretty much sealed the fact he hadn't known his father. And from what he'd told her today, his aunt in New Orleans had raised him. Had his mother died? She drew in a deep breath, thinking it really wasn't any of her business. Still, she couldn't help being curious about the hunk stretched out on her sofa. The man who had kissed her twice. The man who'd literally knocked sense right out of her brain.

And that wasn't good. That meant it was time for him to leave. Yesterday she had appreciated his help in shopping with her for baby items. Today she appreciated the pizza. There couldn't be a tomorrow.

Easing out of the chair, she crossed the room and gently shook him awake. She sucked in a deep breath when his eyes snapped open and his beautiful dark eyes stared up at her. Pinned her to the spot where she was standing. They didn't say anything but stared at each other for the longest time. She felt his stare as if his gaze was a physical caress.

And while he stared at her, she remembered things. She remembered how good his mouth felt on hers.

How delicious his tongue tasted in her mouth. How his tongue would slide from side to side while driving her to the brink of madness. It made her wonder just what else that tongue was capable of doing.

She blushed and she knew he'd noticed because his gaze darkened. "What were you thinking just now?"

Did he really expect her to tell him? Fat chance! Some things he was better off not knowing and that was definitely one of them. "I was thinking that it's time for me to put Sunnie to bed."

"I doubt that would have made you blush."

She doubted it, too, but she would never admit to it. Instead of responding to what he'd said, she reached for Sunnie. "I'm taking her upstairs and putting her to bed." Once she had the baby cradled in her arms, she walked off.

When she had gone up the stairs, Zeke eased into a sitting position and rubbed his hands down his face. Surprisingly, he'd gotten a lot of work done. Sunnie had sat in her car seat and stared at him the entire time, evidently fascinated by the shifting of the papers and the sight of him working on his laptop computer. He figured the bright colors that had occasionally flashed across the screen had fascinated her.

He stood and went back into the kitchen. There was no doubt in his mind that when Sheila returned she would expect him to be packed up and ready to go. He would not disappoint her. Although he would love to hang around, he needed to haul it. There was too much attraction between them. Way too much chemistry. When they had gazed into each other's eyes, the air had become charged. She had become breathless. So had he. That wasn't good.

All there was supposed to be between them was business. Where was his hard-and-fast rule never to mix business with pleasure? It had taken a hard nosedive the first time he'd kissed her. And if that hadn't been bad enough, he'd kissed her again. What had come over him? He knew the answer without thinking—lust of the most intense kind.

By the time he clicked his briefcase closed, he heard Sheila come back downstairs, and when she walked into the kitchen he had it in his hand. "Walk me to the door," he said softly, wondering why he'd asked her to do so when he knew the way out.

"Okay."

She silently walked beside him and when they got to the door, she reached out to open it, but he took her hand, brought it to his lips and kissed it. "I left my card on the table. Call me if you need anything. Otherwise, this was my last time coming by."

She nodded and didn't ask why. He knew she understood. They were deeply attracted to each other and if they hung around each other for long, that attraction would heat up and lead to something else. Something that he knew neither of them wanted to tangle with right now.

"Thanks for everything, Zeke. I feel rested."

He smiled. "But you can always use more. She'll

probably sleep through the night, but she'll be active in the morning. That little girl has a lot of energy."

Sheila chuckled. "So you noticed."

"Oh, yeah, I noticed. But she's a good kid."

"Yes, and I still can't believe someone abandoned her."

"It happens, Sheila. Even to good kids."

He brushed a kiss across her lips. "Go back to bed." Then he opened the door and walked out.

Zeke forced himself to keep moving and not look back. He opened the car door and sat there a moment, fighting the temptation to get out of his car, walk right back up to her door and knock on it. When she answered it, he would kiss her senseless before she could say a single word. He would then sweep her off her feet and take her up to her bedroom and stretch her out on it, undress her and then make love to her.

He leaned back against the headrest and closed his eyes. How had it moved from kissing to thoughts of making love to her? *Easily, Travers,* his mind screamed. She's a beauty. She's hot. And you enjoy her mouth too damn much.

He took a deep breath and then exhaled slowly. He would be doing the right thing by staying away. Besides, it wasn't as though he didn't have anything to do. He had several people to interview tomorrow, including several TCC members who wanted to talk to him. One of them had called tonight requesting the meeting and he wondered what it would be about.

He turned the key in the ignition and backed out the driveway. He looked at the house one last time before doing so. All the lights were off downstairs. His gaze traveled to her bedroom window. The light was on there. He wondered what she was doing. Probably getting ready for bed.

A bed he wished he could join her in.

Sheila checked on Sunnie one more time before going into her bathroom to take a shower. She felt heat rush to her cheeks when she remembered waking Zeke earlier. The man had a way of looking at her that could turn her bones into mush.

A short while later after taking a shower and toweling dry her body, she slid into a pair of pajamas. She checked on Sunnie one last time and also made sure the monitor was set so she could hear her if she was to awaken. Zeke was convinced the baby would sleep through the night.

She drew in a deep breath knowing he'd told her he wouldn't be back. And she knew it was for the best. She would miss him. His appearance at her door tonight had been a surprise. But he had a way of making himself useful and she liked that. Crawford hadn't been handy with tools. He used to tell her he worked too hard to do anything other than what was required of him at his job. Not even taking out the trash.

And she had put up with it because she hadn't wanted to be alone.

Moving here was her first accomplishment. It had been a city where she hadn't known anybody. A city where she would be alone. Go figure. She had gotten used to it and now Zeke had invaded her space. So had Sunnie. The latter was a welcome invasion; the former wasn't.

As she slid into bed and drew the covers around

her, she closed her eyes and ran her tongue around her mouth. Even after brushing her teeth she could still taste Zeke. It was as if his flavor was embedded in her mouth. She liked it. She would savor it because it wouldn't happen again.

The next day, Zeke leaned back on the table and studied the two men sitting before him and tried digesting their admissions.

"So the two of you are saying that you also received blackmail letters?"

Rali Tariq and Arthur Moran, well-known wealthy businessmen and longtime members of the TCC, nodded. Then Rali spoke up. "Although I was innocent of what the person was accusing me of, I was afraid to go to the authorities."

"Same here," Arthur said. "I was hoping the person would eventually go away when I didn't acknowledge the letters. It was only when I found out about the blackmailing scheme concerning Bradford that I figured I needed to come forward."

"That's the reason I'm here, as well," Rali added.

Zeke nodded. What the two men had just shared with him certainly brought a lot to light. It meant the blackmailer hadn't just targeted Brad, but had set his or her mark on other innocent, unsuspecting TCC members, as well. That made him wonder whether the individual was targeting TCC members because they were known to be wealthy or if there was a personal vendetta the authorities needed to be concerned with.

"Did you bring the letters with you?"

"Yes."

Both men handed him their letters. He placed them

on the table and then pulled out one of the ones Brad had received. It was obvious they had been written by the same person.

"They looked the same," Rali said, looking over Zeke's shoulder at all three letters.

Arthur nodded in agreement.

"Yes, it appears that one person wrote them all," Zeke replied. "But the question is why did he carry out his threat against Brad but not on you two?"

He could tell by the men's expressions that they didn't have a clue. "Well, at least I'm finally getting pieces to the puzzle. I appreciate the two of you coming forward. It will help in clearing Brad's name. Now all we have to do is wait for the results of the paternity test." An hour later he met Brad for lunch at Claire's Restaurant, an upscale establishment in downtown Royal that served delicious food. A smile curved Brad's lips after hearing about Zeke's meeting with Rali and Arthur.

"Then that should settle things," he said, cutting into the steak on his plate. "If Rali and Arthur received blackmail letters, that proves there's a conspiracy against members of the TCC. There probably are others who aren't coming forward like Rali and Arthur."

Zeke took a sip of his wine. "Possibly. But you are the only one who he or she carried out the threat with. Why you and not one of the others? Hell, Rali is the son of a sheikh. I would think they would have stuck it to him real good. So we still aren't out of the woods. There's something about the whole setup that bothers me."

He studied Brad for a moment. "Did you and Abigail Langley clear things up?"

Brad met his gaze. "If you're asking if I think she's

still involved then the answer is no. Now I wished I hadn't approached her with my accusations."

A smile touched Zeke's lips. "I hate to say I told you so, but I did tell you so."

"I know. I know. But Abigail and I have been bad news for years."

"Yeah, but someone getting on your bad side is one thing, Brad. Accusing someone, especially a woman, of having anything to do with abandoning a child is another."

Brad held his gaze for the longest time. "And you of all people should know, right?"

Zeke nodded. "Yes, I should know."

Zeke took another sip of his wine. As his best friend, Brad was one of the few people who knew his history. Brad knew how Zeke's mother had abandoned him. Not on a doorstep, but in the care of his aunt. Although his aunt had been a godsend, he'd felt abandoned those early years. Alone. Discarded. Thrown away. No longer wanted.

It had taken years for him to get beyond those childhood feelings. But he would be the first to admit those childhood feelings had subsequently become adult hang-ups. That was one of the reasons he only engaged in casual affairs. He wouldn't let anyone walk out on him again. He would be the one doing the walking.

"Abigail certainly took my accusation hard," Brad said, breaking into Zeke's thoughts. "I've known her since we were kids and I've never known her to be anything but tough as nails. Seeing her break down like that really got to me."

"I could tell. You seemed to be holding her pretty tightly when I walked in."

He chuckled at the blush that appeared in Brad's features. "Well, what else was I supposed to do?" Brad asked. "Especially since I was the reason she'd gotten upset in the first place. I'm going to have to watch what I say around her."

Especially if it's about babies, Zeke thought, deciding not to say the words out loud. If Brad wasn't concerned with the reason the woman fell to pieces then he wouldn't be concerned with it, either. Besides, he had enough on his plate.

"So how's the baby?" Brad asked, breaking into his thoughts yet again.

"Sunnie?"

"Yes."

He leaned back in his chair as he thought about how she had wet him up pretty good when he'd given her a bath. He'd had to throw his shirt into Sheila's dryer. "She's fine. I checked on her yesterday."

"And the woman that's taking care of her. That nurse. She's doing a pretty good job?"

Zeke thought about Sheila. Hell, he'd thought about her a lot today, whether he had wanted to or not. "Yes, she's doing a pretty good job."

"Well, I hope the results from the paternity test come up quickly enough for her sake."

Zeke lifted a brow. "Why for her sake?"

"I would hate for your nurse to get too attached to the baby."

Zeke nodded. He would hate for "his" nurse to get too attached to Sunnie, as well.

"She is such a cutie," Summer Franklin said as she held Sunnie in her arms. Surprisingly, Sunnie hadn't cried when Summer had taken her out of Sheila's arms. She was too fascinated with Summer's dangling earrings to care. Sheila liked Summer. She was one of the few people she felt she could let her guard down around. Because Sheila had a tendency to work all the time, this was the first time she'd seen Summer in weeks.

"Yes, she is a cutie," Sheila said. "I can't imagine anyone abandoning her like that."

"Me, neither. But you better believe Zeke's going to get to the bottom of it. I'm glad Darius brought him on as a partner. My husband was working himself to death solving cases. Now he has help."

Sheila nodded, wondering how much Summer knew about Zeke, but didn't want to ask for fear her friend would wonder why.

Although Sunnie had slept through the night, she herself, on the other hand, had not. Every time she closed her eyes she had seen Zeke, looking tall, dark, handsome and fine as any man had a right to be. Then she also saw another image of him. The one sleeping peacefully on the sofa with the baby lying on his chest. She wondered if he would marry and have children one day. She had a feeling he would make a great dad just from his interaction with Sunnie.

"Oops, I think she's ready to return to you now," Summer said, breaking her thoughts. She smiled when she saw Sunnie lift her little hands to reach out for her, making her feel special. Wanted. Needed.

"You're good with her, Sheila."

She glanced over at Summer and smiled. "Thanks."

"I wonder who her real parents are."

"I wondered that, as well. But I'm sure Zeke is going to find out," Sheila said.

Summer chuckled. "I believe that, as well. Zeke comes across as a man who's good at what he does."

Sheila held the baby up to hide the blush on her face.

She knew for a fact that Zeke was good at what he did, especially when it came to kissing a woman.

Zeke let himself inside his home with a bunch of papers in his hand, closing the door behind him with the heel of his shoe. He'd been busy today.

He dropped the papers on his dining room table and headed straight to the kitchen to grab a beer out of the refrigerator. He took a huge gulp and then let out a deep breath. He'd needed that. That satisfied his thirst. Now if he could satisfy his hunger for Sheila Hopkins the same way...

Twice he had thought of dropping by her place and twice he had remembered why he could not do that. He had no reason to see her again until it was time to open the paternity test results. Considering what he'd discovered with those other two TCC members, he felt confident that the test would prove there was no biological link between Brad and Sunnie. But he was just as determined to discover whose baby she was. What person would abandon their child to make them a part of some extortion scheme? It was crazy. And sick. And he intended to determine who would do such a thing and make sure the authorities threw the book at them as hard as they could.

His thoughts shifted back to Sheila as he moved from the kitchen to the dining room. He had a lot of work to do and intended to get down to business. But he couldn't get out of his mind how he had opened his eyes while stretched out on her sofa only to find her staring down at him. If he hadn't had the baby sleeping on his chest, he would have been tempted to reach out and pull her down on the sofa with him. And he would have taken her mouth the way he wanted to do. Why was he torturing himself by thinking of something he was better off not having?

He drew in a deep breath, knowing he needed to put Sheila out of his mind. He had been going through various reports when the phone rang. He grinned when he saw it was Darius.

"Homesick, Darius?" he asked into the phone, and heard a resounding chuckle.

"Of course. I'm not missing you, though. It's my wife. I'm trying to talk Summer into catching a plane and joining me here—especially since there's a hurricane too close to you guys for comfort, but they're shorthanded at the shelter."

"So I heard."

"She also told me about the abandoned baby. How's that going?"

He took the next few minutes to bring Darius up to date. "I know Bradford Price and if he says the baby isn't his then it's not his," Darius said. "He has no reason to lie about it."

"I know, that's why I intend to expose the jerk who's out to ruin Brad's good name," Zeke said.

Chapter 6

Three days later Sheila sat glued to her television listening to the weather report. It was the last month of hurricane season and wouldn't you know it… Hurricane Spencer was up to no good out in the gulf. Forecasters were advising everyone to take necessary precautions by stocking up on the essentials just in case the storm changed course. Now Sheila had Sunnie to worry about, and that meant making sure she had enough of everything especially disposable diapers, formula and purified water in case the power went out.

Sunnie had pretty much settled down and was sleeping through the night. And they were both getting into a great routine. During the day Sheila had fun entertaining the baby by taking her to the park and other kid-friendly places. She enjoyed pushing Sunnie around in the stroller. Sunnie would still cry on occasion when others held her, but once she would glance around and lock her gaze on Sheila, she was fine.

Sheila had put the baby to bed a short while ago and was ready to go herself if only she was sleepy. Over the past couple of days she'd had several visitors. In addition to Summer and Jill, Dr. Greene had stopped by to check on the baby and Ms. Talbert from Social Services had visited, as well. Ms. Talbert had praised her for volunteering to care for Sunnie and indicated that considering the baby was both healthy and happy, she was doing a great job. The woman had further indicated there was a possibility the results of the paternity test might come in earlier than the two weeks anticipated. Instead of jumping for joy at the news, Sheila had found herself hoping that would not be the case. She had been looking forward to her two weeks with Sunnie.

She heard a branch hit the window and jumped. It had been windy all day and now it seemed it was getting windier. Forecasters predicted the hurricane would make landfall sometime after midnight. They predicted that Royal would be spared the worst of it.

She glanced around the room where she had already set out candles. The lights had been blinking all day; she hoped she didn't lose power, but had to be prepared if she did.

She was halfway up the stairs when the house suddenly went black.

The winds have increased and we have reports of power outages in certain sections of Royal, including the Meadowland and LeBaron areas. Officials are working hard to restore power to these homes and hope to do so within the next few hours…

Zeke was stretched out on the sofa with his eyes closed, but the announcement that had just blared from the television made him snap them open. He then slid into a sitting position. Sheila lived in the Meadowland area.

He knew he had no reason to be concerned. Hopefully, like everyone else, she had anticipated the possibility of a power failure and was prepared. But what if she wasn't? What if she was across town sitting on her sofa holding the baby in the dark?

Standing, he rubbed a hand down his face. It had been four days since he'd seen or talked to her. Four days, while working on clearing Brad's name, of trying hard to push thoughts of her to the back of his mind. He'd failed often, when no matter what he was working on, his thoughts drifted back to her.

What was there about a woman when a man couldn't get her out of his mind? When he would think of her during his every waking moment and wake up in the middle of the night with thoughts of her when he should be sleeping?

Zeke stretched his body before grabbing his keys off the table. Pushing aside the thought that he was making a mistake by rushing off to check on the very woman he'd sworn to stay away from, he quickly walked toward the door, grabbing a jacket and his Stetson on the way out.

Sheila glanced around the living room. Candles were lit and flashlights strategically placed where she might need them. It was just a little after ten but the wind was still howling outside. When she had looked out the window moments ago, all she could do was stare into darkness. Everything was total black.

She had checked on Sunnie earlier and the baby was

sleeping peacefully, oblivious to what was happening, and that was good. Sunnie had somehow kicked the covers off her pudgy little legs and Sheila had recovered her, gazing down at her while thinking what the future held for such a beautiful little girl.

Sheila left the nursery and walked downstairs.

She had the radio on a station that played jazz while occasionally providing updates on the storm. It had stopped raining, but the sound of water dripping off the roof was stirring a feeling inside her that she was all too familiar with—loneliness.

Deciding what she needed was a glass of wine, she was headed to the kitchen when she heard the sound of her cell phone. She quickly picked it up and from caller ID saw it was Zeke.

She felt the thud in her chest at the same time she felt her pulse rate increase. "Yes?"

"I'm at the door."

Taking a deep breath and trying to keep her composure intact, she headed toward the door. The police had asked for cars not to be on the road unless it was absolutely necessary due to dangerous conditions, so why was he here? Did he think she couldn't handle things during a power failure? She was certain Sunnie was his main concern and not her.

She opened the door and her breath caught. He stood there looking both rugged and handsome, dressed in a tan rawhide jacket, Western shirt and jeans and a Stetson on his head. The reflections from the candles played across his features as he gazed at her. "I heard the reports on television. Are you and the baby okay?" She nodded, at the moment unable to speak. Swallowing deeply, she finally said, "Yes, we're fine."

"That's good. May I come in?"

Their gazes stayed locked and she knew what her response should be. They had agreed there was no reason for him to visit her and Sunnie. But the only thing she could think about at that moment was the loneliness that had been seeping through her body for the past few hours, and that she hadn't seen him in four days. And whether she wanted to admit it or not, she had missed him.

"Please come in." She stepped aside.

Removing his hat, Zeke walked past Sheila and glanced around. Lit candles were practically everywhere, and the scent of jasmine welcomed his nostrils. A blaze was also roaring in the fireplace, which radiated a warm, cozy atmosphere.

"Do you want me to take your jacket?" He glanced back at her. "Yes. Thanks."

He removed his jacket and handed it to her, along with his hat. He watched as she placed both on the coatrack. She was wearing a pair of gold satin pajamas that looked cute on her.

"I was about to have a glass of wine," she said. "Do you want to join me?"

He could say that he'd only come to check on her and the baby, and because they seem to be okay, he would be going. That might have worked if he hadn't asked to come in…or he hadn't taken off his jacket. "Yes, I'd love to have a glass. Thanks."

"I'll be back in a minute."

He watched her leave and slowly moved toward the fireplace. She seemed to be taking his being there well. A part of him was surprised, considering their agreement, that she hadn't asked him to leave. He was glad she hadn't. He watch the fire blazing in the fireplace while thinking that he hadn't realized just how much he had missed seeing her until she'd opened the door. She looked so damn good and it had taken everything within him not to pull her into his arms and kiss her, the way he'd done those other two times. Hell, he was counting, mainly because there was no way he could ever forget them.

And as he stood there and continued to gaze into the fire, he thought of all the reasons he should grab his jacket and hat and leave before she returned. For starters, he wanted her, which was a good enough reason in itself. And the degree to which he wanted her would be alarming to most. But he had wanted her from the beginning. He had walked into the hospital and seen her standing there holding the baby, and looking like the beautiful woman that she was. He had been stunned at the intensity of the desire that had slammed into him; it had almost toppled him. But he had been able to control it by concentrating on the baby, making Sunnie's care his top priority.

However, he hadn't been able to control himself that day at his place when she had gotten in his face. Nor had he been able to handle things the last time he was here and he'd nearly mauled her mouth off. Being around her was way too risky.

Then why was he here? And why was his heart thumping deep in his chest anticipating her return? At that moment he had little control of what he was feeling; especially because they were emotions he hadn't ever felt before for a woman. If it was just a sexual thing he would be able to handle that. But the problem was that he wasn't sure it was. He definitely wanted her, but there was something about her he didn't understand. There were reasons he couldn't fathom as to why he was so attracted to her. And there was no way

he could use Sunnie as an excuse. Sunnie might be the
reason they had initially met, but the baby had nothing
to do with him being here now and going through the
emotions he was feeling.

"Do you think this bad weather will last long?"

He turned around to face her and wished he hadn't.
She had two glasses in her hands and a bottle of wine
under her arm. But what really caught his attention was
the way the firelight danced across her features, combined with the glow from the candles. She looked like
a woman he wanted to make love to. Damn.

She was temptation.

Zeke moved to assist her with the glasses and wine
bottle, and the moment their hands touched, he was a
goner. Taking both glasses, as well as the wine bottle,
from her hands, he placed both on the table. And then
he turned back to her, drew her into his arms and lowered his mouth to hers.

Sheila went into his arms willingly, their bodies fus-
ing like metal to magnet. She intended to go with the
flow. And boy was she rolling. All over the place.

She could feel his hand in the small of her back that
gently pressed her body even closer to his. And she felt
him. At the juncture of her thighs. His erection was definitely making its presence known by throbbing hard
against her. It was kicking her desire into overdrive. And
she could definitely say that was something that had never
happened to her before. Since her breakup with Crawford she had kept to herself. Hadn't wanted to date anyone. Preferred not getting involved with any living male.

But being in Zeke's arms felt absolutely perfect. And
the way he was mating his mouth with hers was stirring

a yearning within her she hadn't been aware she was capable of feeling. And when he finally released her mouth, he let her know he wasn't through with her when his teeth grazed the skin right underneath her right ear, causing shivers to flow through her. And then his teeth moved lower to her collarbone and began sucking gently there.

She tilted her head back and groaned deeply in her throat. What he was doing felt so good and she didn't want him to stop. But he did. Taking her mouth once again.

He loved her taste.

And he couldn't get enough of it, which was why he was eating away at her mouth with a relentless hunger. He was driven by a need that was as primitive as time and as urgent as the desire to breathe. He could feel the rise and fall of her breasts pressed to his chest and could even feel the quivering of her thighs against his. He hadn't had the time or inclination to get involved with a woman since moving to Royal. Brad's problems meant putting his social life on hold. He had been satisfied with that until Sheila had come along. She had kicked his hormones into gear, made him remember what it felt like to be hard up. But this was different.

He'd never wanted a woman to this extreme.

And kissing her wasn't enough.

Keeping his mouth locked to hers, he walked her backward toward the sofa and when they reached it, he lowered her to it. Pulling his mouth away, he took a lick of her swollen lips before saying, "Tell me to stop now if you don't want what I'm about to give you."

She gazed up at him as if weighing his words and his eyes locked with hers. His gaze was practically drowning in the desire he saw in hers. And then he knew that she wanted him as much as he wanted her. But still, he was letting her call the shots. And if she decided in his favor, there was no turning back.

Instead of giving him an answer, she reached up and wrapped her arms around his neck and pulled his mouth back down to hers. He came willingly. Assuaging the hunger they both were feeling. At the same time, his hands were busy, unbuttoning her pajama top with deft fingers.

He pulled back from the kiss to look down at her and his breath caught in his throat. Her breasts were beautiful. Absolutely beautiful. He leaned down close to her ear and whispered, "I want to cherish you with my mouth, Sheila."

No man had ever said such a thing to her, Sheila thought, and immediately closed her eyes and drew in a deep breath when he immediately went for a breast, sucked a hardened nipple between his lips. She could feel her breasts swelling in his mouth. Her stomach clenched and she couldn't help moaning his name. She felt every part of her body stir to life with his touch.

Her response to his actions was instinctive. And when he took the tip of his tongue and began swirling around her nipple, and then grazing that same nipple with the edge of his teeth, she nearly came off the sofa. She began shivering from the desire rushing through her body and when he moved to the next nipple, she felt every nerve ending in her breast come alive beneath his mouth. This was torture, plain and simple. And with each flick of his tongue she felt a pull, a tingling sensation between her legs.

As if he sensed the ache there, he pulled back slightly

and tugged her pj bottoms down her legs. Then he stared down at the juncture of her thighs when he saw she wasn't wearing panties. He uttered a sound that resembled a growl, and the next thing she knew he had shifted positions and lowered his mouth between her legs.

He went at her as if this had been his intent all along, using the tip of his tongue to stir a fervor within her, widening her thighs to delve deeper. What he was doing to her with his tongue should be outlawed. And he was taking his time, showing no signs that he was in a hurry. He was acting as if he had the entire night and intended to savor and get his fill. And she was helpless to do anything but rock her body against his mouth. The more she rocked, the deeper his tongue seemed to go.

And then she felt it, that first sign that her body was reaching a peak of tremendous pleasure that would seep through her pores, strip her of all conscious thought and swamp her with feelings she had never felt before. She held her breath, almost fighting what was to come, and when it happened she tried pushing his mouth away, but he only locked it onto her more. She threw her head back and moaned as sensation swept through her. She felt good. She felt alive. She felt as though her body no longer belonged to her.

And as the sensations continued to sprint through her, Zeke kept it up, pushing her more over the edge, causing a maelstrom of pleasure to engulf her; pleasure so keen it almost took her breath away. She began reveling in the feelings of contentment, although her body felt drained. It was then that he released her and slowly pulled back. With eyes laden with fulfillment, she watched as he quickly removed his own clothes and sheathed his erection in a condom. And then he returned to her. As if he wanted her body to get used to him, get to know him, he straddled her and gyrated his hips so that the tip of him made circles on her belly, before tracing an erotic path down to the area between her legs.

Sensuous pressure built once again inside her, starting at the base of her neck and escalating down. And when he eased between her womanly folds and slowly entered her, she called his name as his erection throbbed within her to the hilt. It was then that he began moving, thrusting in and out of her as if this would be the last chance he had to do so, that she could feel her body come apart in the most sensuous way.

He stroked her for everything she was worth and then some, making her realize just what a generous lover he was. She locked her legs around him and he rocked deeper inside her. And then he touched a spot she didn't know existed and just in the nick of time, he lowered his mouth to hers to quell her scream as another orgasm hit.

Then his body bucked inside her several times, and he moaned into her mouth and she knew at that moment that both of them had gone beyond what they'd intended. But they couldn't turn back now even if they wanted to. He kept thrusting inside her, prolonging the orgasm they were sharing, and she knew at that moment this was meant to be. This night. The two of them together this way. There would be no regrets on her part. Only memories of what they were sharing now. Immense pleasure.

Entering Sheila's bedroom, Zeke's gaze touched on every single candle she had lit, bathing her bedroom in a very romantic glow. He had gotten a glimpse of her bedroom before, when he'd been in the room across the hall putting the crib together. Evidently she liked flowers, because her curtains and bedspread had a floral pattern.

He turned back the covers before placing her in the center of the bed. He joined her there and hoped Sunnie slept through the night as Sheila predicted she would. They had made a pit stop by the nursery to check on the baby and found her sleeping in spite of all the winds howling outside.

"Thanks for coming and checking on us," Sheila said, cuddling closer to him. He wrapped her into his arms, liking the feel of having her there. Her back was resting against his chest and her naked bottom nestled close to his groin.

"You don't have to thank me."

She glanced over her shoulder at him. "I don't?"

"No."

She smiled and closed her eyes, shifting her body to settle even more into his. He stayed awake and, lifting up on his elbows, he stared down at her. She was just as beautiful with her eyes closed as she was with them open. He then recalled what Brad had said about Sheila getting attached to Sunnie and could definitely see how that could happen.

He couldn't help wondering how she was going to handle it when Sunnie was taken away. And she would be taken away. Although Sunnie didn't belong to Brad, she did belong to someone. And if no one claimed her, she would eventually become a part of the system.

That was the one thing that had kept him out of trouble as a kid growing up, the fear of that very thing happening to him. Although he now knew his aunt would never have done such a thing, he hadn't known it then and had lived in constant fear that one day, if he did something wrong, his aunt would desert him in the same way his mother had.

But Clarisse Daniels had proven to be a better woman than her younger sister could ever be. A divorcée, which made her a single mother, she had raised both him and Alicia on a teacher's salary. At least child support had kicked in from Alicia's father every month. But neither his mother nor his father had ever contributed a penny to his upbringing. In fact, he'd found out later that his aunt had on several occasions actually given in to his mother's demand for money just to keep her from taking him away.

His father. He hadn't been completely honest with Sheila that day when he'd said he hadn't known his father. Mr. Travers was his father. He might not have known the man while growing up as Ezekiel "Zeke" Daniels, but he certainly knew his identity now. Matthew Travers. One of the richest men in Texas.

It seemed his mother had gotten knocked up by the man who hadn't believed her claim. In a way, considering what Zeke had heard, his father could have been one of two men. His mother hadn't known for certain which one had sired her son. She had gone after the wealthiest. Travers's attorney had talked her out of such foolishness and pretty much told her what would happen if she made her claim public. Evidently she took his threat seriously and he had grown up as Ezekiel Daniels, the son of Kristi Daniels. Father unknown. His birth certificate stated as much.

It was only while in college attending UT that there was a guy on campus who could have been his identical twin by the name of Colin Travers. When the two finally met, their resemblance was so uncanny it was unreal. Even Brad had approached the guy one day thinking it was him.

Zeke was willing to let the issue of their looks drop, but Colin wasn't. He went back to Houston, questioned his father and put together the pieces of what had happened between Matthew Travers and Kristi Daniels many years before, and a year or so before Travers had married Colin's mother.

When Zeke had been summoned to the Travers mansion, it was Brad who'd convinced him to go. It was there that he'd come face-to-face with the man who'd fathered him. The man, who after seeing him, was filled with remorse for not having believed Kristi Daniels's claim. The man who from that moment on intended to right a wrong, and make up to Zeke for all the years he hadn't been there for him. All the years he'd been denied. Abandoned.

He'd also found out that day that in addition to Colin, he had five other younger brothers and a sister. His siblings, along with their mother, Victoria, immediately accepted him as a Travers. But for some reason, Zeke had resisted becoming part of the Travers clan.

He'd always been a loner and preferred things staying that way. Although his siblings still kept in contact with him, especially Colin, who over the years had forged a close relationship with Zeke, he'd kept a distance between him and the old man. But his father was determined, regardless of Zeke's feelings on the matter, to build a relationship with him.

It was Brad and his aunt Clarisse who had been there for him during that difficult and confused time in his

life. It was they who convinced him to take the last
name his father wanted him to have and wear it proudly.
That's the reason why on his twenty-first birthday, he
officially became Ezekiel *Travers*.

That's why he and Brad had such a strong friendship. And that was one of the main reasons his aunt
meant the world to him. The first thing he'd done after
being successful in his own right through lucrative in-
vestments was to buy Aunt Clarisse a house not far
from the French Quarter. Alicia and her husband, both
attorneys, didn't live too far away. He tried to go visit
whenever he could. But now, he couldn't even consider
going anywhere until he'd solved this case.

He glanced down at Sheila. And not without Sheila.
He immediately felt a tightening in his stomach. How
could he even think something like that? He'd never
taken a woman home to meet his family before. There
had never been one he'd gotten that attached to, and he
didn't plan to start doing so now.

He would be the first to say that tonight he and Sheila
had enjoyed each other, but that's as far as things went.
It just wasn't in his makeup to go further. Suddenly feeling as though he was suffocating and needed space, he
eased away from Sheila and slid out of bed.

Tiptoeing across the hall, he went to where Sunnie
was sleeping. She was lying on her stomach and sleeping peacefully. He wasn't sure what kind of future was
in store for her, but he hoped for her sake things worked
out to her benefit.

All he knew was that the woman who'd given birth
to the beautiful baby didn't deserve her.

Chapter 7

"You want us to go to your place?" Sheila asked to make sure she'd heard Zeke correctly.

They had awakened to the forecaster's grim news that Hurricane Spencer was still hovering in the gulf. And although Royal was not directly in its path, if the storm did hit land, there would be a lot of wind and rain for the next day or so. The local news media had further indicated that although the electrical company was working around the clock, certain areas of town would remain without power for a while. Meadowland was one of them.

"Yes, I think it would be for the best for now especially since you don't know when your power will be restored. I have a generator in case the power goes out at my house."

Sheila nibbled on her bottom lip. What he was offering made sense, but she was so used to having her own place, her own stuff. She glanced over at Sunnie, who was sitting in the middle of the kitchen table in her car seat. She had just been fed and was happy. And she hadn't seemed bothered by seeing Zeke. In fact, it seemed as if she smiled when she saw him.

"Sheila?"

"I was just thinking of all the stuff I'd have to pack up and carry with us."

"We can manage. Besides, I have my truck."

How convenient, she thought. She knew his idea made perfect sense, but going over to his place meant leaving her comfort zone. "Sunnie has gotten used to being here," she said.

"I understand, but as long as you're within her sight, she'll be fine."

Sheila nibbled on her bottom lip as she gave her attention back to the baby. Yes, Sunnie would be fine, but she wasn't sure she would be. Waking up in Zeke's arms hadn't been exactly what she'd planned to happen. But it had been so natural. Just like the lovemaking that had followed before they'd heard Sunnie through the monitor that morning.

She had just finished feeding Sunnie when Zeke had dropped what she considered a bomb. She had been thinking how, in a nice way, to suggest they rethink what had happened between them last night and give each other space to do so, when his idea had been just the opposite. Moving her and Sunnie into his house until the storm passed was not giving them space.

Deciding to come out and say what she'd been thinking, she glanced back over at Zeke. He was sitting across the kitchen, straddling a chair. "What about last night?"

He held her gaze. "What about it?"

Sheila's heart thumped hard in her chest. "W-we slept together and we should not have," she stammered, wishing she hadn't been so blunt, but not knowing what else she could have said to broach the subject and let him know her feelings on the matter.

"It was inevitable."

Her eyes widened in surprise at his comeback. "I don't think it was. Why do you?"

"Because I wanted you from the first and I picked up on the vibes that you wanted me, too."

What vibes? "I was attracted to you from the first, I admit that," she said. "But I wasn't sending off vibes."

"Yes, you were."

Had she unconsciously emitted vibes as he claimed? She tried to recall such a time and—

"Remember that day you woke me up when I'd fallen asleep on your sofa?"

She nodded, remembering. They had stared at each other for the longest time. "Yes, I remember."

"You blushed but wouldn't tell me what you were thinking, what was going through your mind to make you do so?"

"So you assumed…"

"No, I knew. I think I can read you pretty well."

"You think so?"

"Yes. I can probably guess with certainty the times we've been together when your thoughts of me were sexual."

Could he really? She didn't like that and to hear him say it actually irritated her. "Look, Zeke, I'm not sure about the women you're used to getting involved with, but—"

"But you are different from them," he finished for her. "And I agree you're different in a positive way."

"We've known each other less than a week," she reminded him.

"Yes, but we've shared more in that time than a lot of people share in a lifetime. Especially last night. The connection between us was unreal."

Sheila immediately thought of her friend Emily Burroughs. If she could claim ever having a best friend it would have to be Emily. They had been roommates in college. And she believed they had a special friendship that would have gotten even stronger over the years...if Emily hadn't died. Her friend had died of ovarian cancer at the young age of twenty-three.

Sheila had been with Emily during her final days. Emily hadn't wanted to go to hospice, preferring to die at home in her own bed. And she had wanted Sheila there with her for what they'd known would be their last slumber party. It was then Emily had shared that although she wasn't a virgin, she'd never made out with a guy and felt one gigantic explosion; she'd never heard bells and whistles. Emily had never felt the need to scream. She had died not experiencing any of that. And last night Sheila had encountered everything that Emily hadn't in her lifetime.

"Do you regret last night, Sheila?"

His question intruded into her thoughts and she glanced back over at him, wondering how she could get him to understand that she was a loner. Always had been and probably always would be. She didn't take rejection well, and every time the people she loved the most rejected her, intentionally put distance between them, was a swift blow to her heart.

"No, Zeke, but I've learned over the years not to get attached to people. My mom has been married five times and my sister from my father's first marriage doesn't want to be my sister because my mother caused her father pain."

He frowned. "You didn't have anything to do with that."

She chuckled. "Try telling Lois that. She blames both me and my mother and I was only four when they split."

"Did you talk to your father about it?"

She shook her head. "When Dad left, he never wanted to see me or my mother again. I guess I would have been a reminder of what she did. She cheated on him."

"But it wasn't your fault."

"No, it wasn't," she said, wiping the baby's mouth. "And I grew up believing that one day one of them, hopefully both, would realize that. Neither did. Dad died five years ago. He was a very wealthy man and over the years he did do right by me financially—my mother saw to that. But when he died, he intended to let me know how much I didn't mean to him by leaving Lois everything. I wasn't even mentioned in his will." She paused a moment, glanced away from him to look out the window as she relived the pain. And then back at him and said, "It's not that I wanted any of his worldly possessions, mind you. It was the principle of the thing. Just acknowledging me in some way as his daughter would have been nice."

Sheila glanced over at Sunnie, who was staring over at her, as if she understood the nature of what she'd said, of what she was sharing with Zeke. She then wondered why she had shared such a thing with him. Maybe telling him would help him to realize that she could get attached to him, and why she couldn't let that happen.

"So, no, I don't regret last night. It was too beautiful, too earth-shattering and mind-blowing to regret. But I have to be realistic and accept that I don't do involvement very well. I get attached easily. You might want a casual affair, but a part of me would long for something more."

"Something I can't give you," he said gently. The sound of his husky voice floated across the room to her. "Precisely," she said, nodding her head while thinking that he did understand.

"I could say I won't touch you again, even if we spend time together."

She would have taken his words to heart if at that moment a smile hadn't curved his lips. "Yes, you could say that," she agreed.

"But I'd be lying. Mainly because you are temptation."

"Temptation?" she asked, and couldn't help chuckling at that.

"Yes."

She shook her head. She had been called many things but never temptation. "You can see me in the garden with an apple?"

His eyes seemed to darken. "Yes, and very much naked."

Sensing the change in the tone of his voice—it had gone from a deep husky to a seductive timbre—she decided maybe they needed to change the subject. "How is the case coming?"

Zeke recognized her ploy to change the subject. She had reservations about sleeping with him again and he could understand that. But what she needed to understand was that there were some things a man and a woman could not ignore. Blatant sexual chemistry was one of them—it pretty much headed the list. And that was what existed between them, connecting more than just the dots.

Making love to her and waking up with her last night had affected him in a way he didn't quite comprehend, and because he didn't understand it, he wasn't ready, or willing, to walk away.

And when she'd tried explaining to him why she preferred not getting involved in a relationship for fear of getting attached, it was like hearing his own personal reservations. He had this apprehension of letting any woman get too close for fear she would do to him the very thing his mother had done. Walk away and leave him high and dry…and take his heart with her. He'd been there and done that and would never go that way again.

She was protecting her heart the way he was protecting his, so they were on the same page there. Maybe he should tell her that. Then again, maybe he shouldn't. Opening himself up to anyone wasn't one of his strong points. He was a private person. Few people got to know the real Ezekiel Travers. Brad and his other college friend and Royal resident, Christopher Richards, knew the real Zeke. And he felt comfortable being himself around Darius Franklin. Over the past year, while working through the terms of their partnership, he had gotten to know Darius, a man he highly respected. And he thought Summer was the perfect wife for Darius.

One night over dinner Darius and Summer had shared their story. How things had ended for them due to a friend's betrayal. They had gotten reunited seven years later and intended never to let anything or anyone come between them again. He was convinced that kind of love could only be found by a few people. He would never think about holding out for a love that sure and pure for himself.

He decided to go with Sheila's change of subject. "The case is coming along. I'm still following up possible leads."

He told her about his conversations with Rali Tariq and Arthur Moran and their admissions that they too had received blackmail letters.

"You mean they received blackmail letters claiming they fathered babies, as well?"

"Not exactly. Both are married men and they received letters threatening to expose them as having cheated on their wives, which they both deny doing. But both knew doctored pictures could have shown another story. It would have been embarrassing for their families while they tried to prove their innocence."

Sheila shook her head as she took Sunnie out of the car seat. "But knowing Bradford Price wasn't the only one who got a blackmail letter gives legitimacy to his claim that he's not Sunnie's father, and it's all a hoax to extract money from TCC members, right?"

"In a way, yes. But you'll still have some who have their doubts. The paternity test would clear him for sure." He saw a thoughtful look in her eye. Clearing Brad also meant that Sheila would have to give Sunnie up.

Zeke stood and glanced out the window. "It's stopped raining. If we're going to my place we need to do so before it starts up again."

She frowned. "I never said I was going to your place with you."

He slowly crossed the room to her. "I know. But considering everything, even your apprehension about spending time with me, is there a reason you should subject Sunnie to another night in a house without power?"

Sheila swallowed, knowing there it was. The one person she couldn't deny. Sunnie. She looked down at the baby she held in her arms. In the end it would always be what was best for Sunnie. Right now she was all the little girl had. And she would always put her needs first. Last night hadn't been so bad, but it was November; even with fire in the fireplace, the house was beginning to feel drafty. And she couldn't risk the baby catching a cold all because she couldn't resist a tall, dark, handsome and well-built man named Zeke Travers.

She looked at Zeke, met his gaze. "Will you promise me something?"

"What?"

"That while we're at your place you won't…" He took a step closer. "I won't what?"

She nibbled on her bottom lip. "Try seducing me into sleeping with you again."

He studied her features for a moment and then he reached out and caressed her cheek with the back of his hand while he continued to hold her gaze. "Sorry, sweetheart, that is one promise I won't make you," he said in a low, husky tone. He took a step back. "I'll start loading up Sunnie's stuff in my truck."

Sheila held her breath until he walked out of the room.

Zeke pretended not to notice how well Sheila interacted with Sunnie as he loaded the last of the baby items into his truck. They would probably be at his place only a day at the most. But with everything Sheila had indicated she needed to take, you would think they were moving in for a full year. He chuckled. He had no complaints. He had a huge house and lately he'd noticed how lonely it would seem at times.

He heard the baby chuckle and glanced back over at her. He couldn't tell who was giggling more, Sunnie or Sheila, and quickly decided it was a tie. He pushed his Stetson back off his head, thinking, as well as knowing, she would make a great mother. She always handled Sunnie with care, as if she was the most precious thing she'd ever touched.

She glanced over at him, caught him staring and gave him a small smile. The one he returned had a lot more depth than the one she'd given him and he understood why. She still had misgivings about spending time at his place. He didn't blame her too much. He had every intention of finishing what had gotten started between them last night. By not agreeing to her request not to get her into his bed, he'd pretty much stated what his intentions were and he wasn't backing down.

But as he'd told her, there was no way he could make her that promise. It would have died a quick death on his lips as soon as he'd made it. And the one thing his aunt Clarisse had taught him not to do was lie. She'd always said lies could come back to haunt you. They would catch up with you at the worst possible time. And he had believed her.

He moved from around the back of the truck. "Ready to go?"

He could tell she wasn't ready. But she widened her

smile a little and said, "Yes. Let me get Sunnie into her seat."

He watched as she strapped the baby in her car seat, again paying attention to every little detail of Sunnie's security and comfort. He stepped back as she closed the door, and then he opened the passenger door for her and watched how easily she slid in across the leather. Nice, he thought. Especially when he caught a glimpse of bare thigh. He'd never given a thought to how much he appreciated seeing a woman in a skirt until now.

He got into the truck, backed out of her yard and was halfway down the road when she glanced over at him. "I want to use one of your guest rooms, Zeke."

"All right."

Zeke kept looking straight ahead, knowing she had glanced over at him, trying to decipher the quickness of his answer. She would discover soon enough that physical attraction was a very powerful thing. And now that they'd experienced just how things could be between them, it wouldn't be that easy to give it up. And it just so happened that his bedroom was right across the hall from the guest room he intended to put her in. "I can make a pit stop and grab something to eat.

"What would you like?" he asked her. "Oh, anything. I'm not that hungry."

He looked over at her when he brought the car to a stop at a traffic light. "Maybe not now, but you'll probably be hungry later."

And he didn't add that she should eat something to keep her strength for the plans he had for her after she put the baby to bed for the night. He felt a deep stirring inside him. There was something about her scent that made him want to mate. And mate they would again.

His peace of mind and everything male within him was depending on it. He couldn't wait for night to come.

But for now he would pretend to go along with anything she thought she wanted, and making sure by the time it was over she'd be truly and thoroughly convinced what she wanted was him. Usually, when it came to women, he didn't like playing games. He liked to be honest, but he didn't consider what he was doing as playing a game. What he was doing was trying to keep his sanity. He honestly didn't think she knew just how luscious she was. Maybe he hadn't shown her enough last night. Evidently he needed to give her several more hints. And he would do so gladly. He shifted in his seat when he felt tightness in the crotch of his pants while thinking how such a thing would be accomplished.

"You don't mind if I pull into that chicken place, do you?" he asked, gesturing to a KFC.

"No, I guess you're a growing boy and have to eat sometime," she said, smiling over at him.

Growing boy was right, and there was no need to tell her what part of him seemed to be outgrowing all the others at the moment.

Sheila glanced around the bedroom she was given. Zeke had set up Sunnie's bed in a connecting room. She loved his home. It looked like the perfect place for a family.

She pulled a romance novel out of her bag before sliding into bed. When they arrived here, she had helped him get everything inside. After that was done they had both sat down to enjoy the fried-chicken lunch he'd purchased. After that was done he had gone outside to check on things. The fierce winds had knocked down several branches and Zeke and his men had taken the time to clean up the debris. While he was outside, Sheila and Sunnie had made themselves at home.

So far he had been the perfect gentleman and had even volunteered to watch the baby while she had taken a shower. Sunnie had gotten used to seeing him and didn't cry when he held her. In fact, it seemed that she was giving him as many smiles as she was giving to Sheila.

Now Sunnie was down for the night and it had started raining again. Sheila could hear the television downstairs and knew Zeke was still up. She thought it would be better for her to remain in her room and read. She would see him in the morning and that was soon enough to suit her.

She had been reading for about an hour or so when she decided to go to the connecting room to check on Sunnie. Although the baby now slept through the night, Sheila checked on her periodically. Sunnie had a tendency to kick off her bedcovers while she slept.

Sheila tiptoed into the room. Already the scent of baby powder drenched the air and she smiled. Sunnie's presence was definitely known. When Sheila had come downstairs after taking a shower, Zeke had been holding the baby in his arms and was standing at the window. From Sunnie's giggles she could tell the baby had enjoyed seeing the huge raindrops roll down the windowpane.

It had been a spine-tilting moment to see him standing there in his bare feet, shirtless with his jeans riding low on his hips. A tall, sexy hulk of a man with a tiny baby in his arms. A baby he was holding as gently as if she was his.

She had watched them and thought that he would make a wonderful father. She wondered if he wanted kids one day. He had talked about his cousin's twins and she knew he didn't have an aversion to kids like some men did. Crawford would freeze up whenever the mention of a baby entered their conversation. That had been one topic not open for discussion between them. Pulling the covers back over Sunnie's chubby legs, Sheila was about to exit when she felt another presence in the room. She turned quickly and saw Zeke sitting in the wingback chair with his legs stretched out in front of him. He was sitting silently and watching her, saying nothing.

The glow of the moon flowing in through the curtains highlighted his features and the look she saw in his eyes said it all. She fought not to be moved by that look, but it was more powerful than anything she'd ever encountered. It was like a magnetic force, pulling her in, weakening her, filling her with a need she had been fighting since awakening that morning.

She wished she could stop her heart from beating a mile a minute, or stop her nipples from pressing hard against her nightgown. Then there was the heat she felt between her legs; the feeling was annoying as well as arousing.

Then he stood and she had to tilt her head back to look at him. In the moonlight she saw him crook his finger for her to follow him into the hall. Knowing it was best they not speak in the room to avoid awakening Sunnie, she followed.

"I didn't know you were in there with Sunnie," she said softly.

He leaned against the wall. "I went in there to check on her…and to wait for you."

A knot formed in Sheila's throat. "Wait for me?" He seemed to have inched closer. She inhaled his masculine scent into her nostrils and her nipples stiffened even more.

"Yes. I knew you would be coming to check on Sunnie sooner or later. And I decided to sit it out until you did."

She shifted her body when she felt a tingling sensation at the juncture of her thighs. "Why would you be waiting for me?"

She was warned by the smile that tilted his lips at the same time as he slipped an arm around her waist and said, "I was waiting to give you this."

He leaned his mouth down to hers. And instinctively, she went on tiptoe to meet him halfway.

This was well worth the wait, Zeke thought as he deepened the kiss. There was nothing like being inside her mouth. Nothing like holding her in his arms. Nothing like hearing the sound of her moaning deep in his ear.

And he had waited. From the moment she had gone upstairs to put the baby to bed, he had waited for her to come back downstairs. She hadn't done so. Instead, she had called down to him from the top of the stairs to tell him good-night.

He had smiled at her ploy to put distance between them, and he put a plan into action. He figured there was no way she would settle in for the night without checking on Sunnie. So he had closed up things downstairs and gone upstairs and waited.

The wait was over.

She was where he wanted her to be. Here in his arms where he needed her to be. But he needed her someplace else, as well. His bed. Lifting his mouth from hers, he gazed down into the darkness of her eyes and whispered against her moist lips, "I need to make love to you, sweetheart. I have to get inside you."

Sheila nearly moaned at the boldness of his statement. And the desire she saw in his dark gaze was so fierce, so ferocious, that she could feel an intensity stirring within her that she'd never felt before. His need was rousing hers.

She reached up and wrapped her arms around his neck, brought her mouth close to his and whispered thickly, "And I want you inside me, too." And she meant it. Had felt each and every word she had spoken. The throbbing between her legs had intensified from the hardness of him pressing against her and she was feeling him. Boy, was she feeling him.

Before she could release her next breath, he swept her off her feet and into his arms and headed across the hall to his bedroom.

Nothing, Zeke thought, had prepared him for meeting a woman like Sheila. She hadn't come on to him like others. Had even tried keeping her distance. But the chemistry had been too great and intensified each and every time they were within a foot of each other.

The last time they'd made love had been almost too much for his mind and body to handle. And now he could only imagine the outcome of this mating. But he needed it the way he needed to breathe.

He placed her on the bed and before she could get

settled, he had whipped the nightgown from her body. She looked up at him and smiled. "Hey, you're good at that."

"At what?" he asked, stepping back to remove his own clothes.

"Undressing a woman."

As he put on a condom, he glanced at her. She was the only woman he wanted to undress. The only woman he enjoyed undressing. The only woman he wanted to make love to. Suddenly, upon realizing what his mind had just proclaimed, he forced it free of such an assertion. He could not and never would be permanently tied to any one woman. That was the last thing he wanted to think about now or ever.

He moved back toward the bed. The way she was gazing at every inch of his body made him aware of just what she was seeing, and just what he wanted to give her. What he wanted them to share. What he intended them to savor.

He stopped at the edge of the bed and returned her gaze with equal intensity. Moonlight pouring in through his window shone on her nakedness. There she was. Beautiful. Bare. His eyes roamed over her uplifted breasts, creamy brown skin, small waist, luscious thighs, gorgeous hips and then to the apex of her thighs.

"Zeke."

She said his name before he even touched her. She rose on the bed to meet him. The moment their lips fused, it was on. Desire burst like a piece of hot glass within him, cutting into his very core. Blazing heat rushed through his veins with every stroke of his tongue that she returned.

He lowered her to the mattress and pulled back from

the kiss, needed the taste of her and proceeded to kiss her all over. He gloried in the way she trembled beneath his mouth, but he especially liked the taste of her wet center, and proved just how much he enjoyed it.

She came in an explosion that shook the bed and he cupped her bottom, locked his mouth to her while those erotic sensations slashed through her. And when his tongue found a section of her G-spot and went after it as if it would be his last meal, she shuddered uncontrollably.

It was only then that he pulled back and placed his body over hers. "I like your taste," he whispered huskily. He eased inside her, stretching her as he went deep. Her womb was still aching and he could feel it. Already she wanted more and he intended to give her what she wanted.

He began thrusting inside her, thinking he would never tire of doing so. He was convinced there would never come a time when he wouldn't want to make love to her. He slid his hands beneath her hips to lift her off the bed, needing to go even deeper. And when he had reached the depth he wanted, he continued to work her flesh. Going in and out of her relentlessly.

He threw his head back when she moaned his name and he felt her inner muscles clench him, hold him tight, trying to pull every single thing out of him. And he gave in to her demand in one guttural moan, feeling the veins in his neck almost bursting in the process. Coming inside a woman had never felt this right before. This monumental. This urgent.

He rode her hard as his body continued to burst into one hell of an explosion, his shudders combined with hers, nearly shaking the bed from the frame. This was lovemaking at its best. The kind that would leave you mindless. Yet still wanting more. When had he become so greedy?

He would try to figure out the answer to that later. Right now the only things he wanted to dwell on were the feelings swamping him, ripping into every part of his body, taking him for all it was worth and then some. It had to be the most earth-shattering orgasm he'd ever experienced. More intense than the ones last night, and he'd thought those were off the charts.

And he knew moments later when his body finally withdrew from hers to slump beside her, weak as water, that it would always be that way with them. She would always be the one woman who would be his temptation. The one woman he would not be able to resist.

Chapter 8

Zeke and Sheila were aware that the power had returned to her section of town. Yet neither brought up the subject of her returning home. Four days later and she was still spending her days and nights in Zeke's home and loving every moment of it.

The rain had stopped days ago and sunshine was peeking out over the clouds. Those sunny days were her favorite. That's when she would take the baby outside and push her around in the stroller. Zeke's property was enormous and she and Sunnie enjoyed exploring as much of it as they could. Sunnie was fascinated by the horses and would stare at them as if she was trying to figure out what they were.

Then there were the nights when she would fall asleep in Zeke's arms after having made love. He was the most generous lover and made her feel special each and every time he touched her. She was always encouraged by his bold sexuality, where he would take their lovemaking to the hilt. When it came to passion, Crawford had always been low-key. Zeke was just the opposite. He liked making love in or out of bed. And he especially enjoyed quickies. She smiled, thinking she was enjoying them, too.

Usually Zeke worked in his office downstairs for a few hours while she played games with Sunnie, keeping her entertained. Then when he came out of his office, he would spend time with them. One day he had driven them to a nearby park, and on another day he took them to the zoo.

On this particular day Zeke had gone into his office in town to work on a few files when his house phone rang. Usually he received calls on his cell phone, and Sheila decided not to answer it. The message went to his voice mail, which she heard.

"Hi, Ezekiel. This is Aunt Clarisse. I'm just calling to see how you're doing. I had a doctor's appointment today and he says I'm doing fine. And how is that baby someone left on the doorstep and claiming it's Brad's? I know you said you were going to keep an eye on the baby real close, so how is that going? Knowing you, you're probably not letting that baby out of your sight until you find out the truth one way or another..."

A knot twisted in Sheila's stomach. Was that why she was still here? Is that why Zeke hadn't mentioned anything about taking her home? Why he was making love to her each night? Was his main purpose for showing interest in her to keep his eye on Sunnie?

She fought back the tears that threatened to fall from her eyes. What other reason could there be? Had she really thought—had she hoped—that there could be another reason? Hadn't she learned her lesson yet? Hadn't her father, mother and sister taught her that in this life she had no one? When all was said and done, she would be left high and dry. Alone.

Her only excuse for letting her guard down was that usually to achieve their goal of alienating her the ones she loved would try putting distance between them. That's why her father never came to visit, why Lois preferred keeping her from Atlanta and why her mother never invited her to visit her and her husbands.

But Zeke had been the exception. He had wanted to keep her close. Now she knew the reason why.

She drew in a deep breath. When Zeke returned she would tell him she wanted to go home. He would wonder why, but frankly she didn't care. Nor would she tell him. It was embarrassing and humiliating enough for her to know the reason.

One day she would learn her lesson.

Zeke glanced over at Sheila, surprised. "You want to go home?"

She continued packing up the baby's items. "Yes. The only reason Sunnie and I are here is because of your generosity in letting us stay due to the power being out at my place. It's back on now and there's no reason for us to remain here any longer."

He bit back the retort that she'd known the power was back on days ago, yet she hadn't been in a hurry to leave…just as he hadn't been in a hurry for her to go. What happened to make her want to take off? He rubbed the back of his neck. "Is something going on that I need to know about, Sheila?"

She glanced up. "No. I just want to go home."

He continued to stare at her. He'd known she'd eventually want to return home. Hell, he had to be realistic here. "Fine, we can take some of Sunnie's things now and you can come back for the rest later on in the week."

"I prefer taking all Sunnie's items now. There's no reason for me to come back."

That sounded much like a clean break to him. Why?

"Okay, then I'd better start loading stuff up." He walked out of the room.

Sheila glanced at the door Zeke had just walked out of, suddenly feeling alone. She might as well get used to it again. Sunnie's days were numbered with her either way. And now that she knew what Zeke was about, it would be best if she cut the cord now.

In the other room Zeke was taking down the baby bed he'd gotten used to seeing. Why was he beginning to feel as if he was losing his best friend? Why was the feeling of abandonment beginning to rear its ugly head again?

Waking up with her beside him each morning had meant more to him than it had to her evidently. Having both Sheila and Sunnie in his home had been the highlight of his life for the past four days. He had gotten used to them being around and had enjoyed the time they'd spent together. A part of him had assumed the feelings were mutual. Apparently he'd assumed wrong.

A short while later he had just finished taking the bed down, when his cell phone rang. He pulled it out of his back pocket. "Yes?"

"I just got a call from my attorney," Brad said. "There's a possibility I might get the results of the paternity test as early as tomorrow. Hell, I hope so. I need to get on with my life. Get on with the election."

"That's good to hear." At least it would be good for Brad, but not so good for Sheila. Either way, she would be turning the baby over to someone, whether it was Brad or the system. And the way he saw it, there was a one-hundred-percent chance it would be the system.

"Let me know when you get the results," he said to Brad.

His best friend chuckled. "Trust me. You'll be the first to know."

A few hours later, back at her place, Sheila stood at the window and watched Zeke pull off. He had stayed just long enough to put up the crib. No doubt he'd picked up on her rather cold attitude, but he hadn't questioned her about it. Nor had he indicated he would be returning.

However, since his sole purpose in seeing her was to spy on her, she figured he would return eventually. When he did, it would be on her terms and not his. She had no problem with him wanting to make sure Sunnie was well taken care of, but he would not be using her to do so.

She turned from the window, deciding it was time to take Sunnie upstairs for her bath, when she heard the phone ringing. She crossed the room to pick it up. "Hello?"

"Ms. Hopkins?"

"Yes?"

"This is Ms. Talbert from Social Services."

Sheila felt an immediate knot in her stomach. "Yes?"

"We received notification from the lab that the results of Bradford Price's paternity test might be available earlier than we expected. I thought we'd let you know that."

Sheila swallowed as she glanced across the room at Sunnie. She was sitting in her swing, laughing as she played with the toys attached to it.

"Does Mr. Price know?"

"I would think so. His attorney was contacted earlier today."

She drew in a deep breath. It would be safe to assume that if Bradford Price knew then Zeke knew. Why hadn't he mentioned this to her? Prepared her?

"Ms. Hopkins?"

The woman reclaimed her attention. "Yes?"

"Do you have any questions for us?"

"No."

"Okay, then. How is the baby doing?" Sheila glanced over at Sunnie. "She's fine."

"That's good. I'll call you sometime this week to let you know when to bring the baby in."

"All right." Sheila hung up the phone and forced the tears back.

Zeke entered his house convinced something in Sheila's attitude toward him had changed. But what and why? He went straight into the kitchen to grab a beer, immediately feeling how lonely his house was. It had taken Sheila and the baby being here for him to realize there was a difference between a house and a home.

This place was a house.

He had drunk his beer and was about to go upstairs when he noticed a blinking light on his phone. He crossed the room to retrieve his messages and smiled upon hearing his aunt's voice. Moments later a frown touched his lips. When had his aunt called? He played back the message to extract the time. She had called around noon when Sheila had been here. Had she heard it?

He rubbed his hands down his face, knowing the assumptions that would probably come into her mind if she had. Sunnie was not the reason he'd been spending time with her. But after hearing his aunt's message, she might think that it was.

He moved to the sofa to recall everything between them since returning home that day. Even on the car ride back to her place she hadn't said more than a few words. Although the words had been polite, and he hadn't detected anger or irritation in them, he'd known something was bothering her. At first he'd figured since this was the beginning of the second week, she was getting antsy over Sunnie's fate. He had tried engaging her in conversation, but to no avail.

He drew in a deep breath. Did she know that she had come to mean something to him? He chuckled. *Hell, man, how could she know when you're just realizing such a thing yourself?* Zeke knew at that moment that he had done with Sheila the very thing he hadn't wanted to do with any woman. He had fallen in love with her. He didn't have to wonder how such a thing happened.

Spending time with her had made him see what he was missing in his life. He had enjoyed leaving and coming home knowing she was here waiting for him. And at night when they retired, it was as if his bed was where she belonged.

He had thought about bringing up the subject of them trying their luck dating seriously. But he had figured they would have the opportunity to do that after everything with Sunnie was over. He envisioned them taking things slow and building a solid relationship. But now it looked as if that wouldn't be happening.

He then thought about the call he'd gotten from Brad, indicating the test results might be arriving sooner than later. He probably should have mentioned it to her, but after seeing her melancholy mood, he'd decided to keep the information to himself. The last thing he wanted her to start doing was worry about having to give up the baby she'd gotten attached to.

A part of him wanted to get in his car and go over to her place and tell her she had made wrong assumptions about his reason for wanting to be with her. But he figured he would give her space tonight. At some point tomorrow he would be seeing her, and hopefully they would be able to sit down and do some serious talking. He stood from the sofa, when his cell phone rang. He quickly pulled it off his belt hoping it was Sheila, and then grimaced when he saw the caller was his father. Matthew Travers was determined not to let his oldest son put distance between them as Zeke often tried to do.

The old man made a point of calling often, and if Zeke got the notion not to accept the call, Matthew Travers wasn't opposed to sending one of his offspring to check on their oldest sibling. Hell, the old man had shown up on his doorstep a time or two himself. Zeke had learned the hard way his father was a man who refused to be denied anything he wanted.

Zeke shook his head thinking that must be a Travers trait, because he felt the same way about certain things. He was definitely feeling that way about Sheila. "Hello?"

"How are you doing, son?"

Zeke drew in a deep relaxing breath. That was always the way the old man began the conversation with him, referring to him as his son. Letting Zeke know he considered him as such.

Zeke sat back down on the sofa and stretched his legs out in front of him. "I'm doing fine, Dad."

At times it still sounded strange referring to Matthew Travers as "Dad," even after twelve years. They hadn't talked in a while and he had a feeling that today his father was in a talkative mood.

The next day Zeke got to the office early, intending to follow up a few leads. Regardless of whether Brad was cleared of being Sunnie's father, there was still someone out there who'd set up an extortion scheme and had made several members of the TCC his or her victims.

He hoped he would be able to call it a day at Global Securities by five and hightail it over to Sheila's place. He hadn't been able to sleep for thinking about her last night. And he hadn't liked sleeping in his bed alone. Those days she'd spent with him had definitely changed his life.

He sat down at his desk remembering the conversation he'd had with his father. His father still wasn't overjoyed that Zeke had turned down the position of chief of security of Travers Enterprises to come work here with Darius. As he'd tried explaining to the old man, he preferred living in a small town, and moving from Austin to Houston would not have given him that. *And had he not moved to Royal,* he thought further, *he would not have met Sheila.*

A few hours later while sitting at his desk with his

sleeves rolled up and mulling over a file, his intercom buzzed with a call from his secretary. "Yes, Mavis?"

"Mr. Price and his attorney are here and want to see you."

Zeke glanced at the clock on his desk, a sterling silver exclusive from his cousin. He frowned, not believing it was almost four in the afternoon. He couldn't help wondering why Brad and his attorney would be dropping by. "Please send them in."

Seconds later the door flew open and an angry Brad walked in followed by Alan Nelson, Brad's attorney. Zeke took one look at a furious Brad and a flustered Alan and knew something was wrong. "What the hell is going on?" he asked.

"This!" Brad said, tossing a document in the middle of Zeke's desk. "Alan just got it. It's a copy of the results of the paternity test and it's claiming that I'm that baby's father."

Sheila hung up the phone. It was Ms. Talbert again. She had called to say the results of the paternity test were in. Although the woman couldn't share the results with her, she told her that she would call back later that day or early tomorrow with details about when and where Sheila was to drop off the baby.

Sheila felt her body trembling inside. She was a nurse, so she should have known not to get attached to a patient. Initially, she had treated Sunnie as someone who'd been placed in her care. But that theory had died the moment that precious little girl had gazed up at her with those beautiful hazel eyes.

The baby hadn't wanted much. She just wanted to be loved and belong to someone. Sheila had certainly understood that, since those were the very things she wanted for herself. She hoped that Sunnie had a better chance at it than she'd had.

But not if she ends up in the system. And that thought bothered Sheila most of all. A part of her wanted to call Zeke, but she knew she couldn't do that. He hadn't gotten attached to her the way she had to him. Oh, he had gotten attached to her all right, but for all the wrong reasons.

She moved over toward the baby. Their time was limited and she intended to spend as much quality time as she could with Sunnie. Although the baby was only five months old, she wanted her to feel loved and cherished. Because deep in Sheila's heart, she was.

"Calm down, Brad." Zeke then glanced over at Alan. "Will you please tell me what's going on?" he asked Brad's attorney.

Brad dropped down in the chair opposite Zeke's desk, and Zeke could tell the older man seemed relieved. There was no doubt in Zeke's mind that once Alan had delivered the news to Brad he'd wished he hadn't.

The man took out a handkerchief and wiped sweat off his brow before saying, "The paternity report shows a genetic link between Mr. Price and the baby."

Zeke lifted a brow. "Meaning?"

"It means that although there's a link, it's inconclusive as to whether he is Jane Doe's father."

Zeke cringed at Alan's use of the name Jane Doe for Sunnie. "Her name is Sunnie, Alan."

The man looked confused. "What?"

"The baby's name is Sunnie. And as far as what

you're saying, we still don't know one way or the other?"

"No, but again, there is that genetic link," Alan reiterated.

Zeke released a frustrated sigh. He then turned his attention to Brad. "Brad, I know you recall not having been sexually involved with a woman during the time Sunnie would have been conceived, but did you at any time donate your sperm to a bank or anyplace like that?"

"Of course not!"

"Just asking. I knew a few guys who did so when we were in college," Zeke said.

"Well, I wasn't one of them." Brad stood up. "What am I going to do? If word of this gets out I might as well kiss the TCC presidency goodbye."

Zeke knew the word would probably get out. He'd found out soon enough that in Royal, like a number of small towns, people had a tendency to thrive on gossip, especially when it involved the upper crust of the city. "Who contacted you about the results?" Zeke asked Alan.

"That woman at Social Services," Alan replied. "She's the one who called yesterday afternoon, as well, letting me know there was a chance the results would be arriving sooner than expected. I called Brad and informed him of such."

Zeke nodded. And Brad had called him. "Did she mention she would be telling anyone else?"

"No, other than the woman who has custody of Jane Doe." Upon seeing Zeke's frown, he quickly said, "I mean Sunnie."

Zeke was immediately out of his chair. "She called Sheila Hopkins?"

"Yes, if that's the name of the woman keeping the baby. I'm sure she's not going to tell her the results of the test, only that the results are in," Alan replied. "Is there a problem?"

Yes, Zeke saw a problem but didn't have time to explain anything to the two men. "I need to go," he said, grabbing his Stetson and jacket and heading for the door.

"What's wrong?" Brad asked, getting to his feet and watching him dash off in a mad rush.

"I'll call you," Zeke said over his shoulder, and then he was out the door.

Sheila heard a commotion outside her window and, shifting Sunnie to her hip, she moved in that direction. Pushing the curtain aside, she watched as Summer tried corralling a group of pink flamingos down the street. She had heard about the Helping Hands Shelter's most recent fundraiser. Someone had come up with the idea of the pink flamingos. The plan was that the recipient of the flamingos had to pay money to the charity for the opportunity to pass them on to the next unsuspecting victim, and then the cycle would start all over again.

Sunnie was making all kinds of excited noises seeing the flamingos, and the sound almost brought more tears to Sheila's eyes, knowing the day would come when she wouldn't hear that sound again. She knew she had to get out of her state of funk. But it was hard doing so.

She moved from the window when Summer continued to herd the flamingos down the street. Sheila was glad her friend hadn't ditched the flamingos on her. She had enough to deal with and passing on pink flamingos was the last thing she had time for.

She glanced down at Sunnie. "Okay, precious, it's dinnertime for you."

A short while later, after Sunnie had eaten, Sheila had given her a bath and put her to bed. The baby was usually worn-out by six and now slept through the night, waking to be fed around seven in the morning. Sheila couldn't help wondering if the baby's next caretaker would keep her on that same schedule.

She heard the doorbell ring as she moved down the stairs. She figured it was Summer dropping by to say hello, now that she'd dumped the flamingos off on someone's lawn. Quickly moving to the door so the sound of the bell wouldn't wake Sunnie, she glanced out the peephole and her heart thumped hard in her chest. It wasn't Summer. It was Zeke.

She didn't have to wonder why he'd dropped by. To spy on her and to make sure she was taking care of Sunnie properly. Drawing in a deep breath, she slowly opened the door.

Chapter 9

She'd been crying. Zeke took note of that fact immediately. Her eyes were red and slightly puffy, and when he looked closer, he saw her chin was trembling as if she was fighting even now to keep tears at bay. He wasn't sure if the tears she was holding back were for Sunnie or what she assumed was his misuse of her.

He wanted more than anything to take her into his arms, pull her close and tell her how wrong she was and to explain how much she had come to mean to him. But he knew that he couldn't do that. Like him, her distrust of people's motives didn't start overnight. Therefore, he would have to back up anything he said. Prove it to her. Show her in deeds instead of just words. Eventually he'd have to prove every claim he would make here tonight. He may have been the one abandoned as a child, but she, too, had been abandoned. Those who should have loved her, been there for her and supported her had not. In his book, that was the worse type of abandonment. "Zeke, I know why you're here," she finally said, after they had stood there and stared at each other for a long moment.

"Do you?" he asked.

She lifted that trembling chin. "Yes. Sunnie's asleep. You're going to have to take my word for it, and we had a fun day. Now, goodbye."

She made an attempt to close the door, but he put his foot in the way. "Thanks for the information, but that's not why I'm here."

"Then why are you here?"

"To see the woman I made love to several times. The woman I had gotten used to waking up beside in the mornings. The woman I want even now."

She lifted her gaze from the booted foot blocking her door to him. "You shouldn't say things you don't mean."

"Sheila, we need to talk. I think I know what brought this on. I listened to the message my aunt left on my answering machine. You jumped to the wrong conclusion."

"Did I?"

"Yes, you did."

She crossed her arms over her chest. "I don't think so."

"But what if you did? Think of the huge mistake you're making. Invite me in and let's talk about it."

He watched as she began nibbling on her bottom lip, a lip he had sucked into his mouth, kissed and devoured many times since meeting her. Had it been less than two weeks? How had he fallen in love with her so quickly and know for sure it was the real thing?

He drew in a huge breath. Oh, it was definitely the

real thing. Somehow, Sheila Hopkins had seeped into his bloodstream and was now making a huge statement within his heart.

"Okay, come in."

She stood back and he didn't waste any time entering in case she changed her mind. Once inside he glanced around the room and noticed how different things looked. All the baby stuff was gone. At least it had been collected and placed in a huge cardboard box that sat in the corner.

Not waiting for him to say anything when she saw the way his gaze had scanned the room, she said, "And please don't pretend that you don't know that I'll be turning Sunnie over to someone, as early as tomorrow."

He lifted a brow. "And someone told you that?"

She shrugged. "No, not really. But Ms. Talbert did call to say the results of the paternity test had come in. And since you were so certain Sunnie doesn't belong to your friend, then I can only assume that means she's going into the system."

He moved away from the door to walk over to stand in front of her. "You shouldn't assume anything. My investigation isn't over. And do you know what your problem is, Sheila?"

She stiffened her spine at his question. "What?"

"You assume too much and usually you assume wrong."

She glared at him before moving away to sit down on the sofa. "Okay, then you tell me, Zeke. How are my assumptions wrong?"

He dropped into the chair across from the sofa. "First of all, my aunt's phone call. She knew about the case I'm handling for Brad. And she knows Brad is my best friend and that I intend to clear his name or die trying. She was right. I intend to keep an eye on Sunnie and that might be the reason I hung around you at first. But that's not what brought me back here. If you recall, four days went by when I didn't see you or the baby."

"Then what brought you back?"

"You. I couldn't stay away from you."

He saw doubt in her eyes and knew he had his work cut out for him. But he would eventually make her believe him. He had to. Even now it was hard not to cross the room and touch her. Dressed in a pair of jeans and a pullover sweater and in bare feet, she looked good. Ravishing. Stunning. Even the puffiness beneath her eyes didn't take away her allure. And where she was sitting, the light from the fading sun made her skin glow, cast a radiant shine on her hair.

"Why didn't you tell me there was a chance the test results would come back early, to prepare me?"

"Because I know how attached you've gotten to Sunnie and I didn't want to deliver bad news any sooner than I had to. And what you assumed regarding that is wrong, as well. The test results were not conclusive that Brad isn't Sunnie's father."

She leaned forward and narrowed her gaze accusingly. "But you were so convinced Bradford Price is not Sunnie's father."

"And I'm still convinced. The test reveals there is a genetic link. Now I'm going to find out how. It's not Brad's sister's child, but he did have a brother who died last year. I'd only met Michael once and that was when Brad and I were in college and he showed up asking Brad for money."

Zeke drew in a deep breath as he remembered that

time. "Michael was his younger brother and, according to Brad, he got mixed up with the wrong crowd in high school, dropped out and became addicted to hard drugs. That's when Mr. Price disinherited him."

She nodded. "What happened to him?"

"Michael died in a drunk driving accident last year but foul play was never ruled out. There were some suspicious factors involved, including the amount of drugs they found in his system."

"That's horrible. But it would mean there was no way he could have fathered Sunnie."

"I thought about that possibility on the way here. He would have died a couple of months after she was conceived. It might be a long shot, but I am going to check it out. And Brad also has a few male cousins living in Waco. Like Brad, they enjoy their bachelor lifestyles, so I'll be checking with them, as well."

She leaned back on the sofa. "So what will happen with Sunnie in the meantime?"

"That decision will be up to Social Services. However, I plan to have Brad recommend that she remain with you until this matter is resolved."

He saw the way her eyes brightened. "You think they'll go for it?"

"I don't know why they wouldn't. This is a delicate matter, and unfortunately it puts Brad in an awkward position. Even if Sunnie isn't directly his, there might be a family link. And knowing Brad the way I do, he will not turn his back on her, regardless. So either way, he might be filing for custody. She's doing fine right here with you, and the fewer changes we make with her the better."

He stood and crossed the room to sit beside her on the sofa. Surprised, she quickly scooted over. "Now that we got the issue of Sunnie taken care of, I think there is another matter we need to talk about," he said.

She nervously licked her lips. "And what issue is that?"

He stretched his arm across the back of the sofa. "Why you were so quick to assume the worst of me.

Why you don't think I can care for you and refuse to believe that I'd want to develop a serious relationship with you."

"Why should I think you care and would want to develop something serious with me? No one else has before."

"I can't speak for those others, Sheila. I can only speak for myself."

"So you want me to believe it was more than just sex between us?" she asked stiffly.

"Yes, that's what I want you to believe."

It's a good thing he understood her not wanting to believe. How many times had he wanted to believe that if he got involved with someone seriously, they wouldn't just eventually disappear? And he knew deep down that's why he couldn't fully wrap his arms around the Travers family. A part of him was so afraid he would wake up one day and they would no longer want to include him in their lives. Although they had shown him more than once that was not the case, he still had those fears.

He stood and walked to the window and looked out. It was getting dark outside. He scrunched up his brow wondering why all those pink flamingos were across the street in Sheila's neighbor's yard and then remembered the TCC's fundraiser.

Drawing in a deep breath, he turned around to glance over at Sheila. She was watching him, probably wondering what he was about. What he had on his mind.

"You know you aren't the only one who has reasons to want to be cautious about getting involved with someone. The main reason I shy away from any type of serious relationship is thinking the person will be here one day and gone the next."

At her confused expression he returned to sit beside her on the sofa. "My mother left me, literally gave me up to my aunt when I was only five. In other words, I was abandoned just like Sunnie. I didn't see her again until I turned nineteen. And that was only because she thought with my skills as a football player in college that I'd make the pros and would be her meal ticket."

He saw the pity that shone in Sheila's eyes. He didn't want her pity, just her understanding. "Since Mom left me, for a long time I thought if I did anything wrong my aunt would desert me, as well."

"So you never did anything wrong."

"I tried not to. So you see, Sheila, I have my doubts about things just like you."

She didn't say anything for a moment and then asked, "What about your father?"

He leaned back on the sofa. "I never knew my father growing up. My aunt didn't have a clue as to his identity. My mother never told her. Then when I was in college, the craziest thing happened."

"What?" she asked, sitting up as if she was intrigued by what he was telling her.

"There was a guy on campus that everyone said looked just like me. I finally ran into him and I swear it was like looking in the mirror. He was younger than me by a year. And his name was Colin Travers."

"Your brother?"

"Yes, but we didn't know we were brothers because

I was named Ezekiel Daniels at birth. Colin found our likeness so uncanny he immediately called his father. When he told his father my name, his old man remembered having a brief, meaningless affair with my mother years ago, before he married. He also remembered my mother's claim of getting pregnant when the affair ended. But she'd also made that claim to another man. So he assumed she was lying and had his attorney handle the situation. My mother wasn't absolutely sure Travers was my father, so she let it go."

"When your father finally discovered your existence, how did he treat you?" she asked.

"With open arms. All of his family welcomed me. His wife and my five brothers and one sister. At his request, on my twenty-first birthday, I changed my last name from Daniels to Travers and to this day that's all I've taken from him. And trust me he's offered plenty. But I don't take and I don't ask. Since acknowledging him as my father twelve years ago, I've never asked him for a single thing and I don't intend to."

"And who is your father, Zeke?"

"Matthew Travers."

Her mouth dropped open. "The self-made millionaire in Houston?"

He couldn't help chuckling at the shock he heard in her voice. "Yes. That's him."

"Do you blame him for not being a part of your life while growing up?"

"I did, but once I heard the whole story, and knowing my mother like I did, what he told me didn't surprise me. He felt badly about it and has tried making it up to me in various ways, although I've told him countless times that he doesn't owe me anything.

"So you see, Sheila, you aren't the only one with issues. I have them and I admit it. But I want to work on them with you. I want to take a chance and I want you to take a chance, too. What I feel with you feels right, and it has nothing to do with Sunnie."

He shook his head. "Hell, Sunnie's a whole other issue that I intend to solve. But I need to know that you're willing to step out on faith and give us a chance."

Sheila could feel a stirring deep in her heart. He was asking for them to have a relationship, something more than a tumble between the sheets. It was something she thought she'd had with Crawford, only to get hurt. Could she take a chance again?

"My last boyfriend was a medical-supply salesman. He traveled a lot, left me alone most of the time. I thought I'd be satisfied with his calls and always looked forward to his return. Then one day he came back just to let me know I'd gotten replaced."

"You don't need to worry about that happening," Zeke said quietly.

She glanced over at him. "And why wouldn't I?" He leaned closer to her and said in a low husky tone, "Because I am so into you that I can't think straight. I go to sleep dreaming of you and I wake up wanting you. When I make love to you, I feel like I'm grabbing a piece of heaven."

"Oh, Zeke." She drew in a deep breath, thinking that if this was a game he was playing with her then he was playing it well. Stringing her as high and as tight as it could go. She wanted to believe it wasn't a game and that he was sincere. She so much wanted to believe.

"I will always be there for you, Sheila. Whenever you

need me. I won't let you down. You're going to have to trust me. Believe in me."

She fought back the tears. "Please don't tell me those things if you don't mean them," she said softly. "Please don't."

"I mean them and I will prove it," he said, reaching out and gently pulling her toward him.

"Just trust me," he whispered close to her lips. And then he leaned in closer and captured her mouth with his.

Sheila thought being in Zeke's arms felt right, so very right. And she wanted to believe everything he'd said, because as much as she had tried fighting it, she knew at that moment that she loved him. And his words had pretty much sealed her fate. Although he hadn't said he loved her, he wanted to be a part of her life and for them to take things one day at a time. That was more than anyone before had given her.

And she didn't have to worry about him being gone for long periods of time and not being there for her if she needed him.

But she didn't want to think about anything right now but the way he was kissing her. With a hunger she felt all the way to her bones.

And she was returning the kiss as heat was building inside her. Heat mixed with the love she felt for him. It was thrumming through her, stirring up emotions and feelings she'd tried to hold at bay for so long. But Zeke was pulling them out effortlessly, garnering her trust, making her believe and beckoning her to fall in love with him even more.

She felt herself being lifted into his arms and carried up the stairs. They didn't break mouth contact until he had lowered her onto the bed. "Mmm," she murmured in protest, missing the feel of his lips on hers, regretting the loss of tongue play in her mouth.

"I'm not going far, baby. We just need to remove our clothes," he whispered hotly against her moist lips.

Through desire-laden eyes she watched as he quickly removed his clothes and put on protection before returning to her. He reached out and took her hand and drew her closer to him. "Do you know how much I missed waking up beside you? Making love to you? Being inside you?"

She shook her head. "No."

"Then let me show you."

Zeke wanted to take things slow, refused to be rushed. He needed to make love to her the way he needed to breathe. After removing every stitch of her clothing, he breathed in her scent that he'd missed. "You smell good, baby."

"I smell like baby powder," she said, smiling. "One of the pitfalls of having a baby around."

His chuckle came out in a deep rumble. "You do smell like a baby. *My* baby." And then he kissed her again.

Moments later he released her mouth and began touching her all over as his hands became reacquainted with every part of her. He continued to stroke her and then his hands dipped to the area between her legs and found her wet and ready. Now another scent was replacing the baby powder fragrance and he was drawn into it. His erection thickened even more in response to it. He began stroking her there, fondling her, fingering the swollen bud of her womanhood.

"Zeke…"

"That's right, speak my name. Say it. I intend for it

to be the only name you'll ever need to say when you feel this way."

And then he lowered himself to the bed, needing to be inside her now. His body straddled hers and he met her gaze, held it, while slowly entering her. He couldn't help shuddering at the feel of the head of his shaft slowly easing through her feminine core.

She wrapped her legs around him and he began moving to a beat that had been instilled inside his head from the first time he'd made love to her. And he knew he would enjoy connecting with her this way until the day he took his last breath. He'd never desired a woman the way he desired her.

And then he began moving in and out of her. Thrusting deep, stroking long and making each one count. Shivers of ecstasy began running up his spine and he could feel his hardness swell even more inside her. He reached down, lifted her hips to go deeper still and it was then that she screamed his name.

His name.

And something exploded inside him, made him tremble while wrapped in tremendous pleasure. Made him utter her name in a guttural breath. And he knew at that moment, whatever it took, he was determined that one day she would love him back. He would prove to her she had become more than just temptation to him. She had become his life.

Sheila snuggled deeper into Zeke's arms and glanced over at the clock on her nightstand. It was almost midnight. They had gotten up earlier to check on Sunnie and to grab a light dinner—a snack was more like it. He had scrambled eggs and she had made hash browns.

While they ate he told her more about his relationship with the Travers family. And she shared with him how awful things had been for her with Crawford, and how strained her relationships were with her mother and sister. He had listened and then got up from the table to come around and wipe tears from her eyes before picking her up in his arms and taking her back upstairs where they had made love again. Now he was sleeping and she was awake, still basking in the afterglow of more orgasms tonight than she cared to count, but would always remember.

She gently traced the curve of his face with the tip of her finger. It was hard to believe this ultrahandsome man wanted her. He had a way of making her feel so special and so needed. Earlier tonight in this very bed she had felt so cold. But now she wasn't cold. Far from it. Zeke was certainly keeping her warm. She couldn't help smiling.

"Hmm, I hate to interrupt whatever it is you're thinking about that's making you smile, but…"

And then he reached up, hooked a hand behind her neck to bring her mouth down to his. And then he took possession of it in that leisurely but thorough way of his. And it was a way that had her toes tingling. Oh, Lord, the man could kiss. Boy, could he kiss. And to think she was the recipient of such a drugging connection.

He finally released her mouth and pulled her up to straddle him. He then gazed up at her as he planted his hands firmly on her hips. "Let's make love this way." They had never made love using this position before, and she hesitated and just stared at him, not sure what he wanted her to do. He smiled and asked, "You can ride a horse, right?"

She nodded slowly. "Yes, of course."

"Then ride me."

She smiled as she lifted the lower part of her body and then came down on him. He entered her with accurate precision. She stifled a groan as he lifted his hips off the bed to go deeper inside her. She in turned pressed down as hard as she could, grinding her body against his.

And then she did what he told her to do. She rode him.

Brad glanced across the desk at Zeke. "Is there a reason you ran off yesterday like something was on fire?"

Zeke leaned back in his chair. He had left Sheila's house this morning later than he'd planned, knowing he had to go home first to change before heading into the office. He wasn't surprised to find Brad waiting on him. He'd seen the newspaper that morning. Brad's genetic connection to Sunnie made headline news, front page and center, for all to read.

When Zeke had stopped by the Royal Diner to grab a cup of coffee, the place where all the town gossips hung out, it seemed the place was all abuzz. There must have been a leak of information either at the lab where the test was processed or at the hospital. In any case, news of the results of the paternity test was all over town.

Everyone was shocked at the outcome of the test. Those who thought the baby wasn't Brad's due to the blackmailers hitting on other TCC members—even that news had somehow leaked—were going around scratching their heads, trying to figure out how the baby could be connected to Brad.

"It had to do with Sheila," he finally said.

Brad lifted a brow. "The woman taking care of the baby?"

"Yes."

Brad didn't say anything as he studied him, and Zeke knew exactly what he was doing. He was reading him like a book, and Zeke knew his best friend had the ability to do that. "And why do I get the feeling this Sheila Hopkins means something more to you than just a case you're working on?" Brad finally asked.

"Probably because you know me too well, and you're right. I met her less than two weeks ago and she has gotten to me, Brad. I think… I've fallen in love with her."

Zeke was certain Brad would have toppled over in his chair if it had not been firmly planted on the floor. "Love?"

"Yes, and I know what you're thinking. And it's not that. I care for her deeply." He leaned forward. "And she is even more cautious than I am about taking a chance. I'm the one who has to prove how much she means to me. Hell, I can't tell her how I feel yet. I'm going to have to show her."

A smile touched Brad's lips. "Well, this is certainly a surprise. I wish you the best."

"Thanks, man. And you might as well know one of her concerns right now is what's going to happen to Sunnie. She's gotten attached to her."

He paused a moment and then said, "Since you're here I have a video I want you to watch."

"A video?"

"Yes. I want you to look at that video I pulled that shows a woman placing the car seat containing the baby on the TCC doorstep. All we got is a good shot of her hands."

"And you think I might be able to recognize some woman's hands?" Brad asked.

Zeke shrugged. "Hey, it's worth a try." He picked up the remote to start rolling the videotape on the wide screen in his office.

Moments later they looked up when there was a tap on the door. He then remembered his secretary had taken part of the morning off. "Come in."

Summer entered. "Hi, guys, sorry to interrupt. But you know it's fundraiser time for the shelter and I—" She stopped talking when she glanced at the wide screen where Zeke had pressed Pause and the image had frozen on a pair of hands. "Why are you watching a video of Diane Worth's hands?"

Both men stared at her. Zeke asked in astonishment, "You recognize those hands?"

Summer smiled. "Yes, but only because of that tiny scar across the back of her right hand, which would have been a bigger scar if Dr. Harris hadn't sutured it the way he did. And then there's that little mole between the third and fourth finger that resembles a star."

Her smile widened when she added, "And before you ask, the reason I noticed so much about her hand is because I'm the one who bandaged the wound after Dr. Harris examined her."

Zeke got out of his chair to sit on the edge of his desk. "This woman came through the shelter recently?"

Summer shook her head. "Yes, around seven months ago. She was eight months pregnant and her boyfriend had gotten violent and cut her on her hand with a bowie knife. She wouldn't give the authorities his name, and stayed at the shelter one week before leaving without a trace in the middle of the night."

Zeke nodded slowly, not believing he might finally have a break in the case. "Do you have any information you can give us on her?"

"No, and by law our records are sealed to protect the women who come to the shelter for our protection. I can tell you, however, that the information she gave us wasn't correct. When she disappeared I tried to find her to make sure she was okay and ran into a dead end. I'm not even sure Diane Worth is her real name."

Zeke rubbed his chin. "And you said she was pregnant and vanished without a trace?"

"Yes, but Abigail might be able to help you further." Brad lifted a brow. "Abigail Langley?"

Summer nodded. "Yes. It just so happened the night Diane disappeared, we thought she might have met with foul play. But Abigail had volunteered to man our suicide phone line that night, and according to Abigail, when she went out to put something in her car, she saw Diane getting into a car with some man of her own free will."

"That was a while back. I wonder if Abigail would be able to identify the guy she saw?" Brad mused.

"We can pay Abigail a visit and find out," Zeke said. He looked over at Summer. "We need a description of Diane Worth for the authorities. Can we get it from you?"

Summer smiled. "With a judge's order I can do better than that. I can pull our security camera's tape of the inside of the building. There were several in the lounge area where Diane used to hang out. I bet we got some pretty clear shots of her."

Adrenaline was flowing fast and furious through Zeke's veins. "Where's Judge Meadows?" he asked Brad.

Brad smiled. "About to go hunting somewhere with Dad. Getting that court order from him shouldn't be a problem."

"Good," Zeke said, glancing down at his watch. "First I want to pay Abigail Langley a visit. And then I want to check out those videotapes from the shelter's security camera."

"I'm coming with you when you question Abigail," Brad said, getting to his feet.

Zeke raised a brow. "Why?"

Brad shrugged. "Because I want to."

Zeke rolled his eyes as he moved toward the door. "Fine, but don't you dare make her cry again."

"You made Abigail cry?" Summer asked, frowning over at him.

"It wasn't intentional and I apologized," a remorseful-sounding Brad said, and he quickly followed Zeke out the door.

Chapter 10

"You need a husband."

Sheila groaned inwardly. Her mother was definitely on a roll today. "No, I don't."

"Yes, you do, and with that kind of attitude you'll never get one. You need to return to Dallas and meet one of Charles's nephews."

Sheila shook her head. Her mother had called to brag about a new man she'd met. Some wealthy oilman and his two nephews. Cassie had warned her that they were short for Texans, less than six feet tall, but what they lacked in height, they made up for in greenbacks.

"So, will you fly up this weekend and—"

"No, Mom. I don't want to return to Dallas."

Her mother paused a moment and then said, "I wasn't going to mention it, but I ran into Crawford today."

Sheila drew in a deep breath. Hearing his name no longer caused her pain. "That's nice."

"He asked about you."

"I don't know why," she said, glancing across the room to where Sunnie was reaching for one of her toys.

"He's no longer with that woman and I think he wants you back," her mother said.

"I wouldn't take him back if he was the last man on earth."

"And you think you can be choosy?"

Sheila smiled, remembering that morning with Zeke. "Yes, I think I can."

"Well, I don't know who would put such foolishness into your head. I know men. They are what they are. Liars, cheaters, manipulators, all of them. The only way to stay ahead of them is to beat them at their own game. But don't waste your time on a poor one. Go after the ones with money. Make it worth your while."

A short time later as she gave Sunnie her bath, Sheila couldn't help thinking of what her mother said. That had always been her mother's problem. She thought life was a game. Get them before they get me first. There was no excuse for her cheating on her first husband. But then she had cheated on her second and fourth husbands, as well.

Her phone rang and she crossed the room to pick it up, hoping it wasn't her mother calling back with any more maternal advice. "Yes?"

"Hi, beautiful."

She smiled upon recognizing Zeke's voice. "Howdy, handsome."

She and Zeke had made love before he'd left that morning and she had felt tingly sensations running through her body all day. They had been a reminder of what the two of them had shared through the night.

And to think she had ridden him. Boy, had she ridden him. She blushed all over just thinking about it.

"I think we have a new lead," he said excitedly. "You do? How?"

He told her how Summer had dropped by when he was showing the videotape in his office to Brad, and that she had identified the hands of the woman who had left Sunnie on the TCC's doorstep. He and Brad were now on their way to talk to Abigail Langley. There was a chance she could identify the man who the pregnant woman had left with that night. Then they would drop by the shelter to pull tapes for the authorities. There was a possibility Sunnie's mother was about to be identified.

By the time she'd hung up the phone from talking to Zeke, she knew he was closer to exposing the truth once and for all. Was Diane Worth Sunnie's biological mother? If she was, why did she leave her baby on the TCC's doorstep claiming she was Bradford Price's child?

Abigail led Zeke and Brad into the study of her home. "Yes, I can give you a description of the guy," she said, sitting down on a love seat. "I didn't know who he was then, but I do now from seeing a picture of him flash on television one night on CNN when they did an episode on drug rings in this country. His name is Miguel Rivera and he's reputed to be a drug lord with an organization in Denver."

"Denver?" Zeke asked, looking at Brad. "Why would a drug lord from Denver be in Royal seven months ago?"

Brad shrugged. "I wouldn't know unless he's connected to Paulo Rodriguez." Brad then brought Zeke up to date on what had gone on in Royal a few years ago when the local drug trafficker had entangled prominent

TCC members in an embezzlement and arson scandal. "I think I need to fly to Denver to see what I can find out," Zeke said. He glanced over at Abigail. "I appreciate you making time to see us today."

"I don't mind. No baby should have been abandoned like that."

Knowing that the subject of the baby was a teary subject with her for some reason, Zeke said, "Well, we'll be going. We need to stop by the shelter to see what we can find out there."

They were about to walk out the study, when Brad noticed something on the table and stopped. "You still have this?" he asked Abigail.

Zeke saw the trophy sitting on the table that had caught Brad's eye.

"Yes. I was cleaning out the attic at my parents' house and came across it," she said.

Intrigued, Zeke asked. "What is it for?"

"This," Brad said, chuckling as he picked up the trophy and held it up for Zeke to see, "should have been mine. Abigail and I were in a spelling bee. It was a contest that I should have won."

"But you didn't," she said, laughing. "I can't believe you haven't gotten over that. You didn't even know how to spell the word *occupation*."

"Hell, I tried," Brad said, joining her in laughter. "Trying wasn't good enough that day, Brad. Get over it."

Zeke watched the two. It was evident they shared history. It was also evident they had always been rivals. He wondered if they could continue to take their boxing gloves off and share a laugh or two the way they were doing now more often.

After a few moments, the pair remembered he was

there. Brad cleared his throat. "I guess we better get going to make it to the shelter. Goodbye, Abby."

"Bye, Brad, and I'll see you around, Zeke."

"Sure thing," Zeke responded, not missing the fact this was the second occasion that he'd heard Brad refer to her as Abby. The first time occurred when he'd been holding her in his arms, comforting her. Um, interesting. "So what do you think?" Brad asked moments later while snapping on their seat belts in Zeke's car.

Zeke chuckled. "I think it's a damn shame you couldn't spell the word *occupation* and lost the spelling bee to a girl."

Brad threw his head back and laughed. "Hey, you didn't know Abigail back then. She was quite a pistol. She could do just about anything better than anyone." Zeke wondered if Brad realized he'd just given the woman a compliment. "Evidently. Now to answer your question about Miguel Rivera, I think I'm going to have to fly to Denver. If Diane Worth is Sunnie's mother, I want to know what part Miguel Rivera is playing in her disappearance. I think all the answers lie in Denver."

Brad nodded. "And you think there's a possible connection to my brother, Michael?"

"I'm not sure. But I know that baby isn't yours and she has to belong to someone. And you and I know Michael was heavy into alcohol and drugs."

"Yes, but as a user, not a pusher," Brad said.

"As far as we know," Zeke countered. "When you went to collect his belongings, was there anything in them to suggest he might have been involved with a woman?"

"I wasn't checking for that. Besides, there wasn't much of anything in that rat hole he called an apartment.

I boxed up what he had, if you want to go through it. I put it in storage on my parents' property."

"I do. We can check that out after we leave the shelter." Zeke backed out of Abigail's driveway.

"You're leaving for Denver tomorrow?" Sheila asked hours later, glancing across the kitchen table at Zeke. He was holding Sunnie, making funny faces to get her to laugh. Sheila tried to downplay the feeling escalating inside her that he was leaving her.

This is work, you ninny, a voice inside her said. *This is not personal. He is not Crawford.* But then she couldn't help remembering Crawford's reasons for leaving were all work-related, too.

"Yes, I need to check out this guy named Miguel Rivera. He might be the guy who picked Diane Worth up from the shelter that night. Thanks to security cameras inside the shelter, we were able to get such good shots of the woman that we've passed them on to law enforcement."

The woman who might be Sunnie's mother, she thought.

"How long do you think you'll be gone?" she asked.

"Not sure. I don't intend to come back until I find out a few things. I have a lot of questions that need to be answered."

Sheila nodded. She knew his purpose in going to Denver would help close the case on Sunnie and bring closure. It was time, she knew that. But still… "Well, I hope you find out something conclusive. For Sunnie's sake," she said.

And for yours, Zeke thought, studying her features. He knew that with each day that passed, she was getting attached to Sunnie even more. The first thing he'd noticed when he arrived at her place was Sunnie's things were once again all over the place.

"So what are you going to be doing while I'm gone?" he asked her, standing to place the baby back in her seat.

"You can ask me that with Sunnie here? Trust me, there's never a dull moment." She paused and then asked quietly, "You won't forget I'm here, will you?"

He glanced up after snapping Sunnie into the seat. Although Sheila had tried making light of the question, he could tell from the look on her face she was dead serious. Did she honestly think when he left for Denver that he wouldn't think of her often, probably every single day? And although he would need to stay focused on solving the case, there was no doubt in his mind that she would still manage to creep into his thoughts. Mainly because she had his heart. Maybe it was time for him to tell her that.

He crossed the room to where she sat at the table and took her hands into his and eased her up. He then wrapped his arms around her waist. "There's no way I can forget about the woman I've fallen in love with."

He saw immediate disbelief flash across her features and said, "I know it's crazy considering we've only known each other for just two weeks but it's true. I do love you, Sheila, and no matter what you think, I won't forget you, and I am coming back. I will be here whenever you need me, just say the word."

He saw the tears that formed in her eyes and heard her broken words when she said, "And I love you, too. But I'm scared."

"And you think I'm not scared, too, baby? I've never given a woman my heart before. But you have it—lock, stock and barrel. And I don't make promises I don't keep, sweetheart. I will always be here for you. I will be a man you can count on."

And then he lowered his mouth and sealed his promise with a kiss, communicating with her this way and letting her know what he'd just said was true. He wanted her, but he loved her, too.

She returned his kiss with just as much fervor as he was putting into it. He knew if they didn't stop he would be tempted to haul her upstairs, which couldn't happen since Sunnie was wide awake. But there would be later and he was going to start counting the minutes.

Sheila woke when the sunlight streaming through the window hit her in the face. She jerked up in bed and saw the side next to her was empty. Had Zeke left for Denver already without telling her goodbye?

Trying to ignore the pain settling around her heart, she wrapped the top sheet around her naked body and eased out of bed to stare out the window. Was he somewhere in the skies on a plane? He hadn't said when he was returning, but he said he would and that he loved her. He *loved* her. She wanted so much to believe him and—

"Is there any reason you're standing there staring out the window?"

She whipped around with surprise all over her face. "You're here."

He chuckled. "Yes, I'm here. Where did you think I'd be?"

She shrugged. "I assumed you had left for Denver already."

"Without telling you goodbye?"

She fought back telling him that's how Crawford would do things, and that he had a habit of not returning when he'd told her he would. Something would always come up. There was always that one last sale he just had to make. Instead, she said, "What you have to do in Denver is important."

He leaned in the doorway with a cup of coffee in his hand. "And so are you."

He entered the room and placed the cup on the nightstand. "Come here, sweetheart."

She moved around the bed, tugging the sheet with her. When she came to a stop in front of him, he said, "Last night I told you that I had fallen in love with you, didn't I?"

"Yes."

"Then I need for you to believe in me. Trust me. I know, given your history with the people you care about, trusting might not be easy, but you're going to have to give me a chance."

She drew in a deep breath. "I know, but—"

"No buts, Sheila. We're in this thing together, you and me. We're going to leave all our garbage at the back door and not bring it inside. All right?"

She smiled and nodded. "All right."

He was about to pull her into his arms, when they heard the sound of Sunnie waking up on the monitor in the room. "I guess we'll have to postpone this for later. And later sometime, I need to look through some boxes Brad put in storage that belonged to his brother. His cousins in Waco swear they are not Sunnie's daddy, and since Michael is not here to speak for himself, I need to do some digging. But I am flying out for Denver tomorrow sometime."

He took a step back. "You go get dressed. Take your time. I'll handle the baby. And please don't ask if I know how to dress and feed her. If you recall, I've done it before."

She chuckled. "I know you have. And you will make a great father."

His smile widened. "You think so?"

"Yes."

"I take that as a compliment," he said. "And like I said, take your time coming downstairs. Sunnie and I will be in the kitchen waiting whenever you come down."

Zeke decided to do more than just dress and feed Sunnie. By the time Sheila walked into the kitchen, looking as beautiful as ever in black slacks and a pretty pink blouse, he had a suggestion for her. "The weather is nice outside. How about if we do something?"

She raised a brow. "Do something like what?"

"Um, like taking Sunnie to that carnival over in Somerset."

"But I thought you had to go through Brad's brother's boxes," she said.

"I do, but I thought we could go to the carnival first and I can look through the boxes later. I just called the airlines. I'll be flying out first thing in the morning, and I want to spend as much time as I can today with my two favorite ladies."

"Really?"

He could tell by her expression that she was excited by his suggestion. "Yes, really. What do you say?"

She practically beamed. "Sunnie and I would love to go to the carnival with you."

Considering how many items they had to get together for Sunnie, it didn't take long for them to be on their way. He had passed the carnival a few days ago and had known he wanted to take Sheila and Sunnie there. It had been only a couple of weeks, but Sunnie had become just as much a part of his life as Sheila's.

Although he'd told her how he felt about her, he could see Sheila was still handling him with caution, as if she was afraid to give her heart to him no matter how much she wanted to. He would be patient and continue to show her how much she meant to him. As he'd told her, considering her mother, sister and ex-boyfriend's treatment of her, he could definitely understand her lack of trust.

"And you're sure Brad is okay with you putting the investigation on hold to spend time with me and Sunnie?"

He glanced over at her as he turned toward the interstate. "Positive. A few hours won't hurt anything. Besides, I'll probably be gone most of next week and I'm missing you already."

It didn't take them long to reach the carnival grounds. After putting Sunnie in her stroller, they began walking around. It was Saturday and a number of people were out and about. He recognized a number of them he knew and Sheila ran into people she knew, as well. They ran into Brad's sister, Sadie, her husband, Ron, and the couple's twin daughters.

"She is a beautiful baby," Sadie said, hunching down to be eye level with Sunnie.

And as usual when strangers got close, Sunnie glanced around to make sure Sheila was near. "Yes, she is," Sheila said, smiling. She waited to see if the woman would make a comment about Sunnie favoring her brother or anyone in the Price family, but Sadie Price Pruitt didn't do so. But it was plain to see she was just as taken with Sunnie as Sheila was with Sadie's twins.

They also ran into Mitch Hayward and the former Jenny Watson. Mitch was the interim president of the TCC, and Jenny, one of his employees, when the two had fallen in love. And they had a baby on the way.

But the person Zeke was really surprised to see was Darius. He hadn't known his partner had returned to town. "Darius, when did you get back?" he asked, shaking his business partner's hand.

"Last night. We finished up a few days early and I caught the first plane coming this way."

Zeke didn't have to ask why when Darius drew Summer closer to him and smiled down at her.

"I would have called when I got in, but it was late and…"

Zeke chuckled. "Hey, man, you don't have to explain. I understand." He was about to introduce Darius and Sheila, but realized when Darius reached out and gave Sheila a hug that they already knew each other.

"And this is the little lady I've heard so much about," Darius said, smiling at Sunnie. "She's a beautiful baby." They all chatted for a few minutes longer before parting ways, but not before agreeing to get together when Zeke returned from Denver.

"I like Darius and Summer," Sheila said. "That time when Summer and I worked together on that abuse case, Darius was so supportive and it's evident that he loves her very much."

Zeke nodded and thought that one day he and Sheila might share the kind of bond that Darius and Summer enjoyed.

Chapter 11

Zeke was grateful for the friendships he'd made while at UT on the football team. The man he needed to talk to who headed Denver's Drug Enforcement Unit, Harold Mathis, just so happened to be the brother of one of Zeke's former teammates.

Mathis wasted no time in telling Zeke about Miguel Rivera. Although the notorious drug lord had been keeping a low profile lately, in no way did the authorities believe he had turned over a new leaf. And when they were shown photographs of Diane Worth, they identified her as a woman who'd been seen with Rivera once or twice.

Zeke knew he had his work cut out in trying to make a connection between Diane Worth and Michael Price. Michael's last place of residence was in New Orleans. At least that's where Brad had gone to claim his brother's body.

His belongings hadn't given a clue as to who he might have associated with, especially a woman by the name of Diane Worth. But Zeke was determined to find out if Diane Worth was Sunnie's mother.

The Denver Drug Enforcement Unit was ready to lend their services to do anything they could to get the likes of Miguel Rivera off the streets. So far he had been wily where the authorities were concerned and had been able to elude all undercover operations to nab him.

Since Zeke knew he would probably be in Denver awhile, he had decided to take residence in one of those short-term executive apartments. It wasn't home, but it had all the amenities. He had stopped by a grocery store to buy a few things and was reminded of the time when he had gone grocery shopping with Sheila and the baby when they'd stayed over at his place. He had been comfortable walking beside her and hadn't minded when a few people saw them and probably thought they were an item. As far as he was concerned, they were.

He glanced out a window that had a beautiful view of downtown Denver. He was missing his *ladies* already. Sunnie had started to grow on him as well, which was easy for her because she was such a sweet baby. She no longer screamed around strangers, although you could tell she was most comfortable when he or Sheila was around.

Sheila.

God, he loved her something awful and was determined that distance didn't put any foolishness in her mind, like her thinking he was falling out of love with her just because he didn't see her every day. Already he'd patronized the florist shop next door. They would make sure a bouquet of flowers was delivered to Sheila every few days. And he intended to ply her with "thinking of you" gifts often.

He chuckled. Hell, that could get expensive because he thought of her all the time. The only time he would force thoughts of her from his mind was when he was trying to concentrate on the case. And even then it was hard.

He picked up the documents he had tossed on the table that included photographs of both Rivera and Worth. A contact was working with hospitals in both New Orleans and Denver to determine if a child was born to Diane Worth five months ago. And if so, where was the baby now?

He was about to go take a shower, when his phone rang. "Hello."

"I got another blackmail letter today, Zeke."

He nodded. Zeke figured another one would be coming sooner or later. The extortionist had made good his threat. But that didn't mean he was letting Brad off the hook. It was done mainly to let him know he meant business. "He still wants money, right?"

"Yes, and unless I pay up, Sunnie's birth records will be made public to show I had a relationship with a prostitute."

Of course, that was a lie, but the blackmailer's aim was to get money out of Brad to keep a scandal from erupting. It would have a far-reaching effect not only for Brad's reputation but that of his family.

"I know it's going to be hard for you to do, but just ignore it for now. Whoever is behind the extortion attempt evidently thinks he has you where he wants you to be, and we're going to prove him wrong."

By the time Zeke ended his call with Brad, he was

more determined than ever to find a link between Rivera and Worth.

"You're thinking about getting married?" *Again?* Sheila really should not be surprised. Her mother hated being single and had a knack for getting a husband whenever she wanted one…

"Um, I'm thinking about it. I really like Charles."

You only met him last week. And wasn't it just a couple of weeks ago she'd asked her about Dr. Morgan? Sheila decided not to remind her mother of all those other men she'd liked, as well. "I wish you the best, Mom." And she did. She wanted her mother to be happy. Married or not.

"Thanks. And what's that I hear in the background? Sounds like a kid."

Sheila had no intention of telling her mother the entire story about Sunnie. "It is a baby. I'm taking care of her for a little while." That wasn't totally untrue since she was considered Sunnie's caretaker for the time being.

"That's nice, dear, since chances are you won't have any of your own. Your biological clock is ticking and you have no prospects."

Sheila smiled, deciding to let her mother think whatever she wanted. "You don't have to have a man to get pregnant, Mom. Just sperm."

"Please don't do anything foolish. I hope you aren't thinking of going that route. Besides, being pregnant can mess up a woman's figure for life."

Sheila rolled her eyes. Her mother thought nothing of blaming her for the one stretch mark she still had on her tummy. She was about to open her mouth and say something—to change the subject—when her door-bell sounded.

"Mom, I have to go. There's someone at the door."

"Be careful. There are lunatics living in small towns."

"Okay, Mom, I'll be careful." At times it was best not to argue.

After hanging up the phone, she glanced over at Sunnie, who was busy laughing while reaching for a toy that let out a squeal each time Sunnie touched it. She was such a happy baby.

Sheila glanced through the peephole. There was a woman standing there holding an arrangement of beautiful flowers. Sheila immediately figured the delivery was for her neighbor, who probably wasn't at home. She opened the door. "Yes, may I help you?"

The woman smiled. "Yes, I have a delivery for Sheila Hopkins."

Sheila stared at the woman, shocked. "I'm Sheila Hopkins. Those are for me?"

"Yes." The woman handed her a huge arrangement in a beautiful vase. "Enjoy them."

The woman then left, leaving Sheila standing there, holding the flowers with the shocked look still in place. It took the woman driving off before Sheila pulled herself together to take a step back into the house and close the door behind her as she gazed at the flowers. It was a beautiful bouquet. She quickly placed the vase in what she considered the perfect spot before pulling off the card.

I am thinking of you. Zeke.

Sheila's heart began to swell. He was away but still had her in his thoughts. A feeling of happiness spread through her. Zeke, who claimed he loved her, was too

real to be true. She wanted to believe he was real...
but... She turned to Sunnie. "Look what Zeke sent. I
feel special...and loved."

Sunnie didn't pay her any attention as she continued
to play with the toy Zeke had won for her at the carnival. Sheila was satisfied that even if Sunnie wasn't listening, her heart was. Now, if she could just shrug off
her inner fear that regardless of what he did or said, for
her Zeke was a heartbreak waiting to happen.

A few days later, during a telephone conversation
with a Denver detective, Zeke's hand tightened on the
phone. "Are you sure?" he asked.

"Yes," the man replied. "I verified with a hospital in
New Orleans that Diane Worth gave birth to a baby girl
there five months ago. We could pick her up for questioning since abandoning a baby is a punishable crime."

Zeke inhaled a deep breath. "She could say the baby
is living somewhere with relatives or friends, literally
having us going around in circles. We need proof she's
Sunnie's mother and have that proof when she's brought
in. Otherwise, she'll give Miguel Rivera time to cover
his tracks."

Zeke paused a moment and then added, "We need a
DNA sample from Worth. How can we get it without
her knowing about it?"

"I might have an idea." The agent then shared his
idea with Zeke.

Zeke smiled. "That might work. We need to run it
by Mathis."

"It's worth a try if it will link her to Rivera. We want
him off the streets and behind bars as soon as possible.
He's bad news."

Later that night, as he did every night, Zeke called Sheila. Another bouquet of flowers as well as a basket of candy had been delivered that day. He had been plying her with "thinking of you" gifts since he'd been gone, trying to keep her thoughts on him and to let her know how much he was missing her.

After thanking him for her gifts, she mentioned that Brad had stopped by to see how Sunnie was doing. Sheila had been surprised to see him, but was glad he had cared enough about the baby's welfare to make an unexpected visit. She even told Zeke how Sunnie had gone straight to the man without even a sniffle. And that she seemed as fascinated with him as he had been with her.

Zeke then brought her up to date on what they'd found out about Diane Worth. "It seems she has this weekly appointment at a hair salon. One of the detectives will get hair samples for DNA testing. Once they have a positive link to Sunnie, they will bring her in for questioning."

"What do you think her connection is to Michael Price?" Sheila asked.

"Don't know for sure, but I have a feeling things will begin to unravel in a few more days."

They talked a little while longer. He enjoyed her sharing Sunnie's activities for that day, especially how attached she had gotten to that toy he'd won for her at the carnival.

"I miss you," he said, meaning it. He hadn't seen her in over a week.

"And I miss you, too, Zeke."

He smiled. That's what he wanted to hear. And since they were on a roll… "And I love you," he added.

"And I love you back. Hurry home."

Home. His chest swelled with even more love for her at that moment. "I will, just as soon as I get this case solved." And he meant it.

A few days later things began falling into place. As usual, Worth had her hair appointment. It took a couple of days for the DNA to be matched with the sample taken from Sunnie. The results showed Diane was definitely Sunnie's biological mother.

Although Zeke wasn't in the interrogation room when Worth was brought in, she did what they assumed she would do—denying the abandoned child could be hers. She claimed her baby was on a long trip with her father. However, once proof was presented showing Sunnie was her child and had been used in a blackmail scheme, and that her hand had been caught on tape, which could be proven, the woman broke down and blurted out what she knew of the sordid scheme.

She admitted that Rivera had planned for her to meet Michael Price for the sole purpose of having him get her pregnant. Once Rivera found out Michael was from a wealthy family, he set up his plan of extortion. She was given a huge sum of money to seduce Michael, and once her pregnancy was confirmed, Rivera had shown up one night and joined the party. Throughout the evening at Diane's, he'd spiked Michael's drinks with a near-lethal dose of narcotics and made sure he got behind the wheel to drive home. What had been made to look like a drunk-driving accident was anything but—Michael had been murdered. She also said that up until that night, Michael had been drug-free for almost six months and had intended to reunite with his family and try to live a decent life. With Worth's confession linking Rivera to Michael's death, a warrant was issued and Rivera was arrested.

Zeke had kept Brad informed of what was going on. The Price family was devastated to learn the truth behind Michael's death and looked forward to making Sunnie part of their family. Brad, who had never given up hope that Michael would have eventually gotten his life together if he'd survived, had decided to be Sunnie's legal guardian. He felt Michael would have wanted things that way.

That night when he called Sheila and heard the excitement in her voice about receiving candy and more flowers he'd sent, he hated to be the deliverer of what he had to tell her. Although it was good news for Sunnie, because she would be raised by Brad and kept out of the system, it would be a sad time for Sheila.

"The flowers are beautiful, Zeke, and the candy was delicious. If I gain any weight it will be your fault."

He smiled briefly and then he said in a serious tone, "We wrapped things up today, Sheila. Diane Worth confessed and implicated Miguel Rivera in the process. He then told her how things went down and how in the end the authorities had booked both Worth and Rivera. Since Worth worked with the authorities, she would get a lighter sentence, and Rivera was booked for the murder of Michael Price."

"That is so sad, but at least we know what happened and why Brad had a genetic link to Sunnie," she said softly.

"Yes, and Brad is stepping up to the plate to become Sunnie's legal guardian. He's going to do right by her. Already his attorneys have filed custody papers and there is no doubt in my mind he will get it. That's another thing Worth agreed to do to get a lighter sentence. She will give up full rights to Sunnie. She didn't deserve her anyway. She deliberately got pregnant to use her baby to get money."

Zeke paused and then added, "She claims she didn't know of Rivera's plans to kill Michael until it was too late."

"I guess that means I need to begin packing up Sunnie's stuff. He'll come and get her any day," Sheila said somberly.

"According to Brad, Social Services told him the exchange needs to take place at the end of the week. I'll be back by then. I won't let you be alone."

He thought he heard her sniffing before she said, "Thanks, Zeke. It would mean a lot to me if you were here."

They talked for a little while longer before saying good-night and hanging up the phone. Zeke could tell Sheila was sad at the thought of having to give up Sunnie and wished he was there right now to hold her in his arms, make love to her and assure her everything would be all right. They would have babies of their own one day. All the babies she could ever want, and that was a promise he intended to make to her when he saw her again.

A couple of days later, after putting Sunnie down after her breakfast feeding, Sheila's phone rang. "Hello?"

"Sheila, this is Lois. Are you okay?"

Sheila almost dropped the phone. The last time her

sister called her was to cancel her visit to see her and her family. "Yes, why wouldn't I be?"

"You were mentioned on the national news again. The Denver police and some hotshot private investigator solved this murder case about a drug lord. According to the news, he'd been using women to seduce rich men, get pregnant by them and then using the resulting babies as leverage for extortion. I understand such a thing happened in Royal and you are the one taking care of the abandoned baby while the case was being solved." Sheila released a disappointed sigh. Ever since the story had broken, several members of the media had contacted her for a story and she'd refused to give them one. Why did her sister only want to connect with her when she appeared in the news or something? "Yes, that's true."

"That's wonderful. Well, Ted was wondering if perhaps you could get in touch with the private investigator who helped to solve the case."

"Why?"

"To have him on his television talk show, of course. Ted's ratings have been down recently and he thinks the man's appearance will boost them back up."

Sheila shook her head. Not surprising that Lois wanted something of her. Why couldn't she call just because?

"So, do you have a way to help Ted get in touch with his guy?" Lois asked, interrupting Sheila's thoughts.

"Yes, in fact, I know him very well. But if you or Ted want to contact him you need to do it without my help," she said. "I'm your sister and the only time you seem to remember that is when you need a favor. That's not the kind of relationship I want with you, Lois, and if that's the only kind you're willing to give then I'm going to pass. Goodbye."

She hung up the phone and wasn't surprised when Lois didn't call back. And she wasn't surprised when she received a call an hour later from her mother.

"Really, Sheila, why do you continue to get yourself in these kinds of predicaments? You know nothing about caring for a baby. How did you let yourself be talked into being any child's foster parent?"

Sheila rolled her eyes. "I'm a nurse, Mom. I'm used to taking care of people."

"But a kid? Better you than me."

"How well I know that," she almost snapped. Her mother's comments reminded her that in two days she would hand Sunnie over to Bradford Price. He had called last night and they had agreed the exchange would take place at the TCC. It seemed fitting since that was the place Diane Worth had left her daughter—although for all the wrong reasons—that she would begin her new life there again.

Sheila wasn't looking forward to giving up Sunnie. The only good thing was that Zeke would be flying in tonight and she wouldn't be alone. He would give her his support. No one had ever done that for her before. And she couldn't wait to see him again after almost two weeks.

Zeke paused in the middle of packing for his return home and met DEA Agent Mathis's intense gaze. "What do you mean Rivera's attorney is trying to get him off on a technicality? We have a confession from Diane Worth."

"I know," Mathis said in a frustrated tone, "but

Rivera has one of the slickest lawyers around. They are trying to paint Worth as a crackhead and an unfit mother who'd desert her child for more drugs, and that she thought up the entire thing—the murder scheme—on her own. The attorney is claiming his client is a model citizen who is being set up."

"That's bull and you and I know it."

"Yes, and since he drove from Denver to New Orleans instead of taking a flight, we can't trace the car he used." Mathis let out a frustrated sigh and added, "This is what we've been dealing with when it comes to Rivera. He has unscrupulous people on his payroll. He claims he was nowhere near New Orleans during the time Michael Price was killed. We have less than twenty-four hours to prove otherwise or he walks."

"Damn." Zeke rubbed his hand down his face. "I refuse to let him get away with this. I want to talk to Worth again. There might be something we missed that can prove that now she's the one being set up."

A few hours later Zeke and Mathis were sitting at a table across from Diane Worth. "I don't care what Miguel is saying," she said, almost in tears. "He is the one who came up with the plan, not me."

"Is there any way you can prove that?" Zeke asked her. He glanced at his watch. He should be on a plane right this minute heading for Royal. Now he would have to call Sheila to let her know he wouldn't be arriving in Royal tonight as planned. He refused to leave Denver knowing there was a chance Miguel Rivera would get away with murder.

She shook her head. "No, there's no way I can prove it." And then she blinked as if she remembered something. "Wait a minute. When we got to New Orleans we stopped for gas and Miguel went inside to purchase a pack of cigarettes. The store clerk was out of his brand and he pitched a fit. Several people were inside the store and I bet one of them remembers him. He got pretty ugly."

Zeke looked over at Mathis. "And even if they don't remember him, chances are, the store had a security camera."

Both men quickly stood. They had less than twenty-four hours to prove Miguel was in New Orleans when he claimed that he wasn't.

Sheila shifted in bed and glanced over at the clock as excitement flowed down her spine. Zeke's plane should have landed by now. He would likely come straight to her place from the airport. At least he had given her the impression that he would when she'd talked to him that morning. And she couldn't wait to see him.

She had talked to Brad and she would deliver Sunnie to him at the TCC at three the day after tomorrow. It was as if Sunnie had detected something was bothering her and had been clingy today. Sheila hadn't minded. She had wanted to cling to the baby as much as Sunnie had wanted to cling to her.

She smiled when her cell phone rang. She picked it up and checked caller ID. It was Zeke. She sat up in bed as she answered it. "Are you calling to tell me you're outside?" she asked, unable to downplay the anticipation as well as the excitement in her voice.

"No, baby. I'm still in Denver. Something came up with the case and I won't be returning for possibly three days."

Three days? That meant he wouldn't be there when

she handed Sunnie over to Bradford Price. "But I thought you were going to return tonight so you could be here on Thursday. For me."

"I want to and will try to make it, but—"

"Yes, I know. Something came up. I understand," she said, trying to keep the disappointment out of her voice. Why had she thought he was going to be different?

"I've got to go, Zeke."

"No, you don't. You're shutting me out, Sheila. You act as if I'd rather be here than there, and that's not true and you know it."

"Do I?"

"You should. I need to be here or else Miguel Rivera gets to walk away scot-free."

A part of her knew she was being unreasonable. He had a job to do. But still, another part just couldn't accept he wasn't doing a snow job on her. "And, of course, you can't let him do that," she said snippily.

He didn't say anything for a minute and then, "You know what your problem is, Sheila? You can't take hold of the future because you refuse to let go of the past. Think about that and I'll see you soon. Goodbye."

Instead of saying goodbye, she hung up the phone. How dare he insinuate she was the one with the problem? What made him think that he didn't have issues? She didn't know a single person who didn't.

She shifted back down in bed, refusing to let Zeke's comments get to her. But she knew it was too late. They already had.

Chapter 12

Two days later, it was a tired Zeke who made it to the Denver airport to return to Royal. He and Mathis had caught a flight from Denver to New Orleans and interviewed the owner of the convenience store. The man's eyewitness testimony, as well as the store's security camera, had pinned Rivera in New Orleans when he said he hadn't been there. With evidence in hand, they had left New Orleans to return to Denver late last night.

After reviewing the evidence this morning, a judge had ruled in their favor and had denied bail to Rivera and had refused to drop the charges. And if that wasn't bad enough, the lab had delivered the results of their findings. DNA of hair found on Michael's jacket belonged to Rivera. Zeke was satisfied that Rivera would be getting just what he deserved.

He glanced at his watch. The good thing was that he

was returning to Royal in two days instead of three. It wasn't noon yet and if his flight left on time, he would arrive back in Royal around two, just in time to be with Sheila when she handed Sunnie over to Brad. He had called her that morning from the courthouse in Denver and wasn't sure if she had missed his call or deliberately not answered it. He figured she was upset, but at some point she had to begin believing in him. If for one minute she thought she was getting rid of him she had another thought coming. She was his life and he intended to be hers.

A few moments later he checked his watch again thinking they should be boarding his plane any minute. He couldn't wait to get to Royal and see Sheila to hold her in his arms, make love to her all night. He hadn't meant to fall in love with her.

An announcement was made on the nearby intercom system, interrupting his thoughts. *"For those waiting on Flight 2221, we regret to inform you there are mechanical problems. Our take-off time has been pushed back three hours."*

"Damn." Zeke said, drawing in a frustrated breath. He didn't have three hours. He had told Sheila he was going to try to be there, and he intended to do just that. She needed him today and he wanted to be there for her. He could not and would not let her down.

He knew the only way he could make that happen. He pulled his phone out of his pocket and punched in a few numbers.

"Hello?"

He swallowed deeply before saying, "Dad, this is Zeke."

There was a pause and then, "Yes, son?"

Zeke drew in another deep breath. He'd never asked his father for anything, but he was doing so now. "I have a favor to ask of you."

"Thank you for taking care of her, Ms. Hopkins," Bradford Price said as Sheila handed Sunnie over to him at the TCC headquarters.

"You don't have to thank me, Mr. Price. It's been a joy taking care of Sunnie these past few weeks," Sheila said, fighting back her tears. "And I have all her belongings packed and ready to be picked up. You paid for all of it and you'll need every last item." Sunnie was looking at her, and Sheila refused to make eye contact with the baby for fear she would lose it.

"All right. I'm make arrangements to drop by your place sometime later, if that's all right," Brad said.

"Yes, that will be fine." She then went down a list of dos and don'ts for the baby, almost choking on every word. "She'll be fussy if she doesn't eat breakfast by eight, and she sleeps all through the night after being given a nice bath. Seven o'clock is her usual bedtime. She takes a short nap during the day right after her lunch. She has a favorite toy. It's the one Zeke won for her at the carnival. She likes playing with it and will do so for hours."

"Thanks for telling me all that, and if it makes you feel better to know although I'm a bachelor, I plan to take very good care of my niece. And I know a little about babies myself. My sister has twin girls and I was around them a lot when they were babies."

"Sorry, Mr. Price, I wasn't trying to insinuate you wouldn't take good care of her."

Bradford Price smiled. "I know. You love her. I could

see it in your eyes when you look at her. And please call me Brad. Mr. Price is my father."

A pain settled around Sheila's heart when she remembered Zeke's similar comment. Then later, he had explained why he'd said it. She was missing him so much and knew she hadn't been fair to him when he'd called two days ago to explain his delay in returning to Royal. "Yes, I love her, Brad. She's an easy baby to love. You'll see." She studied him a minute. He was Zeke's best friend. She wondered how much he knew about their relationship. At the moment it didn't matter what he knew or didn't know. He was going to be Sunnie's guardian and she believed in her heart he would do right by his niece.

"I'm looking forward to making her an integral part of my family. Michael would have wanted it that way. I loved my brother and all of us tried reaching out to help him. It was good to hear he was trying to turn his life around, and a part of me believes that eventually he would have. It wasn't fair the way Miguel Rivera ended his life that way."

"No, it wasn't," she agreed.

"That's why Zeke remained in Denver a couple more days," Brad said. "Rivera's shifty attorney tried to have the charges dropped, claiming Rivera wasn't in New Orleans when Michael died. Zeke and the DEA agent had to fly to New Orleans yesterday to get evidence to the contrary. Now Rivera will pay for what he did. And I got a call from Zeke an hour ago. His flight home has been delayed due to mechanical problems."

Sheila nodded. Now she knew why Zeke wasn't there. She understood. She should have understood two nights ago, but she hadn't given him the chance to explain. Now, not only was she losing Sunnie, she had lost Zeke, as well.

She'd pushed him away because she couldn't let go of the past. She was so afraid of being abandoned; she couldn't truly open her heart to him. And now she feared she was truly alone.

She continued to fight back her tears. "I call her Sunnie," she said, fighting to keep her voice from breaking. "But I'm sure you're going to name her something else."

Brad smiled as he looked at the baby he held. "No, Sunnie is her name and it won't get changed. I think Sunnie Price fits her." He then glanced over at her. "What's your middle name?"

She was surprised by his question. "Nicole."

"Nice name. How does Sunnie Nicole Price sound?"

Sheila could barely find her voice to ask. "You'll name her after me?"

Brad chuckled. "Yes, you took very good care of her and I appreciate it. Besides, you're her godmother."

That came as another surprise. "I am?"

"I'd like you to be. I want you to always be a part of my niece's life, Sheila."

Joy beamed up inside Sheila. "Yes, yes, I'd love to. I would be honored."

"Good. I'll let you know when the ceremony at the church will be held."

"All right."

"Now I better get her home."

Sheila leaned up and kissed Sunnie on the cheek. The baby had taken to Brad as easily as she had taken to her and that was a good sign. "You better behave, my sunshine." And before she could break down then and there, she turned and quickly walked away.

Sheila made it to the nearest ladies' room and it was there that the tears she couldn't hold back any longer came flooding through and she began crying in earnest. She cried for the baby she'd just given up and for the man she had lost. She was alone, but being alone was the story of her life, and it shouldn't have to be this way. She wanted her own baby one day, just like Sunnie, but she knew that would never happen. She would never find a man to love her again. A man who'd want to give her his babies. She'd had such a man and now he probably didn't want to see her again. He was right. She couldn't take hold of the future because she refused to let go of the past.

She saw that now. Zeke was right. It was her problem. But he wasn't here for her to tell that to. He had no reason to want to come back to her. She was a woman with issues and problems.

"Excuse me. I don't want to intrude, but are you all right?"

Sheila turned at the sound of the feminine voice and looked at the woman with the long, wavy red hair and kind blue eyes. She was a stranger, but for some reason the woman's question opened the floodgates even more and Sheila found herself crying out her pain, telling the woman about Sunnie, about the man she loved and had lost, and how she'd also lost the chance to ever have a child of her own.

The stranger gave her a shoulder to cry on and provided her with comfort when she needed it. "I understand how you feel. More than anything I'd love to have a child, but I can't have one of my own," the woman said, fighting back her own tears.

"My problem is physical," she continued as a slow

trickle of tears flowed down her cheeks. "Every time I think I've accepted the doctor's prognosis, I discover I truly haven't, so I know just how you feel. I want a child so badly and knowing I can't ever have one is something I've yet to accept, although I know I must."

Sheila began comforting the woman who just a moment ago had comforted her.

"By the way, I don't think I've introduced myself. I'm Abigail Langley," the woman said once she'd calmed down.

"I'm Sheila Hopkins." She felt an affinity for the woman, a special bond. Although they had just met, she had a feeling this would be the start of an extraordinary friendship. She was convinced she and Abigail would be friends for life.

A short while later they managed to pull themselves together and with red eyes and swollen noses they walked out of the ladies' room, making plans to get together for lunch one day soon.

The sun was shining bright when Sheila and Abigail stepped outside. Sheila glanced up into the sky. Although it was a little on the chilly side, it was a beautiful day in November. The sun was shining and it made her think of Sunnie. Thanksgiving would be next week and she had a feeling Brad would have a big feast to introduce the baby to his entire family.

Abigail nudged her in the side. "I think someone is waiting for you."

Sheila glanced across the parking lot. It was Zeke. He was standing beside her car and holding a bouquet of flowers in his hand. At that moment she was so glad to see him. Her heart filled with so much love. He had come back to her, with her problems and all. He had come back.

As fast as her legs could carry her, she raced across the parking lot to him and he caught her in his arms and kissed her hard. And she knew at that moment he was also her sunshine and that her heart would always shine bright for him.

God, he'd missed her, Zeke thought as he continued to deepen the kiss. Two weeks had been too long. And the more she flattened her body to his, the more he wanted to take her then and there. But he knew some things came first. He pulled back to tell her how much he loved her. But before he could, she began talking, nearly nonstop.

"I'm sorry, Zeke. I should have been more supportive of you like I wanted you to be supportive of me. And you were right, I do have a problem, but I promise to work on it and—"

He leaned down and kissed her again to shut her up. When he pulled his mouth away, this time he handed her the flowers. "These are for you."

She looked at them when he placed them in her hands and for a moment he thought she was going to start crying. When she glanced up at him, he saw tears sparkling in her eyes. "You brought me more flowers after how mean I was to you on the phone?"

"I knew you were upset, but your being upset was not going to keep me away, Sheila."

She swiped at a tear. "I'm glad you think that way. I thought your plane had gotten delayed. How did you get here so fast?"

"I called my dad and asked a favor. I needed to get

here for you, so I swallowed my pride and asked my father if I could borrow his jet and its crew to get me here ASAP." He knew the moment the magnitude of what he'd said registered within Sheila's brain. The man who had never asked his father for anything had asked him for a favor because of her.

"Oh, Zeke. I love you so much," she said as fresh tears appeared in her eyes.

He held her gaze. "Do you love me enough to wear my last name, have my babies and spend the rest of your life with me?"

She nodded as she swiped at her tears. "Yes."

It was then and there, in the parking lot of the TCC, he dropped down on his knee and proposed. "In that case, Sheila Hopkins, will you marry me?"

"Yes. Yes!"

"Good." He then slid a beautiful ring on her finger. Sheila's mouth almost dropped. It was such a gorgeous ring. She stared at it and then at him. "But…how?"

He chuckled. "Another favor of my dad. He had his personal jeweler bring samples on the plane he sent for me."

Sheila blinked. "You father did all that?"

"Yep. The plane, the jeweler and a travel agent on board."

She lifted a brow. "A travel agent?"

Zeke smiled as he stood and reached into his pocket and pulled out an envelope. "Yes, I have plane tickets inside. We'll marry within a week and then take off for a two-week honeymoon in Aspen over the Thanksgiving holidays. I refuse to spend another holiday single. Since neither of us knows how to ski, Aspen will be great—we'll want to spend more time inside our cabin instead of out of it. I think it's time we start working on that baby we both want."

Sheila's heart began to swell with even more love.

He'd said she was his temptation, but for her, he would always be her hero. Her joy.

"Come on," he said, tucking her hand firmly in his. "Let's go home and plan our wedding...among other things. And before you ask, we're taking my car. We'll come back for yours later."

Clutching her flowers in her other hand, she walked beside him as she smiled at him. "You think of everything."

He chuckled as he tightened her hand in his. "For you I will always try, sweetheart."

And as he led her toward his car, she knew within her heart that he would. He was living proof that dreams did come true.

Epilogue

Just as Zeke had wanted, they had gotten married in a week. With Summer's help she was able to pull it off and had used the TCC's clubhouse. It was a small wedding with just family and friends. Brad had been Zeke's best man and Summer had been her maid of honor. And her new friend, Abigail Langley, had helped her pick out her dress. It was a beautiful above-the-knee eggshell-colored lace dress. And from the way Zeke had looked at her when she'd walked down the aisle, she could tell he had liked how she looked in it.

As nothing in Royal could ever be kept quiet, there had been mention of the wedding and small reception to be held at the TCC in the local papers. The story had been picked up by the national news wires as a follow-up to the stories about Zeke's heroics in the Miguel Rivera arrest.

Apparently, news of the wedding had reached as far as Houston and Atlanta.

Cassie had arrived with her short Texan in tow, and Sheila could tell she was trying real hard to hook him in as husband number six. Even Lois had surprised her by showing up with her family. It seemed Ted intended to take advantage of the fact Zeke was now his brother-in-law.

Then there were the Traverses. Lois's mouth dropped when she found out Zeke was one of "those" Travers. But she was smart enough not to ask Sheila for any favors. Sunnie was there dressed in a pretty, pink ruffled dress and it was quite obvious that Brad was quite taken with his niece. Sheila was Sunnie's godmother and Zeke was her godfather.

"I can't get over how much you and your siblings look alike," she whispered to Zeke, glancing around. "And your father is a handsome man, as well."

Zeke threw his head back and laughed. "I'll make sure to tell him you think so."

He glanced across the room and saw Brad talking to Abigail. They sure seem a lot friendlier these days, and he wondered if the truce would last when the election for president of the TCC started back up again. But for now they seemed to have forgotten they were opponents.

He glanced back at his wife, knowing he was a very lucky man. And they had decided to start working on a family right away. And he was looking forward to making it happen. "We'll be leaving in a little while. You ready?"

"Yes." Sheila smiled as she glanced over at Sunnie,

who was getting a lot of attention from everyone. She appreciated the time she had spent with the baby.

"What are you smiling about?" Zeke leaned down to ask her.

Sheila glanced back at her husband. "You, this whole day, our honeymoon, the rest of our lives together...the list is endless, need I go on?"

Zeke shook his head. "No need. I know how you feel because I feel the same way."

And he meant it. She was everything he'd ever wanted in a woman. She would be his lover, his best friend and his confidante. The woman who was and always would be his temptation was now his wife. And he would love and cherish her forever.

* * * * *

Reese Ryan writes sexy, emotional love stories served with a heaping side of family drama.

Reese is a native Ohioan with deep Tennessee roots. She endured many long, hot car trips to family reunions in Memphis via a tiny clown car loaded with cousins.

Connect with her on Instagram, Facebook, Twitter or at reeseryan.com.

Join her VIP Readers Lounge at bit.ly/VIPReadersLounge.

Books by Reese Ryan

Harlequin Desire

The Bourbon Brothers

Savannah's Secret
The Billionaire's Legacy
Engaging the Enemy

Dynasties: Secrets of the A-List

Seduced by Second Chances

Texas Cattleman's Club: Inheritance

Secret Heir Seduction

Visit the Author Profile page at
Harlequin.com for more titles.

PLAYING WITH SEDUCTION

Reese Ryan

Dedicated to all the remarkable readers
I've met during my publishing journey.
You support African American and multicultural
romance with your hard-earned dollars,
valuable time, honest reviews and enthusiastic
word of mouth. We are nothing without you.

Acknowledgments

Thank you, Shannon Criss and Keyla Hernandez,
for believing in me and acquiring
Playing with Desire—the first book in my
Pleasure Cove series.

I am truly grateful for your enthusiastic support
of my career and your role in affording me other
opportunities within Harlequin.

It has truly been a pleasure to work with
you both. And it has been an honor to join
the ranks of the remarkable Kimani Romance
authors I have long admired.

Chapter 1

The click of high heels against the hardwood floors prompted Wesley Adams to look up from his magazine.

A mature, attractive blonde extended her hand, her coral lips pressed into a wide smile. "Pleasure to meet you, Mr. Adams. I'm Miranda Hopkins, executive director of Westbrook Charitable Foundation."

"The pleasure is mine." Wes stood and shook her hand. "But please, call me Wes."

"Wes, I'm sorry to tell you Liam won't be joining us for today's meeting." Miranda frowned. "One of the girls isn't feeling well, so he stayed home with her."

"No, I wasn't aware." Wes was surprised his best friend hadn't called him. After all, Liam had hounded him for more than a month to fly in from London for this meeting in Pleasure Cove. The woman looked worried he'd bolt, so Wes forced a smile. "But I'm confident he left me in good hands."

"You've managed some impressive events in the UK," Miranda said in her heavy, Southern drawl as she guided him toward a carpeted hallway. "We're so excited that you're considering taking on our project."

Wes nodded and thanked her, glad his friend had clearly gotten the point. He was here to assess the project and decide whether it was a good fit. Nothing was written in stone.

As they approached an open door of a glass-walled conference room, he heard the voices of two women. One of them was oddly familiar.

"Wes, this is our events manager, Lisa Chastain." He reached out to shake Lisa's hand. Then Miranda drew his attention to the other woman. "And this is Olympic champion and international beach-volleyball star Brianna Evans. Bree, this is Wesley—"

"Adams. We've met." Her expression soured, as if she smelled a rotting corpse. It sure as hell wasn't her glad-to-see-you-again-Wes face.

Bloody hell.

He hadn't seen Bree since the night they met at that little club in London's West End more than a year ago.

Liam, I'm going to strangle you.

He'd tell his friend what he thought of his match-making attempt later. For now, he'd play it cool. After all, he hadn't done anything wrong. But Bree, whose lips were pursed as she stared at him through narrow slits, obviously disagreed.

Wes widened the smile he'd honed while attending boarding school with kids whose parents made more in a month than his parents made all year. He extended his hand to Bree, despite the look on her face that dared him to touch her.

Bree shoved a limp hand into his, then withdrew it quickly, as if her palm was on fire.

What did, or didn't, happen between he and Bree was personal. *This* was business.

"I believe Miss Evans has a bone to pick with me." Wes pulled out Brianna's chair and gestured for her to have a seat.

She narrowed her gaze at him, then took her seat. As she turned toward the two women, who exchanged worried glances, Bree forced a laugh. "Wes predicted my alma mater wouldn't make it back to the Sweet Sixteen, and he was right. I'm convinced he jinxed us."

Nicely done.

Wes acknowledged her save with a slight nod. He slipped into the chair across from her—the only open seat with an information packet placed on it.

The night they'd met in London, her eyes, flecked with gold, had gazed dreamily into his. The coy, flirtatious vibe she exuded that night was gone.

Bree's face dripped with disdain. Anger vibrated off her smooth, brown skin—the color of a bar of milk chocolate melting in the hot summer sun.

Wes only realized he'd been staring at Bree when she cleared her throat and opened her information packet.

"Well, I…" Miranda's gaze darted between Brianna and Wes. "We're all here. Let's get started, shall we?"

The meeting was quick and efficient. Miranda and Lisa were respectful of their time and promised they would be throughout the course of planning and executing a celebrity volleyball tournament over the next six months.

Six entire months.

Liam had laid out a dream project for him. The per-

fect vehicle for expanding his successful UK event
planning and promotions company to the US. However, working with Bree Evans for six months would
be as pleasant as having an appendectomy, followed by
a root canal. On repeat.

The meeting concluded with a full tour of the expan-
sive Pleasure Cove Luxury Resort property. After they
toured the main building, the four of them loaded into
a golf cart. Wes slipped into the backseat beside Bree
and tried not to notice how the smooth, brown skin on
her long legs glistened. But her attempts to keep her leg
from touching his only drew his attention.

The Westbrooks had gone all-out with the property.
In addition to the main building there were four other
buildings on either side of it that housed guests. There
was a pool and spa house, four different restaurants,
a poolside grill, tennis courts and two workout facili-
ties. Large rental homes and a building with smaller,
connected guest houses completed the vast property.

"Here we are at the guest houses, where you'll both
be staying. Your luggage has already been taken to your
individual guest houses," Miranda announced. "Wes
you're in guest house five and Bree, I believe you're
right next door in guest house six."

Of course.

"Makes it convenient to chat about the project whenever you'd like." Lisa grinned.

"It certainly does." Wes loosened his tie and stepped
out of the golf cart. He extended a hand to Bree, but she
stepped out of her side of the cart and walked around.

"See you at the next meeting. If you want to knock
around some ideas before then, just give me a call," Mi-

randa said. She and Lisa waved goodbye as they zipped off in the golf cart.

Wes took a deep breath before he turned to Bree. "Look, I'm sorry I didn't call—"

"You're an ass." She shifted the strap of her purse higher.

She wasn't wrong.

Still, the accusation felt like a ton of bricks being launched onto his chest. "Bree, you're obviously angry—"

"Don't call me Bree. We're not friends." She folded her arms over her breasts, dragging his gaze there.

Wes raised his eyes to hers again. "Okay, what should I call you?"

Psycho? Insane? Ridiculously hot in that tight little black dress?

The corner of her mouth quirked in a grin that was gone almost as quickly as it had appeared. She'd caught him staring and seemed to relish his reaction. "Call me Brianna or Ms. Evans. I don't really care." Though, clearly, she did.

"All right, Ms. Evans." *Ms. Jackson, if you're nasty.* He bit his lip, scrubbing the image from his brain of her moving her hips and striking a pose. "I'd like to sincerely apologize for not calling when I said I would. It was rude of me. I should've called."

"You shouldn't have promised." Her voice was shaky for a moment. "Don't promise something if you don't intend to carry it out. That's one of the basic rules of not being an ass hat."

"Noted." He chuckled as he pulled his shades from his inside jacket pocket and put them on. "We good?"

"As good as we need to be." Brianna turned on her

tall heels, which added length to her mile-long legs. His gaze followed the sway of her generous hips. She opened the door of her guest house and glanced over her shoulder momentarily before stepping inside and closing the door behind her.

Wesley sighed. He'd spent more than a decade building his event-planning-and-promotion business from a ragtag team of university misfits planning pop-up events for a little extra dosh to a company that routinely planned events for some of the hottest celebs and largest corporations in the UK. Taking point on the planning of the Westbrooks' new celebrity volleyball tournament would help him establish a name with major players in the US more quickly.

But would Bree's animosity make it impossible for them to work together effectively?

He'd lived in London the better part of his life, and he loved living there. Still, the blue skies, warm sun and salty breeze drifting in from the Atlantic Ocean made him nostalgic for home.

But then he hadn't really gone home. He hadn't even told his mother he was in North Carolina.

Maybe he only missed the idea of home.

Either way, it was time to find out.

Bree tossed her purse onto the nearest chair and flopped down onto the sandy beige sofa. It was the same color as Wesley's pants. Not that she cared. She just happened to notice the color, and how well the material had hugged his firm bottom.

No. No. No. Do not think about his ass or any other parts of his anatomy.

She kicked off her shoes and headed to the bar. It

was well-stocked, courtesy of Liam Westbrook. But she also had Liam to thank for bringing her and Wes together on this project.

The stunned look on Wes's face indicated that he was just as surprised to see her. Liam obviously hadn't told his friend that he'd invited her to work on the project.

But why?

They were best friends. Which meant Liam probably knew what had happened that night.

Her cheeks stung as she surveyed the bottles of wine. *No.* It was too early to drink chardonnay alone. She pulled out a split of champagne and a bottle of orange juice.

It's never too early for mimosas.

She took a sip of the cocktail and felt she could breathe for the first time since she'd laid eyes on Wesley Adams. His six-foot-three frame had filled out the navy jacket and beige pants as if they were made for him.

Bree checked the time on her phone. It was still early out in California. After a recent shoulder surgery, her best friend and volleyball partner, Rebecca Jacobs wouldn't be following her usual early morning workout routine. Still, it wouldn't hurt to text.

Bree sent a text message with one hand while nursing her drink in the other. Bex, you up?

Within seconds Bex replied. Uh-oh. How'd your meeting go?

Bree sighed. Was she really that transparent? Then again, she and Bex had been partners for the last seven years, so there wasn't much she could put past her friend. Meeting was great. Unfortunately, I would have to work with the devil himself. Don't know if I can do this.

The phone rang within seconds of her sending the text.

"What the hell is going on?"

Bree laughed. "Good morning to you, too."

"Sorry. Good morning. Now, what the hell is going on? Who was at the meeting that would make you want to pass up this opportunity?"

She sighed, her finger tracing the bar. "Wes Adams."

"The guy you met at the bar that night in London?" Bex let out a sigh of relief. "I know you're bummed he didn't call, but he's a guy. Don't take it personally. In fact, you should be glad you guys didn't sleep together. That'd be awkward."

"Today was awkward." Bree balanced the phone between her ear and shoulder as she wrestled with the plastic-wrapped gift basket filled with goodies. She could use some chocolate. Stat.

"Why? Because you guys fooled around a little? You are seriously out of practice, my friend." She laughed. "I told you not having a life would catch up with you."

"Volleyball *is* my life." Bree ripped open a chocolate truffle and stuffed it in her mouth.

"And it's a great life, but it won't always be there. We're approaching thirty. Time to start thinking about life after volleyball."

"You aren't thinking of retiring on me, are you?" Bree mumbled through a mouthful of chocolate.

"No, but this injury has given me a lot of time to think. I don't want to wake up one day and feel like I missed out on the things that are really important."

"Like?" Her friend was surprisingly philosophical. It made Bree uneasy. She was usually the one reminding Bex to be more frugal and save for the future, when tournament money, appearance fees and endorsements were no longer flowing in, something they'd both been forced to think about more lately.

"I dunno. Like a husband. Maybe kids."

"Wow." Bree's mouth curled in a smirk. "So what's his name?"

"Shut up." Bex fell suspiciously quiet before releasing a long sigh. "His name is Nick. He's my physical therapist, and he is so cute."

"Uh-huh."

"But we're not talking about me right now, Bree. This is about you. Why is running in to this guy again such a big deal? Do you have a serious thing for him or something?"

"No." Even to her ears, her response sounded like that of a tween in denial, punctuated by an unladylike snort. Her mother would be so proud.

Bex paused, which told Bree that she heard her unconvincing denial, but chose to ignore it. "Then no harm, no foul. Certainly nothing worth giving up this opportunity. You could become the face of the hottest new beach-volleyball event on the East Coast. Besides, Westbrook International Luxury Resorts is a worldwide organization. This could be the beginning of spreading your brand. *Our* brand. So don't wuss out on me."

Bree gritted her teeth and stared out onto the water. A huge wave licked the shore, the chilly waters chasing away a toy Pomeranian. "Okay, fine. I'll figure out how to deal with it. With him."

"That a girl. Whatever it takes. Just like on the court. Got it?"

Bree chucked the truffle she was about to open back into its box and nodded. "Got it. Whatever it takes."

She talked to Bex for another half hour, getting an

update on her injured shoulder and her hot new physical therapist before finally ending the call. Bree changed into a pair of yoga pants, a T-shirt and a sweater. She stepped out onto the back deck and inhaled the salty ocean breeze. It was sixty-two degrees out. A fairly warm day for early February.

She flopped onto the chaise and tried to remember her friend's words. They hadn't slept together. So why was she still so pissed at him?

Because she'd wanted to sleep with him. God, she'd wanted to. She'd fantasized about it in the wee hours of the morning, when she couldn't shake the memory of his kiss from her brain.

She shuddered, remembering the touch of his hand when she'd been all but obligated to shake it and make up that story about why she was upset with him. There was some truth to the story.

A slight smile played on Bree's lips as she remembered their argument about what football team had a chance of winning the Super Bowl. She just left out the part where he'd asked her to come back to his place. Bree had turned him down. He smiled, his eyes filled with understanding. Then he gave her the sweetest kiss. Sweet and innocent, yet filled with the promise of passionate nights ahead. They'd only spent a few hours together, but he'd managed to make the kiss feel meaningful. Real.

Real enough that she'd stared at her phone for a week afterward, waiting for him to call. Like he'd promised after their kiss.

Her response that night kept replaying in her head. *Sorry, but I'm not that kind of girl.* She laughed bitterly. True, she wasn't the kind of girl who normally believed in one-night stands. In fact, she wasn't the kind of girl who got laid at all. Not for a very long time. Not since…

She tried to erase the memory of the scornful mouth and hard, dark eyes she'd once found so intriguing. Sexy even. She'd been wrong about that asshole. Apparently, she'd been just as wrong about Wesley Adams.

The man was handsome and tall with warm brown skin. An athletic body that had felt incredible pressed against hers on the dance floor. And a killer smile. One worthy of a toothpaste commercial. He had the straightest, most brilliant teeth she'd ever seen.

And she loved his laugh, which he employed often. Because he was funny. And smart. And he liked sports. Just like she did. But he wasn't intimidated because she was knowledgeable about sports and full of opinions she readily shared. He was the kind of guy she could see herself spending time with on those lonely nights she actually got to spend in her own bed back in Huntington Beach.

Wes was the kind of guy she wanted to spend more than one night with, so she'd turned down his offer to go back to his place.

She'd gone to the pub with Bex that night, determined to crawl out of all the insecurities that rumbled around in her head, barely leaving elbow room for her own thoughts.

She went to The Alley that night, intending to take someone back to her hotel. Just once she wanted to be a little naughty. To shed the good-girl image she'd worked so hard to perfect over the past two decades.

She was the scholarship kid who struggled to fit in at a private school, terrified that the kids would find out she lived in the run-down projects. Two of the front stairs missing and not a single blade of grass on their "lawn."

She'd spent the past ten years creating her image as the perfect spokesperson. A successful player with a feel-good story and the kind of good-girl image that garnered endorsements and kept them. Not the kind of girl who would stroll into a club and pick up a random guy for the night.

In the end, she hadn't turned him down to protect her shiny, good-girl reputation. She politely turned down his offer because she liked him.

Really liked him.

So she gambled on there being another night between them. Only there wasn't. Bree was angry at Wes for not keeping his promise. She was angry with herself for not taking him up on his offer.

Bree drew her legs against her chest, wrapping her arms around them. If she was going to be working with Wes Adams for the next six months, she'd have to start thinking with her brain, not her libido. And she couldn't behave like a jilted lover.

Her heart fluttered, just thinking about how her hand felt in his, even for a moment. A glowing warmth arose through her fingers, making its way to her chest.

She put her head on her knees and sighed.

Letting go of her silly crush on Wes would be easier said than done.

Chapter 2

Wes rang Liam's cell four times.

No answer.

His best friend was definitely dodging him. It was probably best. He had a few choice words for Liam. No way it had just slipped his mind to mention that he'd selected Bree Evans to work on this project, too.

Not that Bree wasn't the ideal person to front an annual sports-and-music festival with the potential to be a huge draw for the resort. She was.

Bree was one of the top beach-volleyball players in the world. One of the few players of color to gain endorsements and a huge following. She was genuinely nice. Frequently participated in charity events. And the camera loved her.

Every single inch of her. A gorgeous smile. A curvy frame anchored by her voluptuous breasts and an ass that would give any red-blooded man reason to adjust his trousers. Long legs. Strong, lean thighs. Undulating hips.

Wes scrubbed a hand down his face. Sitting there recounting the finer points of Bree's physique wasn't a productive use of his time, or a very good way to maintain his sanity. He glanced over at the wall that separated their units. Tried not to wonder what she was doing. If she'd slipped out of the thigh-hugging black dress she wore at the meeting.

He'd like to think she'd worn it for him. The surprise on her lovely face meant she clearly hadn't. Wes shook his head and sighed. Liam couldn't dodge him forever. In the meantime, he had business of his own to handle.

Wes grabbed the key to the loaner car Liam left for him and headed to the front door. Time to go home.

The gravel crunched in the driveway of the old bungalow his grandmother once owned. His mother had left England five years ago and returned to North Carolina to take care of his grandmother, who had taken a tumble down the narrow stairs and broken a hip. After his grandmother passed, his mother decided to stay in her childhood home. A home that held lots of memories for him, too.

Wes stepped out of the red Dodge Challenger with black leather. The loaner was another enticement from Liam to take on the project. Perhaps also an apology before the fact for springing Bree Evans on him without warning. He shut the door and headed up the driveway. There was no answer, so he knocked. Twice.

Finally he heard footsteps inside and the turning of locks. The door swung open, releasing a dark, musty odor that made him wonder if he'd arrived at the wrong house.

"Wes? Baby, what are you doing here?" Lena Adams looked tired and slightly haggard. She ran her hand down the soiled apron she was wearing and smiled, then pushed open the screen door. "It's so good to see you."

He wrapped his long arms around his mother, her face buried in his chest. "Good to see you, too, Mom." His gaze traveled around the room. A thick layer of dust had settled on the furniture. Dust bunnies inhabited the corners. Stacks of books and papers were piled on various surfaces around the living room and dining room. If he wasn't holding his mother in his arms now, he wouldn't have believed he was in her house.

Lena had been the house manager for a wealthy family for two decades. She'd administered weekly white-glove tests, making her the bane of the housekeepers' existence. She would settle for nothing less than absolute cleanliness. Which led to much of her frustration with him, as a boy. Even while caring for his grandmother, she'd managed to keep the place immaculate.

What's going on?

His mother finally released him. She squeezed his hands in hers. "I can't believe you didn't tell me you were coming. I would've gotten the place ready and invited your brother up from Atlanta for a few days." She looked behind him. "Where are your bags?"

"This is a last-minute business trip. I'm staying at the new resort Liam's family built at Pleasure Cove." He tried his best to focus on his mother's face, and not the chaos surrounding them. "He wants me to work on a project for the resort. I haven't accepted the job yet, but I'm considering it."

"Really?" His mother pulled him into the room and toward the sofa. Shifting a pile of magazines from the couch to the floor, she made a place for him. She sat, then patted the space beside her. "All these years, you wouldn't take a job from the Westbrooks. Got your daddy's pride." Through years of practice she'd managed to make the last statement without malice. In fact, there was almost a hint of a smile.

Wes wished he could manage even a semblance of a smile at the mention of his father. The man that had up and left them so many years ago.

All because of him.

He cleared his throat. "I wouldn't be an employee. I'd be working with them as a contractor. And nothing is set in stone. We had the preliminary meeting earlier today."

"If it would keep you here, I'm all for it." She patted his hand and smiled. "But you seem worried. Why?"

Wes drummed the pads of his fingers against his knee. Whatever was going on with his mother, her innate sense of when he was perturbed was still intact. "It would mean working with a girl I met more than a year ago. Things didn't quite work out between us."

"Humph." She nodded, knowingly. "If you'd settle down and give me some grandchildren, you wouldn't have to worry about encountering ex-lovers at business meetings."

Wes sighed. "She isn't an ex-lover. We spent one night dancing and hanging out at a club in London. There was nothing to it really."

His mother laughed. "I'm guessing the young lady doesn't agree."

"Yeah, well it's nothing we can't work through."

"If you really believed that, you wouldn't be considering passing up on this job. And if you're considering taking money from the Westbrooks, it must be a game-changing opportunity." Her eyes twinkled. Sometimes he wondered if she didn't know him better than he knew himself.

Liam and Nigel Westbrook had been trying to get him to come on board at Westbrook International Luxury Resorts since his days in university. But he'd been a scholarship kid at the private academy he'd attended with Liam and at college after that. He didn't want a position just because Liam was his best friend. He wanted to earn his way in the world on his terms. Which was why his master's degree in business was collecting dust on the shelf in his flat back in London. During college, he'd discovered his gift for organizing events. Better still, he'd learned he could make a hell of a lot of money doing something he actually enjoyed. So he'd abandoned his plans to scale the corporate ladder at some conglomerate and struck out on his own.

As proud as Wes was of how the business had grown in London, he wanted to expand his business to the US. Another way to prove to his father that he was a success. The kind of person he should never have walked away from.

It was the only reason he'd considered Liam's offer.

Wes smiled. "Think you know everything, don't you?"

"Not everything. Just you." She squeezed his hand. "Why don't I fix us some lunch. You must be hungry."

"Don't go to any trouble on my account. In fact, why don't I take you out to eat? How about we go and grab an early dinner at the restaurant on the waterfront you're always telling me about?"

A slow smile spread across her face. "You sure? I could just as easily cook us up something. Won't take but a minute."

"I'm positive." He stood. "You go on and get ready. When we come back, I'll help with anything you need around the house."

The fair skin on his mother's cheeks pinked slightly. "I know things have gotten a little out of hand around here. Like I said, if I'd known you were coming—"

"It's okay, Mom." The last thing he'd wanted was to embarrass his mother, but there was something going on. Something she hadn't mentioned during their frequent calls. He needed to get to the bottom of it. "I haven't been home in a few years. I just want to help any way I can while I'm here."

Her smile slid back into place. "Okay, baby. Give me a few minutes to get myself together." As she stood, she seemed to lose her balance. He reached for her, but she'd steadied herself on the edge of the couch. "I'm fine." Her tone was defensive. She cleared her throat, then softened her expression. "Just the trappings of old age, I guess. I'll be back in a few. Excuse me."

He watched his mother cross the room and ascend the stairs. Her gait was unsure, and she gripped the banister as if her very life depended on it. The last time he'd visited she was practically taking the steps two at a time. Like always.

A sinking feeling settled in his gut and crept up his spine. Wes walked back into the dining room and surveyed the books and magazines cluttering his mother's table. They were mostly health and nutrition magazines with little sticky notes protruding from them. He picked one up and turned to the marked page. A tightness gripped his chest, making it difficult for him to breathe. He put down the magazine and picked up another and another. Each sticky note marked an article about Parkinson's disease.

He shifted his gaze to the pile of books. The title on the top of the pile sent a chill down his spine. *Parkinson's Disease: A Complete Guide for Patients and Families*. The orange cover of the second book offered *300 Tips for Making Life with Parkinson's Disease Easier*.

A wave of panic rose in his chest. He steadied himself on a chair then flopped down in it. Lena Adams was one of the strongest women he'd ever known, rivaled only by his grandmother. She was wrong about Wes having his father's pride. Every ounce of strength and willfulness he possessed, he'd learned from her. She'd always seemed…invincible, so independent. Thinking of his mother slowly losing herself to this disease terrified him.

Wes heard his mother descending the creaky stairs. He should put everything back so she wouldn't know he'd been rummaging through her things, but he wouldn't. Instead, he turned to face her, brandishing the orange-covered book. "Why didn't you tell me?"

The smile on her face instantly disappeared, replaced by a look of guilt and apology. She didn't bother to chastise him for going through her books. "I—I was going to tell you the next time you brought me out for a visit."

"How long ago were you diagnosed?" He tried to keep his voice even, despite the fact he was so angry he could practically crawl out of his own skin.

Lena lowered her gaze before returning it to his. "Formally? About six months ago. I began to suspect a few months before then."

So she'd known on her last visit to London, just a few months ago. He rubbed his temple. Why hadn't he noticed?

"We need to talk about this."

Lena grabbed her purse off the chair. "No reason we can't talk and eat." Her cheeky smile almost made him laugh.

Wes looped his arm through hers and led her to the door.

"This is why I didn't tell you. You've known all of five minutes, and already you're treating me like an invalid."

"I'm not treating you like an invalid. I just want to make sure you're okay."

"I am." Her genuine smile and eyes shiny with tears warmed his chest. "Especially now that you're here."

On the ride into town, his mother chatted away, catching him up on what his aunts and cousins were up to. Her familiar laugh gave him a sense of solace. But he couldn't help noticing the slight trembling in her left hand as it rested on her knee. Or the limited gestures she used as she spoke. Both were unlike her, giving him more cause for concern.

Wes had been ready to call his friend and tell him he was passing on the project, but this changed everything. His mother needed him, whether she was willing to admit it or not. Establishing his business in the US, so close to his mother, was no longer a matter of ambition or pride.

It was a matter of family.

His mother had made so many sacrifices for him and his brother, a reality that plagued him with guilt. He'd never be able to repay her sacrifices in-kind. Didn't mean he couldn't try.

Not even if it meant checking his ego at the door and working with Bree Evans to put on the best event the Carolina coast had ever seen.

Chapter 3

Bree arrived fifteen minutes early for the meeting. Because she was always early. Also, because she hoped to get a quick word in with Wes. If they were going to work together over the next six months, she needed to keep things civil. Nothing had happened between them. Other than an amazing night together and a kiss that was so hot and sweet that it melted her insides and made her heart skip a beat.

Other than that, nothing at all.

Bex was right. She needed to let go of her resentment toward Wes. Count her lucky stars they hadn't slept together. Then things would've been unbearably awkward.

She would apologize and clear the air. Let bygones be bygones and all of those other ridiculous clichés. Not for him, but for her. Her participation in this event would expand their brand. Help her and Bex maximize the value of what remained of their careers on the volleyball circuit.

Bree entered the room. No one was there, except Lisa, who stood at the end of the table sorting documents. "Good morning, Bree. Can I get you a cup of coffee?"

"Good morning." She smiled brightly as she surveyed the chairs. Where would Wes sit? Probably next to Liam, who'd likely sit at the head of the table. She walked around the other side of the table and hung her bag on the second seat from Liam's probable chair. Lisa eyed at her expectantly. "Oh, the coffee. I'm fine. Thank you."

The corner of Lisa's mouth quirked in a knowing smile. "All right. Everyone should be here in a minute."

Bree's cheeks warmed. The other woman hadn't done a very good job of hiding her amusement over her careful deliberation about where to sit.

Note to self: take it down a notch. Your crazy is showing.

"Can I help with anything?"

"I'm about finished here." Lisa slid a few stapled sheets into a blue folder, then shut it. "There. All done."

Rather than taking a seat, Bree wandered over to the window and gazed out onto the water. She loved her life on the West Coast, but the Carolina coast was certainly beautiful, too. As soon as the water warmed up a bit, she would get out on a kayak and explore the Cape Fear River on the other side of the island. Right now, the water was still too chilly, despite the mild temperature outside.

Finally, Bree heard voices approaching. She waited

until they were in the room to turn around, flashing her biggest smile. "Good morning."

"Good morning, Bree." Liam shook her hand in both of his, a gesture that was warm and welcoming. "Sorry I couldn't make yesterday's preliminary meeting. I had a family emergency, but I'm here now, and I'm thrilled you've decided to come on board with the project. It's going to be an amazing event. Good for the Pleasure Cove community and the sport of volleyball."

"I know. I'm thrilled. Thank you for inviting me to be part of it."

Miranda greeted Bree, then took the seat next to Liam, closest to the door. The seat she would've expected Wes to take. When Lisa slipped into the seat between her and Liam, that left only the seat across from her vacant. Which meant she'd spend the entire meeting pretending not to stare at him.

"Looks like we're all here," Miranda said. "Let's get started."

"What about... I mean, isn't Wes joining us?" The words spilled out of her mouth before she could stop them. She didn't dare look over at the amused half grin that was probably perched on Lisa's mouth.

Liam's eyes twinkled and his mouth pressed into a slow, subdued smile. "Wes had a family emergency of his own. He won't make today's meeting, but he should be here when we meet on Friday."

"Oh." Bree tried to filter the disappointment from her voice. She adjusted in her chair. *Way to look nonchalant.*

There was a brief moment of awkward silence that made Bree want to crawl into a ball and hide in a corner, until finally, Miranda started the meeting. She directed everyone to the agenda placed inside the front pocket of the folders in front of them.

They reviewed various possible formats for the event, based on ideas generated in the previous meeting. Miranda reviewed reports on current beach-volleyball tournaments in California and Miami Beach. Bree shared her insight on what worked at those tournaments and what could be improved, based on her participation in them in the past. Liam stressed that the event needed to entice notable celebrities who would draw people to the resort.

Lisa reminded everyone of the need to draw visitors who were not diehard fans, including locals. That was Wesley's expertise. Together they made a solid plan that they were all excited about.

After the meeting, Miranda leaned in toward Liam, her voice low. "Has Wes committed to the project?"

"Not yet. But I expect he will soon." Liam's polite smile indicated that his vague response was the extent of their discussion on the matter.

Bree had reacted badly to seeing Wes. She realized that now. Was he waffling on the project because of her?

Wes didn't seem like the kind of guy to let a little contention get in the way of something he really wanted. Still, if she was the reason he hadn't committed, it was more important than ever that she apologize to him. Before he walked away from the project.

Bree said her goodbyes and headed down the hallway.

Liam caught up with her. "Bree, can I give you a ride to your guest house? I'm headed out for a lunch meeting."

She wanted to politely reject his offer. Spend the

short walk back to her place lost in her own thoughts. Her feet, already tired of the four-inch patent-leather heels she was wearing, had other ideas. "Sure."

As they walked toward the front door, Liam stopped and turned to her. "I'm meeting with a few influential folks in town to quell their concerns about the commercialization of the island. It would be great if you came along. You'd be doing me a huge favor, if you don't have other plans."

She wanted to say no. She really did. But his pleading dark eyes and brilliant smile won her over. Besides, she'd taken the time to make up her face and wear a sexy outfit. She should get some mileage out of all that effort before heading back to the guest house and slipping into her comfy yoga pants and T-shirt.

"I'd love to meet some of the townspeople. Maybe even get them on board with the project early on. We're going to need a lot of volunteers."

Liam shook a finger, smiling. "I love the way you think. I owe you one."

"Two, actually." Bree held up two fingers. "The other is for not telling me Wes would be working on the project, too."

Liam pressed his mouth into a straight line, an eyebrow raised.

Busted.

"Perhaps I should've mentioned that. But I can't say I'm sorry I didn't. It would've been a shame if either of you begged off because of it. I think you two will make an excellent team." His smile widened.

She sighed. No apology, but at least he'd given an honest response. That, she could appreciate.

"You're right. I would've said no. That would've been a mistake."

Liam grinned. "You're both here. That's what matters."

Bree wasn't so sure. After all, she'd committed to the project; Wes hadn't. Maybe he'd decided that working with her wasn't worth it. She forced a smile and tried not to let the hurt that arose from that thought crack her smiling veneer.

Wes parked the Challenger in front of the guest house, stepped out of the car and stretched his long frame. He'd spent the last two nights in one of his mother's spare rooms. They had a delicious meal on the waterfront. By the time they ordered dessert she finally leveled with him about her Parkinson's diagnosis. She brought him up to speed on her doctor's prognosis and invited him to accompany her to her next doctor's appointment, which had been today.

He'd spent the last two days getting his mother's house back to the standards she'd always kept. He'd sifted through stacks of papers and mail, sorting and filing what was important, dumping what wasn't. He'd vacuumed carpets, scrubbed floors and cleaned the bathrooms and kitchen. Every muscle in his body ached. It reminded him of those brutal days on the rugby field at university. The days when he'd been sure he must be some guilt-ridden masochist to love the damn sport so much.

His mother's doctor appointment was two hours before his meeting with Liam and Bree. He'd hoped to get back in time to catch part of the meeting, but the doctor's office had used the term *appointment* loosely. By the time they got in to see the doctor, got blood tests, a CAT scan and filled her prescription, they were both exhausted. And there was no way he could make the meeting.

Bree had probably been thrilled by his absence.

Liam pulled behind his car, his face etched with concern. "You made it back. Everything all right?"

"Things have been better." Wes forced a weak smile and rubbed his hand over his head. That's when he noticed Bree sitting in the passenger seat of Liam's car. Their eyes met briefly. She forced a quick smile and nodded, then turned away.

"You look like hell. Want to talk about it?" Liam asked, before he could acknowledge the olive branch Bree had extended.

Liam was his best friend. They kept few secrets from each other. But for now, he preferred to keep the news of his mother's illness to himself. As if not talking about it made it less real. A bad dream from which he'd awaken. Besides, he didn't want to discuss it in front of Bree.

"Maybe later."

"Over golf tomorrow? Ten o'clock?"

Wes shook his head and laughed. There were few things in life Liam enjoyed as much as beating his ass in a round of golf. "Yeah, sure."

"Great. I'll pick you up then," Liam said before turning to Bree and thanking her for lunch.

He should've headed inside. After two nights in that too-little bed, he was desperate to sleep in a bed that could accommodate someone taller than a leprechaun. Instead, he remained rooted to his spot, his feet refusing to budge, as he watched Bree exit the car. When Liam waved and pulled away, Wes didn't respond. He was focused on Bree. She looked stunning, and she seemed fully aware of it.

She strutted toward him in mile-high patent-leather heels that gleamed in the sunlight and made her legs look even longer than he remembered. The white wrap blouse hugged her full breasts, revealing a hint of cleavage. The black pencil skirt grazed the top of her knee. Each step she made offered a generous glimpse of her thigh through a slit positioned over the center of her right leg. She came to a stop in front of him. The same exotic scent she'd worn the night they met at The Alley wafted around her. Fruity and floral. He hadn't been able to get enough of that scent as he held her that night.

"Hello, Brianna." His voice came out softer than he'd intended. Wes cleared his throat and elevated the bass in his voice. "How'd the meeting go?"

"Very well. Sorry you weren't able to make it. Looks like you've been busy the past couple of days." She assessed his clothing. Same jacket and pants he'd worn during their initial meeting. Only more wrinkled.

He could only imagine what she was thinking. No point in trying to dissuade her. Besides, he didn't owe her an explanation. Wes ran a hand over his head. "Yeah, I have. It'll be good to sleep in my own bed tonight."

Her cheeks turned crimson. She bit the corner of her lip. The deep red lip color highlighted how kissable her lips were. A fact to which he could attest. "Can we talk?"

"Sure." He reached into the backseat of the car and pulled out two grocery bags. "But I have to get these groceries in the fridge. Mind stepping inside while I put them away?"

Her hair wasn't pulled back into the severe bun she'd worn earlier in the week. Loose curls cascaded over her right shoulder. She shook her head, and the curls bounced. He balled his fingers into a fist at his side at the thought of fisting a handful of her luxurious hair and taking her from behind. He swallowed, his mouth dry.

"You cook?"

He laughed. "A guy's gotta eat, right?"

"Our meals are being comped." He could hear the click of her heels against the concrete as she followed him up the path to his door.

"I know, but I felt like throwing a steak on the grill."

"In February?"

"When a February day is as beautiful as this one, why not?"

Bree followed him into the kitchen and stood beside the counter making idle chitchat as he put away the groceries. Apologizing was the right thing to do. She believed that. So why was it so difficult to say the words? The words of apology had been lodged in her throat since she noticed he was wearing the same clothes from earlier in the week. He smelled like soap. The utilitarian kind you bought in bulk. A familiar scent. It was all her family could afford when she was growing up. So he'd showered, but he'd been too preoccupied to return here for a change of clothing.

The thought of him spending the past two nights in someone else's bed caused a tightness in her chest that made it hard to breathe deeply. Which was silly. Why should it matter what Wesley Adams did in his spare time and with whom? Her only concern was his actions relating to the event. As long as he nailed this event, he could bang the entire eastern seaboard for all she cared.

The sound of Wes shutting the refrigerator door broke in to her thoughts. He gestured for her to take a seat in the living room. She sank into the cushion of the blue checkered sofa and crossed her legs.

She followed his gaze, which traveled the length of her long legs. His tongue darted out to quickly wet his lips before he dragged his gaze back to hers. "You wanted to talk?"

Her pulse quickened and she smiled inwardly. He still found her attractive. A small vindication.

Bree clasped her hands in her lap, looking down at them for a moment before raising her eyes to his. "I wanted to apologize for how I came off the other day. It was childish and petty. This project is important to both of us. If we're going to work together, I don't want things to be weird between us. So I wanted to clear the air by saying I'm sorry."

Wes seemed pleasantly surprised by her apology. He scooted forward on the couch and gave her a sheepish smile. "I accept your apology, but only if you'll accept mine. I wanted to call, I just…" He sighed, then scooted back on the couch again. His tone turned more serious. "Didn't seem like it was the right time for me."

"Oh." She hadn't meant to say it out aloud. Especially not in that sad, wounded-puppy whimper that changed his expression from contrition to pity. When he felt remorse, she had the upper hand. Now that he seemed to pity her, the power had shifted back to him. Bree shot to her feet. "No apology necessary, but thanks. I'll let myself out."

"What prompted the change of heart?"

Her hand was nearly on the doorknob, but his question grabbed her by the shoulders and yanked her back into the room. She turned back to him and shrugged. "For the sake of the project."

He took a few steps toward her. "Why were you so upset about that night?"

"Why does it matter?"

"Curious, I guess." He shoved his hands in his pockets, drawing her attention to the strain the gesture placed on the placard covering his zipper.

"I overreacted. I get cranky when I'm jet-lagged." The space between them was closing too rapidly. She took a few steps backward toward the door.

His self-assured smile suggested that her answer had told him everything he needed to know.

Her cheeks flamed and she swiveled on her heels, but before she could escape, he'd gently caught her by the hand. A familiar heat traveled from his large hand into hers, up her arm and into her chest. She raised her eyes to his.

"Look, I bought more than enough food to share. I'm going to marinate the steaks then get a few hours of sleep. But I should have the steaks on the grill at say—" Wes flipped his wrist and glanced at his watch "—seven thirty. Why don't you join me for dinner? You can assess my cooking abilities for yourself."

His wide grin and close proximity were doing things to her she wasn't proud of. Wesley Adams wasn't a man she should be flirting with. Nor were they friends. He was a means to an end.

Bree glanced down at his hand on her arm and he dropped it to his side and took a step backward. "Thank you for the offer, but I'm pretty tired, too. I should probably just order in and get some rest."

"The invitation is open, if you change your mind."

Bree had turned and run out of there like her hair was on fire. If it hadn't wounded his pride, he would've found it funny.

Wes closed the door behind her and returned to the kitchen. He seasoned the steaks and put them into the fridge.

You invited her to dinner, genius? Really?

They were forced to work together over the course of the next six months. Like Bree said, they needed to play nice. He appreciated that she'd come to that conclusion. That she had no plans to make the next six months a living hell for both of them.

Being cordial was crucial to the success of the project. Getting to know each other, up close and personal, could only lead to trouble. Yet, he couldn't stop himself. His brain had taken a coffee break and the head on his shoulders was no longer in control.

He'd been dying for another excuse to touch her warm, soft skin. The memory of their night together in London blazed brightly in the back of his mind, like an image from an old-fashioned projector. His skin tingled with the sensation of her body pressed to his on the dance floor. Of his mouth on her lips, her neck, her bare shoulder. The unfinished business between them.

It was good Bree had turned down his invitation. Better for the both of them.

Chapter 4

For the past three hours, Bree had tried to take a nap. Instead, she tossed and turned. Thinking of him. And of that damn kiss. The one that had haunted her for more than a year.

Get your head together. It's not like you've never been kissed.

True. But she'd never been so thoroughly kissed. Kissed in a way that made every nerve in her body raw and frayed. Deeply relaxed, yet ready to spring into action. A kiss that made her want him in the worst way. Body and soul.

In that instant, she'd set aside her plan to make Wesley Adams hers for the night. She'd wanted something deeper with the guy who'd been sweet, funny and incredibly sexy. To be kissed like that for more than just one night. So she'd politely refused his invitation to go back to his place.

She'd regretted it ever since.

Given the chance again, she would've accepted his invitation. If only to ease the tension and stress that had her body strung tighter than a new volleyball net.

Bree slipped on yoga pants, a T-shirt and a hooded sweater, then went downstairs to order from one of the resort restaurants. She grabbed a bottle of water from the fridge and took a sip. A mouthwatering scent had infiltrated the kitchen.

Grilled meat.

Her belly churned. She could almost taste the steak. The one with her name on it.

Bree stepped through the double doors and onto the back deck, following the scent.

"Hey." Wes grinned. He stood over the grill on his deck in a black sleeveless shirt that showcased the gun show he called biceps. His right arm was covered with a tribal tattoo. A pair of lived-in jeans highlighted his assets.

It was colder outside than she thought. Her nipples beaded, pressing against the fabric of her bra. Bree offered a half-hearted wave, then pulled her sweater tight against her body. "Hey."

"You eat yet?" His grin widened when she shook her head. "Got your steak on the grill. C'mon over."

No. No. Tell him no.

Her brain was clear on what to do. Her belly objected, rumbling in response to the delectable aroma. "I'm ordering pizza tonight."

"Or you could have a home-cooked meal with me." His voice indicated that his option was clearly the better choice. Her roiling stomach agreed. "Besides, you're on the road a lot. Home-cooked meals must be a rarity."

"You're assuming I don't cook."

Wes raised an eyebrow, his dark eyes lit with amusement. "Do you?"

She didn't, but that wasn't the point. "It's getting late."

"You're a California girl. It's still afternoon there. Besides, it's just a meal. You can leave as soon as we're done. If that's what you'd like." He'd paused before adding that last bit.

Her jet-lagged brain struggled to manufacture another excuse. Nothing came to her. "Okay. I'll be over in a sec." She headed toward the door.

"Or you can hop the banister now." He closed the lid on the grill and held out a hand to her.

Bree chewed her lower lip as she surveyed the banister between their decks. There were wooden benches on either side of the railing. The banister was only a few feet high. She could easily jump it. Still…

She blew out a breath and stepped up onto the bench. Placing her hand in his, she stepped up onto the railing, then down onto the bench on his side. Before she could jump down, Wes planted his hands on her waist and lowered her to the floor. Taken by surprise, she gasped, drawing in his scent—clean man with a hint of juniper and sandalwood.

Bree fought the desire to lean in, her nose pressed to his freshly scrubbed skin, and inhale deeply. She tried not to muse about how delicious it felt to be back in his arms. So close that heat radiated from his brown skin. She stepped beyond his grasp, shaking her head to clear it of thoughts that would only lead to trouble. "So what's for dinner?"

Wes grinned. "Rib eyes, grilled corn, baked potatoes and grilled onions and peppers. Sound good?"

"Sounds perfect. You went all out tonight."

"Just a little something I threw together." He smiled. "Can I get you a beer or a glass of wine?"

"Red or white?"

"Pink." A wide smile spread across his face. "Sampled a great wine at the grocery store today that'll complement the steak nicely. It's chilling in the fridge now."

"I'll take the wine with dinner." If she was going to be alone with Wesley Adams for the next hour, she'd better do it mostly sober. "Can I help with anything?"

The buzzer sounded in the kitchen. "Potatoes are done. Can you take them out of the oven and plate them? Oven mitts and plates are on the counter."

She slipped inside the kitchen and did as he asked, glad to put space between them.

Bree's eyes twinkled with an excitement she seemed eager to hide as she surveyed her carefully loaded plate. She picked up her utensils. "Everything smells so good."

"Tastes even better. Dig in. Don't be shy." He couldn't peel his gaze from her face long enough to carve his own steak, afraid to miss her reaction.

Bree took a bite. An appreciative moan signaled her approval. The deeply erotic, guttural sound triggered an involuntary twitch below his belt. "This is probably the best steak I've ever had. Where'd you learn to cook like this?"

"My mom is an amazing cook. Taught me everything I know." He took a bite of the steak. It was tender and succulent. Seasoned to perfection. His mother would be proud.

"It's good she taught you to be self-sufficient. It's no picnic being with someone who isn't." Her brows knitted, as if a bad memory flashed through her brain.

"Something you know from experience, I gather." Wes took a sip of his beer. He didn't want to delve deeper into her obvious pain. Yet a part of him was curious.

Bree took a generous gulp from her wineglass. "It was a long time ago."

He took the hint and changed the subject. "So how's Rebecca's shoulder? I read somewhere she'd be side-lined for at least four months."

"Could be a little longer. She's going stir-crazy, but her physical therapy is coming along."

"Good." He put butter and sour cream on his potato. "Dealing with an injury can be tough. Especially late in an athlete's career."

"Were you a soccer player, like Liam?" She dug in to her potato, already smothered in butter and sour cream.

"No, rugby was my sport."

"Amateur or professional?"

"I played at university, then on a lower tier regional league. Definitely wasn't in it for the money." He took another swig of his beer.

"Is rugby as rough as they say?"

"Worse. Got half a dozen injuries to prove it."

"Were you hurt badly?"

Wes winced inwardly at the memory of his last injury, but shrugged nonchalantly. "Sprains and broken bones. Typical injuries in a high-contact sport."

"Is that why you quit?" She took another sip of her wine, her expressive brown eyes trained on him.

"Never really had a passion for the game. It was

something to do in university and I was good at it. Mostly, it was a great way to blow off steam."

"Let me guess, you were the misunderstood rebel type." She speared a piece of steak and pointed her fork at him, then put the morsel in her mouth. His eyes followed the motion. He envied that morsel of beef as she savored it, her full lips pursed as she chewed.

"What gave it away?" He chuckled as she eyed the tattoo sleeve on his right arm, part of a large tribal tattoo that also encompassed the right side of his chest and back. "I didn't consider myself a rebel. Too cliché. On the surface, I was a pretty affable guy. Had a lot of anger pent up inside. Rugby seemed like the best way to release it."

Wes cut into his steak and took another bite, chastising himself. He'd invited Bree to dinner to repair the damage he'd caused and build a working relationship. Not to tell her his entire life story.

He seldom discussed his past with the women he dated. And never with the women with whom he did business. He preferred to stick to the casual overview. Fish-out-of-water Southern boy raised in London was usually enough.

So why had he cracked open the door to his past to Bree?

Because there was something about her that put him at ease. Made him feel like he could let down his guard. It was the thing he remembered most about that night. He was attracted to her, of course. She was Bree Evans. Tall. Gorgeous. Miles of smooth, glistening skin the shade of brown sugar. Provocative, yet sweet. She was laid-back and genuine with a smile that could convince an Eskimo to buy a truckload of ice. No wonder sponsors fell all over themselves to get her to endorse their products. Lip gloss, facial cleanser, breakfast cereal and workout contraptions.

Keep your head in the game, buddy. This isn't a date. You're only trying to create some goodwill.

She broke in to his thoughts with a tentative question. "What was it you were so angry about?"

"Life, I guess. The guys I attended boarding school with had the perfect life handed to them on a silver platter. I didn't." He shrugged. "It bugged me."

"Me, too." She was quiet, contemplative. "I was the scholarship kid at an elite private school." She winced, as if the memory caused her physical pain. "Took three buses to get there every morning, but I got an incredible education and a full ride to college because of it. Most importantly, that's where I fell in love with volleyball. That school changed my life, and I'm grateful for it."

"But…" There was something she wasn't saying. The unspoken words were so heavy and dense, they practically hung in the air between them. He should've ignored them, but the word tripped out of his mouth before he could stop it.

"It was hard being thrust into a completely different world. Especially for a gangly girl who wasn't quite sure where she fit in. Who wanted to be liked."

"How could anyone not like Bree Evans, the quintessential girl next door?" He smiled.

Bree glowered at him, then dug in to her potato. "You'd be surprised," she muttered.

Dammit. He walked right into that one. He wanted to make her forget what an ass he'd been. Now they'd come full circle right back to that night. His gut churned from the hurt in her brown eyes, when she raised them to his again.

"Look, about that night—"

Bree waved his words off as she shook her head. "It wasn't the right time for you. I know. I'd rather not talk about it."

Fine. It wasn't like the conversation was his idea of a good time, either. If she didn't want to talk about it, he sure as hell didn't.

They ate in silence for a few minutes. Then Bree engaged him in small talk about the surprisingly mild weather and her lunch with Liam and few of the locals. He nodded politely and responded appropriately. But he couldn't ignore the pain in her eyes, knowing he'd caused it.

He was his own worst enemy. Always had been.

"The time wasn't right because, for me, it never is. Not for anything serious. I'm focused on expanding my business, so I don't get seriously involved with anyone. Ever."

He studied her face, gauging her reaction and whether he should go further. Her lips were pressed into a straight line, her expression devoid of emotion.

Wes pressed his fingertips to his forehead. "When the night began, it seemed we were on the same page, but then… I don't know. It felt like you wanted more. That's not something I can give you. That's why I didn't call. Not because I don't like you. Because I like you too much to start something I can't finish."

Bree drained what was left of her second glass of wine. "Thank you for being so honest and for being so very considerate of my feelings. But I'm a big girl. I can take care of myself." She stood. "Thank you for dinner, but it's getting late. I'd better get back."

"Brianna, don't go. We were having a lovely dinner. I didn't mean to spoil the mood, but I don't want you to feel as if I rejected you. That wasn't it at all."

"I think I'm still a bit jet-lagged." Bree was a terrible liar, but he applauded her effort to remain civil. She took her dishes to the kitchen.

"I'll get it." Wes trailed her to the kitchen and stacked his plate on hers.

"Dinner was delicious. The least I can do is help with the dishes." Bree scraped his plate, then hers, and loaded the dishes into the dishwasher.

He leaned against the refrigerator, arms folded over his chest, as she put away the dirty dishes. She seemed to be processing his words as she rinsed the pots and pans.

Wes held his tongue. After all, how many times could a guy say he was sorry before the words became hollow and meaningless? More importantly, he kept his hands to himself, balled in tight fists beneath his arms.

He ignored the persistent desire to touch her. To taste her mouth and softly caress the skin at the nape of her neck, exposed by her high ponytail. To finish what they'd started that night in London.

He shifted his weight, camouflaging his body's reaction to the tactile memory and the current vision of Bree bent over the dishwasher—her pert, round ass highlighted by a pair of snug, navy yoga pants.

Maybe they should call it a night, before he did something they'd both regret.

"I've got this. Really." He stepped toward her as she turned suddenly, nearly colliding with him. She planted her hands on his chest to brace herself from the impact. He grabbed her arms to steady her. When their eyes met, her cheeks turned crimson. She dropped her hands and stepped backward.

"Then I'll go." She headed toward the patio door.

"Wait, I'll help you over the—" Before he could get through the doors she'd planted her hands on the railing and vaulted over to the other side.

She was practically a blur as she hurried inside, tossing a final "thanks and good night" over her shoulder.

He ran a hand over his head and sighed.

Way to go, Wes.

Bree retreated to her bed. Her heart rate and breathing were still elevated from her vault over the banister and sprint up the stairs. Knees drawn to her chest, she rested her chin on them and hugged her legs.

The grown-ass woman equivalent of hiding in a corner, hugging her teddy bear.

So much for playing it cool.

She'd accepted his dinner invitation, determined to prove the past was behind them. They'd be able to forge a business relationship that was profitable for everyone involved. She needed to prove it to herself, as much as she needed to prove it to him.

Bex was counting on her to remain calm and stick with the plan. She promised her friend she would. After all, her future was riding on this event being a success, too.

Bree groaned as she recounted the evening's events. Her plan went off the rails long before they sat down to eat. It was the moment he'd taken her hand in his, then grabbed hold of her waist. Instantly, she'd been transported to that night in London. Her attraction to him was as palpable now as it was then.

Still, she managed to pull it together and get through an hour of dinner conversation. Civilly. Without staring at his strong biceps or focusing on the rise and fall of his well-defined pecs as he laughed.

Okay, that last part had been a monumental failure. He caught her checking him out more than once.

No wonder he felt compelled to outline exactly where things stood between them. He wasn't interested in starting a relationship. A statement that was in direct opposition to the starry-eyed schoolgirl fantasy she couldn't seem to let go of.

His words made her want to crawl under a chair and hide.

He'd seen straight through her ruse, much as he had the night they first met. She'd walked into that club determined to be witty, flirtatious and cosmopolitan. All the things she wasn't. She'd been able to maintain the illusion most of the night. Until she met Wes. He was charming and funny, and he'd made her so comfortable she'd dropped the pretense and slipped back into her own skin, like a comfy pair of pj's. The facade quickly faded away, as did her illusions of being satisfied with something temporary and meaningless. She'd wanted more.

That night, for the first time in a long time, she'd been hopeful she could have it.

She'd been wrong.

Maybe she was just as wrong to think she could work with Wes and not be affected by his smile. His charm. His incredible body.

Bree shut her eyes and tried not to think of it. Or the

way his hard muscles felt beneath her fingertips, both times she ended up in his arms tonight.

Stretching her legs, she reached for the remote and turned on the television.

Focus on the plan, not the man. She silently repeated the words her high-school volleyball coach would recite to her when she got too caught up with the opponent on the other side of the net.

Don't be fooled by his good looks and charm. Wesley Adams is the enemy.

A frenemy, at the very least. She'd dealt with plenty of those in her career. Had even partnered up with a couple.

Bree closed her eyes and visualized herself facing off against Wes on the volleyball court. As long as she held onto that image, she'd be good. In control of her thoughts and emotions. Her body's response.

Everything will be fine. She headed back down to the kitchen, repeating the words to herself.

She could do this. But first she needed a bottle of wine. No glass required.

Chapter 5

Wes slipped into the passenger seat of Liam's BMW a few minutes before ten and mumbled his greeting. Despite the comfortable mattress and room-darkening curtains, he would've gotten just as much sleep had he slept on a slab of cold concrete below a bustling railroad bridge. At five in the morning he gave up the pointless battle and went for a run on the beach. But his lack of sleep was catching up to him.

"You're all sunshine and roses this morning, I see." Liam grinned as he turned out of the parking lot and onto the main road. "Why do I feel there's a story involving Bree behind your obvious lack of sleep."

True. Though not in the way his friend was imagining. He'd lain awake last night, his words to Bree and her reaction to them replaying in his head on an endless loop. That was twice he tried to do the right thing where Brianna was concerned, only to have it blow up in his face. A vivid reminder of why he avoided serious relationships. He had a special gift for messing them up. It was a trait he'd gotten from his old man.

When he hadn't been thinking of Bree, he'd been worried about his mother. When sleep finally came, he dreamed of Bree's soft, warm, shapely curves stretching those poor yoga pants to their limit. A shiver ran down his spine now thinking of them.

Still, there was no way he'd give his friend the satisfaction of thinking he was right. Sliding his shades down the bridge of his nose, he peered at Liam. "So you admit that inviting Brianna and I both to work on this project was a harebrained attempt at matchmaking?"

"I'll admit nothing of the sort." His friend's voice was insistent, though the edges of his mouth quirked into an involuntary smirk. He cleared his throat and straightened his expression. "You and Bree are the best people for this project. If something more becomes of it—"

"It won't."

"Fine." Liam kept his eyes on the road ahead, another grin sliding across his mouth. "Though some might say the man doth protest too much."

"Save the Shakespeare bullshit. I'm serious." Wes sighed, softening his voice as he ran his hands through his hair. "Look, I know you see love and happy endings everywhere you look, now that you and Maya are about to get married. But I'm fine with things the way they are."

"I used to think that, too." His friend sported a self-satisfied grin. As if he was in possession of all of the universe's answers about love. If Wes wasn't so damn happy for the guy, he'd slap him on the back of his head, Three Stooges-style, and tell him to get a grip.

"I'm not just saying it." Wes stretched his long legs out and leaned into the headrest, his arms folded over his abdomen. "Not everyone is in search of love. Or even believes it exists." He muttered the last part under his breath and closed his eyes.

Liam chuckled. "I used to think that, too."

Wes brushed crumbs from his navy slacks and pushed the sleeves of his heather gray sweater up his forearms. Though it was mid-February, it was nearly seventy degrees. They had breakfast at the club before hitting the golf course. Despite Liam's reminder to bring his clubs, Wes left them back in London, hoping they'd skip the links. But Liam was two steps ahead of him. He'd purchased himself a new set of clubs and loaned Wes his old ones.

Now, he stood at the seventh green trying to line up his shot and cut in to the lead Liam was quickly building. Wes widened his stance, squared his shoulders, drew the nine-iron back above his shoulders and swung hard. He stood back and watched the ball's ascent.

Liam chuckled as the ball sailed, beautifully, but headed for the pond. It landed with an unceremonious plop, water shooting in the air. A handful of birds flapped their wings in protest to the intrusion. "Impatient as ever, I see. I've told you a million times, you can't rush the shot. Gotta let it come to you. It's a lesson that works in love, too, my friend."

Wes cursed under his breath at the wicked angle the ball took, then groaned at Liam's brotherly advice. "Is that why we're here today? For Liam Westbrook's lessons in love?"

Liam laughed. "I don't plan to lecture you, if that's

what you mean. But what kind of mate would I be if I didn't state the obvious?"

"That I'm being a general ass where Bree's concerned?" No point in beating around the bush.

"I'd have put it a bit more delicately." Liam held back a grin as he climbed behind the wheel of the golf cart. Neither of them were the kind of guys who relished sitting in the passenger seat. But the agreement was the winner of their last round drove the next time. It was a sucker bet. Liam was a far better player. Still, his pride wouldn't allow him to concede or stop believing he'd win next time. So here he was riding shotgun again.

"Bree's a great girl, Liam. You know I think the world of her. But I'm not interested in a relationship. A policy we once shared." He gave his friend a side eye, trying to rein in the green-eyed monster that gave him mixed emotions about his friend's engagement. He was happy for Liam. They were best friends. Had been since they were thirteen years old.

They trusted each other with their lives. Told each other the truth, whether they wanted to hear it or not. And if they couldn't tell each other the truth, they'd both learned to avoid the subject altogether.

Like he'd been trying to do now. Not that his friend was picking up on the hint.

"Come on. You act like I betrayed the bro code or something." Liam pulled alongside the tree and parked in the vicinity of where the ball had crossed over into the water hazard.

Liam was right. He was acting like an overgrown child whose best friend had become friends with the kid next door.

"I didn't mean it like that. I just meant, you once

understood that philosophy. Lived by it faithfully. You were the one person I could count on to never give me grief about it being time for me to settle down." Wes shrugged. "I miss that luxury."

"Never thought of that." Liam folded his arms over the steering wheel. His expression was apologetic.

After a few moments of silence between them, he continued. "Back when I shared your philosophy on relationships, I truly believed we were the smartest guys around. But when I fell for Maya I discovered the truth about myself. I wasn't being brave all those years, I was afraid of being hurt again. Too cowardly to take the risk."

Wes climbed out of the cart with his club in hand and dropped his ball. Liam's revelation didn't come as a surprise. He remembered how devastated his friend had been when he discovered his off-and-on girlfriend, Meredith, had fallen for his brother, Hunter. Still, it was unsettling to hear Liam admit it.

Wes turned his back to Liam and concentrated on the game. He took his time and drove the ball again. This time it landed closer to the hole than his friend's had. He slid his club back in the bag and hopped inside the cart.

"Well played, mate." Liam's raised eyebrows knitted together, despite his compliment.

Wes laughed. "Look, I appreciate your concern. I do. And you know I couldn't be happier for you. Maya and the girls are amazing. You're a lucky guy. So I get that you want to see me happy, too. But you're assuming I'm not. That my life is somehow incomplete."

Liam didn't respond. His silence said more than his words ever could.

Wes couldn't argue. He was content with his life the way it was, but he couldn't deny that there were nights when his bed felt cold and empty. Even on nights on the town, in a room brimming with people, he occasionally felt alone. But he'd been content to ignore those moments. To fill the empty space with a warm body or a night of laughter. "I'm focused on growing Adams Promotions and making the Pleasure Cove volleyball tournament a success. Don't have time for distractions. Got it?"

After a long pause, Liam nodded. "All right. Now, you were going to tell me why you looked so awful yesterday. What's going on? You sure as hell didn't look content then."

Wes lowered his eyes, his jaw clenching painfully. "It's my mom. She's sick."

Liam parked the cart and turned his body in the seat toward him. "Maya, the girls, and I had lunch with your mum a couple of months ago. She seemed fine."

"She's done her best to hide it." He swallowed the lump that formed in his throat. "She was diagnosed with Parkinson's six months ago."

"Did you know before you went to visit her?" His friend could understand the anger and frustration he felt. Liam's father hadn't told him about his battle with prostate cancer until he was already through his treatments and in remission.

Wes shook his head and shifted in his seat to alleviate the hole that burned in his gut whenever the inevitable thoughts of what was ahead for his mother came to mind. Increased difficulty with balance and movements. Not to mention the involuntary movements that were side effects of the most common medication given for Parkinson's. If the disease continued to progress at its current rate, she would require constant care in a few years. "She didn't want me to worry. Or to feel obligated to return to America. And she didn't want Drake to give up his career."

Liam squeezed his shoulder, forcing Wes to meet his gaze. His friend's knowing smile eased the suffocating pain in his chest. "Sounds like Ms. Lena. She's strong-willed and independent. And she loves you and your brother more than anything in the world."

"But not enough to tell us about her diagnosis." The reality of those words struck him hard. His mother had always been stubborn and determined. She'd made incredible sacrifices to give him and his brother the best life possible, regardless of the cost to her. Yet, now that she needed him, she wouldn't ask for his help. She didn't want to impose on his life. Had he made her feel that way? That she was a bother to him? Wes slumped in his seat, his gaze lowered again. He sure as hell wouldn't be winning any son-of-the-year awards.

Liam patted his friend on the back, then eased his foot onto the gas pedal, setting the cart in motion. "You know how protective your mother is of you two. Like you said, she didn't want you to worry. Besides, not telling you was probably also her way of retaining her dignity and independence. An illness like that forces us to face our own mortality. Even if it's only for a moment. It was hard for my dad. Must be pretty hard for your mum, too."

Mortality.

That word sent a chill down his spine that settled into his gut, twisting it. His mother had given him everything she possibly could. All he'd done was bring her grief. Her marriage ended because of him, and so did her dream career. It killed him that even now she was making sacrifices. She'd already done so much for them. They could never repay her, but he'd do whatever it took to try. Even if that meant moving back to North Carolina.

"Does Drake know?"

"We called him the same day I found out."

"I know how tough this must be for you and Drake. Anything you or your mum need…just say the word."

His friend's words dragged him out of his daze. Wes sat taller in his seat and nodded.

"You've already helped. If you hadn't invited me onto this project…" He shuddered inwardly, wondering how long his mother would've kept the diagnosis to herself. "I appreciate the opportunity and the generous housing offer while we work on the project. I'd only intended to stay for the weeks of our planned meetings, but things have changed. Despite what she thinks, my mother needs me."

"Will you move here permanently?" Liam couldn't hide the excitement in his voice, though he made a valiant effort.

A grin turned up one corner of Wesley's mouth. It was comforting that his best friend was eager to have him move closer. They'd been separated by an ocean most of the past five years. "I'm not ready to sell my flat in London, but I'm escalating my timeline to expand my business here in the US."

"Let me know how I can help."

"Actually, I do need one more favor." Wes hated asking his friend for special treatment. This was a business deal, and he always treated them as such. But regardless of whom he was working with, he had to act in his mother's best interest. As she'd always done for him. "I need to miss our next meeting. I'm returning to London to set the wheels in motion. Unless some emergency happens with my mother, I don't anticipate missing another."

"I understand. Of course. We'll get you the meeting notes and bring you up to speed. Communicate via email until you return."

Wes breathed a sigh of relief. "Thanks for understanding."

"Does that mean you're willing to overlook my meddling in your love life?" The smile returned to Liam's face, easing the tension they were both feeling.

Wes laughed and shook his head. "You know, after that first meeting, I'd planned to turn down the project. Bree was mad as hell about me leaving her hanging. I didn't think it was possible for us to work together."

Lines spanned Liam's forehead as he parked the cart. "And now?"

Wes stepped out of the cart and grabbed his putter. He shrugged. "Now I need to make this work. Seems she does, too. We've called a truce. She apologized for how she reacted after the meeting. I apologized for being an ass back then. I even invited her over for dinner last night."

Liam hopped out of the cart, grabbed his putter and followed his friend onto the green. A huge grin spread across his face. "And after dinner?"

"I grilled steaks. We chatted. Everything was going well until…" Wes rubbed his neck and sighed.

"Until?" Liam raised an eyebrow.

"I wanted Bree to understand why things didn't work out between us. That it was because of me. Not because of anything she did or didn't do."

"Wait, you gave her the bloody it's-not-you-it's-me speech?" Liam scrubbed his hand down his face and shook his head. "Aww, bloody hell. What were you thinking?"

"She looked so hurt about what happened between

us. I couldn't stand seeing that wounded look on her face. I had to do something to fix things between us."

"And did it?"

Wes blew out a breath, exasperated with himself. "She bolted out of the door like her hair was on fire and I was holding a can of gasoline."

Liam rubbed his forehead and took a deep breath. "Okay, so dinner didn't go so well. Next time…"

"There isn't going to be a next time." Wes turned to face his friend, needing him to understand how serious he was about this. "Bree and I came to an understanding. We both need this project, and we want it to be the absolute best it can be. But there isn't going to be a romance, maybe not even a friendship. Just a good, productive working relationship. We're both okay with that. I need you to be, too." Wes pointed a finger at his friend.

Liam snapped his mouth closed and lowered his gaze. He grunted, shoving one hand into his pocket. He gripped his club and assumed his stance. "If that's what you want, fine. I won't interfere."

Liam's agreement was hardly convincing, but he would respect his wishes. He was sure of it. Liam struck the ball and they watched it roll, landing within a few feet of the seventh hole.

It was his turn.

Wes stood over the ball, lining up his shot. He inhaled deeply. *Focus, man. Get the ball in the cup. Simple as that.* He released his breath, drew back the club and smacked the ball, hitting it long.

Too long.

He bit back a curse and climbed back into the cart. If he could keep his foot out of his mouth and his golf ball on the green, maybe he would survive this project.

Chapter 6

It'd been three weeks since the disastrous dinner with Wesley. She hadn't seen him since. There had only been one meeting during the past few weeks, but Wes had skipped it. Probably because of her reaction to his confession that night.

The time wasn't right because, for me, it never is. Not for anything serious.

God, she felt like an idiot. She hadn't accepted his dinner invitation with the hopes of starting something between them. Still, those hopes had lingered in the back of her mind. Despite her desperate attempts to stamp them out.

There is nothing between us. Not now. Not ever.

She repeated the words in her head over and over as she jogged along the beach. Her pace quickened with each repetition, as if she was trying to outrun the words. Or maybe her feelings for him.

He's attractive. Charming. So what? I can think of half a dozen guys who are, too. Guys who are actually interested in me.

Bree came to a halt, as if she'd run into a solid brick wall. The phone calls from her ex that she hadn't returned, along with a text message she'd left unanswered, were vivid in her mind. She could practically hear Alex Hunt's voice, low and gravelly, uttering the words he'd typed that morning.

Been calling you. You're not at your place. Where are you? I'll only be in town for a few more days. We need to talk.

A knot tightened in her stomach. Her muscles tensed and her palms felt clammy, despite the cool breeze blowing across the water onto the beach. Bree calmed her breath and stood tall, stretching her arms toward the sky for a beat before resuming her run.

She was in control. Not Alex. It'd been more than three years since she'd ended their relationship. They were over and there was no way she was going back to him. Ever.

Still, she couldn't deny the unease she felt at his words. How did he know she wasn't at her place? And why, after three years, would he suddenly call? Had he conveniently forgotten how things had ended between them? With her threatening to get a restraining order.

Alex had taken a job in Kansas City not long afterward. She hadn't seen or heard from him since then. Her threats of filing a complaint against him had obviously worked. So why was he contacting her now?

The truth was, she didn't care and had no desire to

find out. She wasn't afraid of Alex. She'd taken defense classes. She could take care of herself if she needed to. Yet, she'd scrapped her plans to return to California and opted to stay at the resort instead. Liam had comped their housing through the wrap-up meeting following the volleyball tournament, not long after Labor Day. She hadn't intended to take him up on it. But when she heard Alex's voice mail, her blood had run cold. She'd canceled her flight home and hired a trainer to work with her in Pleasure Cove.

Bree came to a stop, hands on her hips, sweat running down the side of her face. She checked her pulse. Good, but not great. Breathing heavily, she plopped down into the sand and pulled her cell phone out of her armband and checked her email. Her sporting-goods sponsor was making the final decision on a new line of volleyball attire branded with her name. She needed to review the designs and give her input on which pieces should make the final cut.

No email from the sponsor yet. There was an email from Lisa Chastain with the subject "Changes to Program." She scanned the email, her heart beating faster. *That jerk.*

Wes apparently hadn't liked her idea about making the event a family-friendly one. It wasn't part of the original plan, but it was important to her and Bex. They planned to lead volleyball camps for kids aged eight to seventeen. What better way to build a relationship with her target clients than to involve them in the Pleasure Cove tournament?

Wes clearly didn't agree. Was this his way of getting back at her?

Only one way to find out.

Bree searched the tournament contact list for Wesley's number. She inhaled a deep breath, then clicked on the number. The phone rang several times then went to voice mail.

"Hey, this is Wes. Not available right now, but leave me a message, and I'll get back to you."

The beep sounded and her heart stuck in her throat, leaving her speechless for a moment. "Wesley, this is Brianna Evans. I just saw the email about the changes you're requesting. I'd like to discuss it. Please call me back as soon as you get a moment."

Bree finished her run, determined not to think of Wes or Alex.

Five hours later, Wes hadn't answered her original message or picked up the two times she'd called since then. Maybe her behavior was coming dangerously close to that of a stalker. Bree didn't care. This was important. There was no way Liam would side with her over Wes. Miranda and Lisa were enthusiastic about her idea during the meeting, but she doubted they'd have much sway over their boss if he was backing Wes on this.

She had to go directly to the source. Make Wes understand why the family-friendly component of the tournament was critical.

Bree sat at the kitchen counter, tapping her short nails against the granite. Wes had returned to London for the past few weeks, but she'd seen him arrive the day before. He was right next door, ignoring her calls.

Bree could hear Bex's voice in her head.

Whatever it takes.

She sighed, then hopped down from the stool. Wes

wasn't answering his phone. Maybe he would answer the door instead. Bree knocked. No answer. She'd smelled food grilling earlier. Maybe he was out back. Bree headed through her guest house and went outside. She looked over the barrier between their back decks. There he was, lounging on a chaise, eyes closed and earphones plugged in.

Bree called his name, but Wes didn't respond or even move an inch. She called him again. Still, he didn't hear her. Finally, she climbed over the barrier. She reached out to shake his arm, but she paused, taking him in.

God, this man is gorgeous.

The temperature was only in the low seventies, but the sun still shone brightly overhead, making it feel much warmer. He'd taken off his shirt and thrown it across the empty chaise. She studied his inked, brown skin. The tattoo on his right arm was part of a much larger tattoo that covered the entire right half of his torso and disappeared below the waistband of the swim shorts, which hung dangerously low on his hips. Just how far down did that tattoo go?

You're not here to ogle him. Get a grip.

Wes cleared his throat. A smirk curled the edges of his mouth.

Damn. Busted again.

"Hey, I was just… I mean I was…" Bree sucked in a deep breath, willing herself to stop babbling. "You didn't answer any of my calls."

"Exactly how many times did you call?" There was slight tension in his voice.

Yep. He definitely thought she was stalking him.

"A couple times," she lied, clearing her throat. "Were you screening my calls?"

"Phone's in the house. Sometimes I like to unplug." He yawned, then shielded his eyes from the sun as he looked up at her. "You should try it some time."

Bree stepped forward, her back molars grinding and her hands balled into fists at her side. "I'll pass on the life advice, thanks. It's bad enough you're taking over my event."

"*Your* event?" Wes raised an eyebrow in slight amusement as he adjusted the chair into a sitting position. "This is Liam's event. You're the celebrity name with the pretty face they hired to front the operation." A smirk lifted the corner of his mouth. "Didn't expect we'd see you beyond the first meeting."

Wes was enjoying making her crazy. If the racing of her pulse and the tightening of her nipples were any indication, he was making her crazy for him, too.

Bree tore her gaze away from the sexy smirk on his lips and forced it upward to meet his, rather than downward to steal another glance at the hard muscles glistening beneath a slight sheen of sweat.

Her nails dug into her palms as she stepped closer. Her shadow fell across him. "This isn't my first rodeo, cowboy. Contrary to what you might think, I'm *not* just a pretty face. I agreed to join this project because Liam wanted my input."

"I was only teasing. Thought it would lighten the mood." His expression was apologetic. Seemingly sincere. He snatched his shirt off the empty chaise and extended his hand toward it. "Why don't you have a seat?"

"I don't want to sit. I want to know why you've vetoed my idea without the courtesy of an email or a phone call." Bree crossed her arms over her chest, where his eyes had wandered momentarily.

Wes climbed to his feet and stretched, giving her an excellent view of the hard muscles of his chest and abdomen, beneath his smooth brown skin.

The man took good care of himself. From head to toe. No doubt about that.

He walked over to the hot tub near the far corner of the deck. After removing the cover, he folded it and placed it on the bench before slipping inside. He closed his eyes as he sank deeper into the bubbling water. The tension seemed to disappear from his shoulders.

Finally, he acknowledged her again, though he didn't open his eyes. "If you want to discuss the idea now, I suggest you grab a swimsuit. Because for the next hour or so, this is where I'll be taking my meetings."

Bree's cheeks flamed and her heart beat so loudly Wes could probably hear it. Her hands tightened into fists at her side, itching with a desire to smack that self-satisfied grin off his handsome face. "I am *not* getting into that hot tub."

"Then I guess we'll talk about this when I return in a week."

"Wesley Adams—"

He gestured that he couldn't hear her, then slipped lower in the water.

Bree gritted her teeth, climbed back over the divider and headed up to her bedroom. If he thought he could drive her off that easily, he was in for a rude awakening.

Wes shut his eyes and allowed the heated water and full-blast jet streams to melt the tension. For as long as he could remember, any stress he was feeling had gone straight to his shoulders. He could still hear his teacher,

Ms. Lively, scolding him for hunching his shoulders around his ears, like they were a pair of earrings.

He'd been a sensitive kid. Always in tune with the feelings of others. Particularly his mother and grandmother. His mother had always put on a brave face and tried to hide her anxiety. But she didn't fool him. Not for a minute. Not even when he was twelve.

Over the years he'd learned to control it. To dial back his reaction to other people's feelings. He reserved that kind of investment for the people who really mattered to him.

Lena Adams was at the top of that list.

Despite the brave face she'd put on, she was scared. Afraid of what the future held when her body no longer complied. The pain that simmered beneath her brave smile nestled in his gut like a five-hundred-pound boulder. He hadn't been able to shake it.

The trip back to London hadn't helped. His event manager, Nadia, wasn't happy about his decision to make Pleasure Cove the new home base of the company. She was aware that he'd planned to expand to the US, but she'd expected him to continue living and working in London for the majority of the year. He had, too. His mother's illness changed his plans.

He wouldn't move to New Bern, where his mother lived. She'd feel he was encroaching on her independence. Instead, he'd make Pleasure Cove his home base, keeping him within an easy two-hour drive of his mother. Besides, with Pleasure Cove as his base he could easily work with Westbrook International Luxury Resorts on future projects, while slowly expanding his reach along the East Coast. It wasn't the fancy, New York office he'd planned, but he'd make it work.

"Looks like you're deep in thought. Hope you're thinking about why my family-friendly tournament is the better option."

His eyes fluttered open. Wes blinked. Twice.

Bree stepped down from the bench in a sexy, black one-piece swimsuit that caused all of the tension that had drained from his shoulders to settle below his waist. He swallowed hard as she walked toward him. The asymmetrical swimsuit had one strap, across her left shoulder. Just below her full breasts, a cut-out veered in, nearly to her navel, then dipped back out again at her waist, revealing the smooth, brown skin on the left side of her torso. Her hair was pulled up in a loose ponytail, high at the back of her head.

She was gorgeous. From the sway of her generous hips and the sly turn at the corners of her pouty lips, she damn well knew it.

The gloves were off, and Bree was prepared to play dirty. There was no way in hell he could concentrate on business while she was standing there in...*that*.

His appreciative assessment of the swim attire clinging for dear life to her undulating curves hadn't gone unnoticed. Bree tried to swallow a grin as she inched closer, then slid out of her sandals.

Wes extended his hand to her, but didn't stand. If he did, his appreciation for her choice of swimwear would become painfully obvious. "You took me up on the offer. Didn't think you would."

"Don't underestimate me. I don't give up so easily." She settled into the seat across from his.

He nodded, his gaze settling on her fiercely determined one. Bree was ready for a battle. "I know. Watched you play for years. I've seen you dig out of some tough spots. Your refusal to concede, it's what I admire most about you as a player."

"But not as a colleague seated across the boardroom table, I take it." She folded her arms beneath her breasts, inadvertently providing him with a spectacular view of her cleavage. His gaze dropped there momentarily and she immediately realized her mistake. Bree lowered her arms and narrowed her gaze at him, one eyebrow raised.

"I appreciate tenacity, even in an opponent. Regardless of the playing field. Apparently you do, too. You teamed up with one of your fiercest rivals, Bex Jacobs." Wes reached behind him and opened the cooler. "Beer?"

She stared at him for a moment, as if the question was a test, then nodded. "Yes, thank you."

Wes grabbed two beers, opened them both and handed one to her. "So you and Bex…how'd that happen?"

"We became friends during a trip to the Olympics with other partners. A couple years later, we both found ourselves in need of new partners. Teaming up was a no-brainer."

"A lot of pundits felt it was a mistake for you two to team up."

"Reporters and analysts who were afraid that without our rivalry, there would be nothing else in women's volleyball to talk about." She practically snorted. He held back a grin. "They were wrong."

"They were, and so was I. I was one of those people who thought it was a mistake. Glad I was wrong." He sipped his beer.

"But you're not wrong now?" She narrowed her gaze when he gestured that her estimation was correct. Her cheeks turned deep red and she pursed her lips. "You summarily dismissed the idea without giving it any consideration."

"I have considered your proposal. It's admirable you want to make the event welcoming to families, but that isn't what we're going for here."

"Why not? Because you say so?" She crossed her arms again, higher this time, blocking his view of her curves. It was a move he appreciated—he didn't need the distraction.

"Because we want to make as much money on this event as possible the first time out. We won't do that selling cotton candy and ice cream. Alcohol—" he held up his bottle for emphasis " *that's* where we'll make our money. Throw in a celebrity chef making gourmet meals. Couple that with overpriced drinks with fancy names. Suddenly we're making money hand over fist our first year."

"You act like there isn't money to be made in family entertainment." The pitch of her voice climbed higher. "Ever heard of theme parks?"

"Of course." He smiled inwardly. She was on the defensive. Not as calm and collected as she'd been when she'd strolled across the deck. "But this ain't a theme park, darlin'. The Pleasure Cove Luxury Resort is geared toward entertainment of the adult variety. I imagine having Junior underfoot would kill Dad's buzz while he's ogling the celebrity volleyball players."

She folded her arms, lifting her breasts again. Then she dropped them and sighed, not responding. He wasn't sure if she was angry with him or herself.

Despite what she seemed to think, he got no joy from raining on her parade. He'd much prefer to see that gorgeous smile of hers. The one that went straight to his chest and made his heart skip a beat.

Wes leaned in, his voice apologetic. "Look, I admire your idea. I'm just not sure there's a market for a family-friendly volleyball tournament. If there is, it's definitely not Pleasure Cove. Besides, our goal is to make this event rival some of the other popular East Coast volleyball tournaments within the next three years. Inviting small children isn't the way to do that."

Her lower lip jutted out a bit. Even her pout was sexy as hell. It made him want to cross to her side and suck on her lower lip. Hear the soft moans that would emanate from her throat when he did. The memory of how she felt in his arms and the taste of those sweet, kissable lips crawled over his skin, unsettling him.

Keep your hands and lips to yourself, man.

Wes set his beer on the hot tub, dragging his gaze back to her eyes. He hated to see her disappointed. Hated being the cause of it. But he was hired to do a job. Not to protect the volleyball princess's feelings.

So why did he feel like shit for killing her idea?

Bree set her beer bottle on the side of the hot tub. "Then we should be more aggressive with our plan. Give it a music festival vibe. Maybe bring in some up-and-coming local bands on rotating stages. That's what they did at the tournament in LA. I played in that tournament a few times. The lure of the bands boosted attendance."

"This isn't LA. We're not exactly known for our music scene."

"Okay, maybe not Pleasure Cove, but we could expand the reach to the rest of the state." She sighed in response to his unconvinced expression. "Are you saying North Carolina doesn't have the talent to pull this off?"

"Not at all. There are a wide range of talented acts here in the state. But it wouldn't have the kind of draw the LA music scene does. We can integrate local acts, maybe have them featured at some of the smaller venues, but we'll need some heavy hitters, including a highly recognizable act to anchor the center stage. I know you're a California girl, but the East Coast has a totally different vibe."

"Well, at the event in New York—"

He shook his head, ignoring the frown tugging at the corners of her mouth. "This isn't New York, either. We're in the Carolinas. Got no illusion we can beat New York or LA at their own game."

Bree folded her arms again. "Then exactly what do you suggest?"

Wes smiled, waving a hand toward the beach. "We create a competitive advantage based on what sets North Carolina apart."

"And exactly what is that?" She stared at him, one eyebrow raised. Ready for battle.

He chuckled. "The fact that you have to ask means a little research is in order."

"You're giving me homework?" The tension in her voice spiraled.

"I'm giving *us* homework." His brain immediately balked at the statement. He was supposed to be creating distance between him and Bree Evans. Not finding a way to spend more time with her. It was a battle his good sense was losing. He raised his chin. "Spend the next week exploring the state with me."

Her mouth opened and her eyes widened, but she

didn't speak. She was considering it. That was more than he'd hoped for. So he pressed further.

"We'll spend a couple of days at the beach, a few in the mountains, and a day or two in Raleigh, Chapel Hill and Charlotte. You'll get a sense of what makes the state unique." She narrowed her gaze at him, so he added, "I'm a North Carolina native, but I've lived in London most of my life. The state is growing rapidly, and so much has changed. That's why I need the refresher. What do you say? Do we have a date?"

Wes regretted his word choice nearly the moment he'd uttered it.

This would be a business trip. Plain and simple. He wouldn't spend the next six months fighting her on every decision they had to make about the tournament. Which celebs to invite. The selection of celebrity chefs. Which bands to hire. Themes. The schedule.

Bree knew volleyball tournaments. She'd competed in plenty of them, competitive and exhibition. But if he could give her a better sense of the venue and what he and Liam were trying to accomplish, she might come around and stop fighting him.

Wes tilted his head, taking her in. This might be the worst idea he ever had. Bree was smart and beautiful. Yet, she was a fierce competitor. Everything about this woman made him want her.

He gripped the sides of the hot tub, determined not to move, when what he really wanted was to take her in his arms and kiss her again. Then take her to his bed.

The physical attraction was enough to battle, but what worried him most was his growing need to be in her company. He felt at ease with Brianna. Her company was a welcome antidote to the anxiety he felt over his mother's illness.

If they could get past the awkwardness of what had happened in London, maybe they could be friends.

"C'mon, it'll be fun."

She raised her gaze to his. "And we'll have separate rooms?"

"Of course. I'll be on my best behavior. I promise."

"Fine." Bree stepped out of the hot tub and dried herself off. She wrapped a towel around her body and secured it. "Email me the itinerary."

She didn't wait for his response, so he didn't offer one. He only hoped he wasn't making another huge mistake that would land both of them in hot water.

Chapter 7

"You agreed to do what?" Bex's voice blared through the speaker on Bree's cell phone, which was propped on the bathroom sink as she detangled her shoulder-length, curly hair. It was a task that took far longer than she cared to admit. "Have you lost your freaking mind? You've got a thing for this guy. Or are we still pretending that you're over him?"

"Hey, you're the one who said do whatever it takes to make this work. That's what I'm doing. Or have you forgotten the plan?" Bree responded, her heart racing. Not because she was arguing with her best friend. Because Bex was right, and they both knew it.

"I know what I said, but I also know you. The girl who wears her heart on her sleeve, and who is really attracted to this guy." Bex sighed. "I don't get this guy. First, he tells you he doesn't believe in anything serious. Next, he's inviting you to spend a week with him exploring North Carolina. What the hell? Is this some kind of sick mind game?"

"Doesn't seem like his style. Besides, now that I've had time to think about it, he's right. I need a better understanding of the locale. Maybe I've been approaching this the wrong way."

"See, that right there is what I'm talking about. He's got you doubting yourself. I thought the plan was to see him as a competitor. The enemy." Bex's Yorkshire terrier, Sheba, barked frantically in the background. Her friend was likely pacing the floor and gesturing wildly, working the poor thing up.

"And don't we always say we need to know our enemy in order to defeat him?"

"If you really mean it, it's a good plan," Bex conceded. "But it feels like you're trying to convince yourself. Are you sure this isn't just about spending some alone time with Wesley Adams?"

Bree stared at herself in the mirror for a moment before dropping her gaze to the phone. "I'm sure."

"Then good luck, but you call me the second you feel yourself falling for this guy. I'll knock some sense back into you, even if I have to fly out there." The smile was back in her friend's voice.

They both laughed. "Promise."

"Good. Anything else I should know about?"

Bree's gut churned. Was she that transparent?

She hadn't told Bex about the messages from her ex. Bree knew how her best friend would react. Without knowing some of the uglier details of the breakup three years ago, Bex had been ready to take a bat to Alex's precious car.

It was just a few voice mails and a text message. He'd get bored and give up when she didn't respond. So why get Bex upset for nothing? Besides, she didn't want to talk about Alex. She'd given him three years of her life, and he didn't deserve another moment of it.

"Everything is fine."

"You're a terrible liar, Brianna Evans," Bex said. "But whether it's Wes or something else that's bothering you, I'm here when you're ready to talk."

Bree ended the call and hoped like hell that everything would be all right.

Wes leaned against the hood of the car, his hands shoved into his pockets as he waited for Bree.

An entire week together. Alone.

What had he been thinking when he proposed this trip?

That there was no way in hell Bree would agree to his request. If he'd bet money on it, he'd have lost his flat back in London and everything in it, because Bree called his bluff. Which left him no choice but to go through with it.

Not one of my better ideas.

Nor was it part of some calculated grand plan. He'd planned this trip two weeks ago, only he'd intended to travel solo. After two decades of living abroad, he was out of touch. He needed this research trip as much as Brianna did. Besides, time on the road alone would've given him a chance to clear his head, still spinning from the reality of his mother's illness.

Then there was the dark truth that he didn't dare admit, not even to himself.

He wanted an excuse to spend time with Bree.

A small part of him hoped that the competitive spirit that made Bree Evans a world class athlete would prompt her to accept his challenge.

Wes glanced at his watch. Five minutes past their scheduled departure.

Maybe she planned to leave him waiting—her retribution for how he'd treated her in London.

Served him right. He'd been an ass, even if he'd done it for the right reasons. Then he heard her voice.

"Sorry I'm late. My mom called as I was leaving." Bree pulled a small carry-on bag behind her. Slim, dark-wash jeans hugged her luscious curves. She wore a red-and-white striped blouse with a wide band at the waist.

"Is everything okay?" He opened the trunk.

"She needed to vent. My dad retired late last year, and he's driving her crazy." A tentative smile settled on her glossed lips.

"That all you're bringing? We'll be gone a week, you know?"

"I have everything I need. When you schlep your own luggage as much as I do, you learn to pack light."

Bree eschewed his offer to take her bag. She lifted the small, black bag into the trunk. The band at her waist rose, providing Wes with a glimpse of the tattoo on her lower right side. A vibrant, purple butterfly landing on a lotus blossom rendered in a deep, rich shade of pink. He'd seen dozens of glossy photos of Bree online and in magazines. That tattoo hadn't been in a single one. He would've remembered. So it was a recent addition. Or maybe she'd always had it airbrushed out of her photos.

What does it mean?

Asking was out of the question. Might as well confess he'd been gawking at her. Not a good move at the outset of their strictly business road trip.

"You're traveling light, too." Her voice broke into his thoughts.

"I'm a simple guy." He closed the trunk and resisted the inclination to open her car door. After her insistence on handling her own luggage, he doubted she'd welcome the action. Instead, he gestured toward the car. "Shall we?"

"Sure." An uneasy smile curled the edges of her mouth. The bravado she'd shown earlier was gone, if only for a moment.

It was a feeling he knew well. They weren't on the road yet, and already the tension crept up his spine.

"Have you eaten?" When she indicated that she had, he slid behind the steering wheel and secured his seat belt. She did the same. "Good. We can hit the road right away. Got a long drive to Asheville."

"I've always wanted to visit there." Her smile deepened into one that lifted her cheeks and lit her eyes from within.

There's that smile. The one he remembered so fondly from their night together in London.

"Good, because we're spending two days there." Wes turned the ignition, then headed onto the road.

"I noticed." She waved a copy of the trip itinerary he emailed her because she'd insisted on one. It was pretty vague. Just a list of the cities he planned to visit and the dates they'd be there. "You're not a man of many details, are you?"

Wes laughed. "You'd be surprised to learn that I'm known for my attention to detail. It's an essential skill in planning and promotions."

"So this list is purposely vague?" She held up the sheet again.

"I was going for Man of Mystery. Apparently, I've failed miserably." He smiled. "So you'll just have to take my word for it."

Bree's laughter warmed his chest. "So, Man of Mystery, what will we be doing in Asheville for two whole days?"

"Everything." He wished he could rescind the word when her shoulder stiffened and her cheeks turned crimson. "I mean, there's a lot to do there. Two days will barely scratch the surface. Got a few activities planned, but I don't want to ruin the surprise."

"Fair enough." Bree stuffed the piece of paper back into her purse, then dropped her bag on the floor. "How long until we're there?"

"It's nearly a six-hour drive."

Her eyes widened in protest. For a moment, he thought she might bolt from the moving vehicle. He held back a chuckle.

"Don't worry, we'll stop for lunch in Raleigh. Give you a chance to stretch your legs out and sample some of the best barbecue in the state."

"Raleigh's in central North Carolina. So will we be having Eastern or Western-style barbecue?"

"Someone's been doing her research."

"You said I didn't know enough about the state." She shrugged. "I decided you were right."

They were silent for a few minutes, then he asked the question that had lingered in his mind from the moment she agreed to the trip.

"So…why'd you change your mind about joining me

on this trip?" Liam would accuse him of looking a gift horse in the mouth. Still, he needed to know.

"Other than the fact that you asked me?" She stared out of the passenger window.

He grinned. "Yeah, besides that."

"Partly because you didn't expect me to say yes. Partly because you were right. We can't beat the Miami or LA tourneys at their own game. We must focus on what sets Pleasure Cove apart. I need a better understanding of the location in order to do that."

"Is that why you haven't gone home between the meetings?"

She didn't reply right away, and he nearly regretted asking. What business was it of his if she hadn't returned home? Yet, when Liam mentioned it, in passing, he couldn't help wondering why she'd stayed.

"Sorry, it's none of my business."

"No, it's fine. I just wondered how you… Ahh, Liam."

Shit.

Should've kept his mouth shut. Now she'd think they were a couple of gossiping men. "We talked while I was in London. He mentioned he saw you at lunch."

She nodded thoughtfully, though he wasn't sure if she accepted his explanation or was simply acknowledging that she heard it. "I was able to conduct all of my meetings via phone or email. Since I had no pressing issues back home, I stayed put. It gave me a chance to familiarize myself with the venue and some spots around town."

"And what do you think of Pleasure Cove?" He was glad to sway the conversation from the fact that he'd been keeping tabs on her.

"The town or the resort?"

"Both."

"The town is idyllic. Charming. There's an eclectic mix of locally owned shops and eateries along the beach and downtown. I admire the fact that they've kept the big-box stores and chains at bay. A lot of those small, quaint shops couldn't stay afloat if they had to compete with them."

"You have been getting to know the locals. And what you say is true. But their reluctance to change also left the town outdated, almost losing its relevance except with the handful of tourists who've been coming here for years, many of them since they were kids. A lot of the old guard fear the evils of commercialization, but the town and its economy needed the shot in the arm that infusion of cash brought."

"I've heard a few debates about it in town. So I understand the careful balancing act we have to do. We have to find a way to bring in the masses without pissing off the locals. That's why I thought a family-friendly event would work best. It's something everyone in town could enjoy."

It was too early in the trip to get into a heated debate about the format of the tournament again. Bree took the hint and changed direction.

"That reminds me, I think we should source goods and services for the event locally. It won't be feasible in every instance, but it may buy us some goodwill with the locals. Besides, it's just the decent thing to do."

"Great idea. My go-to vendors are all in the UK. I need to build a database of stateside vendors anyway. I'd love to patronize local shops."

"Good to know you don't disagree with all of my ideas."

Don't take the bait, man.

An uncomfortable silence settled over the car. Wes turned on the radio and focused on the road.

Maybe their trip wasn't off to a stellar start, but he had seven days to convince Bree they were on the same side.

Chapter 8

By the time they arrived in Raleigh, Bree was restless. Their conversation had been cordial, but thank-
fully there hadn't been much of it during the two-hour
drive up I-40W. She'd taken a series of business calls.

Wes probably thought she was being rude. If he did,
she couldn't blame him. Under normal circumstances,
she would've waited until she arrived to take the calls in
private. However, the creative department for her biggest
sponsor—a major athletic-wear line—was in a panic.

Already three weeks behind schedule getting to production, her latest sportswear line hit another snag. The
team was in crisis mode.

"We're here." Wes pulled into a recently vacated
parking space on the street.

"Perfect timing." Bree hit Send on the follow-up
email to the call that had lasted nearly an hour. She

shoved her tablet in her bag. "I'm done with work and I'm starving."

"Me, too." Wes stepped out of the car and came around to open her door. A wide smile lifted the corners of his sensuous mouth as he extended his hand to her.

Bree slipped her hand into his. A slight shiver trailed up her arm and his scent enveloped her.

She'd been aware of his masculine scent as they rode in the car, but it was subtle. Standing toe-to-toe with him, she was enraptured by the scent. She inhaled the notes of lavender, orange and patchouli, her eyes fluttering closed for the briefest moment. Bree withdrew her hand from his and stepped away, hitching her purse on her shoulder.

Wesley's gaze dropped to the stretch of skin the movement left exposed at her waist. His eyes traced her tattoo. A butterfly alighting on a lotus blossom. Warmth filled her cheeks.

"Sorry, I didn't mean to stare. It's a beautiful tattoo. The colors are exceptionally vibrant, and it fits you."

"Thanks." She tugged down her blouse.

You are not attracted to him. You are not attracted to him. You are not...

Who was she kidding?

Of course she was attracted to Wesley Adams. He was tall, dark, handsome and incredibly fit. A fact not hidden by the gray, lightweight sweater he wore over a pale blue button-down shirt. His dark eyes, framed by neat, thick brows, seemed to stare right through her, exposing her every thought and emotion.

Bree folded her arms and nodded toward a redbrick-and-glass building that looked like a converted warehouse. "This the place?"

A stupid question, but she needed to say something. *Anything.*

"You bet." Wes placed a hand low on her back as he steered her out of the way of a group of people who'd spilled out of the restaurant and onto the sidewalk. "Just wait until you try the chopped barbecue and fried okra."

Bree tried to ignore the heat seeping into her skin and the way her body reacted to his touch.

"Not a fan of okra. It's so…slimy. Human food should not be slimy."

The laughter that rumbled in his chest vibrated against her shoulder. "I don't disagree. In fact, the only way I'll eat it is fried." He ushered her inside.

"I'm not eating anyone's okra." Her tone was definitive.

"That'd be a shame, 'cause our okra is awful good." A gorgeous blonde with sparkling blue eyes flashed her brilliant teeth in a good-natured smile.

"I'm sure it is." Bree tucked her hair behind her ear. "It's just not my thing."

"We got a menu full of options. You'll have plenty to choose from."

They settled into their booth and Bree scanned the menu.

"We can order whenever you're ready." Wes sipped his water.

"You haven't touched your menu."

Wes grinned. "Don't need it. I know exactly what I want."

He hadn't intended to, but as Bree studied the options, her gaze buried in the menu, Wes took the opportunity to study her.

For a moment, why he'd chosen not to call her escaped him.

Right. Because he didn't want to be the asshole who broke the heart of America's volleyball sweetheart.

Being the good guy didn't always pay off.

Bree tugged her full, lower lip between her teeth as she studied the menu.

Sensory memories of that night in London flooded his brain. The flavor of Bree's lip gloss. The warm, sweet taste of her mouth. How her body—with its perfect mix of lean muscles and sexy curves—pressed against his. His pulse raced and heat crawled up his neck.

I'm a bloody masochist.

No other way to explain why he'd torture himself by inviting Bree Evans on this trip.

"I've heard about this place." Excitement lit her brown eyes. "It's supposed to be really good."

"One of the best around. I come here whenever I'm in town."

"You've been living in London. How often do you get to Raleigh?"

"Whenever I visit my mother, we make it a point to come here at least once." He drummed his fingers on the table. "Truthfully? Not often enough. I usually fly Mom out to visit me. I haven't been too keen on returning home."

"Why?" Her intent gaze penetrated him.

He opened his mouth to deliver his usual excuse, that he had been busy, but there was something about Bree. He didn't want to bullshit her. Still, there was no need to relive his entire life story.

Wes rearranged the salt and pepper shakers. "Running from bad memories, I guess."

"Sorry." Bree lowered her gaze. "I shouldn't have pried. I didn't mean to dredge up bad memories."

"No need to apologize. You couldn't have known." He forced a smile, hoping to set her mind at ease. "You know, I haven't thought of New Bern as home in years. I spent most of my life in London and it's felt like home for the past twenty years, but…"

"But this trip home feels different?" Her wide, brown eyes were like a truth elixir.

Wes nodded. "Yeah. When I first got off that plane last month, it was the first time since I was a kid that I felt some sense of nostalgia. Maybe even a little bit of homesickness."

"So will you be coming home more often now?"

"Actually, I decided to move back to the US. I've always known that one day I wanted to establish my event-and-promo business here." Wes dropped his gaze from hers. He wouldn't lie to her, but she wasn't entitled to know everything about him or his family. "Now feels like the time to do that."

"Your mother must be happy."

"Haven't told her yet. I wanted to wait and see how things worked out with the tournament."

"You mean whether you could stand to work with me for an entire six months." She laughed when his eyes widened. "Relax, I'm not offended. I considered backing out, too."

"I'm glad you didn't." His gaze held hers. His pulse quickened in response to the slow smile that spread across her face.

"Glad you didn't, either." Bree tucked her hair behind

her ear. "I think we have the potential to be an incredible team that delivers on everything Liam is hoping for, but that means we need to function like a team. No surprises."

"Fair enough," Wes conceded, thankful the server stepped in to take their order.

Once their orders were complete, she checked her email again.

"Everything okay with your sponsor?" Wes sipped his sweet tea. "I couldn't help overhearing some of your conversation in the car."

"The usual production drama." She shrugged, putting her phone on the table. "Seems there's some sort of drama whenever we roll out a new line. I've learned to roll with it. What about you? Seems like you had some business drama of your own."

"Got a big corporate event coming up. I'll be there for the event and the days leading up to it, but I'm letting my team take the lead on this one. I've been dealing with this client for a while. He's having a bloody meltdown, as he's wont to do during these events."

"But you weren't speaking to him. You were speaking to a woman."

"How'd you…?"

"You turn up that Southern-boy charm when you're speaking to a woman." The corner of her mouth curved in the sexiest smirk he'd ever seen as she swirled her straw inside her glass. "Even if you're not attracted to her."

Wes didn't acknowledge her assessment as he leaned back against the booth. What she'd said was true, though not something he did intentionally.

"I was talking to my event manager, Nadia. She's

second-in-command. She's bright and capable, but she's nervous about taking over the reins."

"Oh." She seemed relieved by his answer. "I liked how you handled the conversation. You conveyed your confidence in her in a way that felt warm and genuine. It seemed to calm her down. I couldn't hear *what* she was saying, but I noticed the shift in her tone," she added when he gave her a puzzled look.

"That charm of yours is dangerously effective." Bree folded her arms on the table and leaned forward. "Because I still can't believe you talked me in to this trip."

"I'm still stunned by that one myself." Wes chuckled. "But I'm glad you agreed to join me. The trip wouldn't be nearly as fun solo."

Bree's mouth twisted in a reluctant smile. "Now that I'm here, I would think I've earned at least a preview of what to expect over this next week."

"All right." Wes leaned forward, holding back a grin. "We're having dinner tonight and we're going hiking in the morning."

"But where are we—"

"That's all I'm giving you." He held up a hand as the server approached their table with the sampler of appetizers he'd ordered. "I want you to be surprised, especially in Asheville. So you're going to have to give me a little leeway here."

Bree opened her mouth to object, but a genuine smile lit her eyes as she turned her attention to the chicken wings, fried green tomatoes and potato fritters.

"I shouldn't be eating any of this." She grabbed a saucer and unwrapped her silverware. "But that won't stop me from sampling every bit of it."

Wes grinned, reminding himself of all the reasons

he shouldn't be attracted to her. His brain agreed, but his body and heart had gone rogue.

He wanted to spend more time with Bree. To learn everything there was to know about her. He couldn't stop the visions of her in his bed, calling his name.

Wes sighed softly. Giving himself the keep-it-in-your-pants speech wouldn't be enough. Brianna Evans had burrowed under his skin and was working her way into his heart.

Chapter 9

Bree stood in front of the mirror in her hotel room and smoothed down her skirt. So maybe the little black dress was sexier than anything she'd normally wear to a business meeting. And maybe she had made a real effort with her makeup tonight.

It wasn't as if she'd flirted with him.

Okay, maybe she had, but only a little. It was certainly nothing serious.

Her phone rang. It was a video call from Bex. Bree cringed. For a moment, she considered not answering, but that would've worried Bex more.

"Hey. You caught me on the way out to dinner." Bree tried to sound nonchalant.

"Obviously, you're not going for pizza and a beer down at the pub." Bex's expression grew wary, as did her tone. "Let me see what you're wearing."

Bree breathed out a long sigh and extended her arm,

holding the phone up so Bex could take in the entire outfit—cleavage and all.

"So this is a date." Bex's tone had gone from wary to alarmed.

"It isn't a date." The objection felt weak, even to Bree. "There's a restaurant in our hotel, and it happens to have a dress code."

"Does that dress code require cleavage? The girls are looking pretty spectacular tonight."

Bree's cheeks stung with heat. She smoothed a hand down the clingy, black draped jersey dress. "You're the one who's always saying I don't show off my assets enough."

"And today is the day you decide to listen?" Bex sucked in a deep breath. "Look, Bree, we both know you *really* like this guy. Hell, I like the guy. In any other circumstance, I'd tell you to go for it. Have a little fun. But there are three really important things for you to remember. Wes doesn't want anything serious, you do and this guy is the one standing between us getting what we want out of the tournament. Don't forget any of that."

"You think I'm too naive to hold my own with Wes."

"It isn't that, and this isn't me scolding you or saying in any way that you should change who you are. You see the good in everyone and you wear your heart on your sleeve. I love those things about you. It's why we make such a good team. You balance out my craziness, and I need that." Bex smiled into the camera. "But for you, *nothing* is strictly business. I doubt Wes shares your philosophy."

Bex wasn't wrong. Bree was playing with fire and she knew it. Still, she was drawn to Wes in a way she couldn't explain. Like they were meant to be together. If not as lovers, at least as friends.

There was a knock at her hotel-room door. A knot tightened in her belly.

"I have to go." Bree lowered her voice. "But I'll remember what you've said. Promise."

"Fine. Have fun." Bex's exasperated tone indicated she knew her advice had fallen on deaf ears. "Just be careful. I don't want to have to come out there and kick his ass."

"'Bye, Bex." Bree ended the call and dropped the phone in her clutch. She surveyed herself in the mirror one last time.

This is business. Relax. Have fun.

It was a hollow claim, because the closer she got to the door, the faster her heart beat.

Bree opened the door. "You're early."

"And you...look amazing." Wes jammed his hands in his pockets and leaned against the doorway.

"You sound surprised." There was a nervous lilt to her laughter. "I'd like to think I cleaned up pretty well the night we met."

"You did, but tonight..." He sucked in a deep breath as he surveyed her from head to toe. "Let's just say you've turned it up a notch."

Brianna looked stunning in a form-fitting little black dress that was ultra-feminine and incredibly flattering on her body. The draped neckline drew his attention to her full breasts. The bow-tie belt detail highlighted her small waist and the clingy fabric hugged every single curve.

He cleared his throat as he took a cream-colored cashmere cardigan from her and helped her into it.

She tied the sash at her waist, grabbed her bag and stepped into the hall.

Wes followed her to the elevator, his eyes drawn to how the fabric hugged her curvy bottom. He dragged his eyes away and punched the down button for the elevator.

"You're going to love this restaurant." Wes stared at the elevator doors rather than looking at her. "And this is one of my favorite places to stay whenever I come here."

"It's a beautiful hotel, and it's right across the street from the Biltmore Estate." Bree ran her fingers through her shoulder-length curls. "Almost makes me wish we were going to be here a bit longer, so I'd have time to visit."

"Careful." He grinned inwardly, determined not to ruin the surprise he had planned for her the next day. "Almost sounds like you're enjoying your time with me."

"Don't get too cocky." She laughed. "It's too early to make that call, but so far…yes. I am enjoying the trip."

"Fair enough." He stepped off the elevator and offered his arm to her. She reluctantly slipped her arm through his and fell in step beside him.

They entered the restaurant, greeted by the enticing scent of savory, grilled meat. The gentle strains of live guitar music filled the air.

"It's like an upscale hunting lodge." Bree surveyed the brown-and-red leather seating and the antler chandeliers hanging overhead. "I honestly wouldn't have thought that was possible."

Wes chuckled. "Wait until you taste the food."

"I've already studied the menu, so I know exactly what I want."

His gaze raked over Bree, his heart beating a little faster. He knew exactly what he wanted, too. But it would be better for both of them if he showed restraint.

They were shown to a table, then placed their orders, falling into an easy conversation about Asheville and some of the activities he enjoyed here.

"Tomorrow morning, I'll take you on a walking tour of downtown. It's called the Urban Trail." Wes sipped his beer.

"You've probably done the trail at least a half a dozen times."

"Actually, I've only done it once with my mother and aunt. Normally, when I come to town I prefer something a little more challenging. Like a brisk hike."

Bree raised an eyebrow, as if she'd been challenged. "Then let's do that instead."

"The hike takes about four hours."

"Then we should get started early."

"The trail can be pretty muddy and it's challenging for a beginner."

"Who says I'm a beginner?" Bree asked incredulously. "You do know I make my living as an athlete, right?"

"Fine." Wes raised his hands, giving in. Bree was determined to go hiking with him. Maybe they'd take the city walking tour later. "Then we'd better make it an early night."

He was disappointed by the prospect.

"Not necessarily." She shrugged. "I'm not in training right now. I can handle staying up past my bedtime.

Unless you're the one who can't function without eight hours of beauty sleep."

"I'll manage. Got hiking clothes and shoes?"

"I do."

Bree for the win.

The server brought out his fried calamari and her roasted pear salad. The look of satisfaction on Bree's face after she took the first bite of her salad did things to him.

"Anything else I need to know about tomorrow?"

Wes dug in to his calamari and tried to shift his mind to something that didn't get him so hot and bothered. Like cold showers and sewer drains.

"We'll be on a tight schedule, and you'll want to wear comfortable and casual clothing and footwear for tomorrow afternoon."

"Okay." The expression on Bree's face indicated that the wheels in her head were turning. "Anything else?"

"No." Wes enjoyed keeping her in suspense. Something about her frustrated little pout made him want to kiss her. He wasn't sure who was torturing whom.

Later, as he dined on grass-fed filet mignon and she ate her pan-roasted duck breast, butternut squash risotto and bacon-braised greens, their conversation fell into a comfortable rhythm.

"You didn't mention what took your family to London." Bree sipped her wine.

"My mother was the house manager for a wealthy family that relocated to London," Wes said, then sighed. "Actually, that's what gave us the opportunity to move to London. The reason we moved is because my mother wanted a fresh start for all of us."

Bree's eyes were sympathetic and kind, like a warm

hug from a dear friend. He could tell she wanted to delve deeper, but seemed unsure if she should.

"My parents divorced when my brother and I were kids. He was a jazz saxophonist who headlined his own band. He and my mom met when he hired her as the band's female vocalist."

"Your parents were musicians? They must've lived an exciting life." She sliced into her duck and took a bite.

"They did," Wes said. "Which is why the old man didn't adjust too well to family life and working in a factory. He stuck it out eight or nine years, but then he became restless.

"He got the band back together and snagged a few local gigs. At first, that was enough. But then he wanted to hit the road and tour again." Wes drained his beer, then signaled for another. "My mother didn't want to drag us all over the world, and she refused to leave us behind. She didn't want anyone else raising her kids— not even my grandmother."

"Is that when they split?"

"Not at first. He hired a new vocalist and his band toured the States, then Europe. His calls and postcards became less frequent. Eventually he sent a letter saying that he loved us, but that this was something he needed to do for himself. The divorce papers showed up not long afterward."

"Wes, I'm sorry." There was comfort and compassion in her voice, rather than pity. "I understand the betrayal you feel when a parent walks away from you like that…it's indescribable."

"I thought your parents were still together."

Bree seemed to carefully debate her next words. "I'm adopted."

Wes straightened in his seat, the hair lifting on the back of his neck. "You're adopted?"

"Yes." She seemed surprised by his reaction.

"I didn't mean for it to sound as if…" He took a breath. *Get it together, man.* "It's just that I've seen some of your interviews and pictures of your family. You resemble your mother quite a bit. I guess we see what we expect to see."

Nice save.

Bree's shoulders relaxed. "My adoptive mother is my biological great aunt. My bio mom had me when she was really young. Her aunt and uncle weren't able to conceive and they couldn't afford in vitro. So when they learned my bio mom was pregnant and didn't want the baby, they talked her out of termination and offered to adopt me. I got lucky twice."

"It's good you were able to stay with family." He assessed her carefully before asking his next question. Her open expression seemed to give him permission. "If you don't mind me asking, what's your relationship with your birth mom?"

"We don't have one," Bree responded matter-of-factly, but the light in her eyes dimmed and her smile lost its radiance.

Wes glided his hand across the table, wanting to touch hers. He wanted to give her the same comfort her smile had given him earlier. He froze, his fingers a few inches from Bree's.

Keep it strictly business. Maintain your distance.

"Sorry to hear that, Bree." He gripped his beer glass instead. "That must be hard."

"It's not that I don't see her. I do. At every family function. She went on with her life and became a successful lawyer. Got married. Had kids of her own." Bree forced a laugh. "And me, I'm this big family secret that everyone except her husband and kids know about."

Something deep in his chest bubbled, like hot lava threatening to spill out of a volcano. How could Bree's mother sit next to her at barbecues and family weddings, pretending they didn't share the strongest human bond? Didn't the woman have any idea how that must make Bree feel?

Wes tried to curb the anger building toward a woman he'd never even met. He'd always known how lucky he was to have his mother. She'd given up everything for him. Put all of her dreams aside to give him and his brother the best life she could. For that, he couldn't thank her enough.

But it was more than just Bree's situation that bothered him. Her revelation that she was adopted set all those wheels turning in his head. The ones that kept him awake at night.

Adopted children usually went to good homes. Better situations. What about the ones who didn't? Even when everything looked good from the outside, who could know what was happening behind closed doors?

Wes didn't realize neither of them had spoken in several minutes until her voice, soft and apologetic, broke through the jumble of thoughts that wrapped themselves around his skull and squeezed like a vise.

"I didn't mean to put a downer on this lovely meal. I'm not even sure why I told you that. I shouldn't have. Only a handful of people outside of my family know the truth. So, please don't tell anyone."

"Not my business to tell." He shrugged. "But I'm glad you felt comfortable enough to tell me."

Bree squirmed. Something in her eyes indicated that the ease she felt with him was a source of concern for her.

They had that in common, too.

As they finished dinner and shared a generous slice of pecan carrot cake, Wes tried to reassure himself that getting to know Bree was simply a team-building exercise designed to fortify their working relationship. But the truth gnawed at him.

He liked Bree. *A lot.*

He wanted her friendship, and a rogue part of his anatomy wanted something more.

Trying to strike the perfect balance between building an amicable, working relationship with Bree and keeping a safe emotional distance was a dangerous game. A lot was at stake. For him. For Bree. For Westbrook International.

He couldn't afford to screw this up.

Yet, when he walked her back to her room, he wasn't prepared to say good-night.

"Thank you for dinner." Bree leaned in, one hand pressed to his chest, and kissed his cheek. Her soft scent and body heat surrounded him.

He hadn't expected the innocent kiss or that he'd be overwhelmed by her nearness.

Bree's mouth lingered near his as she pulled away so slowly he could hear every microsecond ticking in his head. He willed himself to stay in control. To keep his hands shoved in his pockets, where they wouldn't get him into trouble.

"You're welcome." The words came out much quieter

than he'd intended. He dropped his gaze to her sensual lips and she smiled.

"I'd ask you in for an after-dinner drink, but like you said, we've got an early morning." Her voice was soft and captivating, an unspoken invitation.

Wes wet his lower lip and tried to tear his attention away from her mouth and her soft gaze. Tried with every fiber of his being to ignore the fact that he wanted her desperately.

He couldn't.

Slipping his arms around her waist, he pulled her closer. His mouth inched toward hers. Bree's eyes drifted closed as she leaned in, closing the space that remained between them.

His lips were nearly on hers when laughter erupted from a loud group exiting the elevator. Startled, her eyes opened and she stepped beyond his grip.

Her cheeks were crimson and she somehow managed to look both surprised and disappointed.

Feelings he shared.

Still, another part of him was thankful. This was a business trip, not a love connection. Something they'd both do well to remember.

"Bree, I'm sorry, I—"

"Saved by the bell." She forced a smile, then dug her hotel key card out and bid him good-night before closing her door.

Wes dragged a hand through his hair and let out an exasperated sigh. He needed to pull it together or he and the project were in serious trouble.

Chapter 10

Bree hoisted on her backpack and made her way toward the sign that declared their arrival at the Looking Glass Rock Trail head in the Pisgah National Forest.

The forty-five-minute drive to the park had been filled with awkward silence over their near kiss the night before, something neither of them seemed willing to discuss.

She zipped her black jacket up to her neck to ward against the cool, brisk morning air. Bree secured her silk-lined knit hat, tugged on a pair of black gloves and wound a scarf around her neck.

The sun was up and the temperature was rising. By the time they'd hiked to the summit, she'd likely need to shed a few layers. But for now, her breath rose as a visible, steamy cloud in the air.

"Sure you're up for this?" Wes set the car alarm, then

zipped the keys in a backpack he'd stuffed with fruit, protein bars and several bottles of water. "The downtown walking tour is still an option."

"And miss climbing to the top of this…what did you call it again?" They'd seen the view of the commanding rock cliff from the other side. It was a rock climber's dream.

"Looking Glass Rock is a pluton monolith. It was formed when hot magma tried to push its way to the surface, but got stuck underground."

"How could it have been formed underground when it's nearly four thousand feet high?" She fastened the backpack straps that intersected her chest.

"A mountain once shielded the rock." Wes nodded toward the trail. "Over time, it wore away, leaving the igneous rock exposed."

Bree grinned. "Wouldn't have pegged you for a science nerd."

"I'm not." A pained look briefly marred Wesley's handsome face. He flashed an uneasy smile. "We'd better stretch, then get going. Got a full day ahead."

They stretched, then followed some steps. The trail opened onto a forest dominated by the towering trunks of dead hemlock trees. Because of the unseasonably warm weather, many of the newer species of trees that had taken root were in bloom, despite it being late winter.

The ground was dry and the gradual elevation of the trail made for a fairly easy hike. They climbed uphill beside a small stream, then the trail took a right and crossed the creek on a footbridge.

About a mile in, the ground changed from dirt to exposed rock.

Bree squatted down to touch the cool surface. "Can you believe this was once hot, molten liquid?"

"Pretty amazing when you think about it. This could've been an active volcano, spewing hot lava." Wes stepped closer, held out his hand and pulled Bree to her feet.

"Thanks." Bree's cheeks heated as her eyes met his. She tugged her hand free, then went ahead of him on the trail. Her pulse accelerated even more than it had from the exertion of the climb.

The trail rose in a series of hairpin turns, which made it possible to see the trail ahead and below. Switchbacks, Wes had called them. The switchbacks kept the trail from getting too steep.

Bree was thankful for the gradual increase. Despite being a runner and regular strength training, her thigh muscles burned in protest.

Along the way, Wes pointed out the flora and fauna. They'd seen cardinals, blue jays and ruby-throated hummingbirds, whose wings moved so rapidly they were a blur. Suddenly, a streak of white fur dashed across the trail.

"Was that a white squirrel?" Bree tried to pull out her phone and snap a picture, but the squirrel had zero interest in his fifteen minutes of fame.

"White squirrels are the unofficial mascot here in Brevard." Wes grinned. "There's a White Squirrel Festival here on Memorial Day weekend."

Bree scanned the forest, looking for the adorable little furry creature, hoping to snap a shot of it. It would look nice beside the photo of black squirrels she'd taken while visiting Toronto years earlier.

Wes handed her a bottle of water, and she accepted

it gratefully. Bree finished nearly half the bottle as she surveyed the area around them. It was peaceful and beautiful, despite the time of year.

"I see why you love coming here." Bree capped the bottle and stuffed it in her backpack.

"Not yet." He finished his bottle. "But you will. C'mon, we'd better keep moving."

Wes went ahead on the trail and she followed. Finally, they reached a helipad used to airlift injured climbers.

"Is this it?" She looked around. "There's no view here."

"Patience, grasshopper," he called over his shoulder, continuing ahead on a slightly downhill trail. Suddenly, the brush opened onto a rocky platform that offered a view of the valley below. "*This* is the money shot."

"It's incredible." She ventured forward carefully. There was no railing. Just a sheer rock cliff at the edge. "Is it safe?"

Wes tested the surface. "There's no ice and it's dry today, so it shouldn't be slippery. Stay on the flatter area bordering the forest and don't venture too close to the edge. It's a long way down."

Bree inched out farther, enjoying the gentle breeze and the sunshine, and she studied the remarkable view below.

"The view must be stunning when the trees are all green during summer, or in the fall when the leaves are changing colors."

"It is." There was a sadness behind Wes's smile that made her heart ache. "Maybe we'll get a chance to come back here when the tournament is over. Sort of a celebration climb."

"I like that idea." Bree returned her attention to the view, not wanting Wes to see how happy the thought made her. She snapped a few shots of the view with her phone, then pointed to a mountain in the distance. "What's that?"

"Black Balsam Knob and that's Pisgah Mountain." Wes pointed to a ridge with a succession of peaks.

Bree moved forward, taking photos, then suddenly lost her footing. She dropped her phone, but Wes caught it and her before either hit the ground.

"I've got you. You're okay." His voice was calm and reassuring as he steadied her. "You just slipped on a patch of algae."

"But if I'd... I mean, if you hadn't..." Her heart raced as she imagined what could've happened if Wes hadn't been there. She hugged him. "Thank you."

"I'd love to take credit for being the hero, but if you'd fallen, you would've only sustained a few cuts and bruises. I doubt you'd have sailed off the cliff. It's pretty flat here." He held her in his arms. "I'd never put you in jeopardy."

Bree leaned back and met his gaze. "Seriously, Wes, I appreciate what you did."

"I'm letting you go now, so watch your step." His smile reassured her. "Stand over there and I'll get a few shots of you with the mountains in the background."

He took a few photos with her phone, then handed it back to her, and she took a few of him in silly poses that made them both laugh and put her at ease.

"If you aren't a science geek, how do you know so much about pluton monoliths and the kinds of trees up here?" Bree studied his face as a stormy cloud seemed to settle over him, making her regret the question.

"My dad." Wes frowned as he sat down and removed his backpack. He rummaged inside and pulled out an apple. He handed it to her before getting another for himself.

Bree took off her backpack and sat on the ground beside Wes. She nibbled on the apple, hoping Wes would tell her more, but not wanting to push him. The subject of his father was obviously a sensitive one.

"My dad had been on the road traveling with his band for several months. When he finally came home, I'd asked him to stay with us rather than going back out on the road." Wes chewed a bite of his apple.

"He didn't answer, but a couple days later, he brought me up here and showed me this incredible view." Wes looked around, staring off into the distance. "He said there was so much out there, and that he wanted to experience all of it. And he wanted the same for me, even if that took us on different paths."

Bree placed a hand on Wes's arm before she could stop herself. He seemed to find comfort in the gesture.

"Wes, I'm sorry about your dad." She lowered her voice, not wanting the hikers who'd joined them on the rocky cliff to overhear her. "Do you and your dad keep in touch?"

"Barely, but I'm fine with things the way they are." His expression belied his forceful statement, but Bree didn't press.

"What about your younger brother?"

"Drake sees our father as this larger-than-life heroic figure. He followed in his footsteps and became a musician."

"Another sax player in the family?" Bree smiled, trying to lighten the mood.

"A drummer. He practiced on an old set of drums Dad left behind."

"Your mom must've been a very patient woman."

"She was." Wes flashed a genuine smile that made her heart soar. "Guess it paid off. Drake's pretty good. He's been working as a session musician mostly, hoping to eventually start his own jazz trio."

"Excuse me," one of the hikers said. "Would you mind taking a group photo of our family?"

Wes obliged, climbing to his feet and accepting the young brunette's cell phone. He took a series of photos of their family of four before handing it back to her.

"Thanks." The girl beamed. "I'd be happy to take a few shots of you and your girl… Oh my God. Look, Mom! It's Bree Evans. It's so great to meet you. I'm a huge fan."

"Thank you so much. It's a pleasure to meet you, too." Bree grinned, hoping she didn't look like a sweaty, hot mess. "And thank you for offering to take our photo, but—"

"Yes," Wes interrupted. "We'd love for you to take some pictures of us."

Bree handed the girl her phone and she and Wes stood together on the rocky cliff with the trees in early bloom spread out behind them.

The girl frowned after taking the photo. "You both look uncomfortable in this one. Maybe we should try again. Stand a little closer and maybe try smiling."

Wes and Bree looked at each other and laughed, stepping a little closer. He wrapped an arm around her and they smiled.

"Much better." The girl took a few more shots and smiled. She returned the phone and asked that Wes take photos of her and her family with Bree. After Bree autographed the girl's backpack, she and her family began their descent back down the trail.

"We'd better go, too." He picked up both backpacks and handed Bree hers. "There's one more thing I want to show you before we head back to the hotel."

Bree turned and looked one last time at the incredible view, wishing they could stay longer. Or maybe it was just her time with Wes that she didn't want to end.

Chapter 11

Wesley tapped softly on Bree's hotel-room door. She didn't answer right away.

He wouldn't blame her if she'd fallen asleep. After climbing Looking Glass Rock Trail and a quick drive to Looking Glass Falls, they'd grabbed fast food and returned to their respective rooms for a quick shower and change before heading out again.

Wes knocked again, louder this time.

"I'm ready." Bree rushed out of the door, filling the space between them with the scent of fresh summer peaches. Her hair, still wet from the shower, was pulled into a high ponytail.

She wore a casual dress in a bold handkerchief-style print. The vivid orange with accents of pink and teal suited Bree well. A nude leather belt cinched her waist. A tan jacket and nude ballet flats with an ankle strap completed the look.

Casual, but sexy. Funky, but not over the top.

"Something wrong?" Bree's gaze dropped to her feet. She flexed her leg, showing off a sexy, heart-shaped calf.

"Everything's good." Wes steered her down the hallway to the elevator.

The valet brought the car and they went just a little way up the street before he turned onto Biltmore Estate Drive.

"We're going to tour the house?" Bree's eyes lit up. She was clearly thrilled.

"Couldn't bring you to Asheville without taking you for a tour of the largest private residence and the most visited winery in America." Wes chuckled.

They parked and he opened her car door. His gaze instantly followed her mile-long legs to the hem of her dress, which ended well above her knees. Wes extended his hand to her, helping her out of the car. They made their way to the main house.

Wes had toured Biltmore before. But Bree's amazement as they toured the home, with its beautiful atrium, lavish furniture, extensive library and impressive grounds, made him feel he was seeing it all for the first time. There was something about her wide-eyed wonder and pure fascination with the estate that reminded him how genuine she was and how much he enjoyed being with her.

Maybe he wasn't a science nerd, but he was fascinated by history. It was the reason he'd visited the historic property, and several others all over the world, whenever his schedule permitted.

Bree squeezed his arm as she related her enchantment with the estate's incredible library of more than twenty-two thousand volumes.

"Relax, Belle," he teased. "There's a lot more to see."

His *Beauty and the Beast* reference wasn't lost on her. Bree pursed her lips and propped a fist on her hip.

"I happen to love that movie, and I know every single word to every single song. Call me Belle again and I'll start singing to the top of my lungs about the simplicity of this provincial life." She cocked an eyebrow that dared him to try her.

"You win." He couldn't help but grin. "Still, you can't deny the similari—"

Bree spread her arms and opened her mouth, preparing to go into song, when he wrapped his arms around her and pulled her closer.

They both dissolved into a fit of laughter that caused the people around them to give them odd looks.

"You were really going to do it, weren't you?" Wes asked, after they'd regained their composure and rejoined the tour.

"Would've been worth it to see the panicked look on your face." Bree wiped away tears from laughter. "Besides, I need to keep you on your toes. Can't be too predictable."

Wes chuckled. "Mission accomplished."

They toured the remainder of the house and the grounds together. After a tour of the winery, they sampled a variety of wines at the subsequent wine tasting, and purchased their favorites.

"Today was incredible." Bree's face practically shone once they were in the car and heading down the long road that led off the Biltmore property. "Thank you."

"Glad you enjoyed it, but the night's not over. Got someplace special in mind for dinner. You'll love it."

"Let me pay this time," she said. "I know these are business expenses, but still… I should pick up the tab for something."

"You can pay when we get to Charlotte tomorrow." This wasn't a lovers' getaway, it was a business trip. Still, he didn't feel comfortable allowing Bree to pick up the tab for dinner tonight or any night.

"Deal," she conceded. "Where are we going?"

"You'll have to wait and see."

Bree agreed to his terms begrudgingly.

She should be annoyed with his little game. Yet, she'd been delighted by every one of his surprises. No reason to believe he'd disappoint her now.

Bree's belly tightened in a knot. Her anticipation over their mysterious dinner destination rose, along with a growing fondness for Wes.

They were working together as a team on a project that was equally important to their careers. They needed to get along so they could work together seamlessly.

Didn't her fondness for Wes make working together easier?

Bree focused on the scenery as they drove through the streets of the charming mountain town. She could keep telling herself this trip was strictly business. But her attraction to Wesley Adams was blooming like a pretty, but unwanted, weed.

She glanced at Wes. Was it possible he was growing more handsome as the day went on?

Bree wanted him. There was no doubt about that. He wanted her, too. She was equally sure of that. But did he see the potential for more between them? Did he want it the way she did?

"Everything okay? You've gotten really quiet."

"I'm thinking, that's all."

"Anything you want to talk about?"

"Not really."

"Fair enough." Wes was quiet for a moment, as if contemplating his next question. He seemed to ask despite his better judgment. "Then let me ask why making the tournament a family event is such a focal point for you?"

Discussing the tournament was exactly what she needed right now. After all, that was the point of the trip.

"The truth?" She turned to him. "Bex and I want to elevate the game. Pass our expertise on to the next generation of players. We're planning to put on volleyball clinics for kids eight to seventeen years old. Gearing the tournament toward families will allow us to tap in to our market."

"I see." He mulled over her revelation in silence for a moment. "It's a solid business idea. Who wouldn't want their kids to learn the sport from two of its most successful athletes? But in terms of the tournament, your target market doesn't align with the resort's."

"Pleasure Cove Luxury Resort isn't an adults-only destination," she countered.

"It isn't a family-friendly one, either. It's the kind of place parents go to get away from their kids for a week."

"That's awful." She couldn't help laughing.

"It's also true." He chuckled, seemingly relieved the mood in the car had lightened. "That doesn't make them bad people. Let's face it, being a parent is one of the toughest jobs in the world. Sometimes you need to take a break and reset."

"You sound like a man who speaks from experience. Are there any little Wesleys out there I don't know about?" She grinned.

His shoulders seemed to stiffen and his smile vanished for a moment. He pulled up to the valet stand in front of a huge, pink stone building.

"No one out there is calling me Dad, I assure you." He forced a smile, but his eyes seemed sadder than she'd ever seen them. He nodded toward the building. "We're here."

A valet at the Omni Grove Park Inn opened the door and helped her out of the car. Wes handed him the keys.

"Shall we?" Wes waved a hand toward the entrance of the building.

"This building is amazing." Bree surveyed the open front hall, which had two massive stone fireplaces blazing. Most of the furniture was art deco. "How long has this place been here?"

"Over a hundred years. The exterior was hewn out of native granite. The roof is comprised of red clay tiles. Some of the original furniture is still on display throughout the hotel."

Wes led her to the Sunset Terrace—a steak-and-seafood restaurant situated on a large, covered outdoor terrace with an incredible mountain view. The server seated them.

"It's stunning." Bree was mesmerized by the incredible view of the mountains as the sun began to set. "A perfect end to a perfect day."

"I wanted your final night here to be memorable."

Wes smiled sheepishly. He added quickly, "To give you a sense of the area."

"Then why do I feel like I'm on a date?" Bree couldn't help the smirk that slowly spread across her face.

His eyes widened and he coughed. Wes took a deep drink of his water without response.

"Or maybe I just need to get out more." She sipped her water then returned the glass to the table. "Because the last time I had this much fun was the night we spent together in London."

Wes seemed relieved when the server appeared and took their orders. By the time the man left, he'd gathered himself.

"Bree..." He said her name as if it'd taken every ounce of his energy to utter it. "I like you. A lot. And maybe you're right. This was supposed to be a simple business trip, but I've turned it into what feels like something *more*. It wasn't intentional."

"So we stumbled into a romantic getaway?" One eyebrow raised, she sipped her water.

"Maybe I allowed my attraction to you to shape my choices." Wes sighed heavily. "But the fact remains that we'll be working together, and we need to keep things professional."

"Not to mention that you're not in the market for anything serious. *Ever*." She buried her hurt behind a teasing tone and forced smile.

"Then there's that." Wes seemed saddened by the concession. He thanked the server for bringing their bread and decanting their wine. "I wish the circumstances were different."

"What makes you think I'm looking for more?" She

traced the bottom of her wineglass, her gaze on her fingertips.

"Because you can't even look me in the eye when you ask the question." He was clearly amused. "Before I met you, I thought the good girl thing was an act to garner sponsorships. It isn't. That's who you genuinely are. That isn't a bad thing, Bree. But I don't want to be known as the scoundrel who broke the heart of America's volleyball sweetheart."

Bree met his gaze, resenting that he knew her so well. Maybe it was the beautiful, romantic setting, but she wasn't prepared to back down.

That night in London she'd been sure they'd connected. That there'd been the potential for something meaningful between them. The past two days had reinforced that belief.

Something was definitely there. Every moment they spent together indicated Wes felt the same.

What is he so afraid of?

They were attracted to each other. So why couldn't they just be adults about it?

Regardless of what happened between them personally, they could simply agree to maintain a professional working relationship.

Bree formulated a proposal in her head.

Sound confident, not desperate.

When she returned her gaze to his, he was carefully assessing her. There was a distance in his gaze that wasn't there moments before.

She lost her nerve, panic gripping her. What if Wes turned her down? Bree couldn't deal with another humiliating rejection.

"So about the tournament" Wes leaned back in his

chair. "I think we agree now that family-friendly isn't the way to go. But I promise to promote your volleyball clinics any way I can. After all, it's the kids' parents who'll be paying for it."

"True." He'd given her a small concession, likely out of pity. Still, she couldn't afford to turn down his offer. "We'd appreciate that."

"You'll need to have your camp dates, website, organization and promo in place by the time we start printing marketing materials. Think you can handle that?" He'd slipped back into business mode, as if their earlier conversation hadn't occurred.

If only Bree could be so pragmatic and detached.

"We'll be ready," she said resolutely. "Bex is restless. She'll be glad to have a project to take on."

"If you need help with the planning and promo—"

"You'd take on a project as small as ours?"

"For high-profile clients like you and Bex? Sure. But I'm not suggesting you hire me. I'm talking about helping as a friend."

"Friends…is that what we are, Wes?" The stunned expression on his face made her regret her words. Wes hadn't done anything wrong. Hadn't promised her anything more than this…whatever this may be. "Sorry. I shouldn't have said that. Your offer is generous. Thank you. I'll talk it over with Bex."

"The sun is setting." Wes pointed in the distance. He seemed anxious to change the subject.

The sky was streaked with lovely shades of purple and orange. The entire scene glowed like a luminescent oil painting.

"It's beautiful. I could sit here staring at it all day."

"Me, too." Wes wasn't looking at the sky. His gaze

met hers for a moment that felt like an eternity before he finally turned to survey the mountain range in the distance.

Heart racing and hands trembling, Bree did the same, determined to ignore the mixed signals Wesley Adams was sending.

"Dinner was amazing. Thank you again for such a lovely evening." Bree stopped in front of her hotel-room door.

"It was a good day," Wes said softly, leaning against the door frame. His eyes met hers, and were filled with the same longing, desire and frustration she felt.

And those feelings were heightened, as they'd dined on a tower of lobster, shrimp, crab and oysters.

Bree sank her teeth into her lower lip, her heart racing. The idea had been brewing in her head all night, and she'd been emboldened by the longing in his eyes and the gruffness of his voice.

Even now, she could feel the gentle tug between them. So why couldn't she just say what they were obviously both thinking?

"Wes…" Bree reached out to straighten his tie. "I'm not ready for our night to end."

"We could grab dessert. Maybe go dancing—"

"No." She stepped closer, their eyes meeting. Her heart beat faster. "I want you. Here. With me. I know you want that, too."

"I do." He sighed heavily. "But we've been over all the reasons this is a terrible idea. Nothing's changed." He pushed a few strands of hair from her face. "I don't want to hurt you, Bree. And I don't want to jeopardize the friendship we've been building."

"Neither do I." Her eyes met his, her voice soft. "And we won't." *Stay calm. Sound confident, not desperate.* "I don't expect anything more than tonight. No promises, no obligations. Just…us."

Bree slipped her arms around his waist, her gaze trained on his as she tried to read him, hoping he'd say yes.

Chapter 12

Wes was trying to do what was in Bree's best interest, but she wasn't making it easy.

Then again, neither had he. Dinner overlooking the sunset? What the hell was he thinking?

This trip was supposed to be about getting better acquainted with the State of North Carolina. Instead, they'd been reminded of all of the reasons they'd gotten on so well together that night in London. The reasons they seemed perfect together.

"I want you, Bree. You know that, but—"

"You're not looking for anything serious." Her tone was sexy, teasing. She leaned in closer. Her soft, sweet scent teased his nostrils. The heat radiating from her body raised his temperature. "Neither am I."

It was a lie, and they both knew it. A lie he wanted desperately to believe.

Wes gripped her shoulders, drowning in her soft gaze. Thoughts of Bree occupied every available space in his brain. Distracted him from what he should be focused on right now—the tournament.

And yet…he wanted this. He wanted her.

The thud of Wes's heartbeat grew louder, his desire for Bree building. He leaned down and slipped his fingers into her hair as his mouth met hers.

A soft sigh escaped her mouth as she pressed her hands to his back and pulled him closer, melding the warmth of her body to his. He pinned her against the door as he captured her mouth in an intense kiss that made him ache for her.

His tongue delved inside her warm mouth. She welcomed it. Glided her own tongue along his as she gripped his shirt.

The voice in his head that was screaming at him not to do this was drowned out by the thud of his heart, his raging pulse and his feverish desire for her.

The elevator dinged, interrupting them as it had the night before. Wes pulled himself away, his eyes studying hers. This time, he couldn't walk away. He extended his palm, his eyes not leaving hers.

Bree dug out her key card and placed it in his palm. There was a hardened edge to her expression, belied by the slight trembling of her hands and her shallow breathing. Wes ushered them inside her room and wrapped one arm around Bree's waist, tugging her body against his.

He trailed kisses down her neck, inhaling her enticing scent. He pressed a soft kiss to her earlobe, then whispered in her ear, "Mixing business and pleasure is always a risky move."

Bree slid one hand up his chest. Her eyes blazed with passion, desire and a bit of defiance. She had no intention of backing down. At this point, neither did he. "Don't worry. I'm worth it."

The edge of his mouth curled. It wasn't the response he'd expected, but it was a sentiment he shared.

She captured his mouth in a greedy kiss that allayed any doubts about whether this was what she truly wanted. About whether she could accept his terms for engagement.

Good. No more Mr. Nice Guy.

Wes lowered his hands to the swell of her curvy bottom, swallowing her soft murmur in response. His body ached with his need for her. A need that'd been simmering since the night they met in London. But now it was at a full-blown boil.

Bree was responsive to his touch as his hands glided along her body—a perfect blend of feminine curves and athletic muscle. Her desire was a living, breathing, palpable thing that demanded satisfaction. He wanted nothing more than to give it to her.

Though the past two days indicated otherwise, this wasn't a fairy-tale romance. Tonight was about passion and desire, mind-blowing sex and pure satisfaction. Then they would both move on.

Wes turned Bree around and nestled her bottom against him as he trailed kisses down her neck. He slipped her dress slightly off her shoulder, and continued kissing his way down it.

She grabbed the hem of her dress and lifted it, but he stopped her.

"Don't take it off." He growled, his lips brushing her ear. He palmed her breast, tracing the tight bud with his thumb. Wes glided his other hand down her side, then up the inside of her thigh. "All night I've imagined what it'd be like to bend you over in this little dress and take you from behind."

Wes slid his fingertips along the crease of her hip, then across the waistband of her silky underwear. Her nipple beaded as he slipped his hand beneath the elastic band and over the narrow patch of curls. Bree gasped when he stroked the stiff bundle of nerves.

"Damn, you're wet." He breathed in her ear, running his tongue along its outer shell. Wes flicked his finger over the nub, enjoying her small gasp and the way her belly tightened in response. "Been thinking about me, haven't you?"

"No longer than you've been thinking about me." The statement began with defiance, but ended with a sensual murmur that did things to him.

"You're right." Wes chuckled, pulling her tighter against his growing shaft. "Because I've been wanting to do this since the night we met."

Wes splayed two fingers and slipped them back and forth over the hardened nub. Bree sucked in a deep breath and looped an arm around his neck, her hips moving against his hand.

He slipped his other hand beneath her dress and gripped her waist, pulling her tight against him. His eyes drifted closed as he reveled in the delicious sensation of her moving against his shaft.

His mouth pressed to her ear, Wes whispered sweet, filthy nothings in it. She rode his hand, her movement growing frenzied as he related every dirty deed he had planned for their night together. Including how he planned to worship that world-champion body of hers with his tongue.

What was it about Bree Evans that made him crazy with want?

"Oh, my God, Wes." Bree was close. Her knees trembled. Her breath came in short, hard exhalations that made his already taut member hard as steel.

He'd wanted to take her from behind. Keep it impersonal. Like two strangers in the dark. But there was something about the way she said his name. Something about how she felt in his arms. He wanted to see every inch of her. To stare in her eyes while she shattered, his name on her tongue.

He gathered her in his arms and carried her to bed.

Bree's heart raced as Wesley set her on her feet beside the bed and started to remove his shirt, one painstaking button at a time.

"Thought we were keeping it quick and dirty." She'd been disappointed that he'd wanted to make their first time together feel impersonal. Transactional. But she thought she'd done a relatively good job of hiding it. After all, that's what she'd agreed to. A no-strings fling.

"Changed my mind." He tossed his shirt and removed his pants without offering further explanation, then growled in her ear, "Now take that dress off before I do."

"Sounds like fun." Bree couldn't help the grin that curled the edges of her mouth at the thought.

Even in the limited light of her darkened hotel room, she could see that she'd surprised him again.

She squealed when he lifted her and tossed her onto the bed. Suddenly, the dress was off, he'd removed her bra and they were both down to their underwear. Wes trailed kisses down her chest and belly before slowly dragging her panties down her legs.

Before she could react, he'd pressed his open mouth between her legs, his tongue lapping at her sensitive clit. Bree moaned with pleasure at the incredible sensation, calling his name before she could stop herself.

He slid his large palms beneath her hips, gripping them and pulling her closer to his mouth as he pleasured her with his tongue. She writhed as the warm sensation of ecstasy built at her center and her legs started to shake.

Wes pulled away and rummaged on the floor, then she could hear the tearing of the foil packet and make out the silhouette of Wes sheathing himself in the dark. He gripped the base of his length and slowly glided inside of her.

Bree sank her teeth into her lower lip, reveling in the sensation of Wes entering her, inch by inch, until he was fully seated. She cursed, her fingertips pressed to the strong muscles of his back, her fingernails digging into his skin.

Wes held her gaze as he moved his hips. Slowly. Precisely. The friction he created with each thrust of his hips was both torturous and delicious. She arched her back, desperate to heighten the sensation.

Her breathing was rapid and shallow as the pleasure building rose to a crescendo. She came hard, her muscles tensing and her legs shaking as she dug her heels into the mattress and her fingernails into his skin.

The hard muscles of his back tensed as she called his name, her body writhing in ecstasy. His gaze intensified as he moved his hips harder and faster until he'd reached his own edge. Wes's body stiffened and he cursed, his breathing labored. He tumbled on the bed beside her, both of them struggling to catch their breath.

Neither of them spoke.

Finally, Bree turned on her side, facing him. This was her idea, so she should be the one to break the awkward silence.

"Wes, that was…" She pressed a hand to his warm chest as she forced her eyes to meet his. "Incredible."

The edge of his mouth curled in a soft smile as he cupped her cheek. "No, you were incredible." He pressed a kiss to her mouth.

Her racing heart slowed just a bit and her shoulders relaxed. His compliment seemed genuine. Maybe he had enjoyed it as much as she had. Wanted her with the same intensity with which she wanted him.

"I know you're worried that I can't handle casual, but I can."

"Have you ever been in a casual relationship before?" He gave her a knowing smile that indicated he already knew the answer to his question.

"No." Her cheeks heated as she remembered how he'd teased her earlier about being a good girl. "That doesn't mean I'm incapable of being in one. I just hadn't encountered the right opportunity…until now."

Wes pushed a strand of hair off her face. "I want to believe you."

"You can." She kissed his mouth, then trailed kisses down his chest. *Convey strength and confidence.* She looked up at him and smiled in a manner she hoped was seductive. "But by the time I'm done with you, you won't want to walk away from me."

"Maybe you're right." He stroked her hair. "But I

will walk away, and I need to know that you'll be okay with that."

Bree swallowed her disappointment and forced a big smile. "Don't worry. I'm a big girl. I'll be fine."

She resumed kissing her way down his hard chest and his tight abs, reminding herself that they were only having a little fun. Enjoying each other's company. That she shouldn't be falling for Wesley Adams. And ignoring the fact that she already was.

Chapter 13

Bree studied Wesley's handsome face as he rubbed his stubbled chin. They sat at a little table by the window. The sunshine warmed them as they chatted over their lavish breakfast, ordered via room service.

Neither of them had wanted to leave her room. They'd barely wanted to leave her bed.

"This is good." Wes took a bite of his eggs Benedict. He cut and speared another bite and held it out to Bree. "You have to try it."

She smiled, but was still shy about what felt like such an intimate gesture. Even after everything they'd done last night.

Her eyes not meeting his, Bree tucked her hair behind her ear and leaned forward, allowing him to slip the forkful of food into her mouth.

"Mmm…" The rich, flavorful hollandaise sauce

melded with the flavors of the forest ham, spinach and tomato. Her eyes drifted closed as she savored the food. "That is good."

His eyes were dark and hooded when her gaze met his. As if he was reliving the sights and sounds of their night together.

Her cheeks filled with heat at the possibility. She tried to push the vision of them together in bed from her head.

"Try my fruit cup." She speared pieces of strawberry, blueberry and banana on her fork and held it out to him.

Wes accepted the offering, his gaze still on her, as if he was waiting for her to say something.

"So, about last night." She dragged the words out slowly as she surveyed his expression.

"Last night was amazing." He sipped his double espresso, his gaze locked with hers.

"It was," Bree agreed, her cheeks stinging. She dropped her gaze as she sipped her decadent mocha cafe. "And I know you planned this spectacular trip for us, but I'd love it if we just…spent the day here in bed."

She laughed nervously in response to his stunned expression. "Don't worry, I'm not suggesting that this means anything. I'm just saying that I enjoyed our night together and I can't think of a better way to spend the day."

Wes set his mug on the table and shifted in his seat. He tilted his head slightly. "Sounds fantastic, but—"

"The rules we established last night still apply." Bree forced a grin, burying the hurt that simmered in her chest. Last night hadn't changed his feelings. "You made that crystal clear."

It was unlike her to be so forward. She'd been the

shy wallflower who spent most of her school dances hovering in the corner, hoping not to be noticed. But there was something about Wesley Adams that eased her inhibitions.

Something deeper brewed between them, whether Wes acknowledged it or not.

"Now that that's all settled…" Bree strolled over to Wes and straddled his lap, her arms wrapped around his neck.

Wes chuckled as he wrapped his arms around her waist. "Who knew that America's volleyball sweetheart is a tempting seductress?"

"Not my usual MO." She shrugged. "But then my life usually doesn't leave much time for…this."

"Then I guess that makes me special." There was an uneasiness beneath his smile.

"Don't flatter yourself, playboy." She forced a grin. "I just happen to have some time on my hands."

Wes laughed heartily. He seemed to relax for the first time since they'd begun this conversation. "Then I guess I'm just lucky. Like the night we met."

Something about his statement—that he was lucky to have met her—warmed her chest and made her feel things she shouldn't about Wesley Adams. Feelings she should best ignore.

She kissed him and concentrated on all of the things she should be feeling. His hardened shaft pressed to her sensitive clit. The tightening of her beaded nipples, pressed against the hard muscles of his chest. The graze of his whiskers against her skin. The heat rising between them and the electricity that danced along her spine.

Bree wrapped her long legs around his waist as Wes

carried her to the bedroom. He made love to her, and she lost herself in the heat and passion between them. In all of the physical sensations that it was safe to allow herself to feel. While ignoring the nagging insistence that, regardless of what either of them claimed, this was the beginning of something more.

Wes strode back to bed and sipped his beer as he watched Brianna sleeping. He should've returned to his own room last night. Maintained some space between them. But he hadn't. And since they'd chosen to stay another day, they'd only reserved one room. So tonight he had no room to which he could retreat.

He turned on the television with the volume low and studied Bree in the flickering television light. Her hair, loosened from the ponytail and still damp from their earlier shower, was everywhere. Mouth open, one foot hanging off the bed, makeup ruined, and still she was adorable. Probably as much a product of his unsettling feelings for her as her natural beauty.

Bree rolled over, throwing an arm across him. Wes sighed softly and slipped his arm beneath her head, cradling her against him. He stared at the ceiling, listening to the sound of her breathing, and hoped this wasn't a mistake they'd both regret in the weeks ahead.

His phone vibrated on the nightstand beside him. *Drake*. It was late for his brother to be calling. After sunset, Drake was usually preoccupied with a gig or a groupie he'd met during said gig.

"Isn't this the time of night vampires usually hunt their prey?" Wes smirked, teasing his younger brother.

"Usually. But we make an exception when our mothers stumble and fall down half a flight of stairs."

"What happened? Is she all right?" Wes slid his arm from beneath Brianna and climbed out of bed, pacing the floor near the window.

"She got tangled up in the bedding she was carrying downstairs to the wash. Damn lucky to have only fractured her ankle and sprained her wrist." Drake's gravelly voice was that of a man who spent his nights in smoke-filled clubs.

Wes cursed, running a hand over his head. "This happened tonight?"

Drake hesitated before responding. "Last night. We've been trying to reach you, but your phone was off."

"My phone died last night. I've been…preoccupied." Wes glanced back at Bree. "Started charging it about an hour ago."

He'd always been the reliable son. The one who'd drop everything to help out his mother. But he'd failed her when she'd needed him most, a mistake he wouldn't make again.

"Thanks for being there, Drake."

"She's my mother, too." His words were laced with resentment. "Maybe I'm not always there physically, but I do whatever I can for Mom, no matter where I am in the world."

"Didn't mean to imply otherwise. Like I said, I'm just glad you were able to be there." Wes sighed, kneading the tension in his neck. "Is she still at the hospital?"

"Yes. Her doctor wants to hold her one more night for observation, in light of her Parkinson's." His brother cleared his throat. "When do you think you can get here? I'd love to stay, but I have to catch a plane in the morning. The band's got a gig in Germany in a few days."

"I'm in Asheville, but I'll leave first thing in the morning. I'll be there tomorrow afternoon. Is Mama awake? Can I talk to her?"

"She's resting. The pain meds knocked her out. I'll be leaving shortly, but between Aunt May, Dallas and Shay, she's in good hands. So don't worry. And Wes…" Drake's tone had softened, the tension gone.

"Yeah?"

"Don't beat yourself up over this. There's nothing you could've done to prevent this. And no one blames you for taking a little time for yourself. Certainly not Mama."

Wes wouldn't commit to not feeling guilty about allowing himself to be distracted when there was so much on the line professionally and personally. Still, he appreciated his brother's assurance.

Chapter 14

Bree awoke just in time to see Wesley striding out of the bathroom, freshly showered, with a towel slung low across his waist. As he bent over his luggage, the beads of water on his brown skin highlighted the strong muscles of his shoulders and back.

"Good morning." She sat up in bed, pulling the cover up around her.

"You're up. Good." He turned to her, a grave expression tugging down the corners of his mouth. "I'm afraid I have to bail on the rest of our trip. I have a family emergency. I need to be back home in New Bern as soon as possible."

"What happened? Is it your mother?" Panic bloomed in Bree's chest on his behalf. She knew how close they were.

"My mother tripped down the stairs. She fractured her ankle and sprained her wrist. I know the injuries might seem minor, but I'm afraid it's part of a larger problem." He paused as if there was something more he wanted to say. Something he wasn't comfortable sharing with her. Wes sighed. "She was diagnosed with Parkinson's six months ago. I only learned about the diagnosis when I went to visit her after our first meeting about the tournament."

"That's where you spent the night." Bree's cheeks warmed the moment she blurted out the words.

"I stayed to accompany her to the doctor the next day and to help out around the house." A knowing smirk curled the corner of Wes's mouth.

"Sorry to hear about your mother. About the fall and the diagnosis." Bree forced her eyes to meet his rather than take in the brown skin stretched over his muscles. "I'll jump in the shower so we can get out of here as soon as possible."

"I'd appreciate that." He rummaged in his suitcase and produced a pair of jeans and a T-shirt. "And I hope you don't mind me stopping by the hospital to get my mom and then getting her settled at her place. As soon as I'm done, I'll get you back to Pleasure Cove."

"Of course not." She wasn't Wes's girlfriend, so why did she feel uneasy about meeting his mother? He'd probably introduce her as a friend or a business associate.

In little more than half an hour, she'd showered, dressed and tossed everything back into her suitcase. They ordered breakfast sandwiches to go and piled in the car.

"So your mom fell last night?" Bree asked between bites of her breakfast croissant.

Wes frowned and sipped his coffee, returning it to

the cup holder before responding. "She fell the night before. My phone was off. My brother was finally able to reach me last night, after you'd gone to sleep."

"Oh." She nibbled on more of her sandwich. "So that's why you're…distant this morning. I'm the reason you missed the call about your mother."

"It's my fault. No one else's. Between my mother and the tournament… I should've made sure my phone was on. That I was available." Wesley narrowed his gaze, his eyes focused on the road and his jaw tight. She'd definitely struck a nerve.

"So maybe it isn't my fault directly, but it was me that distracted you." Bree echoed the sentiment clearly written on Wesley's face and implied by his words. "I'm sorry about that. If I'd known your mother was ill—"

"It wasn't your business to know. I only told you because…" He sighed, then muttered under his breath. "Don't really know why I told you. So I'd appreciate it if you wouldn't mention it to her when you meet her."

"Of course." Bree nodded, staring out the window. Hoping to hide the deep flush in her cheeks.

Wes was silent for a moment, his tone lower and softer when he spoke again. "Just so we're clear, I'll be introducing you as my friend and business associate."

"That's accurate. The business-associate part, I mean. The friendship…that's still a work-in-progress."

Wes chuckled. "I guess it is."

Bree clutched a vase of flowers as she approached Mrs. Adams's hospital room. She'd suggested that Wes go up ahead of her and make sure his mother was up to meeting someone new. She tapped on the partially open door, her heart racing. Bree stepped inside when a voice called for her to come inside.

"You must be Brianna." A wide grin spread across the woman's face. She was a beautiful older woman who seemed far too young to be Wesley's mother. "I'm Lena Adams. Wes stepped out to talk to someone about finally letting me out of this place. He told me to expect you. He didn't say you'd be bearing gifts."

Bree sighed in relief. The woman's warm, welcoming demeanor put her at ease. "I walked past the gift shop and they were so beautiful. I couldn't resist. I hope you like them."

"Like them? Honey, this bouquet is stunning. How thoughtful. Thank you." She accepted the crystal vase and inhaled the flowers before setting them on the nightstand beside her bed. She indicated a nearby chair. "Please, have a seat."

Bree sat in the chair, suddenly conscious of whether Mrs. Adams would think her blouse was cut too low or her jeans were too tight.

Relax. You're not his girlfriend.

"Speaking of beauty, you're even more stunning in person." Mrs. Adams grinned.

"Thank you." Bree's cheeks warmed. "Do you follow beach volleyball, Mrs. Adams?"

"Only during the Olympics. But I've seen you in at least a dozen commercials over the years." Excitement lit the older woman's eyes. "And call me Lena, please."

"Someone will be along shortly to complete your discharge." Wesley's tall frame filled the doorway. His eyes met Bree's for a moment before he turned them back to his mother. "I see you've met Bree."

"I have. You didn't tell me that she was as sweet as

she is beautiful. Look what she brought me." Lena nodded toward the flowers.

"Thank you, Bree." Wes studied the expensive flower arrangement, then turned toward her. His expression was a mixture of gratitude and suspicion. "They're lovely."

Bree clasped her hands, her eyes roaming anywhere in the room except Wesley or his mother. The elegant bouquet of red roses and orange Asiatic lilies was an expensive gift to a woman she'd never met. But they were beautiful and Wes had said how much his mother enjoyed gardening. So she thought Lena would appreciate them. She hadn't given any thought to the message her gift was sending...until now.

"Yes, they are." Lena emphasized the words as she eyed her son sternly. She returned her warm grin to Bree. "I hope you'll join us at the house for lunch, Brianna. It won't take me long to throw something together. We'll just need to make a quick stop at the grocery store." She turned to Wes.

He frowned, his arms crossed. "The doctor made it very clear that you should get some rest and stay off your feet as much as possible."

"Relax. It'll be fine." She squeezed his arm, then turned to her. "Brianna?"

"I'd love to join you for lunch, but Wes is right. You should be resting. So why don't you let me fix lunch for you?"

Lena's eyes lit up and her smile widened. "That's so thoughtful, Brianna. But I can imagine how busy you must be. I don't want to be any trouble."

"It's no trouble at all. It'd be my pleasure."

"Then we have a date."

The attendant arrived and helped Lena into a wheel-chair. They followed the attendant down the hall as he pushed Wes's mother and they chatted.

"Look, Bree, I appreciate your willingness to come here and the flowers…but you don't have to fix lunch. I can pick up something that's already prepared." His voice was hushed.

"Are you afraid to eat my cooking?" Bree teased, hoping to lighten his mood.

Wes held back a smirk. "Should I be?"

"Probably." Bree smiled. "Actual cooking isn't my gift. But, I can assemble a mean chicken salad. Don't worry. I'll pick up a rotisserie at the grocery store."

"Bree." He grabbed her arm, stopping her, so that their eyes met. Wes sighed. "I just want to make sure you understand that nothing has changed between us. We're still just business associates and friends—"

"With benefits." Bree narrowed her gaze, her chin tipped so her eyes met his. "You were crystal clear about that. I'm not an idiot, and I'm not trying to get to you through your mother—if that's what you're thinking."

Wes's stare signaled that he didn't buy her story.

"I got the flowers because they were pretty. I thought your mother would like them. I offered to make lunch because it was clear that if I didn't, she was going to insist on making lunch for us. And because she seems sweet. And I like her. But if you don't want me to have lunch with your mother, fine. I'll rent a car and head back."

"No. Don't. I'm sorry. I'm usually not so ungrateful. I swear." Wes rubbed the back of his neck. "Thank you for the flowers and for offering to make lunch. Maybe you can distract her while I move her bed downstairs. Otherwise, she'd insist on helping me."

Bree nodded and fell back in step with Wes as they caught up with the attendant and his mother.

Her cheeks flamed and a knot tightened in her gut. She hadn't been completely honest with Wesley. She wasn't actively pursuing Wes through his mother, but she wanted very much for Lena Adams to like her.

Wes finished the last bite of his second helping of Bree's cranberry-walnut chicken salad served on warm, fresh, buttery croissants from the local bakery. So maybe Bree couldn't cook, but she could *assemble* a damn tasty meal.

He'd wanted to get started on rearranging the house while Bree fixed lunch, but his mother had insisted he sit down with them until his cousin Dallas could come over and give him a hand with moving her bed. Though she didn't much like the idea of moving her bed downstairs, even temporarily.

"I know you're worried, son, but I still think you're making too big of a deal about this. I fell. Accidents happen. I'll be more careful from now on."

"You can't trudge up and down those steps in an air cast." He lowered his voice. "Not in your condition."

"I was recently diagnosed with Parkinson's," his mother explained to Bree, then turned her attention back to him. "There's a banister. Besides, it's not as if I can't put any pressure on the foot. And I need my stuff. You don't plan to bring my entire bedroom down, do you?"

Bree excused herself and left the kitchen as he and his mother continued to debate the topic. It was one argument Lena Adams wouldn't win. She was going to sleep on the ground floor, whether she liked it or not.

"Excuse me." Bree returned a few minutes later, smiling. "But I think I might have a solution that'll satisfy you both."

"I'm all ears." His mother gave Bree her attention.

"By all means." Wes gestured for her to continue.

She asked them to follow her to the front of the house.

"Your kitchen has ample eating space, but you also have a formal dining room, which it seems you don't use much." Bree indicated the piles of papers and books that had accumulated on his mother's table again since his last cleaning.

"Point taken." His mother chuckled. "Go on."

"Well, it's such a lovely space. It's a shame you don't get more use out of it. The room is spacious and the pretty bay window faces that lovely little park across the street."

His mother nodded thoughtfully. "It's a sizable room and it does have a beautiful view. But it doesn't have a door and it's right at the entrance. Visitors will have full view of my bedroom."

"That's a simple fix." Bree's eyes lit up. "You could add a wall here and put in a door."

"What happens if she decides to sell the house? Not everyone will want a first-floor bedroom in lieu of a formal dining room." Wes appreciated what Bree was trying to do, but he had to be practical. He wanted his mother to be comfortable, but they couldn't ruin the resale value of the house.

"A valid point." Bree tilted her head, her chin resting on her fist for a moment. She snapped her fingers.

"Add a pretty set of French doors instead of a traditional door."

"Guests would still be able to see into my bedroom."

"Not if you mount thick curtains on the door." Bree's gaze shifted from his mother, then to him, and back again.

A wide smile spread across his mother's face, her eyes dancing. "That's a brilliant idea, Brianna. My nephew Dallas is a contractor. He mentioned yesterday that the job they were supposed to work on for the next few days got rescheduled. Maybe he can squeeze me in. He'll be here soon, but I'm going to call him now, so he can give his crew plenty of notice. Besides, I don't want him to give someone else my spot."

"You object?" Bree asked when his mother left the room.

"No. Seems you have everything figured out."

"Why do I have the feeling we're not talking about the plans to relocate your mother's bedroom anymore?" Bree stepped closer.

Her sweet, citrusy scent—like mandarin oranges and orange blossoms—filled his nostrils. The two nights they'd spent together in Asheville rushed to mind with a vivid clarity. A knot tightened low in his belly. His heartbeat quickened and his temperature rose as he recalled the way her brown skin glowed in the moonlight. It took every ounce of willpower he could muster to refrain from leaning down and kissing her soft, glossy lips.

Bree seemed to relish her power over him, and the fact that with his mother just a few feet away, he was forced to keep his hands to himself.

Pure torture.

"Dallas says he can have his crew here in the morning." His mother returned, saving him from the need to respond to Bree's statement. "He'll be here soon to take measurements. The job should only take a couple of days."

"We still need to move your bed downstairs for now." Wes folded his arms.

"Not necessary. I can sleep right here." His mother patted the sofa she was seated on.

"That thing is hard as a rock. I know." Wes clutched his back as he remembered the last time he'd crammed his long frame onto the uncomfortable pull-out sofa.

"I'm half a foot shorter than you, so I think I'll be all right." She held up her open hand when Wes objected. "This is my compromise. Take it or leave it."

"Fine." Wes blew out an exasperated breath. "But don't complain when your back muscles are as stiff as bricks."

"Deal." She indicated that he should kiss her on the cheek.

He did, then sat beside her, draping an arm over her shoulder. "You've eaten and Dallas will be here shortly. This is a good time for me to take Bree back to Pleasure Cove."

"What a shame." His mother frowned. "I was hoping she'd be here to see the finished result of her idea. Besides, I could use her help decorating the new room."

"Bree's a busy woman. She doesn't have time to hang out here and play interior decorator." Wesley's shoulders tensed.

"Actually, since the rest of our trip is canceled, I don't have anything planned for the next couple of days." Bree smiled at his mother, her eyes not meeting his. "I'd love to help."

Wes turned to his mother, who was as excited as a kid at Christmas. If it made his mom happy and Bree didn't object, why should he?

They'd shared a bed for two nights. Surely he could deal with her being at his mother's house for two days.

"You sure about this?" Wes gave Bree one last out.

"Positive." Bree grinned. "This will be fun."

Between his mother and Bree, Wes didn't stand a chance.

Chapter 15

Lena Adams was an indomitable spitfire who wouldn't allow minor inconveniences like a fractured ankle or a sprained wrist to keep her from cooking a full meal for her guests. Bree was sure that if she hadn't insisted on helping the woman, Lena would've soldiered through the entire process herself.

She admired Lena's drive and determination, traits her son had obviously inherited.

In the course of an afternoon helping Lena prepare a three-course meal, Bree had doubled her cooking repertoire.

Bree stole another glance out of the kitchen window at Wes working in his mother's backyard. It was the end of winter, yet the North Carolina sunshine beat down overhead, making the already mild temperature feel considerably warmer. Wes had stripped off his T-shirt. The deep brown skin of his bare back and chest glistened with sweat. His black athletic shorts hung low on his hips.

Bree swallowed hard, then sunk her teeth into her lower lip. Her cheeks warmed and a sudden burst of heat crept down her torso and sank low in her belly.

Lena chuckled.

Shaken from her temporary haze, Bree returned to her work of dicing more potatoes for the potato salad.

"Business associates, eh?" The woman could hardly hold back her laughter. "Is that what they're calling it these days?"

Bree froze for a moment, unsure how to answer her.

"Don't know whether you two are trying to pull the wool over my eyes or your own, but in either case, it ain't working."

"I hate to disappoint you, Ms. Lena." Bree emptied the rest of the diced potatoes in a pot of water on the stove, then washed her hands. "But we really are business associates and friends."

"I hope that isn't true." Lena had a sad smile as she poured two icy glasses of syrupy sweet tea. She handed them to Bree. "It's obvious to anyone with one eye and half a brain that you two are into each other."

"Wes isn't looking for a relationship. He's made that abundantly clear." Bree's gaze drifted back to Wes outside. "Neither am I."

"Sometimes we don't know what we want until the situation presents itself." Lena nodded toward Wes. "My boys mean everything to me. But before Wes came along, I was set on a very different life. One that didn't include children or a stable home. I was terribly wrong because being their mother is the best thing that's ever happened to me."

Bree's chest ached and tears stung her eyes. It was clear why Wes loved his mother so much.

"I wish my birth mother felt the same way about me." Bree said the words before she could stop herself.

Her adoptive mother loved her with all her heart. She was grateful for that. Still, she couldn't shake the deep-rooted pain over her birth mother's inability to muster the slightest maternal affection toward her. The woman had two other children, whom she doted on, so clearly she possessed the capacity for maternal feelings. Evidently, Bree wasn't worthy of them.

"If she doesn't, she's either misguided or a fool." Lena squeezed Bree's arm. The woman's words were filled with indignation, but her tone and expression were filled with compassion. "Any woman would be grateful to have a daughter as kind and thoughtful as you."

Bree blinked back tears as she forced a smile. "Thanks."

Lena glanced out at Wes again. "He's probably dehydrated and doesn't even realize it. He gets so focused on the task ahead of him that he sometimes forgets how important it is to stop and take care of himself."

She dipped a towel into a bowl of icy water, wrung it, then draped the cool cloth over Bree's arm. Lena propped open the screen door and nodded toward Wes.

Bree made her way to the garden, where Wes had been working for the past few hours.

"Your mom thought you might like these." She handed him a glass of sweet tea and the cool towel.

He thanked her, then mopped his brow with the towel

before hanging it around his neck and nearly draining the glass of tea.

"Your mom was worried you might be getting dehydrated. I can get another glass, if you'd like." She turned to go back to the house, but Wes caught her elbow.

"Thank you. For everything." He stared at her with a heated gaze that lit a flame inside of her and caused her breath to come in quick, shallow bursts. "I know you have better things to do with your time, but you've been great with my mom. I can't tell you how much I appreciate that."

"I'm enjoying my time with her. Besides, she's taught me a lot today." Bree glanced over her shoulder toward the house and saw the kitchen curtains stir. She eased her arm from his grip and took a step back.

"What's wrong?" Wes narrowed his gaze.

"Your mom is convinced there's something going on between us. I don't want to add fuel to the fire." She took a sip of her tea.

"I'll bet." Wes chuckled. "My mother seems genuinely taken with you, and she isn't an easy woman to impress."

"She doesn't strike me as a volleyball fan."

"It's not about what you do. If she's impressed, it's because of who you are. For her, it's all about character. The person you are when no one else is around." Wes frowned, his voice fading at the end.

Bree wanted to ask him if he was all right, but before she could he'd thrust his empty glass into her outstretched hand.

"It was kind of you to offer to stay tonight, but I really don't mind taking you back to Pleasure Cove.

And don't worry about my mother, she'll understand. I promise."

"No." Bree shook her head, then smiled. "I'm enjoying my time with her. And you." Her eyes met his heated stare. "I want to stay. Unless it's uncomfortable for you. My being here, I mean."

Wes leaned against the metal rake, still sizing her up, but not responding right away. The awkward silence stretched on between them for what felt like forever before he finally shrugged. "It's...different. Been a while since I brought a girl home. For any reason. So I'm not surprised that my mother is trying to make something bigger out of this. I hope she hasn't made you uncomfortable."

"No, of course not." Bree forced a smile, not wanting to reveal her discomfort at Wesley's words.

Wes tried to ignore the sound of the shower running in the Jack-and-Jill bathroom between his room and the guest room Bree would be sleeping in. Tried to ignore the vision of water sluicing down Bree's back, between her firm breasts and into the valley between her long legs.

He tried, but failed miserably. His body ached with want and left him with an unsettled feeling in his chest.

He wanted her. In a way that made it clear that what he craved was more than just her body. No matter how many times he tried to tell himself otherwise.

"Wes?" There was a knock at the bathroom door that led to his room.

He cleared his throat and edged closer to the door.

"I hate to bother you, but I can't find another towel."

"Sorry about that." Wes groaned. He meant to restock the towels after he'd taken his shower earlier. "I'll get you one."

Wes retrieved some towels from the hallway linen closet and returned to the door. He took a deep breath before he knocked. "Got them."

Bree cracked open the door slightly. The room was still filled with steam and her hair hung in wet curls that clung to her face.

"Thank you." She reached one arm out while shielding her body with the door. "I'll be out in a second, if you need to get in here."

"All I want is you." His gaze held hers. "Naked. In my bed."

Her eyes widened with surprise. She closed the door and bustled around the bathroom, but still hadn't answered him.

Wes groaned, his forehead pressed to the bathroom door. Brianna had gotten under his skin in a way no other woman had. Maybe it was good she hadn't accepted his proposition. She was saving him from himself.

Suddenly, the door opened and she stood before him in one of the fuzzy, cream-colored towels he'd just given her. She gave him a shy smile, but heat raged in her brown eyes.

"I believe you invited me to your room. Does the offer still stand?" Bree seemed to enjoy the stunned look on his face.

He didn't speak. Didn't nod. Instead, he leaned down, cradled her head and pressed his mouth to hers. Slipped his tongue inside her warm, minty mouth. Pressed his body against hers.

Bree wrapped her arms around him, her hands

pressed to his back as she murmured softly, her head tilted.

Her skin was soft and warm and she smelled sweet and sensual. He wanted to taste every inch of her heated skin. Make love to her until they were both sweaty, exhausted and fully satisfied.

Wes slid his hands to her back, then down to her bottom, pulling her against him. He let out a soft sigh at the intense pleasure of her wet heat pressed against him there. He slid his hands beneath the towel, gripped her naked flesh before he lifted her into his arms and carried her to his bed.

Bree's smile was hesitant. Filled with want and need. And something more. Something that tugged at his chest and felt oddly familiar.

He didn't have time to ruminate over it. She took his face into her hands and pulled his mouth down to hers. Kissed him slow and sweet in a way that revved up his body and ignited a flame deep in his chest. It was a feeling that could only mean trouble for both of them.

Wes stripped Bree of her towel and shed his T-shirt and boxers. He trailed kisses from her neck to her center, wet and glistening. Tasted her there. Lapped at her with his tongue while teasing her with his fingers. Until she shattered, her knees trembling and her lips pressed together to muffle her whimpers.

He kissed his way back up to her belly. Laved her hardened, beaded nipples as he slid inside her and rocked them both into a delicious abandon that made him want to forget everything but her.

"You're an incredible woman, Brianna Evans. In every way." Wes kissed her damp forehead and held her tight against him. "Thank you."

Bree was silent for a moment before she pressed a hand to his chest and lifted her head so her eyes met his. "Thank you for what?"

"For being here with me." Wes pulled the damp, curly strands of hair back and tucked them behind her ear so he could study her elegant features in the moonlight. He kissed her cheek. "For being so kind and thoughtful to my mother."

She smiled softly. "Thank you for letting me meet her. I know that isn't something you usually do."

He chuckled. "Try never."

"Why?" Bree hesitated before continuing. "Most guys who feel that way…to be honest, they're probably doing womankind a favor by not getting deeply involved with anyone. But you aren't like that. You're a genuinely good man. You deserve to be happy. To have a full life. So why are you so dead set against getting involved?"

Wes sighed heavily, folding one arm behind his head as he stared at the ceiling. "The men in my family haven't had a very good track record of being good mates."

"My mother gave me up at birth and hasn't wanted anything to do with me since." Bree shrugged, resting her chin on his chest. "Doesn't mean I'd do the same to my kid. Besides, we aren't our parents, Wes. Who we are is based on the decisions we make every single day. Like you making the choice to be there for your mother as she battles her illness. That's why this tournament is so important to you, isn't it?"

"Yes." He traced her bare shoulder with his calloused fingertips. "And I'm not basing my decision on parental history alone."

"We all make mistakes, Wes." Bree was quiet for a moment when he didn't respond. "Doesn't mean that's who we are or that we don't deserve happiness. What matters is that we try to rectify our mistakes and that we learn from them."

"A caged bird escaping its gilded cage." Her gaze dropped to the tattoo on the left side of his chest. The bird was designed of sheets of musical notes. The door it escaped looked like facing capital letter Gs. She traced the ink lightly with her fingertips. "Is that you?"

"No. Got it not long after I graduated university as sort of a tribute to my mother."

"You hoped your mother would go after her dreams again, once you and your brother were no longer her responsibility. That's sweet. *You're* sweet." She leaned in and kissed his mouth.

"But you shouldn't feel guilty about your mom missing out on the life she might've had. You should see the glow on her face when she talks about you and your brother. She doesn't seem to regret a moment of her life. I can't imagine she'd want you lugging around this burden of guilt on her behalf." Bree studied his face, waiting for his reaction.

It was a weight he'd been carrying for years. One not easily budged. He met her gaze. "This is who I am, Bree. It's who I've been most of my life. Sorry if that's not what you wanted to hear."

"I'm sorry, too." She sighed softly, the corner of her mouth tugged down in a slight frown. "Good night, Wesley."

Bree climbed out of bed, gathered her towel and wrapped it around her again.

"Are you angry with me?" He sat up in bed, pulling the sheet up around his waist.

"No, of course not." There was pity and sadness in her voice. "I just think it's better if I sleep in my room. In case your mother comes looking for one of us in the morning."

Her excuse wasn't very convincing to either of them.

"I don't expect her to hobble up the steps. That was the whole point of moving her downstairs. If anything, she'll call upstairs." Wes kept his voice even. It needed to sound as if he was stating a fact, rather than the passionate plea it was.

He liked the idea of waking up to Bree in his arms.

Bree didn't acknowledge his statement. "See you at breakfast."

She exited through the bathroom door. He groaned when the distinct click of the door locking on the other side of the bathroom indicated she had no intention of returning.

Wes groaned, one arm folded behind his head. He should be glad Bree was honoring his request to keep their relationship casual. Instead, he was pouting like a child whose favorite toy had just been taken away.

Chapter 16

"Another trip with Wes, huh?" Bex's observation was more than a passing interest.

"Uh-huh." Bree turned away from Bex. They were using the video messaging app on her phone, which was propped on the nightstand. She stuffed her makeup bag into her luggage and zipped it. When she finally turned back to the phone, her friend had her arms crossed and one eye cocked. "What?"

"You know what. This isn't just business anymore, and it's obviously escalated beyond banging-buddy status. I'm worried about you. I don't want to see you get hurt." Bex's tone had shifted from exasperation to genuine concern.

"I won't." Her statement lacked conviction.

"Even you don't believe that."

It'd been more than a month since she and Wes had

taken their trip to Asheville. They'd continued their affair in secret, not even telling their best friends. But Bex knew her too well. She'd threatened to hop the next plane to Pleasure Cove if Bree didn't level with her.

So she'd told Bex the truth. She and Wes were friends who just happened to also enjoy sleeping together. A lot. But they were not a couple. Nor would they become one, because that wasn't what either of them wanted right now.

That part was a lie. One Bex saw right through. It was the reason she was so concerned.

Though she tried to allay her friend's concerns, they both knew the truth. In the recesses of her heart, Bree quietly believed Wes to be The Trifecta. The elusive man who would satisfy her body, heart and mind.

Each moment spent with Wesley Adams convinced her that he was the man with whom she could happily spend the rest of her life.

Though their no-strings agreement still stood, Bree was sure Wes cared for her more than he was willing to let on.

It was in his kiss. In his touch. In his voice when he whispered in her ear in the wee hours of the morning. It was in the depths of his dark eyes when he made love to her. In his stolen glances at her when he thought no one else was looking.

What they shared was more than sex or even friendship.

Bree wouldn't call it love, but it was deeper than lust or affection. Still, if Wes wasn't willing to explore his feelings for her, what did it matter? The end of summer would bring the volleyball tournament they'd both worked so hard on, and eventually, the end of their relationship. He'd stay in Pleasure Cove and she'd return to California, as if what they'd shared over the summer meant nothing.

The thought made her chest heavy with grief.

"I can handle whatever happens between us this time." Bree hoped her tone was more convincing.

"Then go to London and have a good time with your *friend*." An uneasy smile curled the edges of Bex's mouth. "How's his mom?"

"She's doing well." A wide smile tightened Bree's cheeks when she thought of Lena. Wes had hired an aide to help his mother around the house. Still, he'd visited Lena each week and Bree had accompanied him twice—at Lena's insistence. She went gladly, because she genuinely enjoyed Lena's company. "The air cast came off yesterday and she's getting around well. Still, I hate that neither of us will be here."

"You sound like a dutiful daughter-in-law." Bex peered into the camera, one eyebrow raised.

"She's an amazing woman. Funny and interesting. I can't help but adore her."

"Just don't get too attached. Walking away from Wes at the end of the summer means walking away from his mother, too."

The doorbell rang and Bree said goodbye to her friend, glad not to have to respond to Bex's very salient point.

It was too late. She'd already fallen for Wes and his mom.

A noise startled Wes awake. According to his mobile, it was a little after three in the morning. Yet, Bree was no longer in bed. He followed the sound to his sitting room.

The lights were off, but he could make out Bree's form as she stood in front of the large windows that had enticed him into purchasing the flat. She stared into the distance at London's skyline.

"Is everything okay?"

"Everything is fine." She turned toward him, her face barely visible in the light streaming through the window. "Sorry, I didn't mean to wake you. I couldn't sleep. Figured it was a good time to take in this beautiful view."

"I fell for this place the moment I saw that view." He studied her silhouette in the moonlight. Wearing the sheer white lingerie he'd surprised her with, she managed to look naughty and angelic all at once.

"You look amazing." He stood behind her, slipped his arms around her waist and planted soft kisses on her warm neck. Inhaled her scent. Her soft murmur vibrated against his chest, making him want her more. Wes pressed his body to hers as he slipped the white fabric from her shoulder and trailed kisses there. "And as much as I love seeing you in this, what I'd really like is to see you out of it again."

Bree blushed in the moonlight, the corner of her mouth curling in an adorable grin that warmed him.

He couldn't resist smiling in response.

They'd been carrying on their affair for more than a month. Bree had initiated things that night in Asheville. Yet, at her core she was demure and, at times, bashful. He loved that she could be both a wily, determined temptress and the sweet, blushing girl next door.

"You have a big meeting this morning, remember?"

"It's this afternoon," he whispered in her ear, his lips brushing her skin. "Gives me plenty of time to spend with you."

"I like the sound of that." Bree turned around, her gaze meeting his as she slid one hand down his chest and beneath his waistband, taking him in her palm.

Wes sucked in a deep breath as she palmed his heated flesh. Her cool hand warmed as it glided up and down his shaft.

Her nostrils flared and the corner of her mouth curled with satisfaction. She seemed to enjoy the power she had over him as she stroked him, bringing him closer to the edge.

He cradled her face and claimed her mouth in a frantic kiss. Bree had him teetering on the edge. But he was desperate to be inside her again. To stare into those brown eyes, her bare, sweat-slickened skin pressed to his, as he erupted with pleasure.

Wes scooped her in his arms and she squealed, looping her arms around his neck so she wouldn't fall. He carried her to his bed, each of them shedding their clothing. He settled between her thighs and trailed kisses down her neck and between her breasts.

"You do realize I wasn't finished in there."

"But I nearly was, and we couldn't have that."

Scraping one beaded tip between his teeth, he gently teased it with his tongue. Bree squirmed beneath him. Her soft, sensual murmur stoked the fire building inside him.

Wes hated that he'd pulled the heavy curtains shut. He wanted the satisfaction of seeing Bree's lovely face as she called his name in the throes of her climax. A delight he never tired of.

He sheathed himself, then entered her slowly, groaning with pleasure as her snug heat welcomed him.

They moved together, heat building between them and a light sheen of sweat clinging to their skin. Bree's murmurs grew louder. Her breath came faster. She repositioned her legs and pressed her bare feet to his shoulders, allowing him to penetrate deeper.

She clutched the sheets, her back arched as she called his name, riding the wave of her orgasm. Nearly there, he continued his thrusts until his spine stiffened and he shuddered, cursing and moaning. Calling her name.

Breathless and sweaty, he gathered her in his arms and kissed her damp hair.

Bree Evans was the first woman who'd made him question the wisdom of his commitment to remaining unattached. She made him want to believe he was capable of giving her the things she wanted.

Love. Marriage. A family.

More and more, he'd allowed himself to imagine what it would be like to have those things with her. And it didn't feel stifling or confining. The images in his head filled him with warmth and contentment.

He could get used to having Bree in his bed every night, but he wouldn't delude himself by believing he could become something he wasn't. He'd already ruined one woman's life and caused them both irrevocable harm. He wouldn't do that to Bree. No matter how much he wanted her.

Chapter 17

"He's a pretty spectacular fellow, isn't he?"

The woman's voice startled Bree from what she often found herself doing these days—stealing loving glances at Wesley Adams when she thought no one was looking. His event manager, Nadia, obviously was.

The woman had done a poor job of hiding her disbelief when Wes had introduced her as a friend. Standing in the corner, staring at Wes like a lovelorn fool, didn't help.

"He is…very good at what he does, I mean," Bree clarified as she sipped her champagne. Wes and his team were working the party. So they weren't drinking. She had no such constraints. "I've learned a lot from him since we started working on the project together."

"I'll bet." Nadia was barely able to hold back her grin. "He's taught me quite a lot about the event-planning and promotions business. Still, I've a lot to learn before I'll be anywhere near as gifted as he is."

"Well, he's certainly confident in you," Bree reassured the woman with a smile. "He'd never have entrusted his business to you if he wasn't."

"Thank you." Nadia beamed. "And if you don't mind me saying so, I've known him long enough to realize that what he feels for you is special." She looked over at Wes, who stood on the other side of the room staring at Bree. "I've never seen him light up the way he does when he looks at you. He's completely smitten and it scares him half to death."

A soft smile curved the edge of Bree's mouth and her cheeks warmed as she returned his affectionate gaze. Bree wanted to believe that what Nadia was saying was true. That Wes reciprocated her growing feelings for him.

The warmth she'd felt moments earlier gave way to a dull ache in her chest and a knot in her belly.

She returned her attention to Nadia. "It's not what you think."

"Maybe. Or maybe I'm right and you two are both wrong about what this is." Nadia squeezed her arm and disappeared into the crowd.

Bree released a long, slow breath, her heart beating quickly. They'd grown closer during their two weeks in London. Each day together had felt more intimate, but now their trip was coming to an end.

They'd fallen into an easy rhythm. Making love in the mornings and chatting over breakfast. Dinner together and nights that ended in the same manner they began. In each other's arms.

While Wes worked with his small team to hire more

staff and finalize plans for a huge corporate party, Bree worked on the tournament and her own projects. She'd had video and phone conferences with Bex and the marketing consultant they'd hired to help them plan and promote their volleyball camps the following year.

Still, Wes had insisted on taking her to see all of the tourist attractions she hadn't been able to squeeze into her previous working trips to London. Visits to the Tower of London, Kensington Palace and Westminster Abbey. A turn on the London Eye—the giant Ferris wheel on the south bank of the River Thames. A romantic evening stroll across London Bridge and a view of the city from the hauntingly beautiful attached skyscraper—the Shard.

She'd been incredibly happy, and it seemed that Wes was, too. So why did he seem so terrified by the prospect of exploring the feelings they had for each other?

It was a question she'd revisited time and again. Yet, she hadn't wanted to broach the subject with him. She'd willingly agreed to a secret, no-strings-attached fling with Wes. Insisted that she was cosmopolitan enough to handle such an affair. So she'd grin and bear the pain that knotted her belly whenever she considered what would happen once the tournament had ended and they went their separate ways.

"Enjoying the party?" Wes stood beside her.

"Yes." Bree finished her glass of champagne and set it on the tray of a server walking by. "But I think I'll head back to your place. I feel like I'm a distraction to you. Besides, I need to call my mother and yours."

"You're a pleasant distraction. My favorite kind." He smiled warmly. "And as for my mom, I'm grateful you've been so patient with her, but if she's become a nuisance, I'll talk to her."

"Don't you dare. I enjoy spending time with her. I promise." She double-checked that the spare key Wes gave her was in her clutch, then snapped it shut. "See you back at the flat?"

"At least let me hail a taxi for you." Wes frowned.

"I'll be fine." Bree made her way to the exit, hoping that Nadia was right. And that Wes missed her as much as she was already missing him.

Despite all of the noise and movement swirling around him, Wes was focused on one thing—Brianna Evans walking away from him. A thought that had occupied a growing space in his brain.

He shouldn't worry about what would happen at the project's end. He should just enjoy every moment they had together. Stop worrying about the future and commiserating over his past. Live in the now.

Yet, losing her was all he could think of.

Though he couldn't rightly claim to be losing her when they'd be parting ways at his insistence.

"She's even nicer in person." Nadia had a way of sneaking up on him. "I see why you fancy her so."

Wes didn't respond to Nadia's attempt to gauge his relationship with Bree. It was safer to talk business instead.

"How are the two potential new hires doing?" His gaze swept the room, in search of any small details that might have fallen through the cracks.

"Smashing. It's too bad we can only afford to bring one of them onboard. Don't know how we'll choose."

"Maybe we won't have to." Wes held back a grin

when Nadia's eyes widened. He'd been so preoccupied with business and Bree that he hadn't told her the news. "I've been talking with the Westbrooks over the past few weeks. They'd like to make us the official event-planning professionals for their London headquarters."

Nadia squeezed his arm and mimicked a silent squeal. "I thought you were determined to do this without them."

"I love and admire the Westbrooks, but I didn't want to feel beholden to them. I went against everyone's advice in starting this business—including Liam and his father. I needed to show them I could make it a success without their family's power and wealth behind me." He shrugged. "I've done that here."

"And in the US? I know your best mate begged you to help him out on short notice, but I get the sense there's more to it than that. Was working with Brianna the carrot that finally won you over?" Nadia grinned.

"Didn't realize she was involved when I agreed to it," he reminded her. An involuntary smile tightened his cheeks. "But working with her has turned out to be a highlight."

"I knew it. You're completely gaga over her, aren't you?" Nadia could barely contain her excitement.

"How is it you're more excited about this than my news about Westbrook International?" He raised a brow. "Especially since I'm promoting you to president of UK operations by the end of the year if everything works out in the US."

This time Nadia's squeal wasn't silent. With the ruckus going on around them, few people noticed. She hugged him.

"I can't believe it. Thank you for your faith in me.

I was sure you'd bring some heavy hitter in to head things up here if the project went well across the pond."

"You've been with me since the beginning. Back when we were working out of that mangy old flat. You were there every day and worked solely on commission. How could you think I'd trust anyone else to head up the business here?"

"You're making me blush." Nadia swiped a finger beneath the corner of her eye and sniffled. "Don't expect this to put a stop to me meddling in your love life."

"I don't have a love life."

"Precisely. But you deserve to be happy with someone like Brianna. I quite like her. So don't you dare let her get away." Nadia elbowed him playfully, but then her voice turned somber. "If you care for her the way it seems you do, you'll never forgive yourself if you let her go."

Wes massaged the knot that had formed at the back of his neck.

If only it was that easy.

Chapter 18

Brianna stood at the window taking a mental picture of the view from Wesley's flat. She was trying to memorize it and everything about their past two weeks together in London.

The soft strains of Duke Ellington and John Coltrane's version of "In a Sentimental Mood" drifted from the multi-room audio wired throughout his flat. She'd been listening to the song on repeat. It was Wesley's favorite classic jazz standard. She'd heard it often in the weeks they'd been together, each time with more appreciation than the time before.

On their final night in London together, the song captured her mood brilliantly. Ellington's ethereal piano notes combined with Coltrane's smooth, somber sax made for a brooding, introspective piece reflective of both joy and sadness.

Exactly what she was feeling now.

Her chest filled with warmth as she reflected on the two weeks they'd spent together in London. Yet, a pervasive sense of sadness made her heart ache.

They'd never be in London together again. The city that had originally brought them together.

She inhaled the unbuttoned blue oxford shirt she wore over her bra and panties. The same shirt he'd been wearing before they'd stripped each other naked and made love.

"I'm officially packed and ready for our early morning departure. I'm surprised you're not asleep." Wes joined her at the window.

"Committing this remarkable view to memory." Bree fiddled with the collar of the shirt, hoping Wesley hadn't caught her sniffing its scent moments earlier. They'd shared so many special moments in London. Moments in which they'd grown closer.

London was now inextricably linked with Wesley Adams.

"It isn't as if you'll never return. To London, I mean." His gaze drifted from hers. They were silent for a moment before he shifted the topic. "I've obviously convinced you of the many virtues of 'In a Sentimental Mood.'"

"It's brilliant. Evocative of so many powerful emotions."

"Come here." Wes moved toward the center of the room and extended his hand. When Bree joined him, he took her hand in his and looped an arm around her waist. "Dance with me."

His soft, intimate plea filled her body with heat. A charge of electricity ran along her skin.

She swayed with Wes, her ear pressed to his chest, listening to the thud of his heart as it beat against his strong chest. Her eyes drifted closed for a moment as they swayed and turned about the room ever so slightly with each step.

His chin propped on her head, Wes cradled her closer, neither of them speaking.

The connection they shared was more than sex. More than friendship.

So why was Wes so determined to walk away from the very thing they both seemed to want and need? What was Wes really afraid of?

Bree wanted to ask, but the words wouldn't come. To quiet the pervasive questions that danced in her head, she shifted attention back to the song.

"You said Miles Davis and Thelonious Monk are your favorite jazz artists. So why is a collaboration between Ellington and Coltrane your favorite jazz song?"

"Aside from the brilliance of the collaboration and the complexity of the piece?" Wes's voice rumbled against her ear. "Got my own sentimental connection to the song." He paused so long it seemed he'd decided against divulging it. "My favorite memory of my parents is them dancing to this song."

"That's beautiful." Something about his admission made tears instantly well in her eyes. Bree wasn't sure if she was moved by the poignancy of the story, or by his willingness to share it with her.

"Your mom showed me some old family pictures." Bree hadn't mentioned it before because Wes wasn't inclined to reminisce about his dad. But tonight, he seemed open to it. "Lena is gorgeous now, but she looked like a glamorous movie star in all her photos. And you guys all look so happy."

"In the beginning, my mom was, and I think my dad wanted to be. But his passion was music, being on the road traveling. Maybe he really did love us. But he loved music and life on the road more."

"Wes, I'm sorry." She squeezed him tightly. Bree understood the pain and rejection Wes felt. It was a pain that could only truly be understood by someone who'd endured it, too.

"Don't be." Wes slid his hands beneath the shirt she wore. His rough hands glided along her warm skin. He traced a scar from an old surgery with his thumb.

Bree tensed, self-conscious about the ugly scar. She'd had it incorporated into the tattoo on her side to camouflage the imperfection.

"Does it hurt?" His soft, warm gaze met hers.

"No, and neither does this one." She slipped the shirt from her shoulder enough to reveal a scar that remained from her shoulder surgery a few years ago. "But they've ruined my bikini game." She tried to keep her breathing even as she maintained his heated gaze.

"I assure you that nothing could possibly mar the sight of you in a bikini. Besides, with a one-piece like the one you wore in my hot tub that day…who needs one?" He gripped her bare waist and pulled her closer to him again as he leaned in and whispered in her ear. "By the way, that swimsuit…you weren't playing fair. A man with less willpower would've caved."

"Your concept for the tournament was best, so it's good you were strong enough to resist my charms." She glided a hand up his bare chest. "But I won when it really counted."

"I assume you're talking about when I gave in on other aspects of the tournament—like the stage layout and the celebrities we invited." His sexy mouth curved in a knowing grin that did wicked things to her. Made her want to do wicked things to him.

"Then, too." Bree's cheeks tightened as she tried to hold back a smirk.

Wes kissed her, tightening his grip on her waist as one hand drifted down to squeeze her bottom, pulling her hard against the ridge beneath the fly of his jeans.

She parted her lips and he slipped his warm tongue inside her mouth. Her heart beat faster and her temperature rose as he kissed her hard and deep, with a passion that made her dizzy with want.

Wes turned her around and slipped the shirt from her shoulders. He loosened her bra and let it drift to the floor. When he teased her hardened nipples, her spine stiffened and she sucked in a breath.

He turned her head, capturing her mouth in a bruising kiss that made her core pulse. Wes trailed a hand down her belly, slipping it inside her panties, damp with her desire for him. He teased the bundle of nerves as she moved against his hand. Her heart beat faster as pleasure built in her core. When he pulled his hand away, she released an involuntary whimper, desperate for release.

His eyes met hers, his chest heaving. What she saw there made her weak with want. Wes's gaze radiated heat, passion and raw emotion.

His gaze mirrored everything she'd been feeling. An emotion she hadn't wanted to name. One that felt a lot like love. And looked like what she saw reflected in Wesley's eyes.

Wes took her to his bed and made love to her. It was intensely passionate, but also deeply emotional, in a way it hadn't been before. Things had shifted between them.

Body trembling and her climax building as he held her gaze, something suddenly became very clear.

She wanted to be his. Now and always.

He seemed to want it, to ache for it, too.

Bree blurted out the thing that was on her heart. The one thing she hadn't wanted to say aloud.

"Wes, I love you."

Wes, still recovering from his own release, seemed stunned by Bree's admission.

She'd read him wrong. Had seen what she so desperately wanted to see.

Wes lay beside her, awkward silence stretching between them, making the seconds feel like minutes. Finally, he turned on his side, his head propped on his fist. "Bree, I—I..."

"It's okay." Bree sat up abruptly, her words accompanied by a nervous laugh that only seemed to make him pity her. She dragged her fingers through her hair. "I shouldn't have said that. I was just...you know." She swiped a finger beneath her eye. "Let's talk about something else while I pretend not to be embarrassed that I just said that."

"You have nothing to be embarrassed about, Bree." He stroked her arm. "It isn't you, I swear. I just can't—"

"Please...don't." She inhaled deeply, then forced a painful smile as tears sprung from her eyes. She quickly wiped them away. "Let's talk about something else. Anything. Please."

"Okay." He sat up, too. "Can I get you a glass of wine or something?"

"Wine would be great. Thank you."

While he moved about the kitchen, Bree turned on the bedside lamp, retrieved her underwear and slipped on a T-shirt and a pair of his boxers, since her pajamas were already packed in her luggage. She sat in one of the chairs near the window in his bedroom.

"The French Bordeaux Sauternes we bought at Borough Market." He handed her a glass.

Her hand trembled slightly as she accepted the glass. She took a long sip. Concentrated on the balance of sweetness and acidity. The flavor notes of apricot and honey. *Anything* but the fact that she'd just admitted to Wes that she loved him.

Wes joined her in the sitting area by the window, the space where he often sat and read in the mornings before he would start his day.

He swallowed hard. The words he wanted to say lodged painfully in his throat.

I love you, too.

He had no business saying them. Wouldn't give her false hope.

"You wanted to talk about something else." He set his glass on the small, shabby chic table between them. A salvaged piece he'd held onto from his college days because it was the first piece of furniture his mother had ever refinished. "So tell me, what's next in your career?"

Bree narrowed her gaze at him. It was another loaded topic. He'd known that before he asked her.

She'd been playing volleyball professionally for well over a decade. With each passing year and each new injury, speculation about the end of her career swirled.

Something it seemed Bex was experiencing as she fought to come back from her latest injury.

Still, he really wanted to know. Since they both seemed prone to deep introspection and spontaneous confession tonight, it seemed the perfect time to inquire.

"I hope to play a few more years. So now's the time for me to begin the transition from professional volleyball player to whatever comes next."

"And what is that?" Wes wasn't satisfied with her non-answer. "Will the volleyball camps be your full-time pursuit once you've retired?"

"That's what Bex wants."

"But what does Brianna want?" His voice softened.

"I'm not sure." She shrugged. "Volleyball has been my entire life since I was in middle school. I've sacrificed so much to be the best at what I do. I'm not completely sure where I go from there. Professionally speaking."

They were both silent for a moment, then he asked, "In your heart of hearts, what is it you'd like to be doing, more than anything, outside of playing volleyball?"

"I don't know..."

"I think you do." He swapped his untouched wineglass with her empty one, then sat back in his chair and surveyed her. "Maybe you're reluctant to share it with me, but—"

"What I'm doing now," she said quickly, picking up her wineglass and taking a sip. "Not *this*, obviously." She held up the wineglass and they both laughed. A little of the tension between them eased. "I mean being a spokesperson for important causes. Helping people. Making a difference." A genuine smile lifted her cheeks and lit her eyes. "Going to visit with sick children at hospitals. Talking to high-risk children at inner-city schools and at boys' and girls' clubs. Helping them see that they matter. That no matter how big their dreams are, they're attainable. They just need to believe in themselves and be willing to work for it. But a good support system helps. And I'd like to be that for those kids."

Bree caught Wes staring at her and her cheeks flushed. She took another sip of her wine as she gazed out of the window. "I sound like a corny do-gooder, right?"

"Look at me, Bree." He shifted forward in his seat as her gaze met his. "Never apologize for who you are. Every character trait, every physical scar…they all make you the remarkable warrior goddess you are. So don't apologize for any of it. Got it?"

She was silent for a moment, then nodded.

"Good." He smiled and her shoulders relaxed. "If that's what you really want to do, do it. Kids like us, who came from nothing, they desperately need someone to believe in them. To support their dreams and give them opportunities they wouldn't have had otherwise."

Bree took another sip of her wine. "The trouble is, if I don't keep playing, in some capacity, I'm no longer relevant, and I won't get opportunities like this."

"Make your own. Start your own organization."

"It's not that simple."

"Isn't it? It's not like you'd have to do everything yourself. A charity is like any other business. Hire the best people to run it for you."

Bree seemed unconvinced.

"Seems you've given this some thought, but something about the idea scares you. What is it?"

"It seems overwhelming, to say the least. Besides, it's such an important task. I can't let them down. What if I fail?"

"What if you succeed? Think of how many lives you could change?"

"Have you always been this confident?" She crooked an eyebrow as she studied him.

For a moment, he was sure she could see right through him to the scared little boy wearing hand-me-downs at a boarding school filled with children of the rich and famous. "I had to learn. Survival of the fittest, you know?"

She nodded. "I was one of only a handful of minority kids at my entire private school. The only one there on scholarship. So, I worked hard to prove that I was this perfect little girl. That I belonged there as much as anyone else. Still, there's always this part of me that wonders deep down if I'm really good enough." Bree stood quickly and swiped dampness from the corner of her eyes. "It's late. I need to get ready for bed."

Wes sighed as she disappeared behind the bathroom door. If only he could tell Bree the truth. It was him who wasn't good enough for her.

Wes lay awake, more than an hour after they'd gone to bed, watching Bree as she slept. He cared for her more than any woman he'd ever known. And he wanted to believe he deserved her. That they could be happy together forever.

He turned onto his back and stared at the ceiling, trying to quiet the voice that implored him to trust her with the truth.

That he wanted her, and only her.

He had his rules. Rules designed to keep him from ever needlessly hurting anyone again. He was determined not to break those rules by falling for her.

And yet…he already had.

He'd tried to pretend that what they shared was a symbiotic fusion of sex and friendship. One they could both easily walk away from.

But Bree had changed the game.

She'd shown him how gratifying it was to forge a deep connection with someone who knew him in ways no one else did.

But if he truly cared for her, he'd stick to the plan.

He wouldn't take a chance on disappointing her the way his father had disappointed his mother. Or the way he'd once disappointed someone who'd loved him more than he deserved.

Wes glanced at Bree again. They'd had an incredible time in London. It would be hard to return to this flat without thinking of her in his home, in his bed and in his life. And how happy it made him.

But he'd been playing a dangerous game with Bree's heart. Fooling himself into thinking they could do this without either of them getting hurt.

He did love Bree. And because he loved her, he would let her go.

He'd never hurt anyone that way again. The price was far too steep.

Chapter 19

Brianna had broken the rules of their little game, and now Wes was making her pay.

They'd both downplayed her misstep the previous night. However, the next morning, he was polite, but withdrawn. At the very least, distracted. Though they'd both slept during much of it, their nonstop flight home had been uncharacteristically quiet.

Bree silently cursed herself again for saying those three little words their final night in London. It was the perfect way to ruin a sublime trip and kill the mood with her no-strings-attached lover.

Wes put the last of her luggage upstairs and returned to the living room, where she sifted through a stack of mail and a few postcards. He shoved his hands into his pockets, his gaze not quite meeting hers.

"Look, I know you must be tired. Why don't I stay at my place tonight?"

A stab in the heart would've been less painful.

"Of course. I'll see you… I'll guess you'll let me know when."

She put down the mail and went to the kitchen. Bree opened the fridge, pulled over the trash can and tossed spoiled and expired food into it.

"Bree, I don't want to hurt you. You know that. But maybe this was a mistake." Wes made his way to the kitchen.

"I know we agreed not to let things get serious, and I'm the one at fault here. I made the mistake of thinking you had, you know…feelings. Like a regular human." Bree poured the remainder of a half gallon of milk down the drain, rinsed the bottle and tossed it in the recycle bin.

"You think I'm saying this because I *don't* have feelings? You couldn't be more wrong."

"Then level with me. What's this really about?"

"I am leveling with you, but you won't believe me."

Bree closed the fridge. She struggled to be calm and mature about this. After all, what was the difference between her and her stalkerish ex if she couldn't accept that it was over?

"If you've tired of me and you're ready to move on… fine. And maybe I'm wrong, but I don't think that's it. You act as if you don't want intimacy or a real relationship, but I know that isn't true. I see the truth in your eyes whenever we're together. What I can't figure out is what you're so afraid of?"

He narrowed his gaze, as if she'd struck a nerve, but he didn't respond.

"Talk to me, Wes. Whatever it is, just say it." She

stepped closer to him, stopping short of touching him. "Is there someone else?"

"Bree, there's no one in the world I'd rather be with. But I'm not prepared to make the kind of promises you're looking for."

"What the hell does that even mean?" Bree stood tall, her arms folded, despite wanting to dissolve into tears. She refused to give him the satisfaction of knowing how deeply his rejection cut.

"I'm trying to be completely honest with you, Bree. I won't be like my old man, making promises he couldn't keep. I won't do that to you. To us. I need to be sure."

"Of what? That no one better will come along?" She glared at him. "And what am I supposed to do? Warm your bed, fingers crossed, hoping one day you'll be ready? No thank you."

"It's not like that. Believe me."

"I don't. And I don't believe this is just about your dad walking out on you. People get divorced. Parents leave. And yeah, we both got saddled with a shitty parent. But we don't have to be them. I'm certainly not going to just lie down and die because I'm afraid I'll be like mine."

Wesley's eyes widened, his mouth falling open. She'd stunned him with a strike to the jugular.

Maybe it wasn't fair for her to bring up his dad, but Wes had opened the door to it when he'd used his old man as an excuse.

Bree sighed, no longer able to take the silence between them.

"I think maybe you're right. This was a mistake. I take full responsibility. You were very clear from the beginning. I should've taken your word for it instead of pushing you."

"I'm not saying we can't be friends."

"Nor am I." Bree held her head high. "But right now, let's just focus on putting on a kick-ass tournament. Okay?"

Wes's eyes reflected every bit of the pain it caused her to utter those words. He didn't move or speak.

"So that's it?" Wes cleared his throat, his hands shoved in his pockets.

"I think it has to be. But we'll always have London, right?" She forced a smile, not allowing the tears that stung her eyes to fall.

"Always." He cradled her face and kissed her good-bye.

She waited for the click of the door closing behind Wes before she crumbled onto the sofa, tears streaming down her face.

She'd gambled and lost.

Maybe she'd played her hand too soon. Or perhaps the real mistake had been that she'd dared to play the game at all.

Wes straightened his collar and closed his eyes briefly as he exhaled a long, slow breath. It was exactly two weeks before his best friend's wedding and nearly three weeks since he and Bree had ended their affair.

He'd been in Las Vegas for two days with Liam and around twenty of their friends. But it hadn't been enough to lift the testy mood he'd been in since last he'd seen Bree. She'd returned to California the day after they'd ended things, and she'd attended the last two meetings about the volleyball tournament via video conference.

Yet, she'd kept her promise. She'd kept things civil and pleasant between them. As if nothing at all had happened. He'd called her directly a week prior to get her opinion on a change to the celebrity-chef lineup. Brianna answered the phone and had been as syrupy sweet as the sweet tea his mother made. With the issue resolved, he'd tried to make small talk, but she'd politely excused herself to take another call.

She'd saved him from himself. Had he spoken to her at any length, he'd have confessed to missing her every single day.

It was best that Bree was there in California and he was in Vegas celebrating his best friend's impending nuptials.

Wes had expended a tremendous amount of effort the past two days trying to be a proper best man. Immersing himself in the celebratory spirit. But he'd spent most of the weekend attempting to mask the cavernous hole Bree's absence left in his heart.

Wes knocked on the door of Liam's hotel suite. His friend answered the door in the midst of a video chat with his fiancée's daughters, the two little girls he adored as if they were his own.

"Say hello to Uncle Wes." Liam turned the phone toward him.

Sofia and Gabriella waved at him. "Hi, Uncle Wes!"

His mouth curled in an involuntary smile. His first genuine smile of the day. Since he'd been living in Pleasure Cove he'd gotten to know the girls and he now understood why Liam adored them.

He chatted with Sofie and Ella briefly before Liam

finished his conversation and promised the girls he'd see them soon.

"Go ahead and say it, mate. They've got me wrapped around their little fingers." Liam grinned.

"That's like saying the earth is round. It's already an established fact." Wes sat on the huge sectional sofa, avoiding the cushion that reeked of beer. Liam's brother, Hunter, had spilled some on it the night before. "Besides, I'm happy for you. You know that."

"I do." Liam poured each of them two fingers of Scotch, then handed him one. He sat in a nearby chair. "I also know you thought I'd gone off my trolley for giving up my confirmed bachelorhood to become an instant dad."

"Also an established fact." Wes chuckled softly, taking a sip of the premium Scotch—Liam's preferred drink. "But I'm man enough to admit when I'm wrong."

"I should expect an apology, should I?" Liam raised an eyebrow incredulously. "Well, for goodness sake, man, get on with it."

"I honestly believed you'd be sacrificing your way of life and your independence when you took on Maya and her daughters. I was wrong. You weren't giving up your life, you were gaining a fuller, richer life. One that's made you happier than I've ever known you to be."

"That's saying a lot since we've known each other since we were thirteen." Liam grinned. "I used to hear chaps say that some woman or other was the best thing that ever happened to them, and I'd think to myself they must have lived sad and dreary lives before marriage. But now I understand, because Maya and the girls are truly the best thing to ever happen to me."

"No cold feet, then? Not even a little?"

"Not even the tiniest little bit." A broad smile lit Liam's eyes. "We already have such a wonderful life together. I look forward to making it official."

"I envy you, my friend."

"I'd much prefer you find your own." Liam tilted his head as he assessed him. "Tell me this foul mood you've been in for the past few weeks has nothing to do with Bree returning to California."

"Why would it?" Not a lie, simply a question.

"You tell me." Liam wore a supremely smug expression.

"I know it's your stag party weekend, but that doesn't mean you get a pass on being a nosy, obnoxious bastard." Wes finished his Scotch and set the glass on the table.

"No? Why should it be different from any other day?"

"Don't tempt me to launch a lamp or something at that big head of yours." Wes picked up a pillow and flung it at his friend and he tossed it back.

The lock clicked and Hunter stepped into the room along with Liam's two brothers-in-law to-be, Nate Johnston and Dash Williams.

"Don't remember seeing a pillow fight on the agenda for the weekend." Hunter put two cases of bitter on the bar and plopped down on the sofa. "Are you two going to braid each other's hair next?"

Wes and Liam picked up pillows and tossed them at Hunter simultaneously.

"Guess that makes us the only two grown-ups in the room," Nate said to Dash, as he put a case of imported beer on the bar and sat on a bar stool.

"Then we've definitely moved up in the world. The girls will be glad to hear it." Dash chuckled.

Wes checked his watch and stood. "The party limo will be here in ten. Where is Maya's brother Cole?"

Liam scrolled through the messages on his phone. "Cole will meet us at the limo."

"Then we'd better head downstairs. Everyone else is meeting us at the limo, too."

They loaded the beer onto a luggage cart and headed out into the hallway. Dash pushed the cart onto the partially full elevator. Nate and Hunter got on, too. Wes was about to join them when Liam grabbed his arm.

"You go on. We'll catch the next lift." Liam turned to him as the elevator doors closed.

"Look, I know we were joking around in there, but Bree really is phenomenal. If you're this miserable because she's gone, that should tell you something, mate."

"I like her, okay?" Wes looked away from his friend. "I maybe even love her. But what if I'm wrong? What if in six months or two years I feel differently?"

"Love is a gamble, my friend. None of us knows what will happen tomorrow or next year. But if you truly care for her, tell her how you feel and why."

"What if I tell her the truth and she hates me for it?"

"Then you'll know she's not the one for you."

Wesley's chest felt hollow at the thought of peering into his favorite brown eyes and seeing genuine contempt.

Still, in light of the pain her absence had caused him, it was worth the risk.

Chapter 20

Bree stood on her back deck watering her poor, neglected flowers and enjoying the California sun. She put down the watering can and sat at the patio table with Bex, who was reviewing samples for the camp logo.

"Another cup of coffee?" Bree offered.

"No thanks." Bex studied her for a moment, then sighed. "Look, I'm just going to say this. I was wrong about you and Wesley."

"No, you weren't. You were exactly right. You said I would get hurt and I did. I should've listened."

"But you were so happy. You practically glowed on video chat." Bex closed her laptop. "It was annoying."

"Then you should be happy I'm…" Bree sighed, not wanting to finish the sentence.

"Miserable?" Bex squeezed her arm. "I could never be happy about that."

Bree checked her phone. No calls or text messages from Wes.

"He hasn't contacted me, so obviously he doesn't feel the same."

"Maybe that's because you cut him off so abruptly last time he called." Bex had been there when she'd taken the call.

"It doesn't matter. He doesn't want a relationship, and I do. So there's really nothing for us to talk about."

"Start there. Wes doesn't seem like the typical guy who just can't be bothered to keep it in his pants. Something's got this guy spooked about being in a relationship. You need to find out what it is."

"I can't make him tell me."

"Then ask his mother. She adores you."

"I won't pry into his life behind his back. When he's ready to tell me, he will."

Bex pulled up a photo Bree had sent her. It was her and Wesley at the top of the Shard. She scrolled to another of them atop Looking Glass Rock.

"See what I mean? You never looked that happy when you were with that jerk Alex. Not even in the beginning. Can you believe he had the audacity to email me about you?"

Bree dropped her gaze, sinking her teeth into her lower lip.

"What aren't you telling me, Bree? Has Alex been bothering you?"

"He's left messages. I haven't answered any of them, but he keeps calling. And while I was in London, he sent a postcard to me in Pleasure Cove."

"He's stalking you?" Bex's nostrils flared. Her forehead and cheeks reddened.

"I wouldn't call it that. He's just having a really tough time taking no for an answer. Something I can relate to."

"You were *not* a stalker. A determined seductress? Yes. A stalker? Definitely not."

Bex picked up Bree's phone and handed it to her.

"You want me to call him?"

"No, I want you to call the police."

"Let's just take a minute and breathe, Bex. Alex will eventually get the message or he'll find someone new to harass."

"So you admit he's harassing you?"

"Yes… I mean, no. Look, I don't want to end up on some tacky gossip show, and that's exactly what's going to happen if I make that call." Bree tried to reason with her friend. Bex knew from experience how persistent the paparazzi could be.

"I don't know, Bree. Alex sounds a little unhinged right now. What if his behavior escalates?" Bex folded her arms, her eyebrows drawn together.

"If things get worse, I swear you'll be the first to know."

"What time does your flight leave tomorrow?"

"Ten."

"You should, at least, tell Wes about this guy." Bex frowned.

"It isn't his problem. It's mine. It'll be okay. I promise. Now, let's see those logo samples."

Bree opened Bex's laptop and studied the artwork proofs as if they were the only worry she had in the world.

Wes stepped outside his door as Bree descended her front stairs.

"Good morning, Wesley." She offered a polite wave.

Her willingness to speak first was a good sign, despite the formal address and schoolteacher tone.

"Hi." He caught up with her and fell in step as she walked toward the main building, where the meeting was being held. "Wasn't sure you'd be here in person for today's meeting."

"It's the last one before Liam goes on his honeymoon. So I thought I should be here."

"I'm glad you're here, Bree. I've missed you."

Bree didn't break her stride or in any way acknowledge his words.

Maybe Bree had found someone else. Someone who wasn't afraid to commit. Someone with less egregious sins in his past.

"I'm sorry about before. I was an ass—"

"On that we can agree." Bree gave him a quick glance.

"But not for the reasons you might think," Wes said quickly. "It's just that when you said…well, what you said, I panicked. Relationships aren't my usual MO. I wasn't sure how to respond."

She stopped and turned to him. "You seemed sure about it being a mistake for us to have gotten involved."

When Wes lowered his gaze, Bree walked away.

"Bree, I'm trying to explain how I felt…how I feel."

She stopped again and glared up at him. "I'll admit, maybe I said it too soon. But the fact that you seem incapable of saying the words doesn't bode well for us."

Bree checked the time on her phone.

"Look, if you want to talk about what went wrong with us…fine. But let's do it after the meeting. I need to have a clear head right now and this isn't helping."

"I'll throw some steaks on the grill, and we can talk over dinner." That would give him time to get his

thoughts together. He couldn't afford a repeat performance of his blabbering-idiot show.

She shrugged her agreement.

It wasn't an enthusiastic acceptance, but at least she
hadn't turned him down.

Chapter 21

Bree kicked off her heels and unzipped her skirt. It'd been a long, but productive meeting. They'd sold out of the majority of their sponsorships and were at nearly three quarters of their registration capacity.

They'd gotten the local shop owners onboard by opening the vendor opportunities up to them first at a special rate. Everything was organized and running smoothly and many of the local townsfolk had signed up to serve as volunteers for the event. They were in excellent shape.

Bree changed into shorts and a tank, then grabbed her phone to respond to a few emails before dinner. She opened the patio door and let the cool breeze drift in. The smell of charcoal indicated that Wes had already fired up the grill.

She opened the front door to get a nice cross breeze in the guest house.

"Hello, Brianna."

Bree froze, a chill running down her spine. Her hands trembled and her heart raced. She didn't need to look in those icy blue eyes to know whose voice it was.

"Alex, what are you doing here?"

His toothy smile quickly dissolved into an equally disturbing frown. "I've been trying to reach you for months. You haven't responded to any of my messages."

She stood taller, narrowing her gaze. "Then you should've taken the hint."

The frown morphed into a scowl. "I understand why you're treating me this way, Bree. But I just want to talk."

"There is *nothing* for us to talk about. Not now. Not ever." She stuffed her hands in her pockets, hoping he couldn't see how badly they were shaking.

"I've come all this way to talk to you. The least you could do is let me take you out to dinner, so I can explain. I know I wasn't the best person back then, but I'm different now. I just want to show you that I'm not that man anymore."

"Maybe you are different now. If so, that's great. But you put your hands on me, Alex. I can never trust you again."

"It was one time, and I told you how sorry I was. That I didn't mean to do it. I was so stressed out back then, you know?"

"That's not an acceptable excuse for how you treated me. I should've left you long before I did."

"I told you, I'm not that guy anymore." A vein bulged in his forehead. "If you can't go to dinner, we can talk now. I only need ten minutes. Let me come in. We can sit down and hash this out."

"I don't want to hash things out. I don't miss you or us or the way things were. I don't want any of it, and I don't want you. Please, just go away." She scanned the room for something she could use as a weapon if he tried to force his way inside the door. "I don't want to get the police involved, but I will if I have to."

Bree recognized the signs of rage building. The muscles of his neck corded, his pale skin was mottled and his nostrils flared.

"I'm simply asking for a chance to explain myself, and you're threatening to call the cops on me?" he practically shouted as he dragged his fingernails through his dirty blond hair.

Bree didn't flinch, determined not to show any fear. It was fear that fed the monster.

"I'd do it in an instant and happily watch them drag your ass to jail. That probably wouldn't go over too well with that investment bank of yours."

"You wouldn't."

"Try me." She stood her ground. Her chest heaved and her breath came in noisy pants as her own anger overtook any fear she might have had facing him again.

"Everything all right, babe?" Wes was suddenly behind her. He wrapped his arms around her waist possessively.

"Peachy." She wasn't sure when Wes had entered through her patio door, but she was grateful he was there.

"Who is this?" Alex's gaze shifted from Bree to Wes and back again.

"The man who plans to marry her. And the owner of an aluminum bat with your name on it if you don't turn around right now and walk your happy ass outta here. While you still can." Wes's voice was calm and his tone icy as he dropped his hand from her waist and stepped in front of her.

Alex huffed, his jaw clenched. "You're as crazy as she is. Who needs this? You two deserve each other."

He turned and stomped down the stairs to his Mercedes-Benz parked outside. Neither of them moved until he drove away.

When Alex's car left the lot, Bree released a noisy breath, her hands to her mouth.

"Are you okay, baby?" He gripped her shoulders gently. When she nodded, he pulled her into his arms and held her. Wes closed and locked the front door. "Here, come sit down."

He got her a bottle of water and sat on the sofa beside her.

She took a sip, her hands still shaking. "I can't believe he showed up here."

"Tell me everything you know about this guy."

"The short answer? Biggest mistake of my life. That's what happens when you don't listen to your gut," she added under her breath.

"Go on." He leaned forward intently.

Bree brought Wes up to speed on her history with Alex Hunt, and his persistent attempts to contact her over the past few months.

She drank more of her water. "That line about the bat…that was good. Sounds like something your mother would say."

"Who do you think gave me the bat?" Wes walked over to the window and looked out of it again. "I don't trust this guy to act in his own best interest. You're staying with me tonight."

"Wes, I appreciate what you did. I really do. But I'm fine. Alex won't be back."

"Didn't seem like he was too good at taking a hint or following instructions." Wes crossed his arms, his expression grave. "Guys like that are unpredictable. You never know how far they'll take things. Do you have a restraining order against this guy?"

She shook her head. "No."

"Then get one."

"I don't want the negative publicity, especially with the tournament coming up. Nor do I want to be seen as a victim." She paced the floor. "That would tank my endorsement stock ten times faster than a male athlete being convicted of an actual crime."

"You don't want to be seen as a victim. I get that, but I'm far more concerned about you actually becoming one." A deep frown made his brows appear as angry slashes. "This isn't something to play with."

"And it isn't fair. I never asked for this."

Wes cupped her cheek and spoke softly, his eyes filled with concern. "I know it isn't, honey. But the priority is to keep you safe. You believe that taking action against this guy will make you look weak, but it will empower you. You, in turn, can empower other women dealing with the same bullshit. You want to help people? This is a way to do it."

"Okay." Bree nodded begrudgingly. "I promised Bex I'd get the police involved if the situation escalated."

"You should've told me about this guy earlier. We could've put a halt to this before it got this far."

"I know that we're friends, and you want to help, but I'm not looking for a man to save me. And I don't need a knight in shining armor who walks away the first time he gets freaked out or things get tough."

"Fair enough." Wes wiped his palms on his black basketball shorts. "Now, about why I have trouble saying…" He sighed, then stood again. "It'll be easier if I show you."

Wes led Bree through the patio door and over to his place. He went to his bedroom and retrieved the most precious thing he owned. A black leather photo album with gold lettering on the front.

His heart hammered in his chest as he handed the photo album to Bree.

What would she think of him once she knew the truth?

He didn't doubt her discretion. But would she look at him differently? See him as the monster he saw in the mirror?

Bree seemed as nervous as he was. She opened the book reverently. As if it was an artifact that needed to be handled with care.

She studied the pictures on the first two pages. Pictures of the same little boy at various ages from newborn to about twelve years old.

"He's your son." She nearly whispered the words, her fingers delicately tracing the boy's nose and mouth. Mirror images of his own.

"Yes." Wes nodded, taking the seat across from her. "His name is Gray Grammerson."

Her eyes lit with recognition. "The facing capital *G*s that form the door of the cage on your tattoo. That's for your son."

Wes didn't answer. He didn't need to.

She turned more pages. "Most of these photos were taken from a distance. So you obviously don't share custody of him."

"Right again."

"So he lives with his mother?" Bree stopped turning the pages.

"Not his bio mom. She gave him up for adoption without ever telling me. In fact, I'd never have known about my son had it not been for a mutual friend from university."

"That's awful. Why would she do that?"

"Probably because she didn't think I was worthy of being a father to our child. We weren't together by the time she learned about the pregnancy. I think she also wanted to punish me for hurting her."

Bree raised an eyebrow. "What did you do to make her hate you?"

"I was young and selfish. My life was about meaningless hookups. I wanted her, and she didn't want to be with someone who didn't love her. So I told her I did." He swallowed hard. "We were together a few weeks. Maybe a month. When I was ready to move on, she was devastated."

Bree's eyes were misty. Her expression relayed both disappointment and compassion. "What happened to her?"

"She was an American expat, too. She returned to America. At the time, I was a selfish little prick. I thought, good riddance. I had no idea…" He winced, his eyes not meeting hers. "I had no idea she was pregnant with my son. A few years later, a fellow classmate contacted me. She'd run in to my ex, who told her about the baby. Our baby. She'd given him up without notifying me. I was devastated."

"Where's his mother now?"

"She's an international-aid worker stationed at one of the largest refugee camps in Uganda."

"Have you talked to her since you learned about your son?"

Wes's jaw clenched involuntarily at the thought of confronting Janine. He shook his head. "It's a conversation I can't imagine going well."

Bree studied a photo of Gray being pushed on a swing by his adoptive mother. "How'd you find him?"

"It's one of the few times I readily accepted help from the Westbrooks. Liam helped me find a detective, who tracked down my son. When I found him, he was in a loving, wonderful family with good parents. I didn't have the heart to disrupt their lives."

"So how'd you get the pictures? The detective?"

"He dug up everything he could find at the outset. A lot of the pictures were on his adoptive parents' social-media pages. I have him do a checkup twice a year, just to make sure everything is okay with my son."

"He's so handsome. Just like his father." Bree smiled faintly as she thumbed through the book, and Wes felt as if she'd given him a lifeline.

She hadn't condemned him or walked out in disgust at the pig he'd been back then. When she reached the end of the book she closed it carefully and set it on the coffee table. She stood in front of him, opened her arms and embraced him.

He hugged her tightly, overwhelmed with a sense of relief and gratitude.

"I'm so sorry." She kissed his head. "It makes sense

now, how you feel. But, honey, you can't punish yourself for the rest of your life. What you did was wrong, but you're *not* the one who gave your son away. And look at the effort you put into finding him and into making sure he's safe."

Wes didn't speak. Pain, shame and regret swirled inside him, along with a deep affection for her. Bree's warmth and compassion soothed his soul.

Made him feel human again.

"You aren't the person you were then, Wes. Let go of the guilt and forgive yourself. I know your son wouldn't want you to torture yourself this way."

"What makes you believe that?"

"Because I'd give anything for my bio mother to love me even half as much as you love your son." Her voice broke, tears running down her cheeks.

Wes pulled her onto his lap and kissed her. A kiss that started off tender and sweet. Two people comforting one another over their loss and grief. It slowly heated up. Her kiss became hungrier. His hands searched her familiar curves. Her firm, taut breasts filled his hands.

His tongue danced with hers, the temperature between them rising. He'd missed the feel of her. The taste of her warm, sweet skin. He wanted to lose himself in the comfort of their intense passion. But not before he'd told her everything.

He pulled his mouth from hers, their eyes meeting. "There's something you need to know."

Bree stared at him, her chest heaving, her face filled with apprehension. "All right."

"I love you, Bree. And I'm not just telling you that because you said it first. I'm saying it because it's true. I've waited my entire life to feel like this about someone. I've been miserable without you. I'm afraid I was an awful best man during Liam's stag weekend."

Bree grinned.

"What's so funny?"

"I've been miserable without you, too."

Wesley closed the vent on the grill and locked the patio door. He took Bree upstairs and made love to her, in the fullest sense of the words.

Dinner would have to wait.

Chapter 22

Brianna smoothed down the hem of her skirt, her heart beating rapidly. "Are you sure you want to do this tonight?"

Wesley squeezed her hand and grinned. "The way I see it, this is long overdue."

He pressed a warm, lingering kiss to her lips, one strong hand cradling her face.

Bree leaned into his touch and angled her head, allowing Wes to deepen the kiss. His tongue slid between her lips and glided along hers. He released her hand and planted his on the small of her back, pulling her in tighter against him.

She should pull away. Show a little self-control. After all, though they'd declared their love to each other, they'd yet to tell their family and friends.

Kissing openly outside the resort wasn't very discreet. Still, she couldn't pull herself away, reluctant to allow a single inch of space to separate her from the man she loved madly.

They'd spent the majority of their first three days as a bona fide couple in Wesley's bed. Talking, eating, making love. Taking small steps toward planning for a future together.

The prospect of slowly building a life together was exhilarating and terrifying. And she couldn't think of anything that would challenge her more or make her happier.

Wes pulled his mouth from hers reluctantly and groaned. "We'd better not be late. Liam will never let me hear the end of it."

They rounded the corner and entered the pathway that led to the outdoor patio where Liam and Maya's rehearsal dinner was being held. They were greeted by teasing woots and loud kissing noises.

Bree pressed a hand to her open mouth, her cheeks stinging with heat.

"Guess the secret's out." Wes squeezed her hand.

"No matter. It was just about the worst kept secret in the history of secrets." Liam met them on the path and grinned. "And I should know a thing or two about clandestine relationships."

Wes grinned. "Well, I'm glad you and Maya aren't a secret anymore. I'm excited for you both, Liam. I know you'll continue to be very happy together."

"I'm thrilled for you, mate." Liam's self-congratulatory smile could light the entire Eastern seaboard. He held his arms open and hugged them both. "I knew you two were absolutely perfect for each other."

"Does this mean you're confessing to being a meddling matchmaker?" One corner of Wesley's mouth curved, as he tried to hold back a smirk.

"Now that it's worked? Absolutely." Liam chuckled. "Now, if my best mate has had his fill of snogging this lovely young lady—for the time being—I say we get on with this rehearsal. I'm quite in a hurry to marry a lovely young lady of my own."

Liam's eyes practically glowed as he looked at Maya Alvarez. The woman he would stand beside on the Pleasure Cove Beach and make his wife in less than twenty-four hours.

A table of children squealed with joy, and everyone laughed.

"Those are Maya's daughters—Sofia and Gabriella. That's Kai—the bride's nephew. That's Madison—the bride's niece. The little one is Liam's niece Emma and that's her older brother, Max." Wesley gave Bree a breakdown of all the children in attendance.

"Bree, I'm so glad you're here." Lena's eyes sparkled as she approached, gathering them both in a hug. "You two belong together. I've known it since the day I met you. Saw the love he had for you in his eyes. Saw the same in yours."

Bree smiled, her eyes misty with tears as she glanced up at Wes. "You're a very wise woman, Ms. Lena. And you've raised a truly wonderful man."

Wes leaned in and gave Bree a quick kiss on the lips before deftly moving her through the group of family and friends.

They congratulated Maya, whom Bree had met at a previous business dinner. Wes introduced her to the matron-of-honor, Kendra, and her husband Nathan Johnston, a pro football player. Next, he introduced her to Kendra's and Maya's brother Dash Williams and his fiancée Mikayla.

She met a variety of additional relatives. Liam's father, Nigel, and Mrs. Hanson—the woman who had been Liam and Hunter's nanny since they were boys, but now seemed to enjoy a much more personal relationship with their father. The groom's brother, Hunter, and his wife, Meredith. Kendra and Dash's mother, Ms. Anna. The Johnston family, comprised of Nate's parents and several of his siblings, including his fraternal twin sister Vi. Maya's parents—Curtis and Alita Williams, and her brother Cole.

The rehearsal was lovely. Filled with laughter and tears of joy. During the delicious meal that followed, there was more of the same.

Bree felt at home, like she was among family and old friends. She'd been nervous about the prospect of uprooting her life and moving to Pleasure Cove so that she and Wes could be together and close to his mother. But there was so much love, friendship and good-natured teasing here. And they'd gone out of their way to make her feel like she was part of their extended family.

At the end of the night, she and Wes said their goodbyes, saw Lena to her room at the resort, and strolled along the beach hand-in-hand.

London would always be special for them. It was the place where they'd first met and where they'd both realized they'd fallen in love. But here on the sandy beaches of Pleasure Cove among friends who were already beginning to feel like family…this somehow felt like home.

Not his home or her home, but *theirs*. The place where they could make a life together.

Epilogue

Wes was head over heels in love with the girl who was in his arms. She'd stolen his heart in a way he hadn't thought possible.

He wanted to give her the entire world wrapped in a neat little bow. He'd do anything for her.

The edge of her mouth curled as she slept, mimicking a smile. She seemed to know instinctually that she was safe in his arms. That he'd do everything in his power to protect her and provide for her.

He stroked her soft, downy hair and kissed her forehead.

"Mackenzie Alena Adams," he whispered softly. His lips brushed her warm skin as he inhaled her scent. "Do you have any idea how much you mean to me?"

Mackenzie yawned and stretched, her dark eyes opening for a moment before she closed them again and pressed her fist to her lips in a failed attempt to suck it.

"Hungry again, baby girl?" Wes secured the blanket around his daughter, only a few hours old.

Bree grinned as she stroked their daughter's cheek. "She's beautiful, Wes."

"Just like her mama." Wes pressed a soft, lingering kiss to Bree's lips.

He sat on the edge of Bree's bed and wrapped an arm around her as he cradled their daughter in his arms.

They'd been together for two years and were already engaged when Bree had shown him the positive pregnancy test. With the help of their family and friends, they'd managed to coordinate a simple, but elegant ceremony on Pleasure Cove Beach. The same place they'd witnessed Maya and Liam taking their vows two years earlier. They'd both stood barefoot in the sand, the soft sea air rustling her hair, and declared their commitment to each other.

Even now, he got choked up thinking of how beautiful she'd been in her wedding dress. A sleeveless, cream-colored ball gown with a sweetheart neckline that showcased her breasts, enlarged by the pregnancy.

Wes hadn't thought he could be any happier than he was the day Bree stood there on that beach in front of the world and agreed to be his wife.

He'd been wrong.

Witnessing the birth of their daughter had been even more touching, eliciting tears from both of them.

As a husband and a father, his life had taken on new meaning. Bree had given him the life he'd convinced himself he hadn't wanted. Yet he was happier than he ever imagined possible.

"Would you like to hold your baby sister?" Wes

beamed at the handsome boy who was nearly fifteen with a face that looked so much like his own.

The boy who'd washed his hands and had been waiting patiently bobbed his head and took the newborn in his arms.

Wesley's heart felt as if it would burst. *His son.* It still didn't feel real. But Bree had made it happen. She'd written letters to Gray's adoptive parents for more than a year before she'd finally gotten a response.

Gray had learned he was adopted and he wanted to meet his biological parents. He'd been angry with Wes at first, but they'd slowly built a relationship over the past year. And four months ago, Gray had finally met his biological mother—Janine.

Wes had been nervous to see her again. He was uncertain of how he'd react to the woman who'd given away their son without telling him. But when he'd laid eyes on Janine and seen the pain and fear on her face, they both had tears of regret in their eyes.

He and Bree had sat and talked with Janine for an hour before Gray arrived with his adoptive parents. And when they parted ways, he managed to hug his son's mother and wish her well. Something that was only possible because of the love and grace he'd learned from his mother and from being with Bree.

They'd been through a lot. Marriage, a growing family and the expansion of two successful businesses. Bree had become a vocal activist for organizations that raised money to battle his mother's illness and those that protected women from boyfriends and exes like Alex Hunt—whom they hadn't heard from since Bree filed a restraining order against him.

A wide smile spread across Gray's face. "I think she just smiled at me in her sleep."

"She knows she's safe. That her big brother will always be there to protect her." Bree wore a white-and-green hospital gown with a crusty, baby-puke stain on one shoulder. Her curls were secured in a messy top-knot.

She looked happy, but exhausted. Still, she was the most beautiful woman he'd ever seen.

The love of his life.

Maybe he didn't deserve Bree, the kids, or the life they were building together, but he was damn grateful for it. And he'd never, ever let any of them go.

* * * * *

SPECIAL EXCERPT FROM

◆ HARLEQUIN

DESIRE

*Shy housekeeper Monica Darby has always had
feelings for handsome chef and heir to his family's
fortune Gabe Cress. But one unexpected night of
passion and a surprise inheritance changes everything.
With meddling families and painful pasts, will they find
their happily-ever-after?*

Read on for a sneak peek at
One Night with Cinderella
by nationally bestselling author Niobia Bryant!

"Hopefully everyone will get home safe," she said.

Gabe took in her high cheekbones, the soft roundness of her jaw
and the tilt of her chin. The scent of something subtle but sweet
surrounded her. He forced his eyes away from her and cleared his
throat. "Hopefully," he agreed as he poured a small amount of
champagne into his flute.

"I'll leave you to celebrate," Monica said.

With a polite nod, Gabe took a sip of his drink and set the bottle
at his feet, trying to ignore the reasons why he was so aware of her.
Her scent. Her beauty. Even the gentle night winds shifting her
hair back from her face. Distance was best. Over the past week he
had fought to do just that to help his sudden awareness of her ebb.
Ever since the veil to their desire had been removed, it had been
hard to ignore.

She turned to leave, but moments later a yelp escaped her as
her feet got twisted in the long length of her robe and sent her body
careening toward him as she tripped.

Reacting swiftly, he reached to wrap his arm around her waist
and brace her body up against his to prevent her fall. He let the hand
holding his flute drop to his side. Their faces were just precious

inches apart. When her eyes dropped to his mouth, he released a small gasp. His eyes scanned her face before locking with hers.

He knew just fractions of a second had passed, but right then, with her in his arms and their eyes locked, it felt like an eternity. He wondered what it felt like for her. Was her heart pounding? Her pulse sprinting? Was she aroused? Did she feel that pull of desire?

He did.

With a tiny lick of her lips that was nearly his undoing, Monica raised her chin and kissed him. It was soft and sweet. And an invitation.

"Monica?" he asked, heady with desire, but his voice deep and soft as he sought clarity.

"Kiss me," she whispered against his lips, hunger in her voice.

"Shit," Gabe swore before he gave in to the temptation of her and dipped his head to press his mouth down upon hers.

And it was just a second more before her lips and her body softened against him as she opened her mouth and welcomed him with a heated gasp that seemed to echo around them. The first touch of his tongue to hers sent a jolt through his body, and he clutched her closer to him as her hands snaked up his arms and then his shoulders before clutching the lapels of his tux in her fists. He assumed she was holding on while giving in to a passion that was irresistible.

Monica was lost in it all. Blissfully.

The taste and feel of his mouth were everything she ever imagined.

Ever dreamed of.

Ever longed for.

Don't miss what happens next in
One Night with Cinderella
by nationally bestselling author Niobia Bryant!

Available February 2021 wherever
Harlequin Desire books and ebooks are sold.

Harlequin.com

Love Harlequin romance?

DISCOVER.

Be the first to find out about promotions, news and exclusive content!

f Facebook.com/HarlequinBooks

𝕏 Twitter.com/HarlequinBooks

◯ Instagram.com/HarlequinBooks

𝓟 Pinterest.com/HarlequinBooks

You Tube YouTube.com/HarlequinBooks

ReaderService.com

EXPLORE.

Sign up for the Harlequin e-newsletter and download a free book from any series at
TryHarlequin.com

CONNECT.

Join our Harlequin community to share your thoughts and connect with other romance readers!
Facebook.com/groups/HarlequinConnection

HSOCIAL2021